REBEL VAMPIRES

REBEL VAMPIRES

THE ROYALE VAMPIRE HEIRS, BOOK ONE

by

GINNA MORAN

SUNNY PALMS
PRESS

For Inquiries Contact:
Sunny Palms Press
9663 Santa Monica Blvd Suite 1158
Beverly Hills, CA 90210, USA
www.sunnypalmspress.com
www.GinnaMoran.com

To those who love a good morning wakeup call.

This is for you. ;)

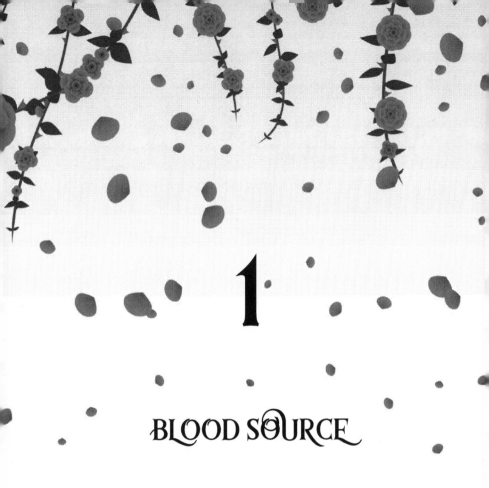

1

BLOOD SOURCE

"THAT'S A SHIT-TON OF BLOOD, Gwen," my brother Kyler whispers, clutching his silver stake tighter.

I wish he would put the thing away and trust me to take care of him. If any vampire in this hellish city sees him with it, they'll know we're not from around here and that we broke the law by sneaking in from the far side through an old drain.

But Kyler would never go unarmed, and guns are too loud to risk right now. Because the stake belonged to our dad, he thinks it somehow gives him the strength of all th

Blood Rebels who held it before him. Such a crock. He's too old to believe in that shit. He's never even used the damn thing. All it does is remind me that Dad died trying to punch out a vampire's heart. And failed.

Kyler waves the stake at the floor again. "There's more. Damn."

From the look of the mess, the blood belongs to a person who didn't even put up a fight. And why would they? Most humans grow up thinking it's best to comply with a vampire's fangs. To fight back means to die. Chances are, the vampire who attacked this human plans to hold onto them. From what my blood source told me, private donors cost too much for the normal shadow dweller. One of the ruling covens wouldn't resort to risking getting caught taking from the general donor population pool.

Unlucky for this vampire, he's about to get caught by me.

How do I know it's a dude? I've encountered a female vampire once. One time. I only know of a couple of human women too. Three to be exact. The male population in the Donor Life Corp territory is huge. I don't know by how much, but my dad used to suspect at least by five times. My blood source says ten. But I can't be sure if the vampire who currently gives me his blood tells the truth. The last one lied. A lot.

I touch my finger to the sticky spot of red fluid. "It's fresh." Training my eyes to the floor, I follow the streak of blood with my gaze to the back of the dark warehouse. "They're still here. Look."

Kyler follows my finger with his eyes, readying his stake. It sparkles in the soft light trickling in through the broken window, a sign that this isn't a vampire hideout. If it were, the glass would be tinted and shatter-proof to protect the blood drinkers from the sun and their blessed sunlight sensitivity. This place belongs to humans, probably ones in desperate need of help to get out of this damn city. And that's what we plan to do.

A shadow moves next to me, seemingly materializing out of thin air. "Smells like more than one human. Possibly four or five."

Swinging my arm out, I clock my blood source in the sternum just hard enough to make him wince. He snatches my hand and drags me to him before I can attempt to punch him again for surprising me.

"Calm down, my dhampir. It's just me," Laredo says, engulfing me in an annoying hug to restrain me to him. He risks pressing my head into his shoulder, knowing that if he pisses me off enough, I'll bite. Hard. He won't survive trying to bite me back. "And you two need to shut up. Someone will hear you."

"All of you shut the hell up," Grayson, my eldest brother says from a dozen feet behind us. He narrows his gaze on me in my blood source's arms, baring his teeth through his unkempt beard. "Put Gwen down and never call her that again, asshole. It's dangerous. You know she doesn't like that shit."

Laredo softly chuckles. "She does if I—"

I widen my mouth on his shoulder and bite but not hard enough to break his skin. "Don't put words in my mouth. He's right, Laredo."

Mostly because if the world knew that I was born half-human, half-vampire, I'd be caged. I carry some traits of vampirism, but I'm a genetic anomaly. I look human and eat solid food. I can go out into the sun. I rarely get sick. But I drink blood. Vampire blood. Some suspect my birth was a gift to humanity, turning someone who should be prey into a predator to fight back against the vampires who control us. If only I wasn't alone.

My ancestor, Gwyneth Gallagher, caught the Blood Hunger Plague while pregnant during the vampire uprising. She died, unable to handle the transition, but her son was born a carrier of the dhampir mutation—his immunity strengthened by the plague. It wasn't until my birth that my family discovered the truth of our lineage—that the symptoms show themselves in some females. If my great-great-grandfather hadn't escaped the division of humans and taken refuge among Blood Rebels, humans and vampires against the uprising, I'd already be dead. So, yeah. My fucking luck.

Laredo slides his hand into my hair, slightly bending his neck to tease me. "Mmmhmm. Keep telling yourself that—"

A guttural cry sounds from behind a cracked door, cutting off Laredo's words before he says something that'll have my eldest brother, who is my formal protector guardian, attempting to gut him. I could be fifty and my brothers would still treat me like a kid because I'm the youngest.

And it wouldn't be the first time Grayson stabbed my blood source. Just last week, Grayson caught me sucking on Laredo's neck after Laredo wound me up enough to bite him instead of drinking his blood from a glass. Grayson shanked him with a fork in the side. Talk about overprotective.

If Laredo were any other vampire, Grayson would be dead. Grayson wouldn't have even been allowed to touch him. But Laredo knows the rules. He's my blood source, and as long as he helps assure I get the blood I need, he'll reap the benefits—mostly an unlimited blood supply from my six brothers. Never from me.

Laredo also thinks he might wear me down one of these days. He can fantasize all he wants but that shit isn't happening and not only because my brothers would stake him. I couldn't trust myself not to get caught up in his charm. He's hot. Muscular. And delicious as hell, way better than my last blood source. That son of a bitch got staked a few years ago on my eighteenth birthday when he assumed he could try to bite me. It was the moment that changed everything—the reason my dad died. He was my first vampire kill. It was then that my brothers knew I was ready to face the world outside the bunker we've lived in all my life, far away from any vampire regions.

Another cry sounds out, and I grimace, turning to Laredo. "That sounds like a kid."

"Shit, Gwen. Come on."

My brothers don't even have a chance to stop us before Laredo dashes us forward at an inhumanly fast pace to the back of the warehouse. If Grayson didn't want to risk ruining our surprise attack, he'd be swearing up a storm that we're taking the lead.

Laredo sets me on my feet and thrusts open the door. A snarl sounds through the air. Laredo disappears, his motions too fast for me to focus on. Something crashes to my right, and I finally catch sight of my blood source shoving a disgusting blood and dirt covered shadow dweller into the wall.

"Gwen, behind you!" Laredo calls.

Instead of spinning, I uppercut a swing straight in front of me, sucker punching the shadow dweller in the chin as he tries to trick me, thinking I'll listen to my blood source. As his head jerks back, I knee him in the stomach, sending him sprawling to the floor.

Saying the opposite of what he wants me to do has been Laredo's thing for months. What started out as me being stubborn toward his suggested fighting methods turned into a pretty effective way to catch these quick suckers off guard.

Laredo closes the space to the shadow dweller, but the jerk dodges past him and disappears, choosing to flee over fighting. If it were just me, he'd continue to try to get to me, but with Laredo, he's choosing self-preservation.

Too bad for him my brothers lay in wait.

An ear-piercing shriek sounds through the air, and I watch the shadow dweller at the door spin Grayson off him. Kyler attacks next, going after the vampire from behind. But he doesn't get within a foot of him. The shadow dweller gnashes his sharp fangs, making Kyler hesitate long enough to escape.

Gunshots pop, and I startle. "Damn it, Declan! What did we say? No fucking guns!"

But it's too late.

My middle brother chose to risk the noise to shoot at the shadow dweller. Now, we'll surely get all the vampires in the area rushing toward us, attracted to the sound of the fight.

A loud siren rings through the air, and Laredo bends forward, experiencing the ear-shattering noise far worse than any of us. I dash toward him instead of my brothers to help him cover his ears. The noise suddenly snaps off, and a few figures appear in the doorway. Silver eyes flash from the two front figures.

Laredo growls. "We have to go."

"But my bro—"

The world spins around me as Laredo lifts me off my

feet and relocates me too fast to orient myself to the shift in our surroundings. Shouts call out for him to stop, but it only pushes him harder, faster. My sudden fear instincts ignite—the icy dread that tells me when a vampire draws near, stalking us—washing down my back.

"Gwen, listen to me," Laredo whispers, keeping his mouth near my ear. "We're being followed. I don't know the city well enough to evade the authorities. They're fast and outnumber me."

I dig my nails into his back. "I'm not afraid to fight. We can do it."

He sucks in a few deep breaths, slowing down to turn into an alley. Pressing my back into the wall, he cages me in. "No. You can't fight. You fight, and they'll kill you."

I tilt my head up to search Laredo's dark gaze. His eyes flash silver, poking at my very nature. "Then I'll die. My brothers—"

"They'd want you to live, Gwen."

Soft footsteps sound out, and Laredo squishes me harder into the wall like he could push me through and into the building to hide us.

"I'll die anyway. You know I will. I can't just pretend to be a donor. I need blood to survive." I cup his face, my chest heaving with gasps so hard that it thumps against his. "Please, fight with me."

Laredo presses his chin into my shoulder, keeping his voice nearly inaudible. "Tell them you're a minor, Gwen. I kidnapped you."

"No," I say. "I'm not letting them take me."

"Gwen." He growls my name, his fingers digging deeper into my sides.

A bright spotlight shines across the mouth of the alley, though I don't hear any voices. I don't see any shadow dwellers either.

"Come on," I say, reaching into my jacket to pull out the stake I'm willing to risk using. I don't have a choice. If they catch up, I can't lie docile. I can't pray that they show me some mercy. And I fucking won't dare bow beneath these assholes or bare my throat to them. Screw that shit. I'm a dhampir. My family raised me to fight. I will not let them down.

"Don't move, and we'll spare your life," a deep, sultry voice says, drawing my attention away from Laredo to spot the shadow of a figure staying just out of my line of sight. "Let the donor go."

He's talking to Laredo.

Laredo growls again, tightening his hold on me. Leaning closer, he brushes his lips to my jaw so that he can whisper in my ear without the douchebags hearing him. "Gwen, I'm sorry. I'm so sorry. I can't risk you fighting and dying."

What the? The clicks of his fangs sound in my ears, and I try to shove against him. Laredo holds me tighter, pressing his body to mine. His breathing quickens, and he grazes his fangs to my neck without biting me.

"What are you doing? You better not bite me, damn it," I say.

"If you die, your life would be a waste. The rebels have always been so wasteful," he murmurs, freaking me the hell out. "You're my dhampir. I vowed to take care of you—forever."

"Last chance, asshole," the same masculine voice calls.

"Laredo—"

His name barely escapes my mouth before Laredo sinks his fangs into my neck, surprising the hell out of me. I grunt and push against him, a sudden burning sensation exploding from his bite.

"Fuck, that hurts," I murmur. "You lied to me. You said it wouldn't." He always swore I'd love for him to bite me. Shit head.

Laredo pulls away, his eyes now solid silver. A drop of my blood stains his bottom lip. "Damn, you taste as amazing as I imagined. At least I can die knowing."

"You fucker," I snap, smacking him across the face.

He releases a soft laugh and then groans. "I'm sorry, Gwen. I had to. They can't cage you now. You'll never be a donor."

His words swirl through my head, sending my heart racing. I reach up and touch the aching bite mark, pulling my fingers back to stare at my blood. It's the first time I've seen it, the color not unlike my brothers'. I don't know why I was expecting it to resemble the deep crimson of a vampire's.

"Shit, did he just bite her?" The figure from the mouth of the alley steps closer at a human's speed. Then another guy soon follows behind him. "Hey, let her go. If you kill her, you'll meet your final donation. It's against Donor Life Corp law."

"She's a minor," Laredo says, raising his voice.

"The hell I—"

Slapping his hand over my mouth, Laredo cuts off my argument. "I'm sorry I failed you. Be brave, my dhampir. The pain will only get worse. But when it's over, you'll be free. They won't harm you."

Fear clenches my chest as I stare into Laredo's eyes. He doesn't make any sense. I push against him, trying to get him to release me, but something collides hard into his back, shoving into me. The breath knocks out of my lungs, and I can't stop the cry from escaping my mouth. Warmth blossoms across my chest, the strong scent of Laredo's blood tickling my nose.

The silver dissipates from his gaze as he falls away, landing on the ground. The edges of my vision shadow. I scream out, throwing myself forward. My sudden movement catches the two vampires off guard, and I land on my blood source. I press my hands to his chest, my fingers sinking deeply into the empty cavity where his heart should be.

"You killed him!"

Fury steals the shock and grief from me, suppressing

the burning in my neck. Reaching into my jacket, I grab for my stake, coming up empty. It's then that I realize Laredo stole it from me. He grips it tightly in his hand, even in death. I don't get a chance to tug it free. Two strong hands lace around my sides and drag me off him.

Cool breath tickles in my ear. "Hey. Hey, it's okay. I'm not going to hurt you. I want to help you. What's your name?"

Instead of responding, I jerk my head back as hard as I can. The vampire growls and drops me to the ground. I scramble away, trying to get to my feet, but something's wrong with me. Starbursts pepper my vision, dizziness washing over me. I slam my shoulder into the hard concrete wall of the warehouse, my fear driving me crazy as the two vampires stalk me.

"Think he bit her with venom?" It's the first time I hear the other guy speak. I draw my attention to him, catching sight of his silver flashing eyes under the glowing light over-head. He's leaner than the other vampire, shorter too. That's all I can tell. My vision blurs too much.

"He might have," the buff vampire says. He materializes in front of me, tilting his head to search my face. His dark eyes trail down my face and to my throat. He has the nerve to try to touch my hair to move it out of the way.

Big fucking mistake.

My body kicks into action, and I jerk my leg out and slam my boot between his legs as hard as I can. He drops to the ground, cupping his junk, and I twist to dash away.

I don't get far.

The world spins and my back hits the wall. The buff vampire clenches his jaw, baring his fangs at me. He inhales a few deep breaths through his nose and looks ready to murder me.

"Chill out, Bronx. You're scaring her," the other vampire says.

"She kicked me in the dick, Everett," he says, glowering at me. "I don't care if she's scared. She should be."

"If you don't set her down, I'll fucking kick you in the cock next."

I hit my knees on the ground and fall over. Pain radiates through me, begging me just to give in. The other vampire, Everett, kneels beside me and eases me onto my back. He hovers a foot above me, his dark blue eyes capturing mine with his stare. Stubble peppers his cheeks, and I can't stop myself from looking everywhere else. I already know what he plans to do, and if I give away the fact that he can't control my mind because I've consumed Laredo's blood not that long ago, I'll be dead.

Everett's eyes flash silver as he locks me in a vampire staring contest in an attempt to control my mind. "You're safe. I'm not going to hurt you, okay?"

I relax my shoulders the best I can. "Okay." I keep my voice even, acting like a zombie. Laredo and I practiced this technique for over a year.

"What's your name?" Everett asks.

I consider lying, but I know that the closer I stick to the truth, the better. And telling this guy my name won't mean anything. "Gwen."

He smiles without his fangs. "That's a pretty name."

Hell, did he just compliment me? I nearly react by making a face.

"Hurry up, Everett. Morning's coming. We have nine other donors to take in for registration. You can interrogate her when we get to headquarters." The asshole, Bronx, stands over us, glaring down at me.

Shit.

Darting my eyes from Bronx and back to Everett, I pray to the universe that neither of them noticed that I broke Everett's stare, an impossible task if I were truly under mind manipulation.

"Did she...?"

Shoving up my hands, I ram them into Everett's chest, knocking him off me. I scramble to get to my feet, but my legs buckle on me. I roll over and drag myself a few inches away until two black boots stand in front of me.

"She was either bitten with venom or is a Blood Rebel," Bronx says, grabbing me by the wrists. He hoists me up, dangling me a foot off the ground. "That shadow dweller lied. I doubt she's a minor. What do you think? You're the donor expert."

"She is well developed," Everett says. "Under twenty-five, though."

I spit in Bronx's face. "I'll kill you both!"

Bronx laughs, turning to glance at Everett. "Damn. I've never seen anything like her."

Everett materializes right next to Bronx and touches his shoulder. "Be careful. She's hurt already. Scared."

"No way. I've seen plenty of scared donors. She's not one of them. Even all those guys in the warehouse looked ready to piss themselves."

"Yeah, right." My damn mouth. I know better than to talk.

"Still, Bronx. She was with an unregistered vampire, obviously bit against her consent. You don't want to traumatize her even more." This is a first. I've never met a vampire who was concerned about my wellbeing. Who the hell is this moral compass asshole?

Bronx groans without looking at me. It's annoying that they talk like I'm not even here. "Well, Mr. Donor Health Keeper, we can't manipulate her mind. What should we do?"

I thrash, using my last bit of energy to break myself free from Bronx. Either that or the jerk purposely drops me. I crash to the ground, heaving a breath, the force of my fall knocking the air from my lungs.

Everett slides his hands under my knees and around my back, lifting me into his arms. "Just go to the others, brother. I'll handle her."

"What the hell ever. That's your dick on the line," Bronx says. He disappears from sight without another word.

"Hey, Gwen. My name is Everett," Everett says. "We weren't lying about not hurting you, but you need to calm down. The others on my team aren't always as nice."

I clench my jaw without a word, but I stop fighting.

He offers me a small smile. "I see that you're unregistered. If you tell me how you got into Crimson Vista, you won't get interrogated later."

Still, I don't answer.

"Was it the vampire you were with?" he asks. "The one who bit you? Did he claim you?"

I must make a face, because Everett hums under his breath.

"May I take a look at the bite? I have medical training in human health. You're not bleeding much, so I don't think he ripped an artery, but it's better if we make sure just in case. If you need a transfusion, I'll have to call it in." He keeps his eyes trained in front of him instead of at me.

I clear my throat. "I-I'm fine. The others you found...?" I can't get my mouth to finish the sentence. I'm terrified of the answer.

"Five adult males and four minors," he says. "One of the minors was badly injured. It's doubtful that he'll make it, but we'll do our best."

I tense. Not because of the minor, but because he said five adult males. That means one of my brothers is missing.

He mistakes my reaction and inwardly groans, the noise barely sounding on his lips. "I'm sorry. I shouldn't have said it like that. Are they your family?"

I don't respond.

"You will all be okay," he says. "Donor Life Corp will assure it."

I open my mouth to tell him that he's full of shit, but he suddenly tightens his hold on me and stops walking. Everett releases a deep, threatening growl from his throat. The hairs on my arms stand on end, and I can't get my fear instincts to calm the hell down.

"Let her go." Grayson's voice draws my attention away from Everett, and I stretch to catch sight of my brother. "If you don't, I'll punch your heart out."

I don't have time to move or scream. I can't even react. The world spins, and Grayson stumbles away. Everett strides toward him, baring his fangs. Grayson reaches for his gun and yanks it free. Aiming, he pulls the trigger.

But instead of hitting Everett, he shoots another vampire that materializes in front of us. The vampire blurs out of the way and reappears behind my brother. Pulling the trigger again, Grayson fires the gun without realizing the vampire already relocated.

Pain explodes through me.

"Gwen!" he shouts.

I don't get the chance to scream out his name.

The world blurs.

2

BALL KICKER

LIGHT ENGULFS ME AS EVERETT rushes through the tinted door of a towering building. I can't tell how far he ran, but it hasn't been long. At least, I think. I blacked out for what felt like seconds. Could've been minutes.

"Please drink more, Gwen," Everett says, pressing his bleeding arm to my mouth.

I flare my nostrils, my body humming like crazy at the strong, sugary scent of his blood. I don't know if he expected me to hesitate or what, but his eyes widen when I mold my lips and begin to suck. We watch each other in silence, his blood sending tingles through me unlike anything I've ever felt. And hell. I don't like what it does.

"That's enough, Gwen. Your wound is coagulating," Everett murmurs, releasing a soft hum from his throat.

I don't release him. I can't. My body knows better. Because, shit. He or the asshole, Bronx, killed Laredo. I can't survive without my blood source. I can go two or three weeks at the most before I get sick. I once made it to a month in an attempt to see how long I could last, but it's been too long. And I'm seriously injured. I was...

"My brothers." Thoughts of Grayson get my mouth to let go of Everett. "Where are they?"

I lick my lips and stare into Everett's deep blue eyes, now sparkling with flecks of green in the lighting of the quiet building.

Everett searches my face for an uncomfortable minute, his bottom lip puffy with his breathing, his eyes suddenly flashing silver with a hunger I'd recognize.

I shove my hand into his shoulder. "Tell me, damn it."

A whistle cuts through the silent lobby of wherever the hell we are, snapping Everett's attention away from me. Three vampires, including the asshole Bronx, materialize in the building at vampire speed.

From over Everett's shoulder, I lock eyes with the same vampire Grayson shot. Ruby blood creates a blossom on the front of his light blue T-shirt, stretched across his broad chest. The guy's arm muscles flex as he clenches his fingers, his stare capturing mine. He lifts his lips, baring his fangs at me.

The fourth vampire, one I haven't seen before, roars a laugh and smacks the guy on the back. "Careful, Mikkalo. I hear this donor's a real ball kicker."

Bronx shoves the guy into Mikkalo, but neither of them falls over. The fourth vampire materializes in front of me and tilts his head with a smirk.

He doesn't reach for me, though he looks like he wants to. Something stops him. Possibly the fact that Everett tightens his grip on me. "I bet Bronxy deserved it, huh?"

"Get back, Jameson," Everett says, shifting me slightly away. If I didn't know better, I'd think he was protecting me. More like being possessive. I'd recognize that because of Laredo. He always got a little bit clingy after I'd drink straight from him. "She scares easily."

I scrunch my face and glare.

Jameson doesn't heed Everett's warning. Instead, he leans closer to me and whispers, "Boo."

Swinging my arm out, I attempt to punch him in the face, but the bastard snatches my hand like he knew I would try to fight him. Everett roars, and I mean deep, guttural, holy shit I might die by his hands, roars. The world falls out from under me, and I screech, unable to prepare myself.

Someone catches me and tosses me onto their shoulder. I suck in a sharp breath of air through my teeth at the pain exploding in my side. Everett yells, and I arch my back in an attempt to get a better view of the craziness that unfolds.

Bronx and Jameson grab each of Everett's arms, restraining him. He gnashes his teeth at them, struggling to break free. "Put her down. You're hurting her," Everett calls. "Mik, please."

Mikkalo doesn't listen, and I jerk my hand out and slap him right on the ass. He startles at my bravado, flipping me back over and into his arms. "Strong little thing, isn't she?"

"She consumed blood," Bronx says.

Mikkalo raises his eyebrows. "Shit. Everett, you didn't."

Everett snaps his teeth. "She had already done so before me. But yeah, I gave her more. She was shot. So please, just put her down. I need to get another look at her to make sure she's okay."

"I don't fucking think so," Bronx says. "You said she could've been bitten with venom too."

Jameson groans next. "Really? What the hell? I knew I should've been the one to go after the outcast."

"We don't know for certain," Bronx says.

Jameson releases Everett, closing the space to me and Mikkalo. He reaches out and brushes my hair off my neck, ignoring the fact that I try to punch at him. Tightening his jaw, he studies Laredo's bite.

"Looks deep," Jameson says. Turning, he glances at Everett. "You good now, brother? I need your opinion."

Everett squares his shoulders and strolls at a human's

speed next to Bronx. And hell, do I wish they'd all back up. All four vampires crowd around me, searching over my body like they've never seen a bitten human before. Mikkalo rubs his hand across his smooth, dark skin like it'll help him figure me out. His nearly black eyes flash silver. Everett inches closer, cautiously reaching for my neck. He surely thinks I'm a wild animal about to bite. I consider it. It takes everything in me not to. He still smells so good. And he's hot. All of them, actually.

What is wrong with me? I've had years of practice denying Laredo even though he was attractive as hell. And he begged me. These guys don't. My dumb body wants to just throw itself at them and not only to taste them.

Laredo's bite really must have knocked the good sense out of me.

My stomach twists, my muscles tightening with hunger the longer they smolder me with their intense gazes. And not just normal hunger. Batshit blood hunger. The kind after starving myself for a month.

"Don't touch it. It hurts like hell," I say, swatting at Everett's hand. "Don't think I can't break your hand."

Everett stops short, curling his fingers. "Is this your first bite, Gwen?"

Ugh. I wish he didn't ask.

"It is," Jameson says, speaking up. "I'd know that look anywhere."

I blush harder, my cheeks burning so badly that it's

nearly as painful as the bite on my neck. "Shut the hell up. You don't know anything about me."

Jameson puckers out his bottom lip. "I'm sorry that asshole ruined what should have been a pleasurable experience for you."

Ah fuck. Laredo always swore it was supposed to feel good. Maybe for twisted masochist vampires. Nothing about his bite felt good. But damn it if I don't believe Jameson and his wide green eyes. He looks just as concerned as Everett.

Everett releases a soft growl but doesn't do anything else to react. "I'll have to run some tests to be sure, but I think we got to her on time. I don't think she'll transition."

"Transition? What are you talking about? I'm not going to transition. I was vaccinated against the Blood Hunger Plague," I say, licking my lips. My stomach lurches again, and I heave a breath, pain burning through me.

Bronx releases a deep laugh. "Good one."

Everett glowers at him. "She wouldn't know, Bronx."

"Know what?" I know I shouldn't ask. I know better than to talk to these guys, but damn it. They just continue to stand around me, caging me between their muscular bodies while Jameson continues to cradle me.

"All vampires have venom they can release to transition a donor. It's against the law without prior approval from Donor Life Corp," Everett says. "But don't worry. I don't think your...master—?"

"Laredo wasn't my master," I snap. He had a mutual agreement with my family. I know better than to call him my blood source, though. Donors are blood sources, not vampires. At least to those associated with Donor Life Corp.

"Then your keeper," Everett says.

"Enough, Ev," Bronx says. "She doesn't need answers. You need to take her to the clinic, make sure she's good to go, and then send her on for interrogation. She's a criminal. Unregistered."

Mikkalo pats Everett on the shoulder. "He's right, brother. I know she's hot and all, but we have to follow protocol. We wouldn't want Zaire suddenly to renounce and outcast us. You know the board position got to his head."

"Zaire?" My dumb mouth. It's just as rebellious as the rest of me.

All four vampires ignore me.

"You're right," Everett says, tightening his jaw. He looks disappointed. "I'm sorry. One of you should give her a bit more blood to speed up her healing process. The last thing we need is to have to admit we let a donor best us in our own region."

None of them respond. They all just look at Everett like giving me their blood is crazy. And what the hell? Laredo enjoyed it. I didn't think I was that repulsive...what am I even thinking?

I shake my head, trying to control my deep-seated nature that just loves the idea of tasting the rest of these vampires, who look nothing like the usual shadow dweller. I thought Laredo was attractive enough, the fact that his blood was delicious helped, but these guys?

I squirm in Jameson's arms at the thought and inhale a breath.

Fuck. Me. I sniffed him.

"Damn." He meets my gaze, his green eyes a far prettier shade than mine. "Damn it, fine. I'll do it. But turn your backs." His words make me frown. I guess I do repulse him.

"We'll wait outside," Bronx says, slapping his back. "Gotta check on the rest of the donors anyway. Just don't get carried away. I don't need to pry her off you."

My eyes widen, ignoring his last comment. I hope they do have to pry me off. One less vampire to fight. "My brothers are here?"

Bronx ignores my question, motioning to Everett and Mikkalo to follow him toward the door. None of them glance behind them at us, and Jameson continues to stare at me until I return my gaze to his.

"Do you always ignore donors like this?"

His Adam's apple bobs in his throat. "I'm going to sit in the chair."

"I guess that's a yes," I quip. "Why do you sound nervous for being a big, scary blood drinker?"

Ignoring me, Jameson strolls to a small sitting area and eases onto a chair. His stiff posture makes this awkward as hell. He turns his gaze away from me and bites his arm. I can't stop my automatic intake of breath.

"Go easy on me," Jameson murmurs, drooping his shoulders to force them to relax. "It's been a long time since I've done this."

I scowl. "Go easy on you? Are you kidding me? I'm a prisoner. You separated me from my family. Your team or whatever killed my blo—vampire friend. I'm not going to go easy on you. I'm going to devour you. Now, give me your damn arm. You smell delicious already, and I'm in so much pain that it's taking everything in me not to—"

"Damn." The second the word escapes Jameson's tight mouth, a bulge pokes my ass.

I hop up at his sudden erection, heat flooding my face. Jameson lets me go, and I take advantage of the situation and bolt for it, gathering all my strength to get my legs to work despite the burning in my neck and side. My body is in full-on escape mode. I'm getting out of here, even if it means I have to crawl on my hands and knees.

I trip, releasing a string of fucks, and glower at the ceiling. "Come the hell on!" It seems I will have to crawl out of here.

If only a few droplets of dark blood didn't splash on the pristine white tiles. I freeze, flaring my nostrils. My body kicks into action, and I launch at Jameson, knocking him on his back. I straddle his waist, ignoring the fact that he's still turned on by me. He doesn't fight me or push me off either.

Locking me with his intense green eyes, he smiles and licks his lips. And my damn mouth. I smile back at him, caught by surprise at how hot he looks fully prepared to let me ravage the hell out of him.

I've never had a vampire—not even Laredo—lie under me, giving up their control. Of course, my experience with vampires only encompasses nasty-ass shadow dwellers, usually starved beyond sanity. Gross, vicious, growly as all get-out. Animalistic.

"I apologize for my prior hesitation...Gwen, is it? You must understand that blood exchanges of this type usually remain in private. It's been quite a while since I've done this, and to be honest, never with a donor."

I blink at his words. This feels like the kind of admission people say before getting it on. "Of course you haven't. Vampires don't give up their control of humans. You can't manipulate our minds if we consume your blood."

He smiles wider, his fangs flashing in the process. "I'm not great at manipulating minds at all, so your speculation of me is wrong."

I narrow my eyes. "Whatever. Let's get this over with. The sooner I'm healed, the sooner I can get out of here and away from you."

Jameson releases a breathless laugh. "You want to leave so soon? I thought we were having fun—"

Snatching his bloody arm, I yank it to my mouth and suck hard enough to re-open his already healing bite. He snaps his mouth closed, not finishing his thought. His eyes flash silver, and he sucks in his bottom lip. I close my eyes to break his stare, feeling the weight of it penetrate me in a way that leaves me nearly panting and buzzing.

Pulling myself together, I jerk away from his arm and throw myself off him. I should not enjoy a blood exchange so much. This guy will see to it I'm caged. He and his team have my brothers.

I hang my head, closing my eyes, curling my legs to my chest. I already feel tons better. Rolling up my shirt, I gaze at the puckered skin, already scabbing over. And shit. Who knew I could heal so fast? I've never been this injured before, but Laredo once gave his blood to my brother Ashton after getting bitten by a shadow dweller, and it still took him over a day.

"Almost like new, huh?" Jameson asks, sitting up next to me.

"Still hurts," I mutter.

"Serves you right. Your kin shot—"

Anger rushes through me, and I can't stop my arm from swinging out. I smack Jameson across the face. He growls in surprise, his head jerking with my action. He has so much nerve even to say I deserved this. What an asshole.

I don't get a chance to try again. Someone drags me to my feet, restraining my arms at my sides. Jameson looks ready to launch at me, but Everett appears and touches his shoulder.

"She'll be fine. Bronx won't hurt her," he says. Everett's voice trickles to me, but he doesn't move his lips.

Oh, shit. This is new.

I knew that vampires were capable of talking in such a way that humans can't hear them. Most are quiet as hell. But damn. Something's wrong with me. I'm pretty sure I just heard something that I wasn't supposed to. And the fact that Jameson wasn't planning to launch at me and instead at Bronx, who tightens his arms around me as I flail, confuses me.

"Fuck, she's strong," Bronx says, his words tickling my ear. "Ev, you need to sedate her. I don't think she's going to stop."

"Can you blame her?" Jameson says, finally speaking up. He trains his eyes on mine and pushes his light brown hair from his forehead.

Bronx growls. "Everett, the sedative. Do not make me call headquarters for backup. We have a job to do. You guys can't get attached to her. She's a criminal. There's a protocol we must follow." His reminder makes both Everett and Jameson's features harden.

"Yes, brother," Jameson says first. "I'm sorry. It won't happen again."

"We're all set to head to the BMC," Mikkalo says from the door. "They're preparing the testing now."

I frown. "BMC?"

No one answers me, and then Everett appears in front

of me, holding a syringe. He frowns. "My apologies, Gwen. This will all be over soon. As long as you don't fight, I'm sure you'll get transferred to someone from a good coven. There is already interest in you."

I blink a few times. "What the hell are you talking about?"

He tightens his jaw and ignores my question. "I'm sorry again. Now take a breath. This will sting."

3

CRIMINAL

"KYLER!" I CAN'T CONTROL MY mouth as I spot my brother through a small window in a door to a room with a single desk and computer against the wall.

Kyler doesn't react, keeping his eyes trained on the screen. I try to stop walking to bang on the door, but a strange vampire pops in front of the glass and scowls, flashing his fangs. Mikkalo gently touches the small of my back, forcing me to keep walking.

"He can't respond to you," Mikkalo says, nudging me along without full-on forcing me to move. "He's been manipulated to take the Blood Match test."

I frown. "The what?"

"It's a test to see if a donor matches to a vampire to become a permanent, exclusive blood source. There is a questionnaire, physical, blood sampling, and sometimes an interview. In your cases, you'll skip the final portion as your relatability isn't necessary. You've been sentenced by Donor Life Corp to proceed compared to those donors who apply willingly. Your family will also not receive any benefits or exemption if you do match."

I inhale a sharp breath. I've heard about this Blood Match Program before. My dad once told me about an entire human-only community, placated by vampires under the idea that they're somehow better than the rest of us for their family member's sacrifice to willingly give their blood—and sometimes body—to a vampire exclusively. Yuck.

"You can't do this," I say.

Mikkalo stops in front of a room. "I'm sorry, Ms. Gallagher. It's this or being put up for auction to the highest bidder for a final donation. And it wouldn't be pleasant. You could be kept alive for months. Those covens who spend that type of money aren't exactly...let's just say this is a far better option. The vampire you match with won't know the extent of your offense. All they'll know is that you didn't volunteer, so it might take a bit more effort to establish a bond."

Oh, my God. The thought sends my heart racing. I knew that vampires were terrible to donors, especially ones they deemed criminal. My family once helped a man who managed to escape his fate during a crazy-ass, barbaric party game called finders keepers, where vampires hunt and kill criminals for entertainment. And just knowing that Mikkalo thinks he's showing me mercy by forcing me into the Blood Match Program says something.

"Fuck," I whisper to myself.

"I'm sorry, Gwen. I know none of this was really your fault and your family dragged you along with them into the rebel life. If there was something more I could do—"

"Just let me go," I say. "Take me to my brothers and pretend you didn't find us. Blame it on Laredo. Please."

I don't know why I beg, but something about Mikkalo's dark eyes gets under my skin. I've never been apologized to so much—and never by a vampire—I can't stop myself from trying to reason with him.

Without responding right away, he opens the door by pressing his hand to the glowing palm device. He nudges me inside, shutting the door behind us.

"This room is soundproof. Keep your voice low, because vampires can still hear you," he whispers. His eyes search over my face as he stands so close that my chest touches his with every deep breath.

"Why are you—"

He brings his finger to my mouth, silencing my question. "Gwen, please don't make this harder. I can't help you as much as I want to. You entered a quarantined city and jeopardized the entire donor population here. Your brothers killed one of our finest security heads. Grayson shot me. He shot you. He along with the rest of your brothers have already been transferred for auction."

Fury sneaks up on me, and I fly at Mikkalo and shove him into the wall. My fingers dig into his solid chest, and I glower. He lets me pin him, though I know he could easily overpower me. And now I can't figure him out.

"And Kyler?" I ask, pushing him again. "Why is he here?"

"He just made the age cutoff to enter the program with you. My brothers and I agreed that it'd be safe enough after manipulating his mind," he says, locking his gaze to mine. In the lighting overhead, I catch sight of a ring of copper around the near black iris of his eyes.

"What age?" I ask.

"Anyone between eighteen and twenty-two to give matches the most time possible with a personal donor. A Blood Match is lifelong."

I scoff and smack his chest. "Who told you we were under twenty-two? I'm not. I'm twenty-three. Kyler is twenty-four. You should just send us all to auction." Because if we're together, we can fight. We can get out of this. I know it.

Mikkalo narrows his eyes at me.

I keep my face expressionless as to not give away my lie. I've played the role of a minor a dozen times in the last few years, because minors are safer under Donor Life Corp law, so aging myself up is new to me. I doubt Mikkalo can even tell. Most vampires can't be certain. That's why all donors are marked with bracelets with the information. Minors don't get them, so that's always been the role I played.

"One of your brothers already gave you away," he says softly. "Gwen Gallagher, age twenty-one, youngest of seven and the only female in your family. Your father's deceased, and you currently live a nomadic lifestyle. Your permanent residency is far outside the former Bellamy Region and the Donor Life Corp territory."

He recites the facts about me, thankfully leaving out the one I'm most afraid to hear—the one calling me out as the dhampir I am. But my brothers would never be able to tell another vampire. My old blood source ensured it. It was the only time my dad ever let him manipulate my brothers' minds, putting a block in place so they'd be incapable of spilling my secret, even under mind manipulation.

I clench my fingers into fists. "I don't care if I'm eligible for this fucking match program. Just send us to auction."

"I'm sorry, Gwen. Please take a seat at the computer. If you refuse to comply, you'll leave me no choice but to keep you here until my brothers' blood runs out of your system."

"So you can force me," I say, trying to stay calm. My

breath quickens despite my best efforts. I risk glancing over my shoulder to get a better look at the room. It's bare. I could hit him with the chair, but that still leaves me with a locked door.

Mikkalo steps forward, proving that he only let me pin him to the wall and motions me toward the computer. "I'd prefer not to, Ms. Gallagher. I don't like manipulating minds."

"Why not?" I ask. I shouldn't test my luck, but this guy confuses me. "Why treat me differently than my brother?"

His face softens. "Because I'm hoping you'll realize that we're not the bad guys. The situation you were in, how that vampire used you, it was unfair. We're doing our best to help you."

Help me? He's gotta be fucking kidding me. I don't get the chance to say so, because a buzzer sounds on the door, making me jump. Mikkalo groans under his breath and turns to face Bronx peering at us in the window. Bronx's eyes flick to mine for a split second before he opens the door.

"She hasn't started yet? What's taking so long?" he asks, combing his fingers through his dark hair, longer than Mikkalo's buzzed cut. The light catches Bronx's strands, highlighting streaks of golden brown like his skin. "I don't want to be here all night. Zaire said he'd stay. Apparently he's applying to match."

I crinkle my nose. This is the second time I've heard

him mention Zaire.

"What about the rest of us?" Mikkalo asks, stiffening. He stares at Bronx, silver flashing in his eyes. It's hard to tell, but he might actually look like he's nervous to hear Bronx's response.

Bronx's jaw twitches. "We were all denied due to conflict of interest. It must be Zaire."

I open my mouth to ask them what the hell they're talking about, but then I notice I don't see Bronx's mouth move with his flexing jaw. Shit. What the hell did Laredo do to me? What if these douches were right and he bit me with venom? What if I'm currently transitioning? Laredo did mention something about me being free when this was all over. But—

I push the thought away and tap my tongue to my teeth. No signs of fangs. I flick my gaze to my blurry reflection in the small window in the door. No silver eyes either. I touch my throat and groan. Still hurts like hell. I wish I could get a better look at the bite.

"What are you waiting for?" Bronx says, catching me gawking. "Go sit down, Gwen. Take the damn test."

I narrow my eyes at him. "Fuck off."

"I will once you sit the hell down."

Huffing a breath, I force my legs to obey my brain and stroll across the room before Bronx yanks me off my feet to plop my ass in the chair himself. He looks ready to do it. I peer at him over my shoulder again, and he meets my annoyance with his own, his eyes flashing silver. Twirling his finger, he motions for me to turn around.

"Enough, Bronx. I got it handled," Mikkalo says.

Bronx growls, mostly at me, and I spin around to look at the computer screen and raise my hand to flip him off.

He has the nerve to chuckle. "Okay, rebel. I got it. You're tough. Now just take the fucking test. Be honest. If you lie, it only increases your chances of getting placed somewhere intolerable to you."

"Like you even care," I say, staring at the screen in front of me.

"I don't, so shut up. Take the test."

A moment later the door slams. I don't turn around. I don't have to see for myself to know that Bronx left, and Mikkalo hovers near the door, his heart thumping as fast as mine.

Sighing, I lean on my elbows and tap the screen.

"Welcome to the Blood Match Program where you'll soon discover if you're a true match to a vampire," I read out loud. "All participants must match eighty percent or higher to become official Blood Matches. Good luck."

I roll my eyes.

"Don't worry, Gwen," Mikkalo repeats. "You won't need any luck. I have a good feeling about this."

I close my eyes. "I don't."

"I guess we'll see."

Slumping forward, I bang my head on the desk. "I don't even know what this is."

Mikkalo's shadow shrinks on the wall in front of me as he steps closer. "If you tap on the screen, it'll read the question."

I swivel and look up at him. "I can read fine, thanks. I just—what the hell is reverse cowgirl? Why would someone want to pretend to be a female cow...in reverse?"

Mikkalo tips his head back and laughs. His whole face lights up with the action, and I can't stop gawking at him. I blush with embarrassment and turn back around to face the screen.

"Never mind. Go away. I'll just guess," I mutter.

His shadow remains in place and then he touches my shoulder. "I didn't mean to laugh. I wasn't making fun of you. I'm well aware that under your circumstances, you probably haven't had much sexual experience."

I roll my eyes and don't respond. I can't tell if he's trying to bait me or if he really thinks I've been sheltered otherwise.

"I mean, no man would stand a chance with your brothers around. They seemed—overprotective," he muses.

Still, I ignore him. There is no way I'm announcing the status of my sexual prowess, which has sat in a standstill since the few times after I lost my virginity to... I squeeze my eyes shut, pushing the thought away. Every time I think about how Laredo walked in and killed my brother's best friend, thinking he was hurting me—ugh. I can't go there. Porter hadn't spoken or even looked at Laredo since. He barely looked at me.

"The lotus? The bandoleer? Afternoon delight? What the hell?" I whisper.

Mikkalo clears his throat in an attempt not to chuckle. "Just fill out what you know, Gwen. This portion isn't put on record. It's compiled into a series of percentages. Your future match won't ever get to see it."

"Yeah, right," I say, quickly tapping my finger across the screen. I can feel Mikkalo's presence behind me, and I jerk my hand back and hit him in the stomach, regretting the action immediately. Because damn. His abs are hard as all get-out. Like slapping rocks.

His shadow disappears, and I shake out my hand, sliding lower in my chair. The screen suddenly lights up with the word *complete*, and I roll back and stand up. Turning around, I train my eyes to the tiles, not wanting even to humor the idea of meeting Mikkalo's gaze again. Not after that awkward as fuck section where I'm certain he saw that I clicked on the only familiar position I knew the name of.

Another beep sounds on the door, and it swings open. I still don't look up. I can't. My eyes won't let me.

"I'll walk her to the exam room, Mik," Everett says. "Zaire wants to see you in his office."

A figure appears next to me, and I expect to raise my gaze to Everett, but Mikkalo stands a few inches away and smiles. "To be fair, the vampires responsible for the questionnaire were quite creative, even for me."

I groan and whack his arm, making him smile wider. "Shut the hell up."

He brings his index finger to his mouth. "It's our secret. Now, follow Everett. It's a shame I couldn't apply to Blood Match with you. We'd have had a great time."

Mikkalo disappears before I have a chance to tell him yeah-fucking-right, and I turn my attention to Everett. He remains expressionless, standing a few feet away. Extending his hand, he holds it out to me. I don't know what comes over me, but I take it and slide my fingers through his.

He gapes at our hands but doesn't tug away. And then I step even closer, intruding his space like he's done to me. His heart jumpstarts, thrumming in a soft melody I hadn't noticed before. And it gets crazier the longer I stand, holding his hand.

He licks his lips. "I hope you don't mind if I perform your physical. Your application wasn't expected, and those applying refuse to wait another day until we can request a human practitioner."

I don't respond, letting him tug me along the hallway. We pass the room I last saw Kyler, but it's now empty. Everett notices my gaze and gently squeezes my hand, drawing my attention to him.

"He's already in the final phase of his Blood Matching. The results thus far are looking good. He was surprisingly in impeccable health. Most applicants tend to be undernourished, uncared for, and not exactly donors that vampires..." He snaps his mouth shut. "I'm sorry."

I try not to react. "You apologize a lot. I don't know why. It's not going to change the fact that you saved my life only so that I could end up in a cage and fed upon over and over again. You should've left me alone. I'd be better off dead."

I'd think I had slapped the guy. His face flushes unlike anything I've seen before. Straightening his back, Everett stiffens and keeps his eyes trained on the hallway in front of us. He doesn't reply to my comment, choosing to not say anything to me instead.

"I knew I was right," I mutter.

One second, Everett holds my hand, and in the next, he drops it and steps a few feet ahead to put some space between us. He keeps his back facing me, not even peering over his shoulder to see that I follow.

So I stop and turn the other way.

I run.

I make it all of twenty feet and only because Everett lets me. There's no way I can outrun a vampire, only outsmart them, and with Everett, I'm not so sure I can. He acts nothing like a starved shadow dweller on a mission to bite and run, hoping not to get caught tapping into the general population blood source for a snack.

"Wrong way, Ms. Gallagher," Everett says, his voice no longer soft as he speaks to me.

I frown. "It's Gwen."

"I don't have all day to perform the physical. Please, turn around and head to the fifth door on the left. You'll find a medical gown to change into. I'll also proceed with the blood draw to speed up the process. The lab is currently closed due to your unexpected arrival here." Everett points down the hall. "The sooner we finish, the sooner you can get rid of me and never see me again."

I raise my eyebrows. "Are you upset with me? You cannot be fucking upset."

Everett doesn't respond. He doesn't even look at me.

Clenching my fingers into fists, I storm past him and stride down the hallway in the direction he told me to go.

"I don't know why you're so damn offended. Look what you did to my family," I call. "Don't think I'll give you an ounce of gratefulness. You and your team—"

"My brothers," Everett corrects.

"I don't care who they are. You guys ruined my life." I heave a few breaths, trying to jiggle the doorknob on the door, but it doesn't budge.

Everett materializes at the one next to me and opens it for me, pissing me off.

I know I counted five doors and he's at the sixth, making me feel dumb. Pursing my lips, I shove past him and into the room where a tall cot rests against the wall with a privacy curtain to pull around the bed. On the edge lies a tiny as all get-out blue piece of fabric.

I hold it up and shake it out. "Where's the rest of it?"

Everett stands in the doorway. "This is a physical, Ms. Gallagher. I'll be performing a health check. You have had one of those, correct?"

My breath quickens at the memory of the one and only time Dad took me into a small rebel village to visit with their health keeper. I had to take off my pants then too, but that old man wasn't as hot as Everett. He was also a professional, descended from one of the top human doctors from the back-world with the old, yellowing certificate to prove it. He also had successfully delivered over a hundred babies in his life.

But Everett? I have no idea, and I'm not going to find the hell out.

"I have decades of human health experience, Ms. Gallagher," Everett says, clearing his throat. "If you'd like, I can walk you through the exam first. But I need you to change."

I shake the gown at him again. "This thing isn't even big enough to cover my vagina!"

He inwardly groans and turns to face the wall, lacing his hands behind his head. "Ms. Gallagher, please."

I throw the gown at him. "The only way you're getting me out of these clothes is if you take yours off too. I will not be put at a disadvantage."

Everett spins and meets my gaze. "This is a medical exam, not a date."

My mouth drops open as I gape at him in shock. His frown pulls up into a smile, and he has the nerve to laugh and shake his head.

I compose my expression. "Humans don't have the privilege of dating when we're on the run for our lives. And so you know, it'll take a lot more than one date to get my pants off."

His eyes trail down my body, drinking me in, a new expression overtaking his face. Rubbing his forehead, he drags his fingers into his blond hair and tips his head back to stare at the ceiling. I can't tell what the hell he's thinking.

After another moment of silence, he glances into the hallway and proceeds to shut the door. I shift on my feet but not from fear.

My heart picks up speed, and I remember the sugary taste of his blood. My body reacts, goosebumps prickling over my skin.

He clears his throat and strolls to the backless rolling chair and sits down. "Gwen, this wasn't exactly how I wanted to finish my shift. I usually don't go out on calls with my brothers. I know my apology is useless and doesn't mean shit to you, so why don't you just let me draw your blood and sign off on your paperwork? You can fill out as much information as you feel comfortable."

I blink in surprise. "Wait, really?"

He releases a small breath and leans his elbows on his knees. "Yes, really. I can't pretend to know what your life was like before today, but with how fiercely you fight and how almost outrageously brave you are, I can only assume you've dealt with a lot of outcast vampires."

"You can say that. Shadow dwellers are ruthless," I say, finally getting my body to chill the hell out and sit down before it decides to close the space to Everett.

"The outcast ones, yes. They've been banished from the cities by Donor Life Corp for a reason. Donors—humans—remain within cities and in vampire households for their safety. Not all of us are uncivilized, uncontrolled blood drinkers."

"Oh." I knew that. Laredo was usually pretty good.

"And so you know, your results have been narrowed down to three. None of the contending vampires would cage you...unless you give them a reason. You'll be well cared for, and you'll never have to fight again. Think of this as a chance to start a new life." Everett lifts his eyes to meet mine, gauging me for a reaction.

"But my brothers—"

"We tried our best, okay? There's only so much we can do under these circumstances. Your older brothers are the kind of rebels that would rather die than enter the system. But you and Kyler? You both proved to be different. Your results confirmed it. You specifically showed impressive in-telligence, compassion, and open-mindedness." Shifting on his seat, he pulls out a small com device. I've never seen one in person. He taps the screen a few times. "And so you know, Kyler matched into the Anderson Coven of Crescent Ridge in this region. They are some of our allies, which is good to know."

"What region is this anyway? My bl—vampire friend never said. He wasn't familiar with this area," I say.

"Because the Royale Region is fairly new. If he hasn't been around recently, he wouldn't know."

I hum under my breath, wishing he'd go on. The more information I can gather, the better chance I have at figuring the way out.

He doesn't. Instead, he gets to his feet and rolls a metal table toward me. I try not to look at the shiny instruments on the tray, my mouth going dry.

Everett fiddles with the equipment a moment. "Now, if you'd allow me, I'd like to draw your blood."

I bob my head, feeling all sorts of weird. "I've never donated blood before."

"Never?" he asks. "You were with a vampire."

"My brothers fed him."

He remains expressionless to my comment. "Why don't you close your eyes then? I'll be as fast as I can."

A wave of dizziness washes over me, the edges of my vision darkening.

I don't even get a chance to tell him before I watch my vibrant blood flow through a tube and into a vile. I fall forward off the cot, only to land in his arms.

The vile shatters on the floor, spilling my blood.

"Shit," Everett says. "Bronx, I need some help. Take Gwen out of here. I think I got enough of her blood."

The last things I see are Bronx's flashing fangs and ceiling lights.

4

BLOOD MATCH

A SOFT KNOCK SOUNDS ON the door, drawing my attention away from my hands. I've been locked in this room for who knows how long, but at least Bronx left me with a banana, a piece of toast, and the biggest glass of orange juice I've ever seen—actually the first one I've ever seen.

Fruit has always been a special occasion thing, but especially these last few years. Laredo would steal us some from whatever orchards we happened upon, but it was nearly a fight to the death to get more than a piece with my brothers—and I always fought hard.

"Gigi, I'd like to come in," a familiar, melodious voice says. "I have missed you so. I hope my brothers have been treating you well."

"Gigi? Did you forget my name already, *Jamie*?" I ask from my spot without getting up. Not like there's a point. I can't unlock the door myself. I've tried.

A strange-ass noise comes through the door, and Jameson swings it open. He stops short upon seeing me, his gaze sweeping from my brushed hair all the way down to my toes. He doesn't say anything for a moment while he drinks me in.

"You better keep at least three feet of space between us. I can still kick your ass in this stupid dress," I say, sweeping the billowing white fabric back and forth. "Which I wouldn't be wearing if one of your sneaky asshole brothers hadn't stolen my clothes while I was in the shower."

He chuckles. "You can't tell me that you wanted to change back into those grimy clothes."

I twist my lips, hating that he's right. "But this ridiculous dress? Where'd you all find it? A back-world bridal shop?"

"You're familiar with back-world history?" he asks instead of answering my comment.

"Probably better than any human you know." I slip off my chair and stand with my hands on my hips. "So, this dress...? It's gotta go."

Jameson's eyes flash silver, and he takes a step closer and then catches himself. "It's inappropriate to request I undress you when I'm supposed to escort you to your Blood Match announcement."

Swiveling on the balls of my feet, I scoop up my fork and throw it at him. "You think I'm being inappropriate?"

Jameson catches the utensil and stakes it into the wall with a laugh. "Okay, okay. Come on. We're both about to get into trouble if we don't hurry up. I would hate for my brothers to think we ran away together—though after our little blood exchange, I'd be lying if I said the thought hasn't crossed my mind."

His voice softens with the words, his lips smirking.

I don't mean to react, but his reminder of my blood consumption sets my body the hell off. Laredo never made me feel this way. He tasted delicious, but something about this dude makes my mouth water.

"You like the idea," he murmurs.

That's enough to put me in check, because there is no damn way I'd ever willingly run away with him unless... "Love it." I can't stop the words from coming out, but hell. If I can convince this guy to risk breaking the law, I might have a chance to escape. He doesn't even look like he'd put up that much of a fight, not if I suggest he feeds me.

He makes that strange-ass noise again—almost like he's purring. I've heard vampires growl and snarl—shriek like crazy—but to purr like a cat? But deeper, rumbly almost. Why is that so sexy sounding to me? Maybe because it feels like he's inviting me to get closer. And if I get close—

I hadn't realized how hungry I was until I jump into Jameson's arms and bury my face into the crook of his neck. What the hell is wrong with me? I can usually go weeks without blood. But now? I'm suddenly feeling bitey. It takes everything in me not to test my luck. Vampires don't like the action reciprocated most of the time because I don't have fangs—I should know. I've bitten quite a few vampires since we've been infiltrating cities to help desperate donors find a way out.

Jameson slides his hand down my back but stops short of my ass, allowing my thighs to do all the work as I hang onto him. He groans but not in a bad way. "Gigi, what are you doing?"

I take another breath, making him shiver. "Please, Jamie. I don't want to find out who I Blood Match with. I'm scared." I keep my voice intentionally low. "I like being here with you."

He eases me away from him, setting me on my feet. "Gwen."

Damn it. Something shifts in his green eyes, turning their vibrant color more aqua with the flash of silver. "Jameson."

"Maybe if you actually did like me, I'd consider risking my life to steal you away to keep you to myself, but I know what you're doing. I'm a master at playing games," he whispers, pushing my blond hair behind my ear. "I also know that you'll stake me the second you get the chance."

"Would not. I need you," I say. It's technically true. A girl's gotta eat. I don't say as much though.

"I can see why you managed to hypnotize the vampire we found you with," he murmurs. "You're quite alluring. The thought—"

A chime rings through the air, and Jameson snaps his attention away from me. He tugs his com device from inside his jacket and glances at the screen. I don't even get a chance to prepare myself as he hooks his arm around my waist and charges from the room, carrying me at a vampire's speed.

I struggle to glance around, my eyes watering from the wind mussing my hair. There is no chance I'll be able to get out of this place, even if I somehow manage to overpower Jameson and force him to let me go. It would be easy enough to throat punch him. I doubt he'd expect it.

Leaning away from him, I swing my arm back to give my punch enough force. I jab my fist forward and stumble, tripping over the long skirt of my white gown. And damn it. I took too long.

A big hand locks onto my wrist, stopping me from eating shit in the middle of a brightly lit lobby. I stiffen, a dozen gazes locking on me. I don't even have to look around to know that I'm in a room full of vampires, now caught mid-attack.

"Jameson, you asshole! Warn a woman next time you decide to turbo run." I straighten the bodice of my gown, ignoring that Bronx stands awfully close—protectively? No. He looks more ready to throw me into a chair to yell at me to sit down and shut up and to mind my place as a donor. But he doesn't, and a soft chuckle sounds through the air.

"Forgive me, Ms. Gallagher," Jameson says, meeting my gaze from his spot standing next to Mikkalo and Everett. "We'd be here until dusk if I had let you walk yourself. Have you never worn a dress?"

His question prods at me, and it takes everything in me not to scowl. What an asshole. He's lucky there is a room full of vampires scrutinizing my every movement—and maybe the fact that he doesn't call me out on my attempted assault—but still.

"She seems rather feisty," a man murmurs to another guy in the corner. His mouth doesn't move, freaking me out just a bit.

"Seems like a lot of work. I was hoping for an obedient female."

Screw. That. Shit.

"I find a wild heart rather enjoyable," another guy says. "It's quite boring otherwise."

Double screw that shit.

Curling my fingers into my palms, I tense myself, preparing to fight to the death. There is no way I'm leaving with any of these blood sucking pieces of shit who think they have the right to parade me around in a white dress and force me into blood servitude.

Flicking my gaze around the room, I search for anything to use as a weapon. I could swing a chair and hope to break it into sharp enough pieces, but the action might take too long. Only one vampire, a strange, utterly still guy who sits at the end of a row of chairs carries an obvious weapon—a dagger. I can work with that. But damn it. His unblinking eyes, now locking on me, freak me the hell out. My fear instincts prickle like crazy.

"Ms. Gwen Gallagher," a sweet, feminine voice calls. It's enough to draw my attention away from the eerie whispers from the group of all male vampires. "Please come to the counter to receive your Blood Matching results."

Bronx clears his throat and motions to a wraparound desk on the far side of the room. I freeze in my tracks, glaring at the glossy tiled aisle that forces me to stride past the sitting area, taking me too close for comfort toward all the vampires—all of whom look hungry as hell. I know that look. I'm nearly certain it's crossing my face as well, though I try to remain expressionless otherwise.

I can't stop wondering if this is how Laredo always felt around my family, like we were a buffet for him but with me being off the menu.

My. Fucking. Head.

What's wrong with me? If Laredo wasn't already dead,

I'd kick him in the balls for whatever the hell he did to me. My sudden anger eases any sort of grief that might threaten to break free—mostly for my brothers. Laredo was my blood source. Sometimes my entertainment. But now? Damn him if he's going to be my undoing.

Bronx nudges my shoulder with his knuckles, and I straighten my back and stomp down the aisle, keeping my eyes trained in front of me. My steps falter a few feet away from the counter as I spot a human woman sitting at the desk. Her dark brown hair with streaks of gray twists into an intricate knot I'd never be able to accomplish. She flicks her gaze from her screen and greets me with a smile.

"Full house today," she says, baring her teeth in an uncomfortable smile. "It's been over seventy-two days since a female entered the program. You should feel lucky to have had such interest."

Bronx's looming shadow stops me from telling her I feel like I've been cursed. Instead, I keep my mouth shut. Grayson always told me my mouth would get me in trouble, but I always assumed he was teasing me about the fact that I bite back. Now, I realize the truth to his words. I need to keep my mouth shut and not say more than I have to.

"Now, let's see." She hums under her breath.

I nearly jump over the counter to tell her to hurry up because of the sudden murmurs of annoyance sounding out behind me. She taps her fingers to the digital keyboard a few more times. I lean in, stretching as far as my neck will allow, trying to glimpse her screen.

"Shit," Bronx whispers beside me.

I can't stop myself from turning to look at him with a frown. His eyes train on the wall in front of us instead of me, and I ease my eyes off the hulking vampire to follow his line of sight. That's when I notice my picture—the worst one I've ever seen in my life—blinking on the wall. A dozen stats appear below my photo along with three different multi-colored circular graphs.

"Congratulations, Ms. Gallagher," the woman behind the counter says. "You're an eighty-two percent match to Z—"

"Zaire Royale?" I can't stop myself from reading the name that pops up with mine.

"Of the Night Palms Castle just outside the city." The woman grins again at me, drawing my attention away from the screen. "Because you have no heirs to contact or belongings to take with you, you may join your Blood Match immediately." The woman stands and looks behind me. "Mr. Royale, all I need from you is to sign the contract stating that you now have Ms. Gallagher—"

"Ms. Royale," a smooth voice says from behind me.

"Oh, yes. My apologies—Ms. Royale. Please sign the contract the states your Blood Match is now in your care. Read the rest carefully as Donor Life Corp issued a few changes a while ago."

"I'm highly aware. Thank you, Ms. Perkins. You are relieved of your duties and may return to your quarters."

The woman nods her head and smiles at me once more. It's like she was manipulated to show off her teeth with every word directed at her. "Congratulations again, Ms. Royale. I hope to see you around."

I bow my head, resting my hands on the cool countertop. Bronx's shadow disappears from beside me, and the room falls utterly silent apart from two heartbeats—one crazy and out of control and the other slow, even, steady. Damn it. I wish mine would relax.

"Ms. Royale, would you be kind enough to turn around so I can get a better look at you. My brothers spoke so...fondly of you that I'm slightly afraid they have raised my expectations quite substantially." Brothers? Shit. Of course the name Zaire sounds familiar. Bronx kept mentioning him. But Royale? Isn't that the name of the region?

Steeling myself, I spin on my feet, keeping my gaze trained to the floor. I can't help it. It's been far too long since I've consumed vampire blood, and it has surely left my system by now. All it would take is simple eye contact to fall victim to a vampire's mind manipulation. And if this guy's any good, which undoubtedly he is with an entire region named after him, I probably wouldn't even know he manipulated me. I think.

A soft, cool hand touches my chin. "You don't have to be afraid. I will not hurt you, Ms. Royale."

I swallow my nerves and look up. Instead of meeting

his eyes, I peer past him at the now empty lobby—all signs of vampires, including his brothers, gone.

"Call me Gwen, please," I say lowly to keep my voice from breaking.

Zaire nods. "That is a lovely name. You may call me Zaire. There's no need for formalities. I expect us to grow quite close with our Blood Matching relationship."

I furrow my brows, finally meeting his brown eyes to study his features. His skin is a shade lighter than the velvety darkness of Mikkalo's and his jaw is more round than the rugged boxiness of Everett's. Through his suit, I notice his bulging muscles, pretty comparable to Bronx's. His lips part in a smile, showing off his straight teeth without his fangs. Silver flashes in his eyes as he drinks me in, looking as confident as Jameson.

It's like a part of each of his so-called brothers—I mean, physically, it's unlikely they were related before catching the plag...transitioning—manifests in Zaire's handsome, ageless face.

I open my mouth to automatically argue with him that despite how attractive he may be or how nice he sounds, or whatever the hell is stated in the contract he just signed—there is no fucking way I'm partaking in any sort of relationship with him.

He rubs his full lips together. "I know this is all new to you, but I hope you'll soon realize that life for you can be much, much worse."

I stiffen at the threat lying beneath his words. He's testing me for a reaction to see if I'll comply. In any other place outside of this damned city, I might. But now? Surrounded by concrete and metal, shatter-proof glass, and of course all of the shadow dwellers just waiting for a stray donor to head their way, I'm unwilling to risk leading my own personal rebellion. Not alone. Not without Laredo or my brothers.

Sucking up my urge to tackle Zaire, I force my mouth to attempt at least a half smile. "I know how to adapt," I say, finally locking my gaze to his. My insides twist and turn, begging me to look away. I don't. "And I would like to personally thank you for sparing my life and giving me this...opportunity."

Because really, it is. I can see more clearly now.

To fight means to die, and I'm sure the hell no longer ready.

Dying was always something I thought I was okay with. I expected my life would end under the fangs of a shadow dweller. But now that I'm standing in front of an okay-ish acting vampire, who has brothers who might be a teensy bit better than okay-ish, I want to wait this out. My brothers would be livid if I just gave up with the possibility of strategizing my way out of this, using whatever I can against this guy to hopefully free myself, and soon. Because Grayson would kick my ass if I don't, and Kyler needs me. All my brothers need me. I was born a dhampir for a reason—to save humanity. And there's still time to try to save my brothers' dumb asses.

I hear the familiar click of extending fangs and catch sight of Zaire's peeking out from beneath his lips. After spending years with Laredo, I know for a fact that Zaire liked what I said. Vampires tend to flash their fangs for various reasons—food, desire, and anger—and I'm nearly certain approval might also be one of them.

Summoning my nerve, I reach out my hand and graze my fingers across his lips. A bold as hell move, I know, but I also know he looks like he'll relax more if I show him some attention to prove my words are true. "So, what now? Are we staying here all day because of the sun?"

Zaire takes my bait and links his fingers around my wrist. Ever so gently, he brings my index finger to his right fang and pricks me just hard enough to summon a drop of blood. I close my eyes not to watch his soft tongue glide across my finger. The sensation is weirdly not as bad as I expected. Not like the bite Laredo gave me. "I'd like to take you to my estate if that's okay. It's close enough to sunset, and we'll travel by car."

"If it's not okay?" I ask, finally opening my eyes.

He releases a soft chuckle. "I have a suite on the top floor here but thought you'd prefer to hurry to see your new home."

I rub my lips together. "You thought right. I'd like nothing more than to get out of here."

"Good," Zaire says, smiling wider. He holds his arms

open for me. "May I carry you where we need to be going? I'll take care of you. I'm far less adventurous than my brother."

I groan. "Yeah, sure. If you feel it's necessary."

Chuckling again, Zaire lifts me off my feet, carrying me like the damn blushing bride I'm dressed like. "I don't, but it's faster."

I release a small screech as he takes off. Closing my eyes, I breathe next to his ear, catching the sultry, almost warm-smelling scent of his blood. My stomach twists, begging me to do something to satiate its need.

I suppress my nature, clenching my jaw while trying to think of a dozen other things besides the feeling of Zaire's arms around me. But thinking about Zaire makes me think of his brothers. I wonder if I'll ever see them again or if this is it.

I push the thoughts away. This isn't it. I'm going to escape. I'm going to survive.

I still have a lot of fight left.

5

ROYALE BROTHERS

THE SUN DISAPPEARS INTO THE horizon as Zaire navigates the vehicle through the main exit of the city. Tall cement walls surround what's left of the place that survived the vampire uprising and then also The Divide. My dad told me that my grandpa said our family was lucky enough to have escaped during the chaos when the supposed Blood Hunger Plague spread and decimated a huge portion of the human population decades ago.

If people were in cities, they were trapped. Towns fared

no better. Donor Life Corp rose after the government collapsed and quarantined what they could to stop the spread of vampirism. They vaccinated every remaining human and corralled them in the cities for protection. Laws went into effect to satiate the new vampire population. The divisions took place to even out donations, and sadly, families were sometimes separated.

Laredo told me it was to keep the vampires who rose into power from starting blood feuds, and it was all random—a lottery of sorts. At least that's what I was told. Now, I'm not sure after what Bronx said about the spread through venom. He made it sound like we weren't vaccinated against the plague. But why haven't I transformed with Laredo's bite? Maybe because I'm half. I don't know.

I shiver at the thought, staring through the dark tint in an attempt to watch the orange sky fade to purple. Swiveling in my seat, I turn to face Zaire. I wonder if he was around during The Divide. I guess he'd have to be. Maybe even before. Who knows, he could even be responsible.

"You look like you have something to say," Zaire says, tapping a few buttons on the dashboard of the silent car, the only noise coming from the tires gliding over the asphalt. Vampire vehicles are nothing like the ones scavenged by Blood Rebels. There are tons of old, gasoline-powered metal beasts of cars in some of the abandoned cities cared for all these years and passed down generations. But they're illegal. And loud. Humans aren't allowed to drive, but that never stopped my dad from teaching all of us.

From the looks of this sleek, shiny, almost bullet-like vehicle, I think learning to drive wasn't that necessary. Zaire slides his seat away from the steering wheel and twists to meet my gaze.

"Um, shouldn't you watch the road?" I ask instead of commenting on his observation about my burning questions.

The last thing I want to do is discover that he was in fact involved in the slaughter of humanity. It's already taking everything in me to keep from attacking him to try to get out of this metal and glass prison.

Zaire smirks at me like my comment is the most ridiculous thing he's ever heard. "I've programmed our destination in to give you my undivided attention. It'll be a bit of time before we arrive at our estate, so I figured I'd take this opportunity to get to know you beyond the results of our Blood Matching."

"So the car drives itself?" It's obvious, but I need confirmation. I might have to drive it myself very shortly. The city grows smaller in the distance, only visible because of the suddenly glowing lights.

"I suppose you wouldn't know that since not many donors have the privilege of riding in vehicles," he says. Zaire motions at the dash. "It is as easy as tapping a few buttons into the navigation system."

I remain expressionless as he shows me the glowing

map with a few stars that indicate nearby cities. And thank God. For being a vampire, he's naïve as hell—or extremely confident in his abilities as to not worry about someone like me.

"Oh, maybe I can try sometime." I meet his dark eyes and offer a smile. "Unless you're too good to let me break the Donor Life Corp law."

That gets a chuckle out of him, and he adjusts his seat more, creating a human-sized space between his body and the steering wheel. I bite my lip between my teeth and smile, waiting for him to invite me onto his seat. It wouldn't be the first time I've played lapsies with a vampire. My family always had to squeeze into a van, which meant I had to sit on Laredo's lap because he followed me everywhere.

"Want to know a secret?" Zaire asks, leaning in closer, lowering his voice.

"Hmmm?" My heart picks up speed under his intense gaze.

"I *am* Donor Life Corp law and a member of their board." Wiggling his fingers at me, he flashes his fangs. "So, come here. I'll let you drive if you want."

This was too easy. I nearly feel bad for the guy for what I'm about to do. But this is life imprisonment and death for my brothers otherwise. My family comes first. They've always put me before them, so I desperately need to put their needs over mine.

"Really?" I ask, beaming my brightest smile. "You're

the best." If I've learned one thing about vampires from my blood source, it's that they love compliments like everyone else. Laredo would sometimes beg me to comment on his strength or speed, his power, even if I wasn't impressed.

Zaire offers me his hand and helps me slide across the empty space in the middle of the seats and onto his lap. He opens his legs wide enough for me to rest between them, his thighs pressing into my hips. He leans into me so that I feel the taut muscles of his chest against my back.

"You're hypnotic, Gwen," he whispers, resting his chin on my shoulder. "I can't stop thinking about how incredible you taste." His breath on my neck makes me shiver, and I stiffen as he adjusts his arm across my stomach.

"Um, thanks?" I say, arching forward to grip the steering wheel. "So, how do you disable the autopilot?" I keep my voice even, staring at the confusing dashboard labeled with indecipherable images instead of words.

Zaire hooks his other hand around me. "We're not going to do that."

"But you said—"

"You are driving, Gwen," he murmurs, his lips brushing my bare shoulder with his words. "And to be honest, it was never my intent. I wanted to be close to you. Is that okay?"

"No." It takes everything in me not to shove my elbow into his gut. But I still haven't figured out how to disable the autopilot. There's no way I'll survive jumping from the vehicle at this speed.

"No?" His voice deepens with his words.

"That's right," I say. "You offered me the chance to drive to trick me. Not cool, man."

He releases a low growl, sending the hairs on my arms rising. "I wasn't tricking you. I made my intentions clear that I wanted to get to know you apart from the test. And to be honest, I'm starving. The process took longer than I expected."

Ah, hell.

"Please relax, Gwen. I promise I'll be far gentler than the outcast who was mistaken in his worth to possess you." Zaire grazes his fangs on my shoulder, ripping the thin strap of my dress.

I grip the steering wheel. "Please don't bite me."

He stops short. "How else am I going to eat? You're my Blood Match. My personal donor. The faster we get comfortable with each other, the more enjoyable it'll be."

"I don't want to get comfortable," I say.

"Gwen, I don't want to force you, but this was the deal. You enter the program and become a blood source or you join the rest of your despicable brothers in a fate where you would fare far worse being a female. I think a few bites would be worth the extravagant life I'm offering." He loosens his hold on my stomach and meets my gaze in the mirror. "You do realize that I hadn't planned to apply to Blood Match. I have plenty of available blood sources at my disposal on my personal staff. But I'm doing my brothers a favor. For some reason beyond my comprehension, they thought you deserved mercy."

"I never asked for it!" My voice screeches through the air.

Jerking my arm back, I try to elbow Zaire, but he catches me, digging his nails hard enough into my skin to make me wince. He slides his other hand around me, pinning me in place so that I can't flail my arms in an attempt to disable the autopilot.

"Calm down!" he yells.

His deep, guttural voice stabs at my fear instincts, and I stop fighting. I know if I continue, he might try to manipulate my mind. And right now, it'd be easy as hell.

Relaxing his muscles, he inhales a few deep breaths. "That's better, Gwen. Just take it easy. The more you fight, the worse off you'll be."

"Please, just stop the car," I whisper. "Let me out."

He scoffs. "Absolutely not. You're my Blood Match, and I'm going to use you as intended. I'm only going to say this one more time. Relax and accept your position as my blood source or I'll cancel your contract."

"You'll send me where you did my brothers?" I ask, hope rising within me.

"No. I'll complete your final donation. I did not pay an exorbitant amount for a criminal not to enjoy a taste of you at least one more time." His eyes flash silver in the rearview mirror. "Now, what will it be?"

I close my eyes. "I don't want to die."

"Then relax."

I don't want to do that either. So I don't. Bending my neck forward, I put enough space between us to slam my head back. Zaire roars in my ear, attempting to retaliate by snapping his fangs. But the surprise head-butt allows me to swivel and shove my hand to his chest. The steering wheel digs into my back as I twist in the seat, blindly punching at Zaire.

Anger pushes me to fight harder, and I manage to strike Zaire in the groin. He hollers and releases me completely to tend to his hopefully bruised as hell junk, giving me the chance to tap as many buttons on the dash as I can.

It only takes four before the car swerves off course and hits the dirt outside the long stretch of smooth road. Instead of trying to bite me again, Zaire shoves me off of him and back into the passenger's seat. I bounce around, uncontained because he didn't even consider to show me how the crazy complicated seat restraints worked.

I press my hand onto the dash to hold myself in place long enough to figure out how to unlock the doors. But I can't. It's a dumb palm print activation, which immediately turns red under my touch.

Zaire slams the brakes, sending me crashing forward. I hit my head on the windshield. Stars burst in my vision, and I manage to lift my leg to kick it into his stomach. My thrashing gets him to open his door and step out. Disappearing from sight, he abandons me in the vehicle, and I search around for anything I can use as a weapon.

Cool air engulfs me as Zaire jerks open my door and drags me out by the back of my dress. The billowing fabric stops me from dashing away, and instead I fall to my knees, scraping my palms on the rough terrain.

I don't even get a chance to get to my feet. Zaire flips me over and straddles me, using one hand to hold my wrists and the other to bend my neck for him. He extends his fangs farther than he needs to bite me to drink. I'd recognize a kill bite anywhere.

I squeeze my eyes shut. "Wait, please. I'm sorry. Please." I never in my life imagined I'd grovel beneath a vampire to spare my life, but it's not my life I'm worried about. If I die here, my brothers are screwed. There won't be anyone left to fight for those who need it. I'm the only dhampir alive. Most die in childhood because people don't know about us—very few vampires. We don't get what we need to survive.

Zaire doesn't loosen his hold, but he also doesn't bite me. "Open your eyes, Gwen."

Ah hell. I know exactly where this will head. If I open my eyes, he'll trap me in his gaze. If he traps me in his gaze, I'm pretty much dead—at least the self that I know. He'll force me to comply. I've heard about humans breaking out of a vampire's mental hold, but no one has ever told me how. Even if I could, Zaire could do it over and over again.

"Open your eyes before I force them open." His deep voice tightens my chest. Shifting his weight, he repositions himself for a better hold on me and runs his finger across my eyelashes. "I don't want to hurt you."

"Liar," I mutter under my breath.

Zaire releases a deep-ass snarl, and for the first time in a long time, I whimper. I can't help it. I've never been this scared. I've lived my life on edge. I've lived cautiously and aware of the threats around me. I know and accept that there's nothing I can do about my natural fear of a predator. But the sudden alarm blazing inside me strikes me in the gut.

This is one asshole. I can take him. I know it.

I just wish he didn't see me afraid. I wish I didn't feel the penetration of his gaze as my eyes uncontrollably water, and I begin to cry.

"Fuck," Zaire whispers under his breath.

"What? Have you never seen someone cry?" I ask, jerking my head in an attempt to fling the stubborn tears off my cheeks.

Zaire's grip on me disappears, and he growls again. Snapping my eyes open, I realize that I was so focused on what felt like his imminent bite and my oncoming demise that I failed to hear the soft thumps of feet.

It wasn't Zaire setting me off. It was the group of quiet as hell shadow dwellers gliding so fast in our direction that they look like they're flying. Not only that, but their glowing silver eyes look hungry as hell, and from the looks of it, I'm the only human in sight.

"Under the authority of Donor Life Corp, I order you to stop and stay back," Zaire says. "I have claim on this donor. She is mine."

I never thought I'd ever think this, but hell yeah, I'm Zaire's. Because I sure as hell am not going to allow any of these gross, snarling, wild-eyed assholes try to stake a claim on me.

Zaire holds his hand out to me, coaxing me to get to my feet. "Come along, Gwen. It's time to go."

It takes everything in me to take Zaire's hand, but what the hell. If I had to pick who gets to perform my final donation, I'm vain enough to pick the nice-smelling, handsome douchebag over a coven that looks like they rip and spit instead of piercing nicely with their fangs.

Zaire lifts me to my feet only to take me into his arms. He manages to hike up my dress before I realize it. I'm left no choice but to straddle him and hold on myself so that he can keep his hands free. More growls sound out, but the shadow vamps keep their distances. They're either waiting for the opportunity for Zaire to let his guard down or they're smarter than they look. If Zaire's anything like his brothers, he'll be able to take them.

"Do you know how to fight, Gwen," Zaire whispers breathlessly in my ear.

"Yes. I've killed thirteen vampires and helped trapped seven more for my brothers to take care of." I don't know why I get all specific. That kind of revelation gets people immediately drained. Something inside me feels the need to prove myself to Zaire.

"I'm going to pretend I didn't hear that and allow you to retrieve the dagger from inside my jacket," he says, easing back toward the car at a human's pace.

"You're seriously going to fight these guys?" I ask.

"Now's not the time for questions. Grab the blade." Zaire adjusts me slightly so that I can reach between us and tug the dagger from its hidden sheath beneath his jacket. The cold metal hilt weighan any stakes I've held, and I lace my fingers around it the same way too.

"Good,' Zaire whispers. "Now, I'm going to flip you over my shoulders. The outcasts will split up, sending at least one of them at you. The rest will attack me. I need you to do your best to defend yourself. I can't protect you and efficiently fight."

I bob my head. "Got it."

"Get ready."

His words leave me zero warning as the world flips with me, and Zaire drops me over his shoulder to land on my feet on my own. I crouch down, my legs caught in the stupid dress, and I do the only thing I can think of. I rip the side zipper down and let the damn thing fall off.

A dirty-ass vampire freezes in front of me, his silver

flashing eyes practically devouring me in my bra and underwear, and I kick into action and jab the dagger upward to get under his sternum to hit his heart more accurately. Only Laredo's ever been able to crack that damn bone for me, but without him, I must channel everything my dad and brothers have taught me.

The vampire wails, thrusting forward at me. I hit Zaire's back, his solid body feeling like a brick wall as it refuses to give in to the force of my weight. The shadow vampire snarls, staking himself for me in an attempt to bite anywhere he can. Instead of yanking my arm back to try again, I thrust my weight back at him, feeling the slime of his insides sliding up my arm all the way to my elbow as I push every strange-ass thing I can through his back and out his body.

The shadow dweller drops, taking me with him, my arm now stuck in his chest cavity. And fuck. His putrid smelling blood slams into my senses, making my already twisting stomach heave. But even with the gross smell, I can't stop myself from tugging my arm free only to shove my fingers into my mouth.

I regret it immediately.

The eerie silence of the night presses against me, drawing my attention away from the dead body of the vampire and to Zaire. He bares his teeth at me in a confused grimace as I continue to lick the gross blood off my hand.

"Gwen, I don't understand—"

A figure blurs behind Zaire, and I jerk my hand out, sending blood spatter across his face. He turns a little too late, distracted by me and my sudden blood hunger that the outcast manages to knock him off his feet. This guy either laid in wait for the chance to attack or was drawn by the commotion of the fight, because by the looks of the pile of bodies, Zaire had taken care of the assholes who attacked.

Zaire roars, bending his knees to kick the guy off him. Another figure blurs toward Zaire, and I jump to my feet as the two guys surround him. The three of them blur in a fight far too fast for my eyes to follow. A body drops to the ground, and I kick the decapitated head of one of the shadow vampires away from me.

"Time to go, pretty donor." A hoarse voice sounds in my ear.

I freeze in place, staring in shock at Zaire as he continues to fight against a vampire. He pauses and yells something to me that I can't hear over the pounding of my heart. A man materializes in front of me, touching my cheek. I don't have time to react as he leans in to try to capture me in his silver gaze.

"Do not fight. Do not scream," he says, flashing his fangs at me.

"Fuck you!" I swing out my arm to punch him, but he grabs my hand, pulling me into him. I can't stop my mouth from shouting, fear engulfing me at the sound of his fangs clicking as they extend.

Spinning me around, the shadow vampire holds me away from him, bending my neck to the side. He doesn't just want to bite me. He's also trying to prove his power to Zaire by claiming me, who he sees as nothing more than a blood source.

Zaire reacts, shoving the vampire he fights away to close the space to us. My back hits into the shadow dweller's chest, the air escaping my lungs. With one hand, Zaire locks his fingers to my shoulder, forcing me down on my knees. Blood splashes over me, and I startle, watching it pool and absorb into the dirt.

My stomach twists and begs me not to waste it, and I scoop up a handful of dirt and shove it into my mouth. The grains crunch between my teeth as I suck the blood a moment before spitting.

"Gwen, what are you doing?" Zaire asks.

"I—" I snap my mouth shut and thrust my arms around his waist, doing anything I can to give me a moment to think of a response apart from my stomach controlling me and begging me to feed it.

I realize that my face presses right into Zaire's crotch as his body reacts to my closeness, choosing now to throb with a raging boner I can feel against my cheek through his pants. I automatically reach up and press my hand to his erection at the same time I pull my face away, and Zaire gawks at me, a mixture of emotions crossing his face.

And then a hand pops through his chest, sending his

heart splattering right between my legs. His eyes widen, his mouth opening and closing in surprise.

His head drops onto me next, a second before his heavy body crushes me, knocking me flat on my back. A shadow dweller grins at me, haloed in the soft moonlight from above. He wiggles his bloody fingers but doesn't drag Zaire's body off me. Instead, he raises Zaire's blade and stakes it into Zaire's back, stabbing it into me far enough to make me scream.

Sinking my teeth into Zaire's severed neck, I silence myself with the blood I crave. The blood I need to survive. The blood I know that will help heal my injuries.

"That's enough, donor. Time to go," the shadow dweller says, finally pulling Zaire's body off me.

He offers me his hand, but I don't take it. Instead, I swing my leg up to try to kick him in the balls. Catching my ankle, he hoists me off my feet upside down. The world blurs as he spins me around so fast that I can't scream and then releases me.

I tighten my muscles, bracing to crash into the ground.

I brace for a shit-ton of pain.

But the vampire appears in my line of sight to catch me.

Instead, I prepare to die.

6

NIGHT PALMS CASTLE

"GOTCHA, DANDELION."

I huff a breath, my body knocking into the burly chest of Bronx as he catches me. A wail pierces the air, making me wince, and I automatically bury my face into the soft cotton of Bronx's T-shirt. And shit does he smell good. A mixture of fresh laundry soap and something fruity tantalizes me, and I inhale a deep breath.

"Did you just sniff my shirt?" Bronx asks, adjusting me in his arms.

The world blurs around us, the cool night wind whipping my hair. I don't respond to him. I can't. My voice remains locked the hell up in my throat. All I can do is continue to inhale and exhale the calming scent that somehow manages to get my heart back in control so that it doesn't escape me.

"Is she injured?" Another familiar voice says, drawing my attention to Everett. "Bring her here."

Bronx stops but doesn't let me go. Actually, it's me who doesn't let him go. My fingers dig so deeply into his shoulders that I'm certain someone's going to have to pry them off to get me to let him go.

But no one does.

"Hey, Gwen. Look at me," Bronx says.

Slowly, I ease my face away from his chest and tilt my chin to look up at him.

His eyes flash silver. "You're safe, okay?" he says, stroking his big hand over the length of my back.

I tighten my jaw. "How can you be sure?"

Bronx groans, flicking his gaze away from mine. "She must've consumed blood—maybe one of the corpses." His mouth doesn't move as he whispers it to Everett, who stands somewhere behind me.

Fury floods through me. "Did you just try to manipulate my mind?" I can't stop the question from spilling from my mouth.

Bronx furrows his brows. "I was trying to help you."

At least he doesn't call me out or question how the hell I knew. "So you did."

He flares his nostrils in annoyance like he's the one that has the right to be upset. "You're in shock. Pinching the hell out of my shoulders."

I finally release his tensing muscles only to smack my hands to his chest. "I don't care."

"Calm down. I wasn't doing it for nefarious reasons. You look ready to pass out. You're shaking."

"Of course I'm shaking! We were attacked. Zaire's head fell on my lap. I thought those assholes were going to devour me." My voice screeches through the air. "So don't tell me to calm down. And never, and I mean *never* try to do that again."

Bronx jerks me away, dangling me out in front of him. Everett gathers me into his arms, taking me from Bronx. Bronx disappears into the night, and I jump at the sound of a car door slamming. A screech cuts through the sudden silence. I shield my eyes from the bright beams of the headlights as Bronx takes off in an unfamiliar car.

"Here, take my jacket, Gigi," Jameson says, materializing next to me. "As much as I wanted to see you without the dress, this wasn't how I imagined it happening."

I close my eyes and release a breathless laugh. "You try fighting in a bridal gown. It's impossible."

Jameson steps closer and hands me his jacket, helping me put it on without asking Everett to set me down. "I don't believe in the impossible, so now as soon as we get you home, I'll have to prove you wrong."

"Home?" I ask. "You don't know where that is."

Everett releases a low groan. "He means to Night Palms Castle, the Royale Coven's estate."

I cover my face with my hands. "Please, just leave me here. Pretend you didn't find me. It's the least you can do."

"I know you're a brave, hot as hell little donor, but no," Jameson says. "Our brother died protecting you when he didn't have to. I'm not going to let you go so that you can get yourself killed. His death will not be a waste."

Shit. While neither of them reacts with grief, I'm sure something must be going through their minds. Jameson's eyes flash silver more than Everett's, but they both look on the verge of snarling. Not at me though. I'd feel sorry if anyone even tries to approach the three of us.

"I—I'm sorry," I say. I don't know why I apologize. Zaire's death was his own damn fault. He was going to bite me. He tried to force me to submit to him—to a life I sure as shit don't agree with. But I won't tell his brothers that. The last thing I need is to piss off more vampires.

"It's not your fault, Gwen," Everett says, finally speaking up. "Now, if it's okay, I'd like to put you in the car."

I press my lips together, still tasting the sweetness of Zaire's blood on my mouth. "Fine," I manage to say.

Everett sets me on the backseat and slides in next to me, leaving Jameson to take the wheel. It's now that I realize

Mikkalo isn't with them.

"Mikkalo went with Bronx to take care of Zaire's remains. You shouldn't have to see that, so we decided it best to split up," Everett says like he can read my mind.

I bob my head.

"Don't look so sad. We're the ones who won in this situation," Jameson says, hitting a few buttons on the dashboard to send the car moving forward. "But Mikkalo will gloat all night if he finds out that you were wondering about him. You're making me jealous, Gigi. I thought we had a connection."

Everett leans forward and backhands Jameson, making him laugh. Jameson catches my gaze in the rearview mirror and has the nerve to wink at me. I sink lower on the cool seat, pulling his jacket around me. I wince at the ache burning across my chest.

"Are you injured, Gwen?" Everett asks, keeping his voice low like any sudden noise will send me back into fight mode.

"It's nothing. Just a stab wound," I mutter, easing the jacket back enough to glance at the blood smeared over my bra and down the line of my stomach all the way to my navel.

Everett sucks in a breath through his teeth while Jameson laughs so loudly that I startle. And I hate that I do. I've never been so on edge in my life. It's also the first time I've ever had to truly rely on myself in a fight, even with Zaire.

Like Jameson said, he didn't have to fight. He could've left me or gave me to the shadow dwellers. But his sudden possessiveness didn't allow him.

Now that I have a moment to breathe, I know it's the truth. It's why my brothers were always so adamant that I keep Laredo at a distance. It's why I was left no choice but to stake my first blood source—a vampire whose name I can't even think of.

"May I please take a look, Gwen," Everett asks, drawing my attention from my wild thoughts.

"No," I say, shifting in place to look away from him.

"But I can help you." He taps his fingers on the seat, a few inches from my bare leg. "Look, I have a medical kit. You won't even need sutures with the synthetic skin in my bag. I also have something to ease any of your pain. You don't have to suffer."

"I also don't have to give you another show of my cleavage," I say.

Everett closes his eyes for a second at my remark and pops open his medical kit anyway. "You're right. You don't. I can show you how to apply it yourself."

I blink in surprise. "Really?"

"I'd never make you do something you were uncomfortable doing—not if it's not a life and death situation, at least."

Bringing my gaze to Everett, I stare into his dark blue eyes for a moment, studying his face. His features remain soft, sincere. He's not even annoyed by my stubbornness.

"Okay," I say, accepting the tube of ointment he proffers to me. "How does this work?"

As Everett explains how to clean my wound for proper care, I glance up at Jameson as he watches me instead of the road. He offers me a smile, and I can't stop myself from returning it. Now that I'm not going to die or get bitten, I feel like I can relax. I hardly know Everett and Jameson, but I don't think they pose a threat. They act almost like Laredo acted with me. But how long this feeling will last about them? I have no idea.

"So, how does it feel now?" Everett says, drawing my gaze to his as I finish applying the numbing cream to the small incision already healing faster than I've ever seen my body do.

"Great, thanks. This stuff is awesome," I say. "Like magic."

Everett chuckles. "More like science. It helps that you...already consumed vampire blood."

"There was no way I was going to let someone manipulate my mind," I say, straightening my shoulders. "It's how my blo—vampire friend used to help me."

"Well, you won't have to worry about that anymore, Gigi," Jameson says. "You're safe with us."

"Especially here." Everett waves his hand, motioning to the looming wrought iron gate guarded by three scary as hell vampires carrying giant guns I've never seen before. It's the first time I've ever actually seen a vampire with a weapon as such.

Jameson notices me gawking and says, "Not every vampire is as powerful and resilient as we are."

"Huh?"

"We're Royales, Gigi. We transitioned with power far superior from the general vampire population."

"Hence the big-ass house?" I ask, leaning forward between the seats.

I stretch to get a better view of the massive white building made from unfamiliar material—some sort of smooth stone. Tall pillars hold up a carved archway with intricate designs. Two figures stand in the glow of the chandelier that sends fractals of rainbow light across the glittering stone ground.

Jameson pulls the car under the grand entrance and kills the engine. "Welcome to Night Palms Castle. Are you impressed?"

I raise an eyebrow at him. "It's a little excessive, isn't it?" I keep my face expressionless. There is no way I'll show him that he's right. I'm more than impressed. I'm astonished.

He chuckles. "You just wait."

Jameson and Everett open their doors at the same time in a race to open mine. Mikkalo beats them to it, offering his hand out for me to take. I stand outside the car and peer up at the outdoor chandelier. Bronx remains in his spot, glowering at me like I'm the last person he wants to see.

At least Mikkalo smiles. His eyes trail from my surely gross face, with remnants of dried blood still on my skin, and to the open jacket, showing off way more skin than I intend to. I hug it tighter against me and playfully kick him with my bare foot.

"Stop looking at me like that," I say.

"I see you lost the dress." His smirk grows wider.

"Too bad it wasn't doing something fun." Did I just flirt with him?

"We'll have to amend that next time you dress up." Yup, I was definitely flirting. Now, so is he.

Bronx sighs and grabs Mikkalo by the shirt, cutting our conversation short. The two of them flash their fangs at each other, making me step back and bump into Everett. Jameson heads to the grand opaque glass and wooden double door, opening it for all of us.

He tips his head at me. "Ladies first."

I hesitate, unsure of what to expect. The last vampire household I went into had a wall of chained humans in the basement. This place is enormous enough that they could have a dungeon. The thought makes me nervous to peer around to see how far I could make it until someone catches me.

A gentle hand touches the small of my back. "Come on, Gwen. Bronx wasn't lying. You are safe with us. I bet you're hungry. How about I show you to your room, find something clean for you to wear, and bring you something to eat?"

I bob my head, my body reacting before my mind. Because Everett's suggestion sounds amazing. I bet this place even has a shower like the one in Crimson Vista.

Everett guides me into the gleaming marble foyer with a huge mural of what looks like some sort of crest with five white and yellow flowers with stems dripping blood off the black shield. The strange delicateness of the flowers makes the crest weird as hell, and I can't stop staring at it.

"You know, I've seen coven crests with lions, tigers, and wolves, but never a cute...bloody flower," I say, tipping my head back to peer up toward a banister of the upstairs floor.

"It was inherited," Bronx mutters. "Zaire picked the bloodroot."

"Of course he did," I say, regretting my quip immediately.

I tighten my jaw and turn away from the four of them gazing at me. I can't read any of their expressions, but I know better than to comment on something one of their dead brothers gave them. I know I'd be upset.

Everett closes the space to me again and motions toward an enormous staircase that wraps around to ascend to the second floor. "It's been a long day. We could all use some extra rest."

I nearly had forgotten they're nocturnal. They just—I shake my head to push the thought away. They're vampires.

They feed on human blood. They're why I'm here and away from my family.

But they're also why I'm alive.

Fuck me.

I try to resist looking over my shoulder at Mikkalo and Jameson, but the weight of their stares burns my back. I sneak a quick peek behind me only to see Bronx's glower. It makes me whip my head forward.

"Give her a break, Bronxy," Jameson whispers. I don't have to look at him to know that the words weren't intended for me to hear. That I shouldn't be able to hear them. "Gigi was separated from her family. You out of any of us should understand."

"She had expected proper protection only to have witnessed Zaire fail her," Mikkalo adds.

Bronx releases a soft groan. "He failed all of us. He should've just listened. It wasn't supposed to be this way. He should've let us help him."

"What he should've done is allowed us all to apply for a Blood Match," Jameson says.

"What are we even supposed to do with her?" Bronx asks, his voice sounding soft, gentle, worried almost.

"I'll look into it," Mikkalo says. "But for now, let's just give her some space."

"You hear that, Everett?" Jameson calls.

"I heard you," Everett says.

"We need a coven meeting," Bronx adds.

Everett catches me looking at him, and he parts his mouth into a smile. "I'm just going to assure she has what she needs. I'll meet you guys in Zaire's office after."

Mikkalo clears his throat. "No more than an hour, brother. I can see how much you already like her. She was Zaire's Blood Match."

Everett releases a soft growl. "Well, she should've had the chance to be mine."

7

ESCAPE PLAN

I TIPTOE ACROSS THE SPACIOUS room Everett promised he'd help make my own once he and his brothers get everything figured out. He didn't even have more than a T-shirt and too baggy shorts for me to wear. Though, I can't really blame him. None of them were expecting a woman to move into their household. It would have been Zaire's job.

I shudder to think about it. I wonder if he'd have given me anything at all. Probably sexy lingerie, though I'd take it right now considering there was no way in hell I was slipping back on the bra and panties covered in vampire blood. So, I'm going without. I guess there's a first for everything.

Testing the doorknob, I attempt to open it, but it doesn't budge. I'm locked in. I suppress my annoyance, knowing why Everett did it—I mean, I am currently looking for a way to escape—but still. I bite my lip and spin on my feet, spotting a floor-to-ceiling curtain across the room. Perfect.

As quietly as I can, I stroll to the curtain and tug it open to find a wall of windows with an inlaid door that leads to a balcony. Hell yes! I stare at the golden handle for a minute and close my eyes, begging to the universe for it to be open. I can already tell the tinted glass is shatter-proof. No vampire coven would leave themselves vulnerable. I've heard of rebels blasting through them with explosives, but I don't have any. I don't even have a weapon. Or shoes. Fuck, I miss my damn panties and bra too. For being in what is probably the most expensive room I've ever stayed in, I feel more without than I ever have.

I push down and the handle gives, letting me swing the door open. An alarm blares through the air, catching me off guard. Panic rises through me, and I do the only thing I can think of. I push away the pain in my ears and swing my leg over the banister and step on the ledge. Using the bars, I grip as tightly as I can and ease my way lower to hopefully shorten the long-ass drop. From this spot, the balcony is higher than I anticipated, but at least a stretch of lawn sprawls below me. I might actually make it without breaking anything if I land just right.

I take a deep breath and let go, pressing my lips together to stop from screaming out. Someone catches me, and I automatically swing my fist. I expect to open my eyes to Bronx from the buff build of the guy holding me, but two strange eyes, under a thick brow, narrow on me while the strange vampire clutches my wrist.

"Well, this was an unexpected surprise," the vampire says, flashing his fangs at me.

Instead of responding, I strike my free arm and manage to punch him in the eye. He roars, dropping me a foot only to adjust me in his arms with my back to his chest.

"You bitch. How dare you disrespect me—"

"Release the donor," a deep, throaty voice says.

The vampire spins around to face Bronx. And shit does he look intimidating as all get-out. He keeps his muscular arms at his sides where I spot a drawn knife. The vein in his neck bulges as he clenches his jaw.

The vampire doesn't listen and says, "Finders keepers. I ca—"

Jerking my head back, I hit him in the nose, sending stars bursting in my vision. I barely rid the headache from head-butting Zaire. I swear this better not turn into a normal thing. I've been injured more in the last two days than I have in all of my twenty-one years of life.

The vampire releases me with a roar, dropping me to

the ground.

I scramble toward Bronx on my hands and knees. "I found him on my balcony," I say, bumping into Bronx's legs.

"You bitch," the vampire says for the second time.

I push harder into Bronx's legs until he shifts them, and I squeeze my way through to get behind him. The vampire looks ready to devour me, and I'm pretty sure the only thing stopping him is the solid wall of muscles that Bronx is made of.

"Brothers, I found Gwen. Will one of you please escort Mr. Bevaldi back to his room?" Bronx asks, raising his voice through the air.

"Not it," Jameson calls. "I'll escort Gigi if you want me to though."

I push to my feet, hoping that Bronx agrees.

"No, I got her. I need to talk to her anyway," Bronx says. "Everett or Mikkalo? Which one of you will it be?"

Mikkalo materializes behind the vampire Bronx called Mr. Bevaldi and grips onto his shoulders. The two of them disappear with a blink of my eyes. Swiveling on his feet, Bronx faces me and extends his hand out.

I just look at it. "You saved me. Why?" He technically didn't save me. He stopped my escape if anything, but I'm not going to let him know that. I just hope they don't let the weirdo vampire who tried to claim me speak.

"Would you have preferred to go with Mr. Bevaldi? If

you do, I can call him back here," he says, still holding out his hand.

I roll my eyes. I can't help it. "You're such an asshole."

"And you're a damn pain in my nuts even without you kicking me, dandelion," he says, using the weird nickname he called me earlier in the night.

Instead of asking him about it, I finally force myself to take his hand. His big fingers engulf mine, and he surprises the hell out of me by launching me into the air only to catch me on his shoulder. I gasp a breath, his bone digging into my stomach. I swat him, smacking him straight on the ass, and he chuckles.

"Careful, Gwen. I like that kind of stuff."

I smack him again. "You look like it."

"I do, huh?" he says, striding so fast along the outskirts of the mansion that I can't get a good look around. "You look like you do too."

Ah hell. My face floods with heat, and I refrain from hitting him again. The last thing I want is to turn him on.

"Do not," I say.

Bronx hums under his breath with another chuckle. "I'm sure you wouldn't even know."

I glower at his back. "Shut up."

"I will after I say what I need to say."

Bronx eases me off his shoulder and sets me on my feet in an unfamiliar room. It's at least three times the size of the one I escaped from and definitely more lived in with old books scattered across a coffee table in a sitting area with a leather couch. A giant projection lights up the wall, the movie frozen on a scene...of a close-up shot of a woman's breasts.

I curl my lips and glance at Bronx. "What the hell kind of movie is that?"

He remains expressionless. "A good one. Your damsel act interrupted my free time."

I really wish I hadn't commented. Bronx's face softens with a laugh, and I gawk at him, wishing I hated how he sounds. Or how he looks with a smile. Because damn. He looks even hotter when he doesn't look like I'm the bane of his existence.

"If you don't do anything to piss me off again, I might even let you watch."

Fucking hell.

He laughs again and crosses the room to lift a tablet from the coffee table. He clicks off the projection and plops down on the leather couch, kicking his boots off. He props his legs on the coffee table and turns his attention to me, just standing awkward as hell in the middle of what I'm pretty damn sure is his room.

"Why don't you sit down?" he says, motioning to the couch. "You make me nervous just standing there, looking at me like that."

I comb my fingers through my hair and shuffle forward to the couch next to him, sitting as far away as I possibly can. I pick up a throw pillow and hug it against me for good measure. "Like what?"

"Like you're going to suddenly grow fangs and devour me," he says. "Did Everett give you enough to eat? I thought I heard your stomach."

I release a small breath and nod even though he didn't. "Yeah, it was fine."

"You're going to have to speak up about your needs, okay?" Bronx says, resting his elbow on the armrest to slightly turn his body toward me. "We've never had to care for a donor before, and I don't want to starve you or some shit."

Twisting in my spot, I swing my leg up and kick his leg. "I'm not some animal. I know how to take care of myself. And others, thank you very much."

He lifts and drops his shoulders. "I didn't say you were an animal. You're clearly a pissed off woman who looks ready to punch my balls. But please refrain. I might enjoy a little rough play but not that kind of roughness."

"What the hell? Is this why you brought me here? To tease me? To try to get under my skin? Make me feel awkward as hell? Because if that's the case—"

Bronx scoots over and touches his big hand to my knee. "Gwen, no. I'm sorry. It's not, and I'll stop. I'm just...like I said before. You make me a bit nervous. I've never been knocked down like that in a fight."

I stare at his hand on my knee, feeling how his fingers

cool my skin while I warm his. "To be fair, I highly doubt you expected me to kick you. Not many do."

"And I thought I was special."

Bronx shifts away from me to scrub his face with his hands, groaning under my silent gaze. I move my legs, pulling them up onto the cushion to tuck under me. His eyes flash silver, and he stares at his door, looking like he has something on his mind, but he doesn't want to tell me.

"I can't do it," he whispers, his mouth unmoving.

"She might take it better than you think, Bronxy." Jameson's soft voice trickles into the room.

"As head of our coven, it should be you, brother," Everett adds. Head of their coven? Oh, shit. He was first in line to Zaire.

I try not to frown at their words or the fact that they can talk to Bronx even through the wall. Or that I can hear them both.

"Gwen," Bronx says softly, my name a breathless whisper on his lips. "I know that you never wanted to be in this position, and I'm sorry for how things turned out."

"You're sorry?" I ask, suddenly feeling all sorts of confused by his apology. Because it doesn't cut it. "My brothers are probably all going to die because of you!"

The softness of his features harden under my anger. "My brother did die."

"And he should've." I can't stop from screaming the words. My eyes burn with my furious tears. I hate how much my eyes betray me like this. Grayson would smack me upside the head for daring to cry in front of a vampire. I was trained better than this. I was trained to look death in the eye and to accept it with dignity.

But that was when I had my family here.

That's when I had my freedom.

But now?

I suck in a shuddering breath and get to my feet, hugging myself so that I can turn away from Bronx. "Just tell me what's going to happen to me now. Are you going to take me back to the Blood Match Center? Auction me off? Take my final donation?"

A hand touches my shoulder. Bronx stands so close to me that his chest brushes my shoulder blades with his soft breathing. "No, none of those things."

I blink the tears from my eyes, a flicker of hope rising through me. Turning around, I meet his gaze straight on. "Are you letting me go?"

I suck in my bottom lip between my teeth, begging with everything inside me that he tells me yes, that he hands me the keys to the car so that I can plan out what I'll do next.

"Gwen." I wish Bronx didn't say my name like that.

My chest tightens, knowing that my life could never be that easy.

"The Blood Match contract that Zaire signed—it has a clause in it with a statement that pertains to what happens to you upon his death," Bronx says. "I had no idea about this, I swear. I thought that you might gain exemption into Haven Springs, but because you were found guilty of several crimes..."

I close my eyes. "Just spit it out."

"Your contract gets passed along to the Royale Coven."

"So you?" I ask.

He shakes his head. "I didn't say that."

I place my hands on my hips. "You're the head of the Royale Coven. Isn't that how this works? You brought me here because you're next in line, probably starving, and are too damn scared to tell me that not only were you responsible for murdering my family, but now I have to expose my neck to you every damn day as your personal blood source."

"Gwen, no. That's not—"

"You should just kill me. Get it over with. Because spending the rest of my life like that—that's hell. That's exactly how I imagine my hell to be."

He takes a step closer while I take one back. "That's the last thing I want. I'm not some heartless asshole. I don't want you to be miserable."

I jab him in the chest with my finger. "Then let me go!"

"You'll die out there."

"I'll die here!"

He releases a soft growl and disappears, swinging his fist into the nearest wall, creating a huge-ass crater in the drywall. I jump at the loud crack of his fist and clutch my hands to my chest.

Bronx turns to look at me with wide eyes. "Gwen, I'm sorry. I didn't mean—"

Spinning on my feet, I rush to the door. I brace myself to attempt the impossible feat of breaking it down, but it opens before I even touch the knob. I glance at Bronx behind me, linking his fingers behind his head.

Then he softly calls out to his brothers.

Mikkalo appears in the hallway, blocking my way.

I twist to walk the other direction, but Jameson and Everett appear next. Taking a deep breath, I turn right back into Bronx's room and rush to the open bathroom. I slam the door shut and lock it, resting my back on the cool wood.

"Gwen," Everett calls, tapping his finger to the door.

"Please, just leave me alone," I say. "All of you."

"But—"

"Come on, brother. Just give her some space," Mikkalo says. "We can try again tomorrow night. And if she's not ready, then the next."

I sigh and slide to the floor, curling my knees to my chest. I can't believe this might be my life now.

8

WAKEUP CALL

SWEAT BEADS ON MY FOREHEAD, dripping down my temple. I snap my eyes open and stare at the cloud of steam above me. The muggy air fills my lungs as I suck in a deep breath, trying to orient myself to where I am.

Shit.

Pulling up one of the towels I found in the cupboard to use as a blanket, I bring it to my face and wipe the perspiration from my skin. Soft humming trickles over the sound of spraying water, and I ease myself up to peek out from my place in the tub where I fell asleep.

Condensation fogs the glass shower, but it's not enough to obscure my view of Bronx's smooth, broad back, tight ass, and muscular legs. And damn it, does my body react. I can't deny how attractive he is despite being a vampire, and I'd be lying to myself if I wasn't curious about seeing the rest of—

I throw myself back, thunking my head on the porcelain tub. Growing up with six brothers, I've seen a lot of unwanted dick. But now? Damn. I can't stop myself from arching back up. Talk about incredibly intimidating. And morning—night? Talk about a raging fucking boner.

And getting caught gawking.

Bronx turns his gaze to mine, remaining utterly expressionless as he shuts the water off and steps out of the foggy shower in all his naked-ass deliciousness. My stomach roars. So loud in fact that Bronx finally reacts and tilts his head.

"If you go to my desk, you can call one of my brothers. You can either ask them to bring you something to eat here or in the dining hall. The front balcony also has a nice view this time of night." He reaches for a towel, coming up empty-handed.

I squeeze my eyes shut and sink into the tub. Bronx's light footsteps pad across the tile where I can tell he stops at the cupboard and opens it up. My cheeks flame like crazy at his sigh that has his footsteps heading in my direction. My eyelids darken as he stands over me, and a few drops of water splash my head. I don't have to even look to know he's drinking me in as I lie on every single towel in the bathroom.

"Mind sharing one?" he asks, so much amusement in his voice.

I bob my head and pull the towel off me and lift it up. He tugs it away from me, but I'm not quick enough to release the damn towel and my hand brushes against something hard yet smooth and suspiciously like...

"Fuck. I'm sorry," I say. "You should watch where you point that thing."

He chuckles. "My wrist?"

Oh, thank God.

I flutter my eyes open to meet Bronx's dark gaze. He smirks at me from over his shoulder, using the towel to dry his hair, still leaving the rest of him exposed like this is the most normal thing. Silver flashes in his eyes, and I rub my hands together, incapable of taking my gaze off of every damn curve of his rock-hard, buff as all get-out body.

He drops the towel to the floor and starts lathering his face to shave. Vampires might be un-aging, but they're very much alive with beating hearts and all. Laredo once told me they're more like a genetic mutation—like myself—super human even, apart from the blood drinking, fangs, and light sensitivity. If only it was more than that. Grayson once proved that vampires don't explode in the sun by locking Laredo out. He was pissed as hell but burn free after a few hours and extra blood.

My stomach growls again, and Bronx shifts to look at me. It's then that I realize his muscular arms have hair the same shade as his head while the most prominent part of him lacks any hair at all.

"Fuck," I whisper to myself. "That was so not his wrist."

His lip curls in the corner. "Like I said, you should go call one of my brothers. Or if you insist on staying here, I can bring you a banana or something."

I pull myself up, using the side of the tub. "Only because you insist on staying naked."

He leans closer to the mirror and smiles at me in the glass. "You chose to sleep in my bathroom, which doesn't remain locked for me. There was no way I was using one of my brothers' bathrooms."

Glaring, I say, "I would've left if you woke me up."

"You were tired. I was hoping you'd feel better with more sleep. And I think I was right. You haven't even tried to attack me."

I lick my lips, unable to respond. Instead, I shift on my feet, rubbing my legs together as I look at him a moment longer. My body chooses now to do all sorts of crazy things. To save myself—or maybe Bronx—because I can't take my eyes off him, I stride toward the bathroom door to head into his room. My stomach turns into a ferocious beast in the process.

"Hey, dandelion," Bronx calls, drawing my attention to

him. "I had the staff pick you up a few things to wear."

"Thank you," I say quietly.

Neither of us mentions the shit show that took place last night, and I do my best to suppress it from my mind. When he's not scowling or tossing me on his shoulder or commenting about his dead brother, Bronx doesn't seem so bad. At least for now.

Sleeping in the cold tub helped me cool off and think more about the status of my life. I hate to admit that Bronx was right. If I do actually escape this place, I'll probably be dead within the week for the sole reason that I know my stomach growls like crazy for more than human food. My dhampir half is mad as hell that it's already been...a long damn time since I drank blood. I can only guess that I slept well over half a day.

Swiveling on my feet, I peer around the room and spot Bronx's small com device sitting on the nightstand next to his unmade bed. I sit on the edge, bouncing for a moment on the way comfortable mattress. I've never sat on something like it. The strange material of the mattress molds to me, inviting me to lie down. I shouldn't—I mean I really shouldn't, especially if Bronx strolls out here naked to catch me snuggling his amazing smelling pillows—but my body wins over my brain's plea, and I swing my legs up. Sinking back, I release a small moan as I stretch. This bed is a million times more comfortable than the tub. Warmer. Nearly intoxicating.

I can't tell if it's because I'm hungry as hell or because I just love the way Bronx smells, but I totally roll over onto my stomach, burying my nose into his pillow. I rest the com device against the headboard and tap the screen.

"It's locked," I call out, frowning as it turns red.

A small intake of breath sounds from behind me, but I don't flip over to meet Bronx's gaze. "Hold your finger on it for a few seconds. It'll open for you."

"You granted me access?" I ask.

He hums his agreement. "To most of the estate. You live here now. You shouldn't have to have one of us escort you everywhere or do everything for you."

My chest tightens at his words. I should be relieved that he's chosen to give me a bit of freedom, but I can't suppress the nagging feeling that reminds me that access to opening doors doesn't make me less of a prisoner. His actions are probably part of some bigger strategy to get me to comply, to accept my position as his blood source. Just because he hasn't demanded I feed him doesn't mean it isn't coming.

"Oh," is all I say.

Pressing my finger to the com device, I watch it light up and unlock just like he said it would. I resist reading over the digital letter left open and click on his contact list. I blink a few times at the first name on the list—Anderson, Corona. The Anderson Coven is the one Kyler was placed into after his Blood Matching. I would never forget that. And this vampire must be a part of it.

Before I realize what I'm doing, I tap the name and watch a photo of a man with wavy brunette hair pop up onto the screen. The com device chirps and a sudden projection lights up across the headboard. The photo comes to life, and the vampire man tilts his head and stares at me.

"Uh, hi," I say.

The vampire doesn't say anything.

I swallow my nerves. "Were you the one to Blood Match with Kyler Gallagher?" Bold, I know, but I have to find out.

"Who gave you access to Mr. Royale's line?"

I ignore his question since he ignores mine. "I'd like to talk to my brother."

"Gwen!" Bronx's voice booms through the room, startling me. "End the call now."

"How interesting," the man muses.

Bronx tries to snatch the com device from me, but I roll over a few times to the other side of the bed, making him hesitate.

"There is nothing interesting about watching over Zaire's Blood Match while he attends to business. As you can see, she's rather wild," Bronx says.

"Might I suggest you control her? Look how content my Kyler is."

The screen blurs to stop on a figure, half slumped in a chair. My heart seizes, pain unlike anything I've ever felt booming in my chest. A strangled cry escapes my mouth a second before a heavy body lands on top of me. Bronx snatches the phone away and disconnects the line.

I gasp a few deep breaths, fear and horror sinking deep into my bones. My whole body trembles uncontrollably. The ache in my heart radiates so intensely that I'm certain I'm dying. My body can't handle knowing that Kyler is imprisoned in the household of a demented vampire who's manipulated his mind to the point that I'm not even sure he's even still in his body. I've never seen his eyes so wide and blank like that, just a shell of himself.

"Gwen," Bronx says softly.

I don't respond to him. I can't.

Two big arms slide under me, rolling me onto my side. Bronx hugs me from behind, resting his face between my shoulder blades as he breathes softly into my hair. My body gives in to his, sinking into his embrace, feeling him cocoon around me like he's trying to keep me together as I fall apart.

"You have to let me leave," I finally manage to say. "I have to save him."

"Gwen, I can't let you."

"Please, Bronx." Twisting in his arms, I roll over to face him. "I can't stand knowing Kyler's like that."

His eyes search mine, but he doesn't respond. I already know his answer even though he doesn't say the words out loud.

Bowing my head, I rest it on his, feeling his soft breath

caress my lips. "Please."

"I can't," he finally says.

I pull away from him, and he lets me go, though his eyes remain on me even as I turn my back on him. My body begs for me to return to his side, to feel his arms around me again, but my mind shouts at me that I shouldn't have allowed him so close in the first place. Look what happened to my brother because of him. Because of this whole coven. This world.

Bronx stays on his bed without a word. He doesn't argue or try to stop me as I head to the door. It opens under my touch like he said it would, and I peer around the hallway. I don't know where I'm going, but I can't stay in the same breathing space as Bronx. I need to get away. And fast.

A small beep resonates through the air as Bronx calls one of his brothers. Mikkalo's voice trickles from Bronx's room, saying he's already on his way to me. I can't stop myself from picking up my pace. I don't need someone else trying to convince me that everything will be okay, and I don't need a fake apology for destroying my life. I most definitely don't need to be told I can't leave again either. Why this coven even cares whether I live or die is beyond me. There are tons of compliant humans willing to feed them. They don't need me.

Footsteps sound from behind me, and I turn my head to peer over my shoulder. I frown at the empty hallway behind me. I expected Mikkalo to be following me, but no one's there.

And then my fear instincts go off like crazy.

Swinging my arm out as I spin around, I punch the solid body of a vampire. Mr. Bevaldi snarls at me, grabbing onto my wrist. I uppercut him with my free hand, jabbing him in the chin, sending his head snapping upward. But the action only pisses him off.

He yanks me to him, hooking his arms around my body, restraining my arms to my sides. I jerk my knee up, hitting him right in the junk, and he drops to the floor and releases me. Hopping over him, I run as fast as I can, ignoring the line of closed doors in the hallway.

A growl sounds out from behind me, and I scream out, knowing that Bronx will hear me. If I had a weapon, I wouldn't resort to begging for help, but damn it. I've never felt so defenseless in my life. I can't kill a vampire with my bare hands. I'm strong, but not bone-shattering strong.

"Gwen?" a soft voice calls, drawing my attention straight ahead of me as Mikkalo appears from an elevator I've never seen.

Now that I think about it, I haven't seen most of this mansion, and it's not until now that I realize there isn't a window in sight. I'm nearly certain I'm underground. I know what it's like—I grew up in an underground bunker. The air just feels different.

Mikkalo closes the space to me, and I throw myself at him, forcing him to embrace me. He chuckles in my ear, resting his chin on my shoulder.

"Did you miss me?" he asks, rocking me back and forth.

"No, I—" My stomach roars, clenching with pain, cutting off my words. I can't even tell him that Mr. Bevaldi was chasing me.

I hunch forward, forcing Mikkalo to give me some space. He crouches low to look at me, his smile fading. Reaching out, he pushes my blond hair behind my ear so that it stops veiling me from him.

"Damn. Let's get you something to eat," he says. "You don't look so good."

I inhale a couple of deep breaths, my body tensing.

Mikkalo touches my hand, trying to take it, and I snap my teeth at him.

He jerks away in surprise but isn't fast enough.

Without even thinking, I launch at him.

I lose control.

9

BLOOD LUST

I STOP SHORT OF MIKKALO'S throat, heaving a breath against his skin.

My. Damn. Mouth.

My lips brush over his neck, making him release the softest, sexiest noise in all of existence. Sliding his arms around my waist, he pulls me closer. The hardness of his desire presses into me, and I inhale a small breath feeling his erection through the thin fabric of the baggy shorts.

"Fuck," he whispers, the soft vibration of his voice dancing across my skin.

Fuck is right.

His words should be too soft for me to hear, and I wish I couldn't, because they prod at my very nature as a dhampir. There's a reason I used to sneak around with Laredo and drink from his body despite my brothers always trying to force me to take it from a glass. I always loved the closeness no matter the danger. Laredo used to enjoy it as well—he speculated that it could be in my very nature to draw vampires to me, and right now, I think he could've been right. It works the same as how vampires used to attract humans during the uprising. They're charming when they want to be.

Now, just being so close to Mikkalo, teasing his attraction, his own nature...it feels good. Amazing. Laredo always told me there was nothing wrong with giving into my needs as a dhampir, and damn it do I so desperately want to now.

I surprise Mikkalo with a kiss, caressing my lips to his, feeling the softness of his mouth as he realizes what's happening. He accepts my sudden affection with an unexplainable passion that awakens more than my hunger. My attraction to him runs deeper than I knew possible. I don't know if it's because of my wild emotions, the situation, or what, but I want to see where this goes.

Kissing him deeper, I test the seam of his lips with my tongue, and he opens his mouth for me, allowing me to kiss him in a way that sends tingles through me in all the right places. Rolling my body to his, I grind against his arousal, stirring mine.

"Gwen," Mikkalo says, my name only a breath from his lips, still meeting mine. "You are so beautiful."

My chest heaves, my breath quickening. I want so badly to bite him, to find out if his blood tastes as good as he smells. If his body feels even better without his clothes.

My damn vagina needs to get its act together.

I nip his bottom lip, pulling it between my teeth. Blood teases my tongue, and I moan so loud that Mikkalo kisses me harder only to bite his lip with his fangs, giving me an even better taste of his blood.

"Damn," a soft voice whispers.

It's enough to snap me out of my blood hunger. Blood lust.

Jerking away from Mikkalo, I throw myself back and scramble a few feet away until I hit my back on the cool wall. I dig my fingers into the palms of my hands so hard that I accidentally make myself bleed.

Two intakes of breath.

Three wild heartbeats.

A jumbled mess of emotions crash through me, my face flaming with my fiery blush. I turn my attention to Everett standing a few feet away at the elevator. Mikkalo sits upright, darting his gaze to mine, but I can't even look at him. I can't look at Everett either.

"I don't know what's wrong with me. I—I'm sorry. This was a mistake," I say, pressing my palms to the floor to push myself to my feet. Spots of blood stain the floor, sending my heart crashing around my chest. I clutch my hands together in an attempt to stop the bleeding.

"You're hurt," Everett says, finally composing himself despite the flicker of emotions crossing his face in an array of expressions I don't recognize.

"I—I'm fine." Except I'm not. I'm confused, starving, and now bleeding even more across the floor.

Silver flashes in Mikkalo's eyes as he watches the droplets fall. One second he's on the floor, and in the next, he disappears. I swallow, suppressing my rising fear. Everett remains calm, his eyes normal.

He steps a bit closer. "I know that you'll survive, but let me help you. Those cuts look painful."

I give in to him and nod my head. "They do hurt just a bit."

"Come on. My room's not far."

Everett doesn't touch me and leads the way down the long hallway in the same direction as Bronx's room. I automatically look at Bronx's closed door, hearing the sound of several voices inside, but I can't hear more than the whisper of my name and a groan—Mikkalo's groan.

"Is he going to get in trouble?" I ask Everett. I don't know why I do. I shouldn't care. "Because I kissed him. It was me."

Everett slows down to let me walk beside him. "Why would you think that?"

I glance at him in my peripheral vision. "Because Bronx said that Zaire's Blood Match contract transfers to him."

"No, not him. It transfers to the Royale Coven...once we declare Zaire's death. Bronx has not staked a claim on you." He keeps his voice even.

"But he's next in line."

"That doesn't matter. We all have an interest in you, Gwen. And if I'm being honest, we all want the chance to accept your contract. Had Zaire allowed us to apply to Blood Match with you, we would have tried." Everett stops at the end of the hall where double doors greet us. "You're...I can't explain it."

"Delicious?" I ask.

"I wouldn't know," he says, his fangs peeking out between his lips. "I can imagine though. But it's not that."

"Then why do you even want my contract?" Because it ensures a life as a personal donor.

"That's a formality. It's not really about the contract or what it means in the eyes of Donor Life Corp. It's you. There's just something about you. It..." His words trail off. "Like I said, I can't explain it."

Or he doesn't want to.

"Well, if we're being honest—I don't want to be here. I wish you'd all just let me go." I keep my voice even, trying my best to stay calm.

"You were always quite clear about your feelings, Gwen." He opens the door to his room and waves his hand, motioning for me to enter first. "And even if it were my decision, I would hope to persuade you otherwise. I just don't understand why you have a death wish."

I stiffen at his words. "I don't have a death wish."

"Then why did you jump from your balcony yesterday? Why risk leaving the safety we've provided you? Do you know how easy it would have been for Mr. Bevaldi to end your lif—"

"I didn't jump. He kidnapped me," I say, cutting him off.

He sighs. "Gwen."

I throw my hands up. "Of course you'd believe his word over mine. He's a vampire, and I'm a donor. A criminal."

"Can you stop it with the bullshit?" he asks, his eyes flashing silver. "I saw the footage, Gwen. And you're lucky Mr. Bevaldi is an ally of our coven."

"I'm lucky? *Lucky?*" My voice rises with my anger. "Are you kidding me?"

Everett turns away from me and laces his fingers through his light hair. "You're right. I'm sorry. Let's just drop this."

I lock my fingers to his shoulder and spin him around. "No. I don't want to drop it. I want you to know exactly what I've been through. I want you to know how lucky I really am."

Everett tightens his jaw, but he doesn't say anything.

He trains his gaze on me, and against my better judgment, I glare right back at him. But I want him to look me in the eyes. I want him to see my pain, my heartache. I want him so desperately to understand what it's like being me.

"You might think I'm lucky for being in this ritzy house or because you guys think you like me and I'm somehow safe in your possession, but that's the thing. I'm considered your possession, Everett. You all want a contract I never agreed to which assures that I'm nothing more than a meal. For *life*." My mouth trembles at the thought, and it takes me clenching my teeth to get it under control.

"Gwen, that's—"

"I'm not done talking," I say.

Everett shuts his mouth, his eyes flashing silver again. I'm pretty damn sure he's never been spoken to like this by a donor.

"For some reason, you think I'm more of a criminal than—than even your own damn brother. If you wanted to really protect me, you wouldn't have entered me into the Blood Match Program. You wouldn't have let Zaire take me to do as he pleases. To treat me like his damn food source not more than a few minutes after being alone with him."

He frowns, the corners of his eyes creasing. "He bit you? But—"

"But what? He told you he wouldn't?" I roll my eyes. "And no, he didn't get the chance."

"That's why there was no damage to the car from the

outcast attack." He whispers the words to himself, his eyes darkening to an almost midnight color between flashes of silver.

"Had I not fought, he would've killed me. He said he'd perform my final donation because I didn't want him to bite me," I continue. "Luckily for me, the other shadow vampires wanted to stake their own claims on me too. That's how lucky I am. But hey, it could be worse, right? I could've been sold at auction or had my mind so messed with that I couldn't even keep my mouth from drooling all over the place."

Tears burn my eyes, finally forcing me to break my stare away from Everett. There's no way in hell I'm going to let him see me cry.

Gentle arms wrap around me from behind, testing me to see if I'll give in to them. I do. I can't help it. I feel so out of control and lost. I've grown up with so many people in my life that now that they're not here, I feel lonely. I desperately crave even the simplest touch.

Everett turns me around, and I fall into his arms, burying my face into his chest. I never imagined I'd snuggle a vampire—let alone do more than drink the blood I need—but something about Everett, about his entire coven, digs deeply into me, leaving me feeling so exposed and confused and vulnerable.

"There's nothing I can do tonight, but if you let me talk to my brothers, maybe there's something we can do for your family, Gwen," he says, keeping his voice even.

I tilt my head up, meeting his gaze. "Really? You'd do that?"

"You have to do something though."

I inhale a small breath, my heart ricocheting against my ribcage. Slowly, I tug my long hair from my shoulders and expose my neck to him. It's what Grayson would do to get help. He's told me many times that we sometimes have to do things we don't want to so that we can survive. "Okay, you can bite me. I'll let you drink my blood."

His brows furrow in confusion before his face softens more, and he shakes his head. "Oh, no. Not that. I need you to have some patience. I need you to stop trying to escape. We can't do everything if we're constantly worrying about you." Reaching out, he pulls my hair back over my shoulders for me like he can't handle seeing the smooth skin of my throat a moment longer. "If someone else were to get close to you like Mr. Bevaldi had, they could break into your mind and learn about Zaire's death. Right now, we can't afford for that to happen."

"Wait, what? It's a secret?" I kind of knew that—the memory of what Bronx told the asshole with my brother rises to the forefront of my mind. I was in too much shock even to think about it, but he made it sound like Zaire was alive.

Everett leans into me, resting his chin on my shoulder. The sudden shift of his body sends my heart racing. It was easy to forget that I was even hugging him. That I still continue to hug him with no intention of stopping.

He brings his lips to my ear. "Zaire is head over the Royale Region. He is a Donor Life Corp board member. If they were to find out..." His voice trails off. "We just need a bit of time to strategize what we're going to do."

I turn my head slightly to look at him, our lips a mere inch apart. "Oh."

He licks his lips and swallows. "But that's nothing you need to worry about as long as you—"

"Behave your cute little feisty ass." Jameson stands in the doorway of Everett's room, carrying a covered tray.

The warm scent of food trickles through the air, drawing me away from Everett. He doesn't let me get far, staying close to my side as I pad across the floor to meet his brother. Jameson raises an eyebrow at me, a smirk dimpling his cheek, and I press my hand to my stomach as it growls for what feels like the billionth time.

"I figured the only way you'd ever get something to eat is if I interrupted to feed you myself. I could hear your stomach all the way from my room," he says, lifting the lid on the tray. "I hope you like what the back-world used to call a continental breakfast. If you don't, I can see what the staff prepared for their dinner. They're on a daytime schedule. I just thought it'd be weird to offer you that considering you're going to be on our schedule."

My eyes dart over the array of different kinds of food

on the plate, some I haven't eaten in years. Like the cup of yogurt. Cold stuff doesn't travel well, and my brothers and I were more like scavengers considering we couldn't buy anything in the cities without being registered. If we stole something, it always had a long shelf life.

I dig my nails into my palms in an attempt to stop myself from snatching the tray of food away from Jameson. Pain shoots through my arms, and I wince. I had nearly forgotten about the cuts, which was the whole reason I came here with Everett.

"Shit, I'm sorry, Gwen," Everett says.

I smirk at him, remembering what it was like to feel his arms around me again. "Don't worry about it. I got distracted too."

"Why don't you come sit down, and I'll get you fixed up?" he asks, motioning to his sitting area.

I glance at Jameson and the tray of food.

"I'll feed you if you'd like, Gigi," Jameson says, his smile widening.

My stomach responds on my behalf, and he chuckles. "I can wait."

He balances the tray in one hand while grabbing the spoon in the other and dipping it into the yogurt. Holding it out, Jameson hovers it close to my mouth, daring me even to try resisting his offer. "Now why would you if you don't have to?"

I take a bite and close my eyes, the burst of fruity flavor

exploding across my tongue. "Okay, fine. Join us. But if you spill—"

"I'll lick it off," he says. "My punishment."

I laugh, the sound of my voice startling me. I can't even remember the last time I've found anything funny. "Be careful, Jamie. I might make you spill on purpose."

The second the words escape my lips, I realize how they must sound. I had intended it to be a joke, because from my time with my blood sources, I know how disgusting vampires find human food. It would be like if they offered me a glass of human blood. It wouldn't kill me but yuck.

Jameson grins and taps my lip with the empty spoon. "It would be worth it."

My body reacts to his words, my nipples hardening with my sudden arousal, and I squeeze my legs together. Because fuck. He thinks it'll be worth it to him, but the risk totally seems worth it to me. I never thought I'd want a vampire's mouth on my skin, but now I can't stop thinking about it.

Everett touches my hand, drawing my attention to him, and I feel guilty that I lost myself to Jameson's playfulness. Smiling, Everett clasps my arm by my wrist to get me to stroll with him to sit down in one of his comfy reclining chairs.

"Your laugh might have been the best thing I've heard in a while, Gwen," Everett says, sitting on the arm of the chair. He rubs his fingers over the inside of my wrist, and I spread my fingers out for him to get a look at my palm.

I blush at his compliment. The only compliments Laredo ever gave me were about how good he thought I smelled or how I made him hungry. I'm pretty sure he didn't like my laugh because he'd cover my mouth and tell me I was loud.

"You're welcome," Jameson says, pulling the coffee table closer so that my knees rest between his.

Everett chuckles. I realize Jameson wasn't talking to me but his brother, responding to his comment. The guilt I had a second ago melts away, Everett obviously unfazed by my interaction with Jameson. And Jameson loves the fact that I gave him permission to join us and feed me—a job I had no idea he'd take so utterly seriously. I hate that I love it. How I don't feel annoyed, threatened, or even like food.

I don't get a chance to say anything to Jameson as he holds up another spoonful of yogurt for me to take. I thought he was only kidding about feeding me and would just wait for Everett to finish cleaning and applying the synthetic skin to my palms but no. And I let him. I'm nearly certain if Jameson wasn't, I might start shoveling the food in my mouth. I knew I was hungry, but I had no idea I was *this* hungry.

I eat the entire tray of food, the portion larger than even Grayson can eat. Everett and Jameson both silently stare at me as I gaze at the yogurt bowl, contemplating whether or not I should steal it from Jameson's possession to lick the damn thing.

Jerking my hand out, I grab for it, but Jameson's faster and pulls it out of my way. "I can get you more to eat if you're still hungry."

I release a breath through my nose. "Don't judge me because I want to lick the bowl."

"Just let her, Jameson," Everett says, absently twirling strands of my hair between his fingers.

Jameson narrows his eyes at me. "Only if she lets me do it."

I groan. "Really?"

He proves he's serious and swipes his finger across the side of the bowl, scraping up the last bit of yogurt. Chuckling at my gaping reaction, he holds his finger out to me, daring me with his silver flashing eyes to lick it.

Everett whacks Jameson's shoulder. "Knock it off."

The glob of yogurt falls from his finger only to splat right on my leg to drip down my thigh. I really wish I hadn't rolled my shorts up to fit better. The three of us jerk our attentions to the damn yogurt, surprise freezing me in place, stopping me from automatically swiping it off.

Everett releases a soft growl. "Shit."

Jameson meets my eyes, his smile fading into a serious expression. "Whoops. Looks like I'm in trouble."

"Me too." I meant to think the words, but my mouth betrays me, and I whisper them to myself.

Jameson studies my face, strands of his light brown hair

hanging across his forehead. His green eyes capture mine with their intensity through the veil of his soft tresses. I hold my breath. So does Everett. Scooting the coffee table back with his leg, Jameson slides onto the floor in front of me and clasps both my knees.

"Jameson," Everett says quietly. "You're going to make Gwen uncomfortable."

He keeps his eyes trained on mine without looking at his brother. "She can tell me to stop." He licks his lips. "You can tell me to stop, Gigi. I know you were only joking."

I swallow, my words staying locked in my throat. I don't know what the hell comes over me, but I slightly ease my legs open, giving him silent permission to continue. Jameson gulps, the sound loud enough to raise my eyebrows. I'm not the only one nervous.

My mouth breaks into a smile, and I release a laugh and pat his cheek. "A nervous vampire. I never thought I'd see the day."

Jameson leans back and groans, covering his face with his hands, pushing his hair up. "Today isn't that day. I just really fucking hate donor food."

"And for a minute, I thought I was worth it," I tease, wagging my fingers at him as he fake-glowers at me.

"You're killing me, Gigi."

I laugh again. "Oh, you'd know if I really was."

"Okay, you know what—"

Everett surprises me by hooking his hands under my

knees to twist me in place until I'm practically on his lap. "Lost your chance, brother. It's my turn to show Gwen that she's definitely worth it to me."

I smile and flush. "You're full of shit like your brother."

Everett rubs his lips together. "Would you like to find out?"

"No, I think she's good, Ev," Jameson says.

I hold my hand up to Jameson to get him to stay in his spot. Turning to Everett, I shrug and say, "Might be worth it if you figure out how to feed it to me. I'm still incredibly hungry."

Everett draws his gaze down my body. "Any way I like?"

"You better not fucking whip out your dick," Jameson says.

I bring my hand to my mouth. That thought never even registered in my mind. "What he said."

Everett backhands his brother on the arm. "I'd never. That's something only you would think of doing."

I flick my gaze to Jameson, and he smirks at me with a shrug, keeping whatever comment he has to himself.

Before I realize what's happening, Everett pulls me closer and lifts me up by the ass to pull me to his face. I squeal in surprise, cracking up, and unintentionally moan at the sensation of his lips gliding over my skin.

"Damn," Jameson whispers. "So hot."

My breath catches as Everett sets me down only to slide

his body between my legs to lie over me. A burst of fruity flavor coats my bottom lip as he rubs his mouth to mine, and I can't stop myself from pulling him to me for a kiss.

Ah, hell. Is this really happening? Am I really that hungry I'd let this sexy-ass vampire feed me with his mouth? Damn straight I am. I'm not only experiencing blood hunger but also blood lust, and the cure is literally on top of me right now. If I don't move, I'm going to bite. Hard. If I bite him, he'll know. Jameson too. Then what?

Everett pulls away, and I flutter my eyes to look at him, my heart thumping so hard that I can feel it pulsing through my whole body. He grins, wiping the remainder of the yogurt from his mouth with a napkin. Nerves and desire explode through me even more, my body going crazy with all sorts of emotions. One second I'm smiling and laughing, and in the next, I'm rolling off the chair and scrambling to get away as fast as I can. I have to leave. I have to. If I don't...I can't think about it.

Laredo used to tease that I was the world's best predator because if I even looked at him a particular way, he had the urge to throw himself at my feet, fully prepared to let me devour him. And I'm starting to wonder if it's more than just them thinking I'm hot or because they love the idea of my blood.

But I'm scared to find out. They still have good sense. I don't actually want to devour and kill them—but I want to bite and suck and do all sorts of things in this moment.

Things I shouldn't. I know better. This could only end badly no matter how amazing it feels.

"Gwen," Everett calls, but he doesn't chase me, probably knowing something like that would set off my human rationale. What he doesn't realize is that it could set off my dhampir half too. "I'm sorry. I—"

Slamming my hand against the door, I get it to open. I turn to peer at Everett and Jameson from over my shoulder. "You d-don't need to apologize."

"Then why are you trying to run?" Everett asks. "I moved too fast, and I'm sorry. I just—I wasn't thinking straight. Please, don't go."

I scrunch my face, trying to control my wild heart. "It's fine, really. Thank you for taking care of my hands. I just need some fresh air now."

I need a moment to breathe.

I shouldn't be joking around and kissing vampires. What the hell is wrong with me?

"Let me escort you," Jameson says, moving closer. He's halfway across the room with a blink of my eyes.

I shake my head. "No, please. Please. Don't follow me."

Before either of them can stop me, I slam the door and run.

10

THE SITUATION

WHEN BRONX SAID I COULD open most doors, he only meant the ones that didn't lead outside. All of the exits—doors, windows, balconies, and even a skylight to the roof wouldn't budge. But all the inside rooms? Apparently I'm free to roam about. Every single door unlocked under my handprint. And I checked out every single one I passed.

Though I probably should've stopped after the last ten.

Because, yikes.

How was I supposed to know there were a ton of people in this place? I've only seen Asshole Bevaldi apart from

Bronx, Jameson, Everett, and Mikkalo. Until now.

I just walked in on four strange vampires in three different rooms in what I guess is the guest wing of the estate. I nearly attacked them all for being in various stages of undress doing things I could've lived my life without seeing.

One vampire was tied up and getting banged by who I assume was a personal blood source. Another two were also amid some seriously freaky sex game that involved a lot of biting and blood—the whole scene first freaking me out, thinking one was a human and then it doubly freaked me out because my stomach growled and drew their attention to me. I never denied an invitation to join someone for an early dinner so fast in my life. Lastly, and I shiver every time the image pops into my mind, was a man bathing in blood in the middle of the room. Like, he yanked the tub from the bathroom in his twisted renovation.

I for sure thought my surprise scream would draw one of the Royale brothers to my side, but so far, they're just lurking around. I can't see them, but I sense them. They think I'm too much trouble to leave alone—and after seeing the bloody guy with an unimpressive boner stand up to yell at me—I'm starting to agree. But this isn't any trouble I want to be a part of.

I reach the end of the wing with doors on each side of the hallway and find a set of stairs that lead down. A prickling sensation washes over the back of my neck, and I spin around, expecting to see one of the guys.

"Okay, I know you're there. Just come out," I say. Usually when being stalked by a vampire, my fear instincts go off like crazy. Right now, the only thing going off is my stomach. The pain worsens by the hour, and I don't know how much longer I can go without consuming vampire blood. Fucking Laredo.

Every time I think about him, I flip-flop between missing and hating him. We weren't best friends or anything, and I know he obviously had a thing for me, but he was good. He protected me and kept me fed. He helped my family when we needed it. But damn it. Whatever he did with his bite really fucking screwed me up. If he planned to transform me to set me free—stupid liar—he failed miserably.

My stomach clenches again, and I hug myself. "Seriously, just show yourself."

"Bronx said not to," Mikkalo says softly. "You have to return to our wing first. Consider this your free space."

"Mikkalo..." My voice trails off. Heat warms my skin as I think about the last time I saw him. How I practically attacked his mouth with mine, nearly got off while I lost control of my blood hunger, letting it turn into lust. Again, another reason my brothers insisted on drinking from a glass.

Mikkalo clears his throat, still not showing himself. "I'm sorry, Gwen. My brothers and I are a bit concerned over our current situation."

"Situation?"

He doesn't respond.

"You mean me." The warmth in my cheeks turns to full-on flames that I half expect to catch my reflection burning in one of the shiny silver light fixtures. "Is this because I kissed you and your brother?" I close my eyes for a second. "I'm really sorry. I don't know what had gotten into me. I've just been—"

"Please, Gwen. Just return to our wing. Here's not a great place to discuss things."

I stare at all the closed doors. He's most definitely right. Mr. Blood Bath Boner might hear us over the shudder-worthy moans of his—whatever the fuck that shit was.

I release a small breath. "Okay. Will you at least walk with me? I don't remember the way back."

A hand links through mine, and I turn to offer Mikkalo a smile. Mr. Bevaldi flashes his fangs and tugs me to him, slapping his hand over my mouth to silence my scream. Dragging me into a room, he quietly closes the door and kicks a dark wooden chest in front of it. I flail my body, attempting to elbow him, kick him, do anything I can to get him to break his hold on me.

Lugging me across the room, he heads toward the balcony. I expect an alarm to go off as he opens it, but the silent night greets us. I snap my teeth against his hand, trying to bite his fingers, but he curls them enough to keep them from my teeth.

Mr. Bevaldi spins me around and shoves my back

against the banister. "Don't—"

I jerk my head forward, trying to head-butt him. He expects my move and returns the gesture with enough force that the world turns black for a few seconds. It was long enough for him to jump from the balcony with me.

"Mikkalo!" I yell. At least I think I do. The ringing in my ears is far too loud to let me hear even my racing heartbeat.

The world spins, and I smash to the concrete, the air knocking from my lungs. My eyes water as I open and close my mouth. Mr. Bevaldi slaps his hand over my lips again, leaning into me while pinning me down.

"Stop fighting," he commands, locking me in his gaze.

To my utter despair, my body slackens, a numbness traveling from my toes and into my fingers. An invisible weight presses down on me, stopping me from moving. Panic tightens my chest, the sudden paralysis the worst thing I've ever felt in my life. I'm utterly helpless beneath this lunatic vampire.

Mr. Bevaldi's eyes flash silver. "Don't make a sound."

I couldn't even if I tried.

"Where is Mr. Zaire Royale?" he asks, leaning into me more.

Pain bursts through me as I try to resist his gaze, but it only takes a second for my mouth to open and say, "Dead."

Raising his eyebrows, Mr. Bevaldi studies my face for a long moment. "Are you sure?"

"Yes." Annoyance washes through me, and I try every-thing I can to look away, but his mind manipulation is too strong.

A smile crosses his face. "Yet the Royale Coven issued an eviction from the premises to me on behalf of Zaire. Which was your fault."

I just continue to gape at him.

"Do you know what that means?" he asks.

"No." Ugh. I concentrate on trying to curl my fingers.

"You owe me." Flashing his fangs, he inches his face closer to mine. "But don't worry. You will enjoy my bite."

A strange emotion floods through me, my mouth au-tomatically whispering a breathless moan at his words. My mind screams to knock that shit off. This isn't real. I don't want this asshole to bite me. The only thing I want is—

All it takes is Mr. Bevaldi flicking his gaze to my throat to break from his stare. Jerking my head up, I chomp down as hard as I can onto his shoulder, surprising the hell out of him. His strangely aromatic blood wafts through the air, but none spills on me. The fabric of his jacket soaks it up, not even offering me a single drop.

I yell and shove my hands hard into his chest, knocking him flat on his back. He snarls at me, and I grab his head in my hands and bend his neck to expose his throat. Leaning down, I bite him again, sinking my teeth in so deeply that he howls a wail. Blood fills my mouth, and I automatically swallow.

Two strong hands link onto my waist to yank me back. My burning hunger takes control of me, and I swing my elbow, hitting whoever holds me right in the nose. A deep grunt huffs in my ear. I break free and rush at Mr. Bevaldi again. Latching onto my bite mark, I suck hard, filling my mouth again, fully intent on drinking every last drop of him.

"Gwen," a soft voice says.

I don't look at Mikkalo. I can't. "He broke into my mind!" My voice screeches through the air, gurgling with the blood still spilling from the artery I tore open. "I can't let it happen again. I can't."

Mikkalo grabs onto me, ripping me away. Mr. Bevaldi stumbles to his feet, clutching his throat. Reaching into his jacket, he pulls out a dagger and holds it out, warning me to stay back. But the fight drains from me as the burning hunger inside me dissipates.

My rising panic explodes through me, and all I can think about is how I attacked a vampire. I broke the law again. I'm dead. I know it.

"Donor Life Corp is going to hear about this, Mr. Royale," Mr. Bevaldi says, his voice deep with his threat. "How long were you going to keep Zaire's death a secret?"

A hulking figure materializes behind Mr. Bevaldi, and Bronx swings a giant-ass sword right through his neck, severing his head off. Jameson catches it in his hands, his jaw tight, his eyes flashing silver, and he proceeds to stick his fingers into the dead vampire's mouth to rip his fangs free.

Everett appears in front of me, and I scream and slap out, startled by his sudden arrival. He frowns and steps close to me, engulfing me in a hug, squishing me against Mikkalo until my trembling body settles down enough for me to stand on my own feet.

I swipe the blood from my mouth with the back of my hand. "You killed him."

Jameson swings Mr. Bevaldi's head in a circle by his hair. "Wish it could've been more merciless."

Bronx punches him in the shoulder. "Stop."

"What? Look what he did to Gigi. He should've been slowly impaled in the sunlight. She's *ours*." His eyes flash silver before he looks at me. And then he groans. "I—fuck!"

Jameson disappears, leaving me with his brothers.

All I can do is close my eyes. Because he said I was theirs. They killed the guy because he touched one of their possessions.

"Please, someone take me inside," I murmur.

"Of course, Gwen," Mikkalo says.

Bronx steps closer. "Allow me, brother. And go find Jameson. The five of us really need to talk."

The second Bronx set me on my feet, I charged for the bathroom and hopped in the shower with my clothes on and all. I wish I had thought things through, because in my hurry to get Mr. Bevaldi's blood off me and also to steal a moment of alone time to gather my thoughts before I face this mess, I forgot to ask about clothes.

And I hear four voices trickling to me from Bronx's room.

They're arguing.

"We can't just leave her mind unprotected, Bronx. She knows too much. Look how fast Bevaldi got to her," Mikkalo says.

Jameson releases a growl. "That wouldn't have happened if you had been paying better attention."

Mikkalo groans. "I was keeping the space Bronx demanded. You try separating all of the noise in the guest wing."

"Which she wouldn't have needed had you three dumbasses kept your damn hands to yourself," Bronx snaps.

"Hey, I did!" Jameson yells. "I wanted so badly to— fuck. You need to decide who gets her contract so that I can work on getting her out of my head. She's so damn—"

A thud sounds through the air, cutting off his words. "Watch it, Jameson. She's listening to your loud mouth." Bronx clears his throat. "Hey, Gwen? It's okay to come out if you want. We have nothing to hide."

Except for the fact that they were totally arguing about me and my contract.

Slowly easing the door open, I peek out. Cool air sends goosebumps over my damp skin, and I stroll from the bathroom, clutching the towel around me. I try to remind myself that they found me in my bra and underwear after Zaire's death, so even in a towel, I'm more covered up.

All four of them inhale soft breaths and drop their gazes to the floor when I turn my head to look at them. My body reacts to their attention, even if they all redirect it. Their quick glances at me are enough to send my skin buzzing.

"I forgot to ask for clothes," I say softly.

Bronx lifts his muscular arm and points to an open doorway across the room. "In the wardrobe. The top two drawers are yours as well as the stuff hanging on the far right. We'll get you a few more things tomorrow evening."

I bob my head and pad my way across the room, strolling past the four of them sitting together in Bronx's sitting area. I notice a covered tray on the coffee table next to Jameson with what smells like food and try to suppress my rising desire—not for the food. For Everett. My thigh tingles at the memory of his mouth.

"Don't worry, Gigi. It's still hot," Jameson says, smiling at his hands, keeping his eyes trained away from me. "And I won't feed you this time."

I suck my bottom lip between my teeth without responding. Picking up my pace, I enter the giant wardrobe that is bigger than the guest room I was first put in. A huge wall mirror on rollers hides what I assume are Bronx's clothes. Shelves of shoes rest under the hanging racks, and a glass case full of accessories sparkles under wall lights.

A six drawer, built-in dresser is tucked into the end with a bench in front of it. I run my fingers across a small section of dresses—nothing like the bridal gown I wore, but still fancier than anything I've ever owned. I skip them all. Right now, all I want is to slip into something comfortable that will cover my skin far better than any of the stuff hanging.

Pulling open the top drawer, I frown at all of the sheer lace, satin, and silk. Knowing that Bronx picked out my undergarments feels incredibly intimate, but I stop myself from complaining. This is the last conversation I want to have—also, a bra is the last thing I want to put on because I'm so tired and hope this little meeting ends so I can just go to bed. The night schedule sucks.

Despite my desire to forgo the bra, I pick out one that won't flash my nipples through the fabric. I totally dread that I'm going to have to ask for pieces that I can wear for normal occasions. Most of this stuff looks like it was intended only to be ripped off in heated passion and my boobs need some support. I won't last my usual hour of training otherwise...if I'm even allowed to workout. Ugh. I'm going to die of boredom staying in a damn room all the time.

Opening the second drawer, I spot a couple of T-shirts, and whisper a thank you to the universe. I slip a plain black one over my head and unfold the clothes to see if Bronx remembered pants. He didn't.

"Everything okay, Gwen?" Bronx asks.

I realize that all four of them listen to me groaning. "You forgot to pick me up pants."

"You don't like dresses?" he asks.

Huffing, I exhale a deep breath through my nose. "They all look like they're intended for special occasions. I just—never mind. I'll just wear one."

"Check the bottom drawers. My exercise shorts will be big, but you can try."

Relenting to his suggestion, I pull open the next drawer and hesitate, spotting his boxer-briefs rolled neatly in rows. I check the next drawer and tug out a pair of black shorts. They're baggy as hell and would hit my mid-calf.

Fuck it.

I snatch a pair of his underwear and slide them over mine and look at the mirror. I hate my life. My hair hangs in a tangled wet mess, and my skin is blotchy with rosy spots from the heat of the shower. The last thing I want to do is to have a conversation with the guys. Especially because I kissed Everett and Mikkalo, thought about kissing Jameson, and my mind can't stop replaying Bronx's naked wakeup call as I stare at myself in his boxer-briefs.

Shit. Why do I care?

My brothers would murder me for even thinking it's because I might kind of like them. I know my vagina does. My nipples. My mouth.

Forcing myself to leave the wardrobe, I make it all of five feet before I halt under the heat of four of the most intense stares I've ever felt in my life. And boy do the guys devour me with their eyes. I shift on my feet, rubbing my legs together while combing my fingers through my hair. If my body doesn't get itself in control soon, I'm surely going to have resort to taking care of myself before I throw myself at all of them. My body's needs have never been so...prominent.

"Those are not your workout shorts," Jameson whispers, keeping his jaw tight, his lips unmoving.

Shit. Please, please, please. I fucking pray they don't whisper something bad about my appearance. I won't be able to control my face.

"Damn. I'm certain she's going to ensure I suffer from an eternal boner," Mikkalo responds.

My fucking eyes. I dart my gaze right to Mikkalo's lap. My face flushes, and it takes everything in me not to run. To him.

"Say something to her, Bronx," Everett whispers. "She's uncomfortable."

"I—" Bronx snaps his mouth shut.

"The shorts didn't fit." My voice cuts through the silence, the words squeaking as they come out of my throat. "I hope this is okay."

Bronx gets himself together and nods his head. Standing up, he opens a seat for me on the couch and sits down on the coffee table. I count my breaths, trying to control my sudden panting. Because, damn. This is the closest I've been to all of them at once, and my body loves the idea way too much. Who am I kidding? So does my mind.

I nestle between Everett and Mikkalo, crossing my legs at my knees to keep an inch of space on both sides of me. Bronx's knees brush mine as he shifts, attempting to give me space without forcing me to sit between his long legs.

"Here, Gigi. I hope you like pizza," Jameson says, pulling the lid off the tray. "I made it myself."

I raise my eyebrows. "Really? It smells amazing. I haven't had cheese in at least a year."

"Don't let him fool you. All he did was heat it up. None of us are great at cooking," Everett says.

Jameson holds the plate out to me. "But I'm determined to learn for you."

"You don't have to do that. Just show me the kitchen. I can cook for myself. My brother, Porter, taught me the basics when I was..." I suppress the rising sadness inside me at the thought of Porter. He'd be so jealous of this pizza.

A gentle hand touches my knee, and I draw my gaze to Everett. "Your brothers are still alive, Gwen. I wasn't lying when I told you I'd start to look into things. Your Blood Matching put a halt on auctions for an entire month."

I frown. "What?"

"Because Zaire's taken a leave of absence to get to know you," Bronx says, leaning his elbows on his knees. "According to the announcement all coven leaders in the Royale Region received an hour ago along with the board of Donor

Life Corp."

My mouth forms an O, hope rising inside me. "You did that?"

He nods. "It was the least I could do, especially after seeing the videos from Zaire's death from the car cams."

Mikkalo rests his hand on mine, pulling my attention from Bronx. "And we're sorry you experienced that, Gwen. We had no idea he was going to be that way. He knew you never donated. He knew—"

"He knew we were all interested in you," Jameson says. "Fucking asshole."

I bring the piece of pizza to my mouth to stop from commenting. They obviously have mixed emotions about their dead brother.

"Served him right to lose a fight. A little cock grazing shouldn't have distracted him so much," he adds.

I chuck the pizza at him, smacking him right in the face with it. I know he could've caught it before it did, but he let it hit him anyway only to catch it on his lap. I surprise the hell out of him by leaning across Everett and picking it back up. He shivers under the closeness of my hand grazing his pants.

"When you grow up unregistered like I have, you don't waste food," I say, snapping my teeth a little too hard into the pizza to tear off a piece. "And I hope you guys don't mind, but I don't want to think about that night anymore."

They frown at me. I've never seen such pouty vampires

before. They look almost human, despite Bronx's fangs peeking out from beneath his lips.

Reaching out, I rest my hand on his knee, drawing his gaze to my fingers. "I'd also like to thank you for what you did. You have no idea what it means to me. Grayson, Declan, Ashton, Silas, and Porter—they've always looked out for me. They're all I have." I lick my lips. "Is there anything you can do for Kyler? Just seeing him like that..." I push the image of him away. "Being under mind manipulation was the worst thing I've ever experienced."

"You were shot," Everett says, reminding me.

I flick my gaze to him. "That was nothing." I set my plate next to Bronx and hug myself. "I never want to experience that again."

"See, Bronx. Another reason why we can't leave her mind unprotected," Mikkalo whispers from beside me. I'm really starting to hate that they whisper in front of me like this. Or that I can't react. They're nice now, but if they found out that Laredo's bite basically enhanced my dhampir abilities...hell, they'd surely cage me for real if they found out I'm a dhampir.

"And neither do we," Bronx says, responding to my comment while ignoring Mikkalo's whisper. "Which is why we need to figure out your Blood Match contract and decide which one of us it'll go to."

I frown.

Mikkalo slides his arm around my back and hugs me to

him. "Don't worry, Gwen. If you pick me, I don't expect you to provide me your blood."

I gape. "Me pick you?"

"I'd like to offer you the same," Jameson says. "But I will most definitely let you suck on me to assure you can't be manipulated."

I inhale a small breath at the memory of the taste of his blood. "Shit."

"I'm sure that goes for all of us." Everett pats my knee with a smile.

Bronx leans forward. "I know we've had a rough start, Gwen, so I just want you to know that I'll do better. I also won't have any hard feelings if you choose one of my brothers."

Huh? I twist in my seat and take a minute to look at all of them individually. "Wait, you want *me* to choose?"

"It's the easiest way. I wasn't lying when I said that we're all attracted to you," Bronx says. "And the idea of taking care of you—"

"I can take care of myself," I snap.

Mikkalo chuckles. "We definitely know—"

"And I'm not choosing any of you." I push to my feet and find myself trapped between way too many muscular legs to easily escape without landing on my ass. "I'm not a piece of property nor am I something you can just sign your name to. I don't even know you guys that well."

Bronx tips his head back and groans, peering at the ceiling. "Okay, okay. Gwen, we're sorry. We just thought you'd like a choice instead of us deciding."

I clench my fingers into my palms. "I do want a choice."

"But—"

I hold up my hand silencing him. "But you can't just throw this at me. This is my life. I need time."

The four of them look at each other, and then Bronx whispers, "Will you three be able to manage giving her time? I know this isn't ideal—"

"But if we don't, she's going to hate whoever gets her contract," Everett responds. "I don't want it if that's the case."

I tighten my jaw, stopping myself from shouting at them to quit talking about me like I'm not here. "So can I please have that? Some time? You said you needed some as well to figure out the whole Zaire situation."

"I'm good with it," Jameson whispers to Bronx.

"But we can't smother her," Bronx says. "We need some rules. Time alone with her."

I groan and push myself between Bronx and Mikkalo's legs. "I'm just going to assume the answer is yes. Now, since you guys obviously want to talk about me or whatever, I'm going to bed."

"I can walk you to your room," Jameson says, standing up.

I shake my head. "After tonight? No. I'm sleeping right

there." I point at Bronx's bed. "The rest of you can decide whose bed I'm stealing tomorrow."

Flopping onto Bronx's giant bed, I roll over, pulling the blankets with me to wrap myself up without getting under them.

"Dibs on tomorrow," both Mikkalo and Everett whisper in unison.

Bronx clears his throat. "You'll stay with Jameson next, Gwen."

I hum under my voice. "Whatever. Goodnight."

"Shit," Mikkalo says, keeping his voice low. "What are we getting ourselves into?"

I groan and cover my ears with my hands. I was thinking the same thing.

11

SIDE EFFECTS

I ROLL OVER AND SMACK into a brick wall...not a brick wall, but pretty damn close. Opening my eyes, I stare at the back of Bronx's head as he sleeps facing the other direction with the blanket he somehow managed to wrangle from me pulled all the way up to his neck.

That must've been some deep-ass sleep for me if I missed him sliding into bed next to me. How he manages to balance his body on the edge while I lie sprawled across the middle? I have no idea.

Stretching my arms over my head, I release a small

moan and roll off the bed to go to the bathroom. Soft music hums from a hidden speaker, possibly from another room, and I quietly listen to it as I pour a glass of water from the sink and swallow, hoping it helps snuff out the burning in my stomach.

From all my years with my blood sources, I know better than to wake up a sleeping vampire, so I busy myself with brushing my hair and teeth and washing the sleep from my face. I do a few stretches and bounce on my feet. I can't tell—because Bronx's room doesn't have any windows—but I'm pretty sure it's still day time. I fell asleep way before the night was over, and now I wish I had tried to stay up longer.

Because now I'm bored. And hungry. And anxious.

Tiptoeing from the bathroom, I peer around Bronx's suite and decide just to head back to the bed. The cool leather couch isn't something I want to plant my ass on, and the view of the TV is much better from the bed.

It doesn't shift at all as I slide back on it and pull the blanket over me. I keep the corner up a bit, unable to stop myself from peeking at Bronx's sleeping form.

I'm such a creep.

But damn it, I can't deny how good he looks wearing only his boxer-briefs. Leaning over him, I snatch what I think might be the TV control from next to his com device. I tense as my hair spills over his head, but he doesn't move, his breathing remaining even. Looks like I'm not the only deep sleeper.

I press my finger to the screen of the control, and it flashes green before the projector turns on. A deep-ass moan sounds through the air as whatever the hell movie Bronx was watching starts playing automatically.

I cover my mouth with my hand, unable to turn my gaze away from the close-up shot of a couple having sex. Shit.

"Tap the top of the screen to bring up the menu," Bronx says, startling me.

I toss the controller into the air like it'll explode, sending it flying to the edge of the bed. Heat floods my face, and I gawk from Bronx to the projector and back to Bronx.

"Or you can just watch this," he says with a chuckle. "Doesn't bother me any. You might like the part coming up." Lifting his hand, he points at the screen.

My rebellious eyes. They disobey my brain and follow his finger to gaze back at the projector just in time to see the woman—a human—release a loud as all get-out moan a second before she sinks her teeth into her vampire lover's chest.

I inhale a soft breath, my stomach flipping in a good way, and I sneak a peek back at Bronx as his eyes linger on the side of my face.

"Ha-ha. Just because I had a vampire friend before, doesn't mean—"

"You mean your blood source," he says, smirking at me. "I'm not unfamiliar with Blood Rebels, dandelion. I know you had blood in your system when I picked you up in the city. That vampire of yours was awfully possessive, and you knew exactly how to bite Bevaldi last night."

I try not to squirm, knowing he's teasing me by the lightness in his voice. But his curiosity about me—disguised as an observation—doesn't go unnoticed by me. And I so don't want him to know that he was right and I might have enjoyed watching the damn sex bite. It made me more than just hungry, and Bronx sits dangerously close.

"A woman has to know how to take care of herself. And Laredo was my blood source's name. He had his flaws, but he respected the rules of our household and saved my ass on more than one occasion," I say, turning to meet his gaze straight on.

"I am sorry I killed him," he murmurs. "I really thought you were in trouble."

I blink a few times and shrug. With the way I grew up, I have kind of always been prepared to lose those in my life. A lot of Blood Rebels die young. It's just the way it is. And Laredo? I can't grieve for him. I just can't. "He wasn't my first."

Bronx raises his eyebrows.

"Blood source that is. I killed my last one because— never mind." I say *our* instead of *mine* because I'm certain he's read into Laredo's near exclusivity apart from the few times he used his blood to help my brothers heal. I heard Bronx and his brothers discuss it. That's why I'm here with

Bronx. Why I'm going to Jameson next. And Mikkalo and Everett after.

"I'm guessing he really fucking deserved it."

"You can say that." It's all I can think to say as the idea of rotating between the four Royale brothers sinks in. Grayson will have a coronary if he hears about this.

Silence falls between us, the movie continuing to play actually has a storyline, but neither of us watches it. I stare at my hands as Bronx gazes at me, sending all sorts of confusing feelings through me. I can barely handle the attention a moment longer and flop back on the pillow and right into the crook of his arm. I hadn't realized how close I was to him. Did he move or did I?

Either way, my body sinks into his side, and he lets me. The sweet scent of his skin draws me closer, and one second I'm looking at the ceiling and in the next I lock my gaze with his, my chin resting on his broad chest. His heartbeat picks up as fast as mine, and he gently combs his fingers through my hair to push it from my face.

"Is this okay?" he asks, his voice deepening. "If it's not, you can tell me."

"You're a lot more comfortable than you look," I say, smirking. Sliding my hand across his stomach, I trace each of his hard stomach muscles.

We both inhale a breath. I'm just as surprised as he is by my wandering hand.

And then I'm on top of him.

His eyes flash silver as I squeeze his hips between my thighs and bend down to brush my lips against his. Sneaking his hands under my shirt, he trails his fingers over my back and pulls me closer, kissing me deeper, reacting to the exploding lust crashing over us.

He slips his tongue into my mouth, awakening my whole body, his lips tasting as sweet as he smells. I caress my tongue to his, grazing my teeth over his bottom lip to pull it into my mouth. I'm tempted to bite down, but something stops me. Either my mind or the burning hunger threatening to unleash the wild, starving dhampir inside me, which one? I'm afraid to find out.

Bronx moans against my lips, his voice vibrating against me as his fingers travel around my hips to pull me into him. My body rubs his, the only thing keeping our skin apart being pieces of thin fabric. I grind into his stiff bulge, feeling the entire length of his shaft. He tightens his fingers around me, rocking me in a way that makes me gasp. The pressure of his erection creates so much good friction that I can't stop imagining what it would be like to lose my clothes. If he lost his.

"Gwen," he whispers, slowing my body down. He flexes his now massively raging boner between my legs. "You're torturing me."

I heave a few deep breaths, easing myself a couple of inches away. "I'm sorry. I—"

Leaning up to close the space once more, he cuts off my

apology with another kiss that ends with me on my back. His body sinks against mine, his weight between my legs sending a burst of electricity through me so intense that I curl my toes and drag my hands down the length of his stomach to feel how hard I make him.

He breaks from my mouth, kissing along my jaw. I stroke the length of his erection over his underwear until his hand slides down my stomach, stopping just before the hem of my bottoms to wait for my reaction. I link my hand around his wrist and push him to continue. He slips his fingers into my underwear and between my legs so that he can feel how warm and wet and excited he makes me as my body begs him for more.

"Gwen," he whispers again. "Is this really okay?"

I hum under my breath and brush my lips to his bare shoulder, moaning softly as he twirls his finger just hard enough against my clit to build pressure to send my nerve-endings exploding with the incredible sensation. I squirm beneath him, completely incapable of staying still under his touch, his lips, his continuous whisper of my name.

I pant and grip the blankets until I can't stop myself from arching up to dig my fingers so hard into his shoulders that my nails break his skin. He releases the sexiest noise, and I lick across the few drops of his blood. And holy shit does he taste as good as he smells. Better. Nearly intoxicating.

Tingles burst over my tongue and to the rest of me, igniting something wild and intense, my deep-seated need suddenly insatiable for all of Bronx—his blood, his body. And then my whole body surprises me by tensing in a crazy way, my muscles clenching as a wave of something indescribable explodes through me unlike anything I've ever experienced in my life. I throw myself back, reaching for a pillow to cover my face as I release a moan I can't control.

Bronx's weight suddenly falls off me, and I lie still with my chest heaving, my body continuing to buzz. I manage to drag the pillow from my face only to find the bed beside me empty.

"Bronx?" My voice comes low, breathless.

"I'm sorry, Gwen." His voice sounds from the open bathroom.

I slide off the bed and pad my way over. I catch sight of him standing in front of the mirror, droplets of blood crawling from ten very noticeable scratch marks on his shoulder blades. "Fuck, I didn't mean to hurt you. I just—"

He releases a breathless laugh. "Hurt isn't the word I'd use to describe myself. That was one helluva orgasm you had. So sexy. You're—" He turns to face me, his desire still prominently pointing at me. "You're incredible, Gwen."

"But you stopped."

His eyes flash silver, his fangs peeking from beneath his lips, and now I know why. He doesn't say anything for a moment and closes the space to me. Hooking his arm around my waist, he draws me so close that I feel every hard inch of him.

I shiver at his closeness, the ecstasy of our moment together weakening my knees all over again. All of my limited sexual experience before now can't even compare. I didn't even know I could feel this way.

"I didn't want to. It took everything in me to do so. But I had to," Bronx murmurs, leaning down to brush his lips to mine. "I don't think I would, but there was no way in hell I was going to test my restraint."

"You wanted to bite me," I say softly, knowing it's the truth, though he doesn't actually say it.

"A lot. And I know you don't want that."

His admission comes as no big surprise to me. Laredo was always pretty honest—which is what really got on Grayson's nerves—because he used to tease me that he'd never bite me like he did my brothers. If he was going to bite me, he swore it would be magical. I thought he was lying.

But now...

I push the thought of Bronx's fangs getting anywhere near my skin from my mind. It's impossible. Laredo did lie to me. The horrible bite mark he left on my neck had proved it. I can still feel the strange sensation as it still heals, hidden under my blond hair.

"So...yeah. I need a cold fucking shower," he adds, swallowing, drawing my attention to his popping Adam's apple and throat.

I can't stop the giggle from escaping my mouth. Standing on my tiptoes, I push harder against him, giving his boner no place to go except between my legs. I glide my tongue along his jaw, every ounce of my good sense gone as my deep-seated desire to satiate my burning hunger rising through me. "Any chance you can tell me where the kitchen is first? I'm starving." I don't know how else to try to control myself besides stuffing my face.

He clears his throat, mapping his hands down to my ass. "I hope this isn't weird, my brothers and I had a long talk last night, and we'd like to start giving you our blood, even before you make your choice. We can supply it however you choose. And after last night, I want to help you protect your mind, Gwen. So can I give you my blood before you go?"

I don't know if that horrible attack by Mr. Bevaldi was fate or the universe testing me only to finally fall into my favor, but whatever it was—the fear, the awfulness—it might have actually saved me. Bronx might want to assure no one can break into my mind—even if it's for his coven's benefit—but he unknowingly will help me survive.

"Only if you admit that your intentions are more than about protecting me," I say. "You killed Mr. Bevaldi because he ripped the truth about Zaire from me." I don't know why I want to hear it, but I do. It helps remind me of who Bronx is and who I really am to him. The moment we just shared was based solely on need and nothing more. If I can't remember that, I'll lose who I was raised to be—which isn't a donor.

His lips quirk up in the corner. "That wasn't the only reason, dandelion. But I won't lie to you. The fact that it did happen does play a part in my decision besides the bastard pissing me off by putting his hands on you." He bows to me, kissing me again. "I want you to be mine, Gwen."

I shiver under his whisper only to have him pull away. Then he surprises me by sinking his fangs into his arm to send rivulets of blood seeping toward his elbow as he grabs for a glass from the stack of cups he has on a shelf near the sink.

I can't take my eyes away from him as he dribbles his blood into a glass.

"You don't have to do it that way," I say, inching my way closer, practically hypnotized by the crimson liquid.

He chuckles. "Oh, yes I fucking do. With the way you look like you want to devour me, I'm certain I'll let you. And if that happens..." He lets his words trail off for a second. "My brothers will not be happy."

I frown. "You think I'll kill you because of who I am?" I can't get myself to say the words. It makes me frown even to think them.

His eyes widen. "Oh, no. Not that. It's...how much do you actually know about vampires, Gwen? I know you say you've had blood sources, but from the vampires I know who choose to take advantage—"

"Laredo didn't take advantage of me," I snap.

Bronx looks at me like I'm crazy. "He did. He took advantage of your whole family. You were his personal donors."

"He helped us save humans. He protected me. He fought with me," I say.

"Because it was worth the trade. You can't honestly think he would've helped with nothing in return. He even took advantage of the situation when you were caught." Bronx's nostrils flare with his words, and I step away from him. "He was probably even the one who called it in. We didn't just show up at random, Gwen."

My chest heaves with his words, the edges of my vision darkening. "He wouldn't."

"If he was helping you, he'd have stayed and fought to help your brothers."

I open my mouth to tell Bronx he's wrong. That Laredo only fled because he was trying to help me. He was trying to keep me alive and free. But Bronx's words get to me. A part of me thinks he's right. It was Laredo's idea to go into Crimson Vista.

"But he ran with you. I bet he didn't expect it being us who showed up that night. We wouldn't have if your family wasn't called in as Blood Rebels," he adds.

With my breath heaving, I glower at Bronx. I don't even know what to say or how to react. I don't even know how this whole conversation started. But I'm so damn ready to end it. I'm ready for my time with him to be over.

"This is too much," I say, my voice quivering as I try to stay calm. "I didn't need to hear your thoughts on my situation, Bronx. It's not going to change anything. I don't even know why you're telling me this. Why you're trying to make me feel bad about believing Laredo had good intentions. He's dead. He's not a threat to you."

Brushing his free hand through his hair, he tips his head back and glances at the light fixtures above. "You're right. And because I even feel he is, is why I—" He shakes his head and shuts up, though I want so desperately to hear what he has to say. Composing himself, he holds up the glass of blood to me. "Here, take this. You'll find the kitchen on the first floor. Head past the foyer and to the swinging door on the far side of the living room. Ask a staff member if you need assistance. Someone should still be around. I'll find you when I'm done getting ready."

Like that, the conversation's over.

Swiping the glass from him, I chug it and hand it back. Tingles explode over me, and I suddenly find myself back in his arms, my body going crazy. "What the hell?"

He presses his lips into a line. "Fuck," he whispers under his breath.

I touch my fingers to his bare chest, lust warring with my annoyance. Stretching up, I attempt to kiss him. "Why do I want to suddenly have sex with you?"

Bronx gently eases back, placing his hands to my shoulders. "It's a side effect of drinking my blood. I—I didn't know it would happen. I've never shared it with any-one before."

"Shit. I have to go." I don't know how I manage to do it, but I throw myself back. "Maybe you shouldn't find me, Bronx. Because this—" I wave my finger between us. "I don't know what this is. And I don't like it."

Without waiting for him to respond, I spin and leave.

I don't look back.

12

WILD

THIS PRISON OF A MANSION is boring as all get-out.
After making breakfast and eating alone in the biggest kitch-
en I've ever seen, I find myself wandering the only hallway
I'm familiar with. There's no chance in hell I'm going exploring again, especially because I don't know how long
Bronx's blood will stay in my system, protecting my mind,
yet I don't want to find Bronx either. Just like I asked, he
never came searching for me.

I haven't seen any of his brothers either. But that's
about to change. I can't stand being alone for another mi-

nute. For one, I'm not used to it. And two, Everett seems way less moody than Bronx. His room happens to be the only other one I know how to locate.

Standing outside Everett's door, I press my ear to it and listen for a moment. I don't even get the chance to knock before it swings inward, and he greets me with a grin I haven't seen on him yet. He's so hot, all happy to see me. My mouth mimics his, and I smile wide enough to show all my teeth.

"Hey you," he says, leaning on the doorframe. "Everything okay?"

I bob my head. "Yeah...just bored."

His blue eyes shift to glance behind me. "Where's Bronx?"

"Don't know. Don't care," I murmur, twisting to look down the hall. I half expect to see Bronx lurking with the way Everett doesn't keep his gaze on me for long. "And I don't want to see him."

His smile fades instead of widening. I would think knowing that I currently want nothing to do with his brother would make him happy. Instead, he asks, "Rough morning?"

"You can say that." I bounce on my feet, suddenly feeling awkward just standing in the hallway, still wearing the same clothes I slept in. "Is it okay if I come in?"

Everett opens and closes his mouth for a moment, his eyes flashing silver. "Actually, I'm sorry, Gwen. I was about to head out with Mikkalo."

"Oh." Ugh. Why am I so disappointed? "Can you tell me where to find Jameson's room then?"

"Don't do it. I can't say no to that pouty mouth of hers." Jameson's soft voice trickles from somewhere behind me.

If Everett wasn't watching me, I'd turn around and look.

"He might be busy," Everett says.

Annoyance rushes through me, and I groan and spin away from him. "Never mind. I'll just—I'll figure out how to entertain myself. But you guys better not get mad if I break something."

I make it all of ten feet. Everett materializes in front of me, and I raise my hands and steady myself against his chest, his sudden movement throwing me off. If he didn't hook his hand around my waist, I would've fallen on my ass.

He's quick to release me and steps back a good three feet, assuring all of the space between us. I'm actually really surprised. I didn't know vampires knew what personal space was with how close they always seem to be to me.

"Gwen, wait. I'm sorry."

"You don't need to apologize for being busy," I say, crossing my arms.

He scrunches his nose, looking way too cute doing so. "No, but I need to apologize for lying to you."

"So, you're not busy?" From Jameson's plea to have Everett cover for him, I should know this.

"I just—we, my brothers and I—set some rules to try to keep this whole situation in control." Closing the space, he reaches out and takes my hand, pulling me closer. I let him. Something in his eyes draws me to him—his sincerity. Everett could have easily just slammed the door on me, but he looks ready to spill his heart. "I don't know if you know this, but vampires tend to be...possessive."

I knew that, but it wasn't even something that dawned on me. And now I'm pretty certain that Bronx was trying to tell me the same thing Everett tells me now before our fight about Laredo. Except with Bronx, it was his reason to pour his blood in a glass.

Now I feel bad. He was only trying to give me his reasoning. But shit. Why not just spit it out?

"So we decided that it would help keep us sane and stop us from fighting or freaking you out if we kept our distance during the time you asked us to give you to get to know us. It's Bronx's night, so..."

I release a small sigh. "So what? I just have to be alone? Because after this morning and the whole weird-ass reaction I had to his blood, I don't know if I can face him again."

He frowns. "You had a reaction?"

"He didn't tell you?" I swing Everett's hand, feeling antsy as his demeanor shifts into concern.

"No, he didn't. Another rule we set. It's better if we

don't know what happens with each other," he says quietly.

I didn't even think about it, and I'm glad to know. Because, shit. How awkward as hell would it be if Bronx said something to his brothers about...

Damn it. My vagina needs to control itself.

I squeeze my legs together as tingles burst through me as the memory of being with Bronx flits to the front of my mind. "That's probably a good thing," I manage to say. "The stuff my brothers used to share—definitely too much information."

I once punched my brother Declan for going into every single detail with the rest of my brothers after he had sex with a woman we rescued from a blood debt. Let's just say she was as pissed as I was and ended up staying behind in one of the smaller towns.

"We'd never share that kind of information anyway, Gwen," he says, his eyes darkening to an almost night sky blue. "But we agreed to the rule in case. Except when it comes to your health or concerns you have. If you bring it up, it's fine. We don't want you to be afraid to talk to us either. If you've forgotten, I'm trained in human health. If something happened after you drank his blood—"

"I wanted to throw myself at him," I blurt. "I nearly did."

His mouth forms an O. "Have you ever experienced that kind of side effect before?"

I shake my head. "Not like that. Sure, I—" I close my

eyes. "I don't want to really talk about drinking blood with you. It's weird."

He chuckles. "How so? Blood consumption is normal to me. Side effects also happen with vampires. Some humans' blood—there's a reason why Donor Life Corp requires donations."

"Apart from keeping humans compliant? You know we'd fight back more if—"

He frowns.

"I'm sorry, Everett. I didn't mean to snap or make you feel bad. It's not like you set the laws..." Or did he? This is the Royale Region.

His face softens. "I *should* feel bad. I can't imagine all that you've been through. I also can't blame you. Your feelings toward how the world works are warranted. You deserve better. I just hope I can help make it so."

His words touch me so deeply that I throw my arms around him and hug him. No one's ever told me that before. Not even my family.

I rest my head against his chest. "You realize you'd have to change the world, right?"

He pulls away. "I accept your challenge. If you pick me..."

"If I pick you what?" I ask, wanting so desperately to know.

Smiling, he says, "I guess you'll just have to find out."

"Mmmhmm." I meet his smile with my own.

Everett releases a small groan, taking another step back. "I hate to have to do this, but you should go find Bronx. I'm sure he'd love to apologize for whatever happened between you this morning."

My cheeks warm. "I can't. The blood."

"You've been away long enough that it shouldn't be so bad. You should also try one more time to see if things change. Sometimes it just takes your body getting used to it. If the side effects don't let up, then I'll think of something to help." He reaches out and caresses my cheek with the back of his hand. "It's going to be okay, Gwen. Promise."

I release a small sigh. "Why are you doing this?"

"Because Bronx is my brother. Don't tell him I said this, but under all his muscles and moodiness, he's just a softy. It's probably driving him crazy that he upset you enough that you've been pacing this hallway for two hours."

"Gotta get my exercise in somehow," I quip.

"Ev, will you tell her she can find me in the gym?" Bronx's whisper trickles through the air. I try not to react. I should've known he was listening.

"We have a place you can do that," Everett says, acting like Bronx didn't just talk to him. The way he can focus his attention on me and the world around us amazes me. No wonder it takes a lot of strategizing to escape crazy shadow dwellers. "It happens to be Bronx's favorite spot. You might find him there."

I want to tell him that I know I will, but then another

familiar voice hums through the air.

"Want me to bring her something to eat?" Jameson asks.

You've got to be kidding me. Jameson's still listening too? Are they all listening?

"She's also still in the clothes she slept in," Mikkalo comments. "You might want to grab her something else."

Ah, hell. They are. This new super hearing is going to drive me crazy. I want so badly to yell at them to stop it. This group effort to make sure my needs are fulfilled is ra-ther...weird? Yeah. I don't know how to feel about it. It's annoying, but a part of me wants to smile like crazy.

I mean, seriously? I know they're coven brothers, but I've never seen a bond like this on anyone outside my fami-ly.

Laredo once said vampires have to put a lot of effort in-to alliances and covens, because it's not easy to get along. But these four? It feels real. I know it's real. They're working together to help Bronx handle me. I expected them to be fiercely competitive, and the fact that they aren't...I like it way more this way.

"I guess that's probably a safer place to see him rather than in his bedroom," I say, wishing I had kept the words to myself. If they've set rules for this situation, I want to re-spect them. The last place I need to be is in the middle of four vampires if things go bad. I could end up literally torn apart.

Everett chuckles, making me feel better about my comment. "Just take this hallway to the end past Mikkalo's room and to the stairs. Once you reach the glass door, exit out and follow the pathway. The gym is in its own building by the basketball courts." Reaching into his pocket, he pulls out his com device and taps the screen before handing it to me. "Remember, you made me a promise about not trying to escape."

"Like I could outrun you," I tease.

"Here, take this too," Everett says, pulling out a dagger from inside his jacket. "You won't really need it, but it's better to be cautious in case."

I gawk at the weapon. "Jeez, maybe you should just walk me."

"I might have agreed if I hadn't seen you take down Bronx in Crimson Vista," he says, grinning. "I think you can handle yourself."

I nod. "You're right. I can."

"Have fun, Gwen. Take it easy on my brother," Everett says.

I laugh, narrowing my eyes. "Never going to happen." I say the words loud enough that it gets a chuckle out of Mikkalo and Jameson. Bronx releases a groan.

Everett squeezes my hand once more, grinning wider at the array of noises coming from down the hall as Jameson teases Bronx. "Good. I guess I'll see you around. I look forward to our time together."

I never in my life imagined I'd say this about a vampire, but so do I. There's just something about Everett that gets to me in a good way. Seeing him smiling at me, how he drinks me in and not in a way that he looks like he just wants to drain me, I can't help but to think maybe my dad was wrong. That my family was wrong. Not all vampires want to use me or cage me.

And thinking about it, with Everett, holding his weapon and com device, getting to turn and walk away from him by my own freewill, I might actually feel a little bit free.

"Whoa." The second the word escapes my lips, Bronx looks up at me from his place sitting on a bench, doing arm curls with weights bigger than my head. His muscles flex and ripple as he sets down the weights and gets to his feet. "Shit," I whisper, my eyes devouring every damn curve on his shirtless body.

I was utterly wrong thinking that the gym would be safer than meeting Bronx in his bedroom. This is worse. Much more dangerous.

"Hey, dandelion. Everett said you were heading this way," he says, waiting for me to close the space to him instead of the other way around. "I'm glad you came."

Because you told him to send me, I think to myself. I try to come up with something to say but end up turning toward the various types of equipment I've never used in my life. Exercise for me consists of cardio and combat. My strength derives from my innate nature as a dhampir, so my brothers were never concerned about strength training. It's not like we had access to proper equipment. My muscles come from all the times I managed to flip Grayson on his ass during practice.

"Gwen?" Bronx keeps his hands to himself and rocks on his heels because of my silence.

I turn away from the equipment to meet his gaze, drinking in his tight jaw and tense posture. He's as nervous as I am. Neither of us expected to take things to the level we had, and I don't want it to be awkward now, especially if I promised Everett I'd stop trying to run away. If I'm staying, I need to sort out all of my wild emotions.

"I'm sorry," we both say at the same time.

"I know the reaction I had toward your blood wasn't your fault," I continue. "And I shouldn't have snapped at you about Laredo."

Stepping closer, he peers down at me. "I should've never brought him up. I was a dick. Jealous even."

I furrow my brows. "Jealous of a dead guy."

He releases a cross between a groan and a laugh. "I know, I know. It's crazy."

"Just a bit." Swinging my arm, I playfully punch him in his rock-hard shoulder. My hand decides it's not going to pull away and takes on a mind of its own to graze up his shoulder blade and to his neck. "So you need to control yourself. I'm not a stranger to possessive vampires, Bronx. Let's get one thing straight. You try to claim me, and you're going to end up on the ground, clutching your cock again. I killed my first blood source for that. The second I turned eighteen, he assumed that gave him permission to control me, claiming that I owed him for his care. He..." I let my voice trail off. He doesn't need to know that our fight turned into my blood source killing my dad first.

His eyes darken more than I thought possible. It almost looks like his dark tan skin reddens under the bright lights. "I'm sorry you went through that."

I shrug. "I barely remember it. Feels like forever ago. I'd prefer to stay in the present."

Bronx takes my hint that I'm done talking about my past and reaches up to tug my hand away from his neck. He links his fingers through mine instead, easing a foot away from me like my closeness gets to him in a good way. His silver-flashing eyes prove it. "Me too. I mean, I never thought I'd ever find myself training with a Blood Rebel."

"Careful, Bronx. I might use whatever you teach me against you," I say, smiling.

"Hopefully not. I'd much rather see you use it on anyone who tries to fuck with you. And they might, which is why we cleared all our guests from the estate and put them up in Crimson Vista."

"So no more blood bather?" I ask, curling my lips at the memory. "Thank God. That shit was—"

Tipping his head back, Bronx roars a laugh louder than I've ever heard. "I thought Mikkalo was joking about Caine. You really saw that?"

"I saw a lot of things I wish I hadn't." I bump my shoulder to his. "Are you as wild?"

He trails his gaze from mine to the rest of me like he needs a moment to decide how to answer my question. My body buzzes just under the weight of his eyes. My heart picks up pace, and I shift on my feet, trying to stay utterly still as he practically undresses me with his gaze. He swallows and licks his lips, and now I can't stop staring at his mouth.

"Probably less so than you, dandelion," he teases, reaching up to tap my bottom lip with his finger. "But I don't mind. This afternoon..." He inches closer, his eyes locking on me. Gently squeezing my hand, he offers me a small, almost shy smile, letting me fill in the rest with my imagination. "Those scratches. Damn."

I gawk at him, darting my gaze to his shoulders, though they're already healed. I clear my throat and shiver, trying to suppress my desire. I need to change the subject. I'm going to do something reckless otherwise, like jump in his arms and attack his face with my mouth. With the way he looks at me, I know he'll let me. I love the idea way too much.

"So that's why you call me that—dandelion. Right?" I ask, deciding to put more space between us.

He chuckles and shrugs, going along with my need to

get my body in check. "Might have a few other reasons."

I fake glare at him and whack him with the back of my hand. Big mistake. My hand doesn't want to return to me and rubs over the spot instead. "Tell me."

He raises his eyebrow, his chest rising and falling under my touch. "Maybe after you get changed. If you can knock me on my ass again—fairly—I'll tell you."

Kill me now. Wrestling is...super dangerous in this moment.

Placing my hands on my hips, I force myself to pull away and say, "Does that mean you're going to fight fair? No vampire speed, teeth, or super strength." I'm doomed. This can't end any other way except for one of us on top of the other. Most likely him on top of me, which I can't have. I suddenly really want to know why he calls me dandelion.

Bronx shifts his attention away from me and to the rest of the gym. "Deal. Now hurry up and change. I can't wait to see what you got." Ah, hell. Me either.

I take a few steps toward the changing room and hesitate. I know my limitations, and even if Bronx doesn't use his enhanced abilities, without the element of surprise, I might never best him. And if I don't, I'm nearly certain he won't tell me why he calls me dandelion. He counts on me losing so that he doesn't have to.

Going against my good senses to even dare a sneak attack, I twist and charge at Bronx. He swivels and stares at me with wide eyes, confusion scrunching his handsome face.

He doesn't even react until I land on top of him.

"Shit," he murmurs, automatically stretching his arms to touch my hips as I straddle him. "Are you okay?"

I laugh and grab his hands, leaning forward to pin them above his head. He freezes under my sudden closeness, my boobs grazing his chest while my blond hair cascades around us to veil our faces from the world. His intense brown eyes rove over my face, flashing with silver, stopping on my mouth.

"Better than okay. You're down. I pinned you." My words come out breathy, and warmth blooms in my cheeks at the way they come out. I clear my throat. "You have to tell me why you call me dandelion now."

The confusion lining his eyes morphs into a fake glare, though something else lingers in his expression. Desire? I shift my body on his, clenching my thighs around his waist in case he tries to throw me off him.

He doesn't. He sucks in his bottom lip instead.

And then I feel his building erection. I was right about his expression.

I throw myself to the mat and lie on my back, closing my eyes for a second. A shadow darkens my closed lids, and I open them to meet Bronx's gaze as he props himself on his elbow, holding himself up enough to peer down at me.

"Would you accept the reason being your hair?" he asks, filling the silence growing between us. Not awkward silence but tense. Heavy in a good way.

I fake glower at him, tightening my mouth before it decides it wants to pucker for a kiss. "Definitely not."

He groans, sitting up completely like he didn't expect me to persist. And he's nervous. More nervous than before. Spilling his thoughts got him sort of into trouble earlier—me too—but I wasn't kidding about not taking it easy on him. I think he prefers that I don't.

"If it's because you think I'm like a weed—"

"Actually..."

I flick him.

"I'm just kidding. But if I'm going to tell you, we gotta stretch or something." He's definitely nervous.

"You're uncomfortable talking to me," I say, letting him help me sit upright.

"No, not uncomfortable." Reaching out, he pulls me to sit across from him so that we face each other.

He doesn't continue right away, just quietly adjusts my legs until the soles of my feet touch each other. Scooting back a bit, he stretches his legs until his feet rest against my shins. He holds out his hands to me and links his fingers to my arms, gently pulling my upper body towards him.

"You know, Gwen. I don't usually have a problem talking to anyone," he says, holding me in a stretch that feels so seriously good. My body has been so tense the last couple of days. He slowly loosens his fingers as I exhale to let me straighten up, but he doesn't let me go.

"Anyone or other vampires?" I ask.

He shrugs. "I'll be honest. I don't talk to many donors. Just the head of the daylight security. The household manager. A couple of other employees."

"It's obvious."

Bronx pulls me into another stretch, and I stare at the mat between his legs. "Which is why I struggle. I don't want to say something to upset you like I did earlier. I know being here isn't easy for you."

"It's...not as bad as I expected," I admit. "I mean, I miss my brothers, and I really don't like the idea of, you know, having a contract or whatever. But you and your brothers have surprised me. I can't figure you out."

"What do you mean?"

"You're not like the vampires I've had experience with. You're even different than Laredo," I say.

"You're worried," he says, recognizing my expression without having to ask.

"Of course I am."

He pulls me into another stretch. "You don't need to be, Gwen. I know it's easy for me to say, but I mean it. There's something about you...it's hard to explain. You're different, and I don't know why. But I feel it."

Because I'm a dhampir. Maybe Laredo was right about my allure and ability to hone my own kind of charm. Most shadow dwellers try to murder me, but only because I act first. I bet if I didn't, things would be different. My brothers—as well as me—never wanted to risk it. Surprise was our strategy.

I don't dare consider telling Bronx this. Instead, I say, "Of course I am. I'm not going to put up with your shit."

He chuckles. "Yeah, I got that, and maybe that's part of it. You're something else."

"A dandelion to you, apparently," I say, wrinkling my nose.

He pulls me toward him again so that he doesn't have to meet my eyes. "It's nothing bad nor am I comparing you to a weed. It was just the word that popped into my head when I saw that asshole trying to steal you after your Blood Matching."

I don't look at him as I exhale again, knowing it's easier for him to open up if he can't read the emotions crossing my face. "But why?"

He pulls me toward him again, gently grazing his thumbs along the sides of my arms. "Like I said, it's hard to explain. Something drew me to you after we found you in the city. You impressed the hell out of me by taking me down."

I tilt my chin just a little to catch him smiling to himself.

"And I don't know. I couldn't stand the thought of sending you to auction. My brothers agreed. We all asked Zaire if we could apply to Blood Match with you."

"But he denied you," I say.

Bronx releases my arms and scoots in closer, crossing

his legs in front of me. He motions for me to do the same until our knees touch. Taking my hands, he guides them to his thighs and presses my hands into his legs until I do it myself. He adjusts his hands on mine, doing the same.

"While the Blood Match Program has been around for years, it's new to our region. Donor Life Corp decided to adapt it to all of the major cities in board member control, allowing us to tailor it how we want," he says. "And Zaire insisted that no more than one vampire per coven could apply to match with a specific donor."

"That's weird. Why? Shouldn't you all get the chance?" I ask.

"I honestly don't know. He was never open about his place on the board." Bronx stretches my legs for a bit longer and stops. "And as you know, the four of us wanted the chance, so Zaire decided he'd do it himself. At first I thought it was so that the four of us wouldn't be disappointed, but—" He groans. "Never mind that. It doesn't matter. I just thought after he matched with you my chance was over."

"It almost was," I say, bowing a bit to send my hair sprawling forward.

"I know. When Zaire sent out the distress call of an attack, I thought you might have been killed." He touches my shoulder, getting me to sit up and look at him. "But then I caught you. It was then that I knew how strong and resilient you were. You came back to me after I thought I lost you...in the most infuriating way. Like a dandelion. Wild too. As fucking hot as the sun."

I giggle and meet his gaze, my smile widening. "You forgot edible."

He sucks in a small breath, his fangs suddenly peeking out between his lips. "Those are dangerous words to say to a hungry vampire."

"Hungry, huh? If you want to call someone in..." I rub my lips together. "I've seen Laredo drink from all of my brothers. I know how to tune it out."

"I don't drink from donors, so it's all good, Gwen. But, if you're hungry and you don't mind, maybe you'll eat with me? The garden is nice this time of night."

I grin and nod my head. "I'd like that."

"Yeah?"

"Mmmhmm," I say, climbing to my feet. "But first, you're going to have to fight me."

"Is that so?"

"And if I win, you have to find me some dessert."

"What if I win?" he asks, smirking.

I glide my tongue over my teeth. "You have to hand feed it to me."

13

POSSESSIVE

AN HOUR BEFORE SUNRISE, I find myself standing with Bronx outside the double doors that lead into Jameson's suite, which is on the opposite side of the long hall where Bronx and Everett stay. Bronx pointed to Mikkalo's room along the way, and he materialized in his doorway to smile at me as we passed.

"Jameson will have everything you need already," Bronx says, keeping his voice low. "Clothes, toiletries, whatever. If he doesn't, just smack him upside the head. He had plenty of time to prepare."

I bob my head. "Will I be drinking his blood since you haven't given me yours?" I hate that I have to bring it up, but I'm starving. He never offered like I expected because of what Everett said of trying again, and I didn't want to ask.

Bronx rubs his lips together. "I figured after earlier it might be better to...have backup. If that's not weird as hell to you."

I laugh. "You're scared of me."

He tightens his jaw, rubbing the back of his neck. "Hell yeah. Do you know how hard it was for me to resist you earlier? Torture."

I step back and give him a once-over. "I'm nearly certain it was harder for me."

"But...I don't want you to want me because of the side effect you have with drinking my blood."

"You know, I didn't drink your blood before the scratches," I say, smiling.

A deep, sexy noise sounds from his throat—almost like a growl but not threatening. Inviting. "Careful, dandelion. It's taking everything in me not to scoop you up and take you back to my room. Give you my blood in bed. Let you find out exactly what you do to me in return." His words come out so softly, his breathless whisper tickling my ear.

I shiver and draw my hands up his broad chest until I can grasp his face in my hands. He meets me for a kiss, brushing his lips to mine, just teasing me without getting carried away. We both want to. It's obvious. But with being outside Jameson's door, Bronx won't. I shouldn't.

Pulling back an inch, Bronx says, "I need you to knock for Jameson. Please."

If he didn't gaze at me so intently, his eyes begging me to do as he says, I might not have. But his beautiful brown eyes flicker silver with something as wild as my beating heart. I know better than to test a vampire. It's dangerous enough that I stand so close, showing off my neck and shoulders with my hair piled in a bun on my head.

I step closer, knocking my knuckles to Jameson's door as I break my stare and hug Bronx. He sinks against me until Jameson opens the door. The two of us turn to greet his brother, and Jameson pats Bronx on the back.

"Bronxy, glad to see you survived. I wasn't so sure you would," he says to his brother. Turning his gaze to me, he offers me the best smile that lights up his whole face. "Gigi, thanks for not murdering my brother. We kind of like having him around. Mostly."

"He did test my nerves a couple of times," I say, bumping my shoulder to Bronx's. "But he made up for it. He gets to live at least a couple more days."

The two of them laugh, and Jameson invites us into his room.

Bronx automatically lets me go while Jameson takes my hand. It's weird how quickly it happens that I don't get a chance to react. Then Bronx disappears.

I stand with Jameson, staring around his room. Dozens

of neatly hung sketches line the dark gray walls that complement the blue rugs over the light tiled floor. Instead of a couch like Bronx's or chairs like Everett's, Jameson's has a square table that looks like he uses as some sort of work station. Wall cabinets line the area behind the table, but I can't see what's hidden inside.

I spot his bed, the same massive size as Bronx's on a raised platform. Only a few feet beside it with a nightstand in between rests a chaise lounge chair. A couple of pillows and folded blankets sit stacked on the end, and nerves suddenly trickle through me.

"So what do you think?" he asks, tugging me farther into the room. "Is it adequate?"

I glance around. "Depends."

"On what?"

Without responding, I pull away from Jameson and cross the room to the bed. I hold my palm out to get him to stay where he is and plop down on the edge of the bed. I bounce on the balls of my feet before lying back and closing my eyes.

I groan and stretch my arms over my head, arching my back.

"Damn," Bronx's voice whispers from next to me.

"Damn is right," Jameson responds to him.

I sit back up, unable to resist the smile crossing my face. Meeting Jameson's gaze, I bob my head. "This is perfect. I never knew a bed could cuddle me."

"If you think the bed's cuddly, you haven't felt any-thing yet."

"I'm sure the chair will appreciate that," I say, smiling wider.

Bronx clears his throat, and I spot him standing in the doorway to a dark bathroom, gingerly holding a glass of dark ruby liquid. My body buzzes, already reacting to the sight of the cup in his hand. He rolls it between his palms without a word.

"Are you just going to tease me with that or are you go-ing to bring it here?" I ask. "I don't bite."

Jameson's laughter fills the air. "Fuck yeah, you do, Gi-gi."

I inwardly cringe, baring my teeth at him. "Okay, I don't bite often."

Bronx shakes his head at the two of us and closes the space, offering the glass to me. It takes everything in me not to start chugging it before asking for more. Instead, I bring it slowly to my lips and take a sip.

Bronx moves a bit closer, watching my every swallow while Jameson turns his back. It's obviously some weird deal between them.

I lick my lips. "Okay, tell me what's up with you guys. Is it against whatever the hell rules to both look at me at once? Am I doing something wrong? You guys were fine yesterday and now you're kind of acting strange."

"Sorry, Gigi. I'm jealous as fuck right now," Jameson

says.

I frown. "I don't understa—" Lust explodes through me, and I swing my gaze to Bronx, my eyes widening. Before I realize what's happening, I'm on my feet and preparing to throw my arms around Bronx.

Jameson materializes between us, releasing a soft growl, but it's enough to make Bronx flare his nostrils.

Fear suddenly sparks inside me, and I get my shit together enough to place a hand on each of their chests. "Bronx, I had a great day, but I'm super tired. See you later?"

Bronx hesitates for a second and nods. "I—fuck."

Bronx disappears, abandoning me in Jameson's room without as much as a goodbye.

I stare in shock at the door, the noise of it slamming still ringing in my ears. "Fuck."

I suck in a breath and fling myself onto the bed, stealing a pillow to cover my head with. I don't know what the hell just happened. Bronx wanted to give me his blood here to have Jameson around in case I experienced the same side effect as earlier—which I did—but then he looked like he was going to start a fight.

Jameson groans, drawing my attention to him. I get up the nerve to pull the pillow from my face. He doesn't look at me as he faces the wall, and I can't help thumping my head against the soft mattress.

"Gwen, I'm sorry," Jameson says, rolling his shoulders,

relaxing a bit at the slam of another door. It's pretty safe to say Bronx isn't coming back to ask me to follow him back to his room, which if my body doesn't chill the hell out, I might. What am I saying?

Jameson turns to face me and runs his fingers through his light brown hair. "I hope you don't hate me that I intercepted you from Bronx. It's what he wanted me to do."

"Didn't look like it," I say, glancing at the door.

"Trust me, he did. And again, I'm sorry," he says. "I know you wanted to go with him."

Tipping my head back, I look at the ceiling. "In that moment, yeah, but now? I know this was the agreement."

His features soften, his full bottom lip popping out a bit in an almost pout. "Oh."

"Is this going to be a problem?" I ask, wringing my hands together. He sounds disappointed by my comment. "You guys looked like you were about to start fighting, and the last place I want to be is in the middle."

"We're good. Promise," he says, stepping closer. "This is just an adjustment for all of us."

"Maybe I should go talk to Bronx," I say.

"Don't fucking let her out of your room, Jameson." Bronx's deep voice sends a shiver through me. "I mean it. I don't want her doing something she might regret. I don't know what she does to me, but I have zero restraint around her. I'm going to talk to Everett now."

Jameson glances at the door and back to me without a

word.

"Or maybe not," I say, forcing my voice to rise a notch, hoping Bronx hears me. "Probably not. His blood tastes way too good. I might accidentally murder him."

Jameson tilts his head, staring at me. I shift awkwardly under his gaze and wonder if I went a little far. I shouldn't have been able to hear Bronx, but I was trying to save both me and Jameson from a conversation I don't really want to have.

"That would be one helluva way to go," Jameson says, finally relaxing completely. The lightness in his voice eases my nerves.

I release my breath. "Sure would. So be careful or you could be next."

Silver flashes in his eyes, and he opens and closes his mouth like he's going to say something but then changes his mind.

We stand in silence for a moment, and I want nothing more than to dive onto the bed and hide my face. What started off as fun suddenly turns uncomfortable, and I'm not the only one who feels it.

Jameson heaves a sigh. "All right. Fuck this silence and awkwardness. Tell me what I can do to fix it. I've been looking forward to our time together, and I don't want to waste it."

"I'm sorry. I've been looking forward to this too," I say. "I didn't mean to make it weird."

"So you're okay being here?"

I nod. "I mean, none of your brothers feed me like you do."

He chuckles. "Don't say that so loud. You'll regret it if they decide to try."

I stick out my tongue at him. "I don't know..."

"All right. It's on."

And like that, he manages to ease the tension.

He wiggles his fingers at me. "Come on. Let's get this slumber party started. We're going to watch a movie, eat whatever the hell you want in bed, and maybe make a damn fort."

I laugh and close the space, hugging him. "If you figure out how to make a castle, I might be okay to share the bed. But it has to be amazing, and I get to pick the movie."

Jameson hums under his breath. "I don't know if I'll have anything you'd like. My collection is quite different than my brother's."

"Jamie!" I say, play-smacking his chest. "That is so embarrassing. I thought you weren't supposed to talk about my time with your brothers."

He taps his ear. "With how loud you had the volume, there was no discussion needed."

"Do you guys hear everything?" Shit. If he heard the TV, he most definitely heard my loud mouth.

Chuckling, he reaches into his pocket, pulling out his com device. He taps a few buttons and music trickles through the air from the hallway. "Not with the music loud enough."

I place my hands on my hips. "And why would we need music?"

Picking me up, he spins me around, making me screech. "That's why."

"You're ridiculous," I say, holding onto his neck.

"Not ridiculous. Determined."

"Determined?"

"Mmmhmm. This is going to be the best day you've ever had."

"So you're the youngest of your brothers?" I ask, staring at the twinkling lights strung across the ceiling over Jameson's bed. He really went all out, hooking blankets from the ceiling. "By how much?"

Jameson rolls on his side, gazing at the side of my face. "I don't want to weird you out, Gigi. Humans don't think of the concept of time like vampires do. I was twenty-four when I transitioned, though."

I flip over to face him, smiling at his nickname for me. After watching a back-world action movie with a human lead Jameson said whose fierceness reminded him of me, I finally got the nerve to ask him where the hell he got Gigi from—my initials G.G. The obviousness of it made me laugh, and I teased that I'd start calling him Junior, which happened to be what his human father called him because they shared the same name.

And now I can't stop asking questions about his life, and he's been more open than I expected.

"So pre or post the divisions?" I ask. It wasn't until after The Divide that the board got their regions under control and stopped the spread of vampirism, according to Laredo.

He grimaces for a split second. "Pre-divisions."

My eyes widen. "That's older than my blood sourc—Laredo was." And like how I don't like to be called a donor, Jameson is pretty set against being called a blood source. He also said there was no way he was ever going to let me drink his blood from a glass for that reason. Fine by me.

"Which is probably why he was helping your family," he says. "Might've been forced into the shadows otherwise."

I reach out and link my fingers through his. "That's not what Bronx thinks."

"I guess we can't know for sure." Bringing my hand to his mouth, he kisses my fingers. He's less reserved than his brothers, not hesitating to touch me, and he definitely keeps closing any space between us. "Doesn't matter now."

"You're right. So tell me, pre or post-uprising?" I ask. Jameson manages to skip over the conversation that might upset me with just enough details to satiate my curiosity, which I'm thankful for. He also lets me change the subject without pressuring me. I can't remember ever having such an easy time talking to someone.

"Post. Only Zaire was pre-uprising," he says.

I crinkle my nose. "So, he was responsible for the supposed Blood Hunger Plague?" I know it wasn't really a plague now, and I know humans who get bit with venom might transition, but it's still hard for me to think about. Laredo bit me with his venom, but I didn't turn. I'm still a dhampir. And now that I think about it, I can't ignore the ache in my stomach.

Neither can Jameson, because he shifts his gaze to look at my belly. "Damn, Gigi. I guess when you stay up all day you get pretty hungry, huh?" He avoids my question for the first time by asking one of his own, and I don't persist with it. I don't want to think any more about Zaire either.

"Don't you?"

His eyes flash silver at my words. "I'm starved, but I'm also so damn comfortable. I don't want to leave our castle."

I smile. "Well, I hear that consuming vampire blood on an empty stomach helps lengthen the time it stays in a person's system. We could prolong this just a bit longer, you know." I can wait for the solid food, but I'm not so sure how much longer I can take without blood.

"You're safe here with me," Jameson says, playing with my hair blanketing the pillow between us.

I can't stop the frown from crossing my face. "Jameson..."

"What, Gigi? You don't believe me?" he asks, propping up on his elbow. "I wouldn't do anything to hurt you."

I inhale a small breath. How am I supposed to respond to that? Because I believe him. I can feel the truth to his words deep in my soul. But I need this. I need his blood.

"I know, it's just—I've been looking forward to it ever since the first time." I lower my voice with my words.

"Are you trying to manipulate me with that sexy mouth of yours?" He shifts closer, trailing his gaze from my eyes down to my lips.

"Is it working?" I lean forward and brush my lips to his, just softly enough to make him sigh against my mouth. He's an amazing kisser, as good as I imagined, his lips just as sweet as his blood was. "Because if it's not, I might just have to bite you."

He releases the sexiest moan, pulling me closer, kissing me deeper for another moment. "Is that a promise?" he murmurs against my mouth.

Holy shit.

His words set off my very nature, and I roll on top of him and bend down, sucking his bottom lip between my teeth to bite him just hard enough to awaken his body under mine. His hands tighten around my waist as he pulls me into him. I knew he wanted me to make a move—the attraction between us intense, but I've been a little nervous with everything that happened with the rest of his brothers.

But my worry melts away as he devours my affection, and all I want to do is give him more—hear his breath quicken, his heart racing, his body begging for my closeness as much as mine begs his.

Straightening my back, I break my mouth from his and trail my gaze down his T-shirt. His chest rises and falls under the weight of my stare, and I link my fingers to the hem, and he eases up a bit and lets me pull it off.

And damn does his body look as good as it feels.

I drag my fingers along the planes of his chest, touching every inch of him, drawing my finger along the line of neatly trimmed hair that disappears into his pajama pants. A strange scar, a series of dark bluish-black lines, decorates his side like a tattoo. It's rare for such an imperfection on a vampire with their quick healing, but I've seen lines like this on some shadow vampires. I never knew what they meant though.

Jameson doesn't let me gape for long nor does he let me ask about them. Arching up, he meets me for another kiss, holding me close while I sit on his lap with my legs around his waist. He plays with the hem of my shirt, twisting it between his fingers. His tongue glides over my bottom lip, testing me, and I part my mouth to let him caress the softness of his tongue to mine.

Grabbing his hands, I guide them up my stomach, getting him to pull my shirt up and over my head. He leans away from me and drinks me in, slowly running his fingers over the cup of my bra before sliding his fingers into it, sending an explosion of tingles through me.

I hear the soft click of his fangs extending, and I suck in

a tiny breath. "Should we stop?" I ask, fighting my sudden desire with the deeply ingrained knowledge that I should never allow a vampire to bite me, no matter how excited I get at the idea—it's the first time I've ever felt this way.

"Only if you want to," Jameson murmurs, stopping to look into my eyes. "I'm not going to bite you if that's what you're worried about...I mean, unless you ask me to."

I moan softly and rest my face in the crook of his neck, smelling the sweetness of his skin. Grazing my lips over his shoulder, I suck hard enough to leave a mark but not draw blood. His hands slide around my back, and he unhooks my bra, kissing my clavicle until he nudges me to lie on my back. His lips work over my heated skin as he kisses and licks and sucks his way to my breasts and twirls his tongue across my sensitive nipples, showing them each attention.

I arch back, pressing my hips harder into his, feeling the length of his erection rub against my thigh. Tightening my legs around him, I roll my body to his and tease him through his clothes. He moans against my skin under the desperate movements, and I can't stop myself from sliding my hand between us to lace my fingers around his raging boner to pull it from his pants.

"Gwen," he whispers. "What are we doing?"

"Is this okay?" I murmur, stroking the length of his shaft, feeling it flex under my fingers.

He brings his mouth back to mine for another hot kiss that leaves my whole body humming. "Whatever you want."

"I don't have a lot of experience," I say, meeting his gaze to see his reaction.

His eyes flicker silver, a mixture of hunger and desire clear in his gaze. "Can I show you what I like?"

I shiver under his words and nod, allowing him to grab a small bottle from inside his nightstand to squeeze a clear gel-like substance into my hand.

I suck my lip between my teeth because I don't know what it is, but I don't want to admit it either. I grew up with six brothers who I'm pretty damn certain scared off most guys who showed interest in me. Which was a lot, considering that rebels protect women fiercely. No man—or vampire—would survive if they hurt a female in front of another rebel.

And the few times I snuck around with Porter's best friend...well, he didn't know much more than I did, but there's a reason. Donor Life Corp banned all contraception and education and our knowledge is passed down. My brothers talked about sex but never with me.

My dad said population growth and control is one of Donor Life Corp's biggest concerns in some of the cities. It's a hard way of life for the general donor population because while contraception is banned, there are also stipulations to having children. More donations are required. If my parents had lived a donor life, I'd have never been born or would have been taken away. I'm not exactly sure, and I won't ask.

"It's lube, if you don't know," Jameson says, rubbing his finger across it in my palm, pulling me from my wandering thoughts like he can read my mind as I try to figure it out. "Amazing stuff."

My cheeks warm at his comment, and he grins at me, leaning closer to kiss me. Guiding my hand over his boner, he releases a throaty moan as I tighten my fingers to feel how stiff he is but not hard enough to stop my fingers from slipping up and down his shaft. I glide my fingers over his tip and back down, familiarizing myself with his body, watching and listening to him to see what he likes.

He slides his hand away from mine and trails it over my thigh, testing to see if I let him continue. I lift my hips for him, and he tugs my cotton shorts just low enough to get them away from my skin until he rips the fabric like they're made from tissue. I gasp, my body so turned on by the softness of his finger as it traces the curve up my hip and between my legs. He teases me, working his finger over my clit in short, quick strokes that have my whole body shuddering.

I lean into him, listening to his breathing quickening to match mine, and I graze my teeth along his shoulder blade. All it would take is for him to pull me closer, and he could be inside me.

I wouldn't stop him if he tried. I nearly do it myself.

My body has another idea as his hand picks up pressure and speed, nearly vibrating. My muscles clench so hard that my toes curl, and I can't stop myself from sinking my teeth into his skin, tasting his blood in the process. I moan loud as hell, my tongue tingling with the rest of my body. I don't stop stroking him, just wanting so badly to feel close, to continue to suck his blood, to get him off as much as he gets me off.

He releases the sexiest noise, almost like a moan but with the deepness of a growl, and then warm liquid splashes across my pelvis and stomach as he cums. He whispers my name in my ear, panting deep breaths until he takes my hand to slow me down. His lips brush my temple, and he hugs me, running his fingers through my hair. Jameson doesn't say anything or try to stop me as I continue to suck his shoulder until I'd have to bite him again to get more blood.

I ease away and touch my fingers to the mark, my heart still beating crazy out of control. His eyes meet mine with such intensity that it feels as if he's gazing through my skin to my blood and possibly my soul.

"This was the hottest thing I've ever experienced," he murmurs, caressing his hands down the length of my back. Our bodies touch, my legs around him, but he doesn't move me. I've never been cuddled like this, just sitting together to enjoy each other's closeness.

I get my racing heart under control with a few deep breaths. "I didn't mean to bite you." It was like my deep-seated nature snuck out, taking advantage of my crazy intense orgasm. And it made it even hotter. No wonder vampires like to bite each other during sex...at least the few I've seen here. Laredo always mentioned it too. Biting isn't always about food.

Jameson chuckles and reaches for his shirt, wiping it along my stomach as we pull apart to gaze at each other. "I obviously liked it. A lot."

I blush under his words, and he stretches close again to kiss me. "Me too," I say, smiling. "I never imagined a night like this. I'm glad I could share it with you."

He grins, his fangs peeking out from under his lip. "I hope there will be many more."

All I do is smile. Because I like him. A lot. And because I like him so much, a part of me freaks out about my situation.

"But you don't have to think about that now unless you want to," he whispers, touching my cheek like he knows the thought crosses my mind. "Can I bring you something to eat? I'm starved. I can clear off the table or we can eat in bed. I'd love to snuggle the hell out of you, Gwen."

I bob my head, my body more relaxed than it has ever been. "I'd like that."

"I'll be quick." Jameson grabs one of the blankets to wrap around his hips instead of getting dressed. "You'll find anything you might need in the bathroom. Don't be afraid to look around. My room is your room while you're here."

I smile. "Just hurry before I bite you again."

He playfully snaps his teeth. "I might ask to bite you back."

Combing my fingers through my hair, I pull it away from my shoulder and expose my neck to him. "You can try," I tease.

He releases a soft moan and heads to the bedroom door. "Careful, Gigi. It's starting to sound like you want me to."

I just smile wider and wave my hand, shooing him away. "I don't think so, Jamie."

"The night's just starting. There's still time."

My body buzzes at his words, and I throw myself back and cover my face with a pillow. Damn. What's gotten into me?

I'm starting to think that I was never really a Blood Rebel after all.

And for once, I don't even care.

14

BREAKING THE RULES

A SOFT TAP SOUNDS THROUGH the air, and Jameson groans from beside me. He slides his arm out from under my neck, carefully trying not to shift me too much. I don't move, keeping my eyes closed and my breath even. I've been awake for an hour, but I don't feel like moving.

"Is Gwen still sleeping? Mikkalo asks, keeping his voice at the pitch of a whisper.

"She's faking it," Jameson responds just as quietly.

I try not to react, feeling them gaze in my direction even though they can't see me from inside the hanging blankets.

Mikkalo chuckles. "You must've annoyed her."

Jameson hums under his breath but doesn't respond to his comment. I roll over to the edge of the bed and crack the blankets to peek out. Mikkalo stands in the doorway, dressed in jeans and a T-shirt. He keeps his eyes trained away from me, but Jameson smiles and winks, and I throw myself back on the bed.

"I think she's good," Jameson finally says, his voice loud enough so that a normal human would be able to hear. "Right, Gigi?"

Taking in a deep breath, I tug one of the blankets down from the ceiling and let it cocoon over me. "Yup. A little out of it."

"She kept me up all day," Jameson says, smirking. "I think we're going to be the ones to adjust to a human schedule instead of the other way around."

I suck my lip between my teeth, the memory of our day flitting through my mind. Mikkalo raises his eyebrows but doesn't comment.

Clearing my throat, I swing my legs over the edge of the bed and slide off. "What time is it? Are you here to pick me up?"

Mikkalo smiles. "It's late but still dark. I came by to talk to my brother actually. I didn't mean to bother you, Gwen."

"It's not a bother," I say. "You can pretend like I'm not

here."

"I'd never," Mikkalo says.

Jameson moves away from the door to allow his brother inside the room, and the two of them stroll over to Jameson's table and sit down. Jameson smiles and motions for me to join them. He slides his chair back and pats his lap for me to sit with him.

I flick my gaze to Mikkalo for his reaction. "Maybe I should sit in my own chair."

Mikkalo brings his eyes to mine. "Sit where you want, Gwen. If you want to be close to Jameson, I don't care. It's your time with him."

Jameson doesn't say anything, but I can tell he's anxious to see what I do. I can't resist his vibrant green gaze, and I let him pull me closer until I sit with him in the chair. He encircles his arms around me, breathing into my shoulder covered by the blanket.

I squirm a little under the weight of both their gazes. "Thanks for saying that, Mikkalo."

"You should be comfortable despite this situation," he says.

"Plus, I'm certain Mik and Ev happened to hear Bronx dropping you off last night," Jameson says to me.

"Give him a break. You know he..." Mikkalo must realize that I devour every single one of his words because his voice trails off.

I reach out and touch his hand. "He what?"

Mikkalo and Jameson both stare at my fingers touching Mikkalo. I jerk my hand away and ease off Jameson's lap. I've never cared about rules or the law, but I know exactly when I break them, and I can't help the annoyance rushing over me.

Sighing, Mikkalo says, "I'm sorry, Gwen. I guess it'll be all right to tell you, but act surprised when Bronx gets up the nerve to tell you himself."

I spin around and glare. I'd think the two of them were scared of me with their wide eyes.

Jameson grimaces. "I don't think that's what bothered her," he whispers to his brother.

"Then what did I do?" Mikkalo asks.

Closing my eyes, I inhale a deep breath through my nose. "You know, it's rude to talk about me like I'm not here."

Jameson's jaw tightens. "What do you mean?"

I sigh and shake my head, crossing the room to flop back onto the bed. "Did you forget that I've spent my life living with a rebel vampire? He told me all his secrets including your capabilities. I know you can talk too quietly for humans to hear. Don't think I don't notice. You make expressions when you do it even if your mouths don't move."

"Shit," Mikkalo whispers under his breath.

Jameson stands from the table and returns to me. "Gigi, if you knew, you should've called our asses out about it."

I shrug. "Would you have stopped?"

"I would've." He groans, and looks at Mikkalo. "At least would have been more discreet."

"Liar," I say, though I know better. I shouldn't call him out, even if I did hear what he said.

And now I'm pissed.

How the hell am I supposed to live like this? It's going to drive me crazy. Hiding that I'm a dhampir was so easy before. I didn't feel so out of control until the Royales came in and crashed my life.

And I can't help feeling stupid. I knew better than to let myself get close to any of them, let alone all of them. Their charm makes it easy to forget where they think my place is. I mean, come the hell on. I can't keep living this way. They can't expect me just to follow some stupid rules they make up as they go along. Those rules benefit them, not me.

"Gigi," Jameson says, staring at me as I glare at my hands, practically seething.

"Don't, Jamie." I turn away from him completely so that he has to look at my back. "You might have fooled me with your charm, but it has worn off."

Jameson risks sitting on the bed. "Mik, give us a couple of minutes, will you?"

He actually says the words for me to hear, and I jerk my attention to Mikkalo still sitting at the table. And damn it if he doesn't look pouty. His dark eyes crinkle in the corners and he scrubs his hands over his cropped black hair.

"Yeah, sure," he says, getting up.

"No, I want you to stay," I say.

"Gwen, this is your time with Ja—"

I throw my hands up and try to scoot off the bed but twist myself in one of the hanging blankets. I screech as I fall off. I brace to eat shit on the ground, the drop higher because of the platform.

Jameson grabs me by my ankles while Mikkalo catches me by the shoulders. We all freeze with my body stretched between them. And then they let go. I hit the ground with a thud and somersault backward, losing the blanket. I lie half between the rug and the cold-ass tiles. My shirt—one I stole from Jameson's side of the wardrobe—rolls up to show off the undersides of my boobs and the sheer pair of bikini cut underwear I chose because I wasn't going to sleep wearing only the strings the other lingerie were made out of.

"Damn it. I'm sorry, Jameson," Mikkalo says. "I shouldn't have touched her."

"You're apologizing to *him?*" I dig my nails into the palms of my hands. "Seriously?"

"I—"

Jameson growls softly. "Give us a minute, Mikkalo. Now."

I don't have a chance even to react before Mikkalo disappears. Jameson materializes in front of me and offers out his hand to help me to my feet. I just gawk at his hand and stay on the ground.

"Come on, Gigi. Let me help you up," he says.

I ignore him.

"Fine, but now I'm just going to join you." Jameson slides onto the ground next to me and stares at the side of my face as I glare so hard at the twinkling string lights now haphazardly hanging from the ceiling.

My eyes burn with my mess of emotions, tangling and fighting inside me with no sign of relenting. My heart rams into my ribcage, the thuds louder than anything in the room, and I touch my chest, half-expecting it to explode through to splat on the high ceiling.

"Look, Gwen. I know you're angry, and I'm sorry. If you know about vampires like you claim you do, then you know how possessive we can be. It's extremely difficult for me not to be jealous, especially after the unforgettable time we had. I like you." Jameson rests his hand over mine, seeing if I'll let him hold it. I do.

"And I like you too," I murmur. "Even if I shouldn't."

He sits up, pulling me with him so that we can face each other. Tugging one of the blankets off the bed, he wraps it around my shoulders but doesn't let it go, just squeezing the rest of the soft fabric in his hands.

"Why shouldn't you?" he asks after a moment. "Is this because I'm a vampire?"

I close my eyes to break his stare. It would be so easy to tell him that yes, of course it's because he's a vampire. My dad would be so upset I let him get so close. He'd yell at me that I was foolish believing anything that comes from Jameson's mouth—that a vampire can like a donor. They don't see us as their equals. We're merely blood sources. It's why my brothers treated Laredo like they had. Why a lot of Blood Rebels treat vampires like that. To show them what it's like to feel less than.

"No," I manage to say. Because it's not. Not really. "I just—I don't know if I can do this."

He frowns. "What do you mean?"

I bend forward and rest my head on his shoulder. "This—the deciding. It's—it doesn't feel fair."

"You getting time to choose was supposed to make it fair, Gwen. It wouldn't be fair if we decide for you." He hooks his hands around me and pulls me closer to hug me.

I sit sideways across his lap and rest my ear to his chest, listening to his heart racing to out beat mine. "Yeah, but..."

"You can tell me what's on your mind," he says, linking his fingers through mine. "I don't know if you realize this, but I love talking to you. And listening."

His words make me smile. "You do make it easy."

"So then tell me what's up. I need to understand what's going on," he says.

I shift to look at him. "I like you, Jameson. A lot. It was an unexpected surprise. The attraction I feel—" I bite my lip. "I enjoy it."

"Good," he says. "I want you to. You have no idea how

much I want to see where this goes."

"But I like Bronx too. And Everett. Mikkalo. I look forward to spending time with the rest of your brothers. At the same time, I feel like—you can't expect me to stick to some half-assed slapped together rules that you haven't even asked or told me about. I felt like a criminal for even touching Mikkalo in front of you." There. I said it. "I know I should be used to it, but—"

"Ah, hell. Gigi, fuck. I'm sorry. You absolutely did nothing wrong. You want to touch my brother in my room, have at it. Kiss him? Shit, I'd be jealous, but I'd get over it. Like I told you before, this is all new. And temporary."

"What happens after?" I ask, keeping my voice low.

He tips his head toward mine. "What do you mean?"

"What if I don't choose you?"

The face he gives me says it all. I don't think he considered it a possibility. I mean, I am snuggled against him in his room, baring thoughts I should keep to myself.

"See?" I say. "I don't want any of you getting hurt. You guys seem so close. If you're anything like my brothers are with each other—"

"Gwen, I love my brothers. You're not going to get between us. If you happen to pick one of...them. Then you pick one of them. They'd deserve you."

"I don't know," I say. "What about them? What about Bronx? He's..."

"Struggling," Jameson says. "He feels the same way you

do. He worries no matter what we tell him. He wanted to back out—he was going to back out—but then you planted that sexy little ass of yours in his bed. Bronx didn't stand a chance."

I laugh. I can't help it. "You forgot the whole lust-inducing side effect to his blood."

He sucks in a breath through his teeth. "I have to say, that's definitely not something I'm jealous of at all." Lifting his hand, he touches his fingers to the bruise, which is the only evidence of my bite left on his skin. "I mean, this bite. He wouldn't be able to resist letting you drain him dry."

I groan. "Hence the cup."

He chuckles. "That's more about the fact that he's never given his blood to anyone before. Nor has he..."

"What?"

"You're the first human he's been this close too. He's only been with other vampires. Now don't tell him I told you. You might never see me again otherwise."

I purse my lips, and he kisses me. I should've guessed Bronx has never been with a human. He did tell me he didn't have much experience with them and had only really talked to very few people. If that's the case, it would mean he definitely hasn't had sex with a human, which explains his reaction after our small moment of intimacy.

"His secret and your sexy ass, stomach, neck, arms—okay all of you—are safe with me. I wouldn't risk never getting to experience another blanket castle with you. Plus, you haven't forgotten to feed me. I'm pretty certain I'd be eating bananas and toast for the rest of my life otherwise."

He snickers, his soft breath tickling my shoulder. "Remember that when you choose."

I bat his shoulder. "Don't remind me."

"Okay, I won't," he says. "I actually would prefer to distract you until the sun rises."

I giggle against his lips, nipping him with my teeth. "I think Mikkalo had something he needed to talk to you about. Maybe you can call Bronx and Everett here too. I need to make some things clear."

"That'll have to wait. Ev and Bronx went to Crimson Vista. They probably won't be back until nightfall," he says.

"Oh."

"But maybe we can call them."

"I'd like that."

Scooping me up with him, he sets me in his bed and retrieves his com device from the table. I hadn't expected him to choose now to do so, but I'm pretty damn sure he knows I'll be distracted otherwise, and I can tell he doesn't want to waste any more time talking to his brothers when he'd prefer to enjoy it with me.

He taps a few buttons, which lights up the wall in front of us. Snuggling his chin into my shoulder, he spoons me from behind while we wait for the line to click.

Jameson's bedroom door flies open at the same time the line connects. Mikkalo rushes into the room and tries to step in front of the projection, but it's too late. I catch sight of Bronx in the video screen, but my eyes don't focus on him.

I cover my mouth. "Oh, shit. Grayson?"

"Gwen?" my brother asks from his spot on the floor. His whole face twists into a snarl. "What the fuck are you monsters doing to her?"

The line drops.

15

KISSING VAMPIRES

"CALL HIM BACK!" MY SHRILL voice cuts through the air, making Jameson and Mikkalo wince.

The two of them look at each other, and I take their moment of distraction to snatch the com device from Jameson's fingers. I throw myself away from him, tumbling off the bed, only to have Mikkalo catch me. Swinging my arm out, I smack Mikkalo upside the head. He freezes in surprise before setting me on my feet.

Jameson comes up behind me, stopping me from spinning away. I find myself caged in between their muscular, way too sexy bodies, which just makes me gasp harder.

"Give me my com device, Gwen," Jameson says. He could easily overpower me and steal it back but he doesn't.

I shake my head. "Nu-uh. I want you to call Bronx back. I want—"

The com device beeps in my hand, and I nearly drop the thing. Jameson takes advantage of my shot nerves and swipes it away, abandoning me to jet across the room at a vampire's speed. Mikkalo steps between us, blocking my way, and I press my hands into his solid chest.

I stop myself from screaming at him and instead sigh and say, "Mikkalo, please. Let me go to him."

"It's not a good idea," Mikkalo murmurs, keeping his voice soft. "Bronx is probably mad as hell that I didn't tell Jameson about him being with your brothers so that he could prepare."

"*He's* going to be mad? You should've told me he was with Grayson," I snap, glowering at him even though I'm pissed off at Bronx. He should've told me the reason he was going to Crimson Vista in the first place. He could've taken me with him.

"Hey, Gwen." Everett's voice draws my attention away from Mikkalo. "I'll let you yell at Bronx all you want in a minute, but can I talk to you first?"

Mikkalo shifts out of my way, and Jameson meets me halfway across the room. We share a look, and Jameson looks like he's just as pissed at his brothers. I bet if he knew, he'd have offered to take me himself. He knows how freaked out I am about them. Jameson possesses something I didn't know vampires could—empathy.

Jameson hugs me and brushes his lips to my ear. "I'm sorry, Gwen. I hope you know I had no idea."

I bob my head and kiss him. "I know."

Easing away, he hands me his com device and hugs me from behind to peer at the screen with me over my shoulder. Everett's face takes up the whole screen, his stubble more noticeable since the last time I saw him. His eyes shift back and forth as he searches my face like he can somehow assess me through the video.

"Where's Grayson?" I ask, wishing I could see past his blue eyes, still managing to capture mine even if he's not in front of me.

"He's in his cell. I'm going to let you talk to him and the rest of your brothers, but Bronx needs a couple minutes," he says, remaining expressionless toward my oncoming annoyance.

"For what?" I ask. My voice deepens with my words. I nearly growl them.

Jameson slides his hands around my stomach, pressing himself completely to me. "I suspect they're quite upset about seeing us together. You can imagine that they might be thinking the worst."

I groan. Jameson's right. My brothers totally are. Knowing Grayson, he's probably assuming that my mind has been manipulated. "That's why I need to talk to him."

"After we go over a few things, Gwen," Everett says, his eyes turning from mine to look at Jameson now close enough to me to appear on screen. "You have to be careful of what you say. Your brothers are smart. They'll try to use anything you say against us. The position you're in—Blood Matching to Zaire—could be used against us by our enemies. We're the ruling coven of the region and many others would love to try to rise to power."

Everett doesn't have to say the exact words for me to know that I better keep my mouth shut about Zaire. If my brothers were to find out, they could easily have their minds manipulated for the information. If that happens? They'll be dead. Bronx, Everett, Jameson, and Mikkalo would be found out, and then there would be nothing they could do...I think. They haven't said exactly what would happen apart from things about my Blood Matching contract and their desire to keep Zaire's death a secret.

"Got it," I say.

"You also need to keep your conversation short. We don't have a lot of time, okay? Just let them know that you're fine. Please don't tell them about Kyler. We don't want to have to subdue them, but we won't be given a choice. If they try anything crazy, it gives their security the right to handle them any way they see fit, including issuing their final donations."

My lip quivers. "What? You said they'd be auctioned

and we'd have time."

"We do. Just keep it short. Remember what I said." Everett rubs his lips together. "I swear. We're doing whatever we can."

I try not to glower at him. "You could just let them go."

Everett closes his eyes for a second without responding to my comment and instead says, "Bronx is ready now if you are."

The video shifts, and Bronx's face takes up the whole screen. I expect him to glare right back at me, but he says, "I'm going to make this up to you, dandelion. I promise. I just need some time."

I lick my lips and swallow. "Okay," is all I can say.

His sad eyes stop me from lashing out at him. In all honesty, I don't want to. I just want to see my brothers and talk to them.

Bronx nods and the video blurs as he sets it down somewhere I can't see. I clutch the com device in my hands, my heart sinking into my stomach the second the video shifts to fall onto my brothers. Grayson sits between Porter and Silas, and Declan and Ashton lean on each other for support, their identical faces drawing up to look in front of them.

"Gwen," Grayson says, his voice quiet. "God. Are you okay?"

My lip trembles, but I suppress my urge to cry. "I'm fine. Uninjured. Safe. A health keeper in the city saved my life. You don't have to worry about me."

"Of course we're going to worry about you, Gweny," Declan says, speaking up, using the name my dad used to call me. He makes me feel incredibly young doing so. "Where are you?"

Jameson squeezes my hand, and I glance to him and realize he doesn't want me to say. "I don't know. But I'm not in a cage or anything, if that makes a difference."

I draw my gaze back to the camera and catch Grayson glaring at me. "Are you being fed on? That vampire—"

"He's my...Blood Match. Zaire." Four soft groans come from every which way, all four Royale brothers hanging on my every word.

"Nice job, Gigi," Jameson whispers.

I swallow. "And Zaire has been...kind." The word makes me want to puke using it in the same sentence as Zaire's name.

My brothers all notice my expression, and if looks could explode the world, I'm nearly certain they'd cause fire and ash to rain through the rest of the universe.

"Will he give you everything you need?" Grayson asks, keeping his words even. He doesn't have to say them for me to know he's talking about vampire blood and my needs as a dhampir. "I know this might be hard to hear, Gwen, but you must do what you have to. I know you have it in you."

I lick my lips. "I know, Grayson. Like I said, don't worry about me. I'm good."

Something dark flashes through his hazel eyes, but he doesn't get a chance to say anything before Bronx picks up the com device and looks at me. "I'm going to need you to say goodbye."

"Wait, Bronx. Just give me another few minutes," I say, pleading with my eyes.

"I can't. I'm sorry," he says. "You know how much I want to, but I promise we'll do this again, okay?"

"Thank you," I whisper.

He turns the video back toward my brothers, who greet me with serious expressions. I shift my gaze from Grayson, practically burning me with his heated gaze and to Porter. I clear my throat. "Keep Grayson calm, Porter, okay? As long as you don't cause any problems, it's going to be fine."

"Gwen, don't kid yourself. We're dead men," Silas says, responding for him.

I clench my teeth. "You're not. Just be fucking thankful that you're there. Kyler, he's—"

"You saw Kyler?" Declan asks.

Tears burn my eyes, but the words stay locked in my throat. I wasn't supposed to mention Kyler. I just couldn't stop myself.

"Damn it." Ashton leans forward to peer at Grayson. "He's dead, isn't he?"

I shake my head. "He's been Blood Matched too."

Grayson groans. "Shit."

"Gwen, I'm sorry," Bronx says. "We have to go."

My brothers yell, their anger getting the best of them. I hear Grayson tell Everett to stay away as I catch sight of him closing the distance. Bronx leaves the com device where it is, and I watch as Porter tries to punch Bronx.

"I'll kill you for doing this, you son of a bitch!" Grayson yells. He manages to grab Bronx by the front of his shirt and shoves Bronx into the wall because Bronx doesn't even try to fight my brother.

"Grayson!" My voice rings through the air, drawing his attention to me. "Stop! Don't hurt him. Please!"

Grayson's eyes widen. "Gwen."

"Please, he's good. He's trying to help us."

Jameson takes the com device from me and tosses it to Mikkalo to spin me in his arms. "Take a breath, Gigi. Your brothers won't understand."

"They will! We can show them you're helping me. It'll stop them from freaking the hell out. Please, Jameson. Just let me see them one more time." I clutch his shoulders and stare into his green eyes. "Please. If you liked me like you said you did, you'd let me."

He sighs. "Not cool to manipulate me like this, Gwen."

I know it's unfair, but I'm desperate. "Please."

He closes his eyes to break my stare. "Come on, Bronx. One minute. She needs this."

Bronx groans. "Fine."

"You're the best, Jamie. I mean it." I hug Jameson with

a smile only to have it melt right off my face. Mikkalo moves and holds the com device too quickly in front of me that my brothers watch me plant a sweet kiss to Jameson's lips.

"Fuck, Gwen," Grayson says.

"Did you hear what she said?" Silas's soft voice hums to me.

Declan groans. "Yeah, she called him Jamie. She's lying to us."

I cringe. "Declan, you're mistaken."

"What the hell? They're manipulating her. Gwen would never kiss a vampire," Porter says. He huffs a breath. "Get out of her head, you assholes!"

"It's not like that, Porter. I swear," I say. "I'm not being manipulated."

Ashton punches at Everett as he tries to keep them calm. "You wouldn't even know, Gwen."

"You wouldn't fucking kiss a vampire if you weren't. You're better than that. You'd rather die than be a damn blood slave," Declan says. "I know you."

"Hang up the line," Bronx snaps.

"No!"

Bronx flashes his fangs. "Now!"

16

STARVED

"THREE HUNDRED AND NINETY-EIGHT. THREE hundred and ninety-nine. Four hundred."

I flop back on the rug, my chest heaving, every one of my muscles aching. Jameson sits at his table next to Mikkalo, drawing while counting my crunches. Mikkalo's been pretty silent, only speaking up to comment when he thinks my form could use work.

"All right, Gigi. I think you've worked out enough," Jameson says, standing from the table. "Can you even get up?"

He offers me his hand, and I don't move to grab it. "Nope. Someone needs to carry me."

Mikkalo materializes next to Jameson. "I'd gladly."

I rub my lips together and nod. "It is late for you, isn't it?"

"Not too bad."

Mikkalo glances at Jameson like he's asking for silent permission. I tap Mikkalo with my foot so that he looks at me and wiggle my fingers. He squats down and slides his hand behind my knees and around my back to pick me up. I groan at the burning in my core.

"Sounds like you could use a soak," Mikkalo says, cradling me like any sudden movement might cause me to swing out and clock him for not being careful. And I can't blame him after I smacked him a few times during the whole incident with my brothers. I did apologize, and he swore it was nothing. He actually teased that he was going to teach me to hit harder.

"Is your tub as big as Bronx's?" I ask Mikkalo, smirking at his suggestion, which actually sounds amazing. I might have slept in Bronx's tub, but I've never taken a bath.

He breaks into a smile. "Much bigger."

"Damn," Jameson whispers under his breath, drawing my attention to him. He smiles when I raise an eyebrow. "Get some rest, Gigi. As soon as my brothers come home, I'll let you know so we can talk."

I reach my hand out to him. "The minute."

He grasps my fingers and kisses my knuckles. "The second."

Tugging my hand from Jameson, I slide my arm around Mikkalo's neck and let him carry me all the way to his room. Listening to the soft music in the hallway is the only thing stopping me from thinking about my brothers or what's happening to them.

Jameson swore that they would be fine, but it's more than their physical state that I worry about. They saw me kiss Jameson. I lied to them and called him Zaire and then messed up to call him Jamie, and they heard me. My brothers aren't stupid. We'd have never survived this long if they were.

Mikkalo attempts to set me on my feet outside his room, but I snuggle against him not even caring that this will be the first time I see where he sleeps. I just want the bath he promised me and to forget that I broke my brothers' hearts. That I betrayed them even.

When they find out that I'm no longer trying to escape and that everything I do is done by my own freewill—they'll deem me a traitor to humanity. And worse, they could very well kill me because of it. It wouldn't be the first time a rebel killed another for growing too close to our supposed enemies. And for me, it's unthinkable. I'm a dhampir. I was born to rise above vampires. I'm supposed to be their worst predator and not falling into bed with them, letting them familiarize themselves with my needs. Shower me with affection I had no idea how much I craved. How it's not only one vampire but an entire coven.

"What do you think, Gwen?" Mikkalo asks, pulling me from my thoughts. "Will you be comfortable sleeping here?"

I trail my gaze from Mikkalo's copper-rimmed eyes and drink in the rest of the room. "I should ask if *you'll* be comfortable with me sleeping here. That's a shit-ton of weapons you have to trust me with. I don't know if you realize, but I have a thing for sharp objects."

He releases a chuckle, carrying me deeper into his room. "That's one of your sexiest qualities. I can't wait to see you in action with some of my favorites."

"Hot and attracted to danger?" I ask him. "This is going to be a fun night."

"I plan on it."

Mikkalo slowly spins me, and I wonder if he's ever going to set me on my feet. I don't mind, but I can't tell if he's more nervous about me and the weapons than he lets on.

Gazing around, I take in the floor-to-ceiling shelves lining an entire wall of his narrow suite. It's twice the length as Jameson's room with an arched entryway that leads into an office with huge glass monitors that flicker with all sorts of images. Behind the desk glows a map that I recognize from the one Laredo drew by hand for me to memorize. It's of the entire Royale Region.

"That's...interesting," I say, trying to glimpse the screens.

"It is if you see what I see," he says, strolling into the office for me to look. "Bronx might kill me if he found out I told you, but this is where I monitor not only our estate but also anywhere in the region. I'm head of our defense."

"Anywhere on the estate?" I ask, pursing my lips.

"I never spied on you in any of the rooms if that's what you think—well, except when you went into the guest wing. And when you tried to make your great escape." He smirks at me as he says it.

I narrow my eyes at him. "What a creeper."

"Not compared to Caine," he teases, flashing his fangs at me. "And I promise there will be no blood involved in your bath."

I tip my head back and laugh. "Shit, thanks a lot for reminding me about Mr. Blood Bath Boner."

"I can replay the feed so you can see your reaction. It was the best," he says, grinning at me. "But don't worry. I only told my brothers about it. They rarely watch any of the feeds."

I scrunch my nose, my mouth opening in shock. "You saved that? Seriously?"

"I keep files and videos on all our guests, just in case. Caine has always been questionable. I needed evidence to prove that he surpassed his allotted gen. pop. supply here, which he had to pay for."

"Gen. pop.?"

"Our on staff donors are off-limits...to even us. They

were Zaire's."

"I bet they're happy."

"He took great care of his blood sources. They enjoyed his company. Not everyone has qualms..." He lets his words trail off, probably because of me twisting my lips. Shrugging, he strolls to his desk, taps the screen a few times, and—

I screech and cover my eyes, surprise washing over me at the glimpse of a bloody Caine standing up from the tub with me gaping at him in shock in the doorway. I forgot that the surprise of it all turned me hysterical to the point that I cracked up.

It's even funnier now than it was at the time. Mikkalo chuckles and spins me away, his distraction totally working to take my mind off his words about the household donors. I almost call him out on it, but when I open my eyes to do so, we're standing in a gleaming metal and dark blue tiled bathroom that leaves me speechless.

An opaque glass shower takes up a good portion of the room with dual showerheads and what looks like a faucet to rain water from the ceiling. Adjacent to the shower rests the huge bathtub that's most definitely big enough for multiple people to soak in together like the hot tubs I've seen in a couple of movies that my dad had for us to watch in the bunker. Each side of the tub curves to comfortably lie inside, and a retractable sprayer curls neatly into the wall.

"Whoa," I say, meeting his gaze. "I'm not sure about

that tub. It looks deep enough that I'd have to know how to swim." Which I don't. The stream by the bunker was never deep enough to try to learn—not that I ever needed to.

Mikkalo sets me on the steps that lead to the platform the tub sits inlaid in, and he reaches into a cupboard and pulls out the softest looking pillow. "You could technically use this as a floatation device."

I snatch the pillow and swat him with it. "Or maybe you could just join me and ensure I don't drown. Death by bubble bath is not the way I want to go."

The second the suggestion leaves my lips, I realize exactly what I just offered. Mikkalo raises his eyebrows, a smirk crossing his face. I squirm under the intensity of his stare and nearly turn my suggestion into a joke, because he looks torn, but then he shrugs.

"Why not?" he says, searching my face. "If you really want my company."

I swallow my nerves instead of changing my mind. "I do." Might as well enjoy myself if I'm going to be deemed a traitor to humanity by my brothers. And it's just a bath...with a guy I'm seriously attracted to.

I bite my lip, thinking about the kiss we shared. No matter how impulsive or blood lust induced it was, or how confused it made me feel, I still enjoyed it. Not to mention that I did ask for time to get to know each Royale brother, and what better way...

Mikkalo beams a smile and hits a few buttons on the

tub, sending water cascading from a waterfall spout from the wall. The most amazing floral scent wafts through the air as the water turns lavender, and then white bubbles foam growing higher than the sides.

I nearly rip my clothes off to jump in. I've never had a bath like this in my life. The shower in the bunker was a tiny box in the same room as the toilet, and it was impossible even to turn around. Sharing the small space with my brothers was even worse. I'll never forget when we were teens, and Dad finally made them head to the stream instead. I used to think that was the best, getting exclusive use of the shower for a few summers, but now? Mikkalo just raised my standards by quite a bit.

Tugging his shirt over his head, Mikkalo doesn't hesitate to undress in front of me, treating it like it's not a big deal to him. And maybe it's not. I try to remain calm. If only my eyes didn't want nothing more than to devour the chiseled curves of his body. His abs flex with his movements, and he has the audacity to stretch his arms over his head, knowing I'm checking him out. He drops his pants next, showing off his muscular thighs and legs in a pair of dark gray briefs that don't leave much to the imagination.

"Gwen, you joining me?" he asks, drawing my gaze from his quite intimidating bulge in his sexy underwear that seems to have really stolen my attention.

"Uh, yeah. But you first," I say, continuing to blatantly stare.

It's then that I notice he has the weird tattoo lines like Jameson has but on the opposite side and twice as many, wrapping around to his back. If I wasn't staring so intently at his amazing body, I might not have noticed the blue lines against his smooth, coppery skin.

"They're ban marks," he says, answering my silent curiosity, slightly twisting so I can see his back. Sneaky. But I love how he inconspicuously gives me a view of the rest of him without calling me out for my uncontrollable need to memorize his body with my eyes. "It's how vampires who break Donor Life Corp law are punished. They must wear the marks until they fade before they're allowed back into the system for gen. pop. blood rations."

"I've seen them before...but always on foreheads," I say. "What did you do wrong? If they're outcast marks—"

"They're not. More like a warning. Let's just say that I might've slept with a few people that don't have an alliance with the Royale Coven," he says.

"A few? That looks like more than that," I say, counting over twenty lines before I mess up and lose track.

Heat blooms on my face at the thought, his sexual experience far exceeding mine. I should know that his would considering he transitioned pre-divisions, but now I'm nervous as all get-out. Why did my mouth invite him into the bath with me?

"They're actually how many times," he says, remaining expressionless.

At least he's honest.

"Oh."

"I hope it doesn't bother you," he adds.

I shake my head, pushing my hair behind my ears. "It doesn't."

Mikkalo smirks at me like he's not sure whether to believe me or not, but he doesn't mention it. Instead, he undresses completely even as I watch him. I suck in a small breath, totally getting turned on just by his boldness. He smiles at me, loving every second I just gape at him. Heat floods my face as he steps into the bath, sending some of the bubbles into the air like clouds of foam. He releases a small groan and presses a button, sending the water whirling.

"So...did you change your mind about the bath?" he asks, his voice lowering. "If it makes you feel any better, I haven't slept with anyone in a while. The growth of our region has been the newest priority."

"You didn't need to make me feel better. And no, I haven't changed my mind." Standing up, I twist the hem of my shirt between my fingers. "But would you mind closing your eyes?"

He chuckles. "Whatever you want, Gwen."

I don't know why I'm so suddenly nervous, but I am. The shock that crossed my brothers' faces floods my mind. I can almost hear them yelling at me.

Mikkalo leans his head back with his eyes closed, and I finally summon the nerve to pull my shirt over my head.

Just as quickly, I strip out of the rest of my clothes and leave them in a heap on the steps, close enough to grab.

I step into the tub, the bubbles making it impossible to see Mikkalo's body. I carefully ease into the hot water and moan as it swallows me into its floral-scented goodness. Jets of water stream from the sides, massaging across my back. It's even more amazing than I imagined.

"What do you think?" Mikkalo asks, his voice sounding soft, deep, almost raspy.

I stretch my leg up to watch the bubbles drip from my skin. "Indescribable. You were right. This was exactly what I needed after—" I snap my mouth closed. "You know."

Mikkalo's hand gently wraps around my foot, and he grasps it between his hands and slides pressure over my arch. "I feel terrible about that."

I tip my head back, clutching onto his ankles as I enjoy the touch of his hands massaging my foot to work up my calf. It's like he knows what my body needs right now. "Please, don't. None of us could've known we'd be in this unexpected position. I should've known better than to beg Jameson to call. I just—I needed to make sure they were okay. You guys make me forget that my life could be a living nightmare, which is surely what my brothers expected."

"I can't blame them," he says, meeting my gaze. "I know what the world outside of Donor Life Corp is like, and I know that even in the cities, sometimes things aren't easy for donors, especially females. We have many laws to protect you, but it's always a power play among covens to acquire what females they can since it's limited to how many leave the general population."

I release a strange, strangled noise from my throat.

Mikkalo splashes water, dragging his hands over his face. "I'm sorry, Gwen. I didn't mean to make it sound—"

"You're just saying the truth," I say.

"It sucks," he says. "I never realized how much it does until I met you."

I offer him a small smile and rub my hand over his muscular calf, distracting myself the best I can, knowing how close his naked body is to mine. "Thanks for saying that."

"It's the truth."

Scooting a bit closer, I slide my legs over Mikkalo's and lean in to kiss him just slow and soft to show him that his realization and admittance mean the world to me, especially now. I want so badly to talk to my brothers again, to tell them that the Royale Coven is different, but I'm not so sure they'd listen. Part of me fears facing them.

Mikkalo slowly breaks away from me, his eyes flashing silver as they capture mine. His heartbeat picks up pace, lust prominent on more than just his face. I can feel his erection touching my leg, but we both pretend it doesn't.

"You're a great kisser," Mikkalo says to cut through the intensity of the silence falling between us.

I smile. "I'm really enjoying my time with you."

"Yeah?"

"Mmmhmm." I accidentally yawn, the bath doing all sorts of good on my body and mind. The tension that bunched my muscles finally easing. It helps that Mikkalo massages my hands between his, assuring I relax.

"What do you say we relocate, Gwen?" he asks lowly after a few more minutes. "While I love being in the tub with you...that kiss. This closeness. I need to cool off."

I giggle and nod, running my hands over my face. "I'm sorry."

"Don't be. This is exactly what I think of as the end of a perfect night." Mikkalo stands up and rinses off, wrapping himself in a towel. "I'll go grab you something to wear, okay?"

I bob my head, watching him go. "Hey, Mikkalo?"

He turns at the door. "Yeah?"

"You've made my night pretty perfect too."

Soft music trickles through the air, and I roll over on the pull-out bed. Mikkalo had it already made after I got out of the tub and got dressed, so I figured I wouldn't make it weird and ask to sleep in his big-ass bed. He might've needed some space of his own after the bath.

But damn. I can't sleep. It's like my brain won't shut off.

Sliding my legs over the side of the bed, I sit up and

peer around the dark room. There is plenty of space to do some more floor exercises, but my body still burns with aches. I don't see where his TV is, and there is no way I'm going into his office with the security feeds. My stomach growls for the second time, and I finally relent to it and pad across the plush rug to where Mikkalo left me a couple of pieces of fruit like he was afraid he might forget to feed me or something. Which he kind of has. But not solid food. His blood.

The fruit will have to do. I just wish I could get my body to control itself. I feel awful the second I'm not distracted. And right now, I'm bored and restless with a mad case of insomnia. It doesn't help that every time I close my eyes, I see my brothers.

"I can get you something else if you want," Mikkalo says, sitting up in his bed. He stretches his arms over his head and yawns. I guess as head of defense, he has to be an incredibly light sleeper.

I dig my nails into the orange, the sweet, tangy juice dripping over my fingers. I automatically pop a slice in my mouth. "This is fine. Sorry if I woke you. I can't sleep."

"Is it the bed?" he asks. "I have never slept on it, so I wasn't sure."

"I don't think so. I can usually sleep anywhere. I slept on the ground for an entire week before you found me." I pop another piece of the orange in my mouth and hum under my breath. While it tastes delicious, it makes the hunger inside me worse. "I just—I don't know."

"You have a lot on your mind," he says. "I get like that too. Have been a little on edge lately with everything going on. Tonight was the first time I actually clonked out."

"It's hard without Zaire, huh?" I ask. Mikkalo hasn't said much about his coven leader—neither has Bronx, Jameson, and Everett—but I can imagine that they feel his absence, even if they don't show me.

"It's more weird than anything. He's always been here, you know? But it's not that."

"What is it then?"

"You."

"Me?"

He smiles at me, his face shadowed in darkness with the only light coming from the glow of screens inside his office.

"Let's just say I feel better knowing I can see you're okay. Knowing that you're here."

I can't stop returning his smile, and I cross the room to close the space. He scoots over and pats the bed next to him. I sit down, sinking against the pillows. "You don't trust your brothers with me?"

Reaching out, he laces our fingers together. "I trust my brothers with my life, yours too, and I know they are plenty capable of taking care of you, but I don't know. Call me overprotective, I guess."

"Or possessive," I say, keeping my voice light.

He chuckles. "Less so than Jameson. I'm not sure about

Everett yet. But you don't have to worry. I'm a master of control. I also find your possessiveness incredibly sexy."

"*My* possessiveness?"

"Maybe it's your need of control. Either way, it's not often someone is brave enough to speak up and tell us what to do, though I was a bit disappointed you didn't demand to sleep in my bed. I had actually made the couch bed for me."

I shift and face him, narrowing my eyes to see if he's joking. His face remains even, his dark eyes flashing. We study each other a moment, our hearts picking up speed the longer I capture him in my stare instead of the other way around.

"Next time," I finally manage to say. "I'm sorry if I disappointed you. I have a lot on my mind."

"Your family?"

I puff a breath through my lips. "I just keep replaying their accusations over and over again in my mind. They just—they don't understand."

Mikkalo gently rubs his thumb over the side of my hand, drawing it closer to hold between both of his. "Understand what?"

"That we were wrong about all vampires."

Mikkalo's face lights up at my words, and he leans closer to me, his gaze flicking from mine to my lips. His desire to kiss me paints his eyes with a flash of silver, and I can't resist wanting nothing more than to give in.

I brush my lips to his without getting carried away, just showing him that I mean what I say. Before he can pull me closer to kiss me more deeply, my body reacts to him, and with more than desire. Pain shoots through me, and I can't stop a whimpering gasp from escaping my lips. I bonk my head on his shoulder as I bow and wait for the rolling hunger to ease up.

"Shit," Mikkalo whispers, pulling back.

Embarrassment floods my face.

"Do I need to call Everett? I've never heard anyone make that kind of freakishly loud internal noise before. Are you sick?"

"Mikkalo, no," I murmur, inwardly cringing. "It's fine. I'm fine. I'm sorry. I'm just hungry."

He raises his eyebrows and stares at my stomach. "Are you sure about that? I might not have experience in donor health, but that was...wild."

I release a breathless laugh and hide my face with my hands. "I'm sure."

"Fuck, that's...shit. I'm embarrassing you." He leans forward and wraps his arms around me. "I'm sorry. I'm an ass."

"Are not. You just didn't know," I say. And he still won't.

"With how hungry you always seem to be, I wonder if Everett should re-evaluate the donor rations in the region. I'm thinking they might be substandard," he says, still caught up on me.

"You can do that?"

"Well, yeah. It's our region. Maintaining good health within the donor population is important."

I frown at his words. I can't help it.

"And saying shit like this is exactly why your brothers won't ever feel the same way as you."

I tilt my head back and gaze into his eyes. "It's more than that. I'm assuming since Bronx knows, that you know at least a little bit about Blood Rebels."

"Less than you'd think. Your family was my first encounter. I mean, there are always donors and vampires who don't register in a region, but I've never met someone who proactively...I don't even know exactly what you were doing, Gwen. It feels wrong to me to list everything you've been accused of under Donor Life Corp law."

I can see that he wants me to tell him, but a huge part of me, one that has ingrained that I must protect my family—others like me—would never allow me to tell him exactly what Blood Rebels do besides break vampire law.

"Honestly, every Blood Rebel is different. Some humans just want to live, you know? But Donor Life Corp can't have that, can they? It's one of the reasons my brothers would never believe that I'm okay with you guys. They will continue to assume that my mind's being manipulated to have me do whatever you want."

He frowns, his chin dimpling with the action. "Most

vampires would never. To completely control a donor takes a lot of strength and mind power. Certain things can break mind manipulation."

My eyes widen. I didn't know. "Like what?"

"Extreme injury is one."

"What else?" Laredo would never dare give away such a secret.

He shrugs. "I don't know, really. It depends on the person."

"Oh."

"I hope you know we'd never manipulate your mind, Gwen. With your reaction to Bronx's attempt after Zaire's death, he made it clear that he'd fuck us up if we even considered it. Not that I would. I much prefer your—ferocity. Hot temper. Bossiness. Your spontaneity."

I turn on the bed, and he hooks his fingers to my legs, sliding them over his so that we sit ultra-close. Our eyes meet, and I can't stop the smile from crossing my face.

"My brothers would still never believe it," I say. "Especially because of all these hours you guys let fall between letting me drink your blood."

He raises his eyebrows. "I have to admit. I forgot. Why didn't you remind me?"

I shrug. "Because that's weird."

He chuckles. "Nah. Blood drinking is normal to me."

Everett said the same thing, but it still feels weird to ask.

"What about offering it?" I bite my lip between my

teeth, anticipating his reaction.

Reaching out, he grazes his fingers along my cheek. "Not as much, but I'm not nervous if you're wondering. I really did just forget."

I scoot closer. "Then come here."

Mikkalo sits up, roving his gaze over my body in only a too big T-shirt—one of his—because I'm nearly certain after seeing me in something of Bronx and Jameson's, he couldn't help himself from seeing me in something of his. He gives me a once-over, his sudden desire pressing into me as the thought arouses him. "Now?"

I trail my gaze from his and down his bare chest. "Yes."

"But—"

"So you are nervous." I can't help from saying the words. The longer I sit with him on his bed, the more my stomach hurts. It's furious at his sudden hesitation.

"Maybe a bit. Not of the act but of how much I want to. I mean, you're in my bed, and I want to...we should wait until dark. No one is going to come into my room now. You're safe."

Pulling away from him, I swivel and slide off his bed. The last thing I need is for him to see how disappointed and frustrated I suddenly am and not just because I feel extra bitey. And now I'm pissed. Not at Mikkalo. Not even at this situation. I'm furious with myself. I'm pissed at the world. At who I am. With how I'm practically on the verge of a melt-down over something that used not to be a huge deal.

I'd be uncomfortable, sure, but not feeling like some savage monster will burst through my skin.

I should have better control—I know I'm capable of it—but my nerves refuse to relax. I'm antsy. In pain. I'm never going to sleep with the ache in my belly. If I can't sleep, I need to put as much space between Mikkalo and me as possible. If I don't, I'm afraid of what will happen.

Mikkalo materializes in front of me, blocking my way. "Gwen, wait. If it's that important to you, then here." Mikkalo bites his arm, sending two streams of blood rolling from his puncture wounds. "I didn't mean to make your feelings seem unimportant. I was only trying to prove to you that you don't need it with me. I want you to trust me."

Something inside me snaps at his words, and I surprise him by crashing into him. He spins the both of us midair, knocking me flat on my back. The sudden movement, the weight of him sinking on my body, ignites my very nature.

I snap my teeth, missing his throat by an inch as he jerks his head.

Mikkalo tenses and rolls off of me, getting to his feet so quickly that his abrupt absence hits me hard. His soft growl sends fear washing over me. My mind whirls, a dozen thoughts spinning through my head.

"Gwen, what the fuck?" he asks, keeping his distance. "Are you okay? What was that about?"

I curl my knees to my chest without responding to him. I can't. Everything that happened with my brothers rams into me. My body and mind war with itself. The fact that Mikkalo's light footsteps draw closer doesn't help.

"Gwen," he says softly, his presence so close that the scent of his blood makes me gasp and clutch my knees. "You're freaking me out. Did I hurt you?"

"Stay back," I whisper. "You have to stay back."

He groans. "I can't. I need to make sure you're okay. Are you injured?"

"Stay back," I repeat.

"Gwen."

Jerking my arm out, I punch him so hard that he flies back several feet. He crashes into the wall, the scariest, most threatening noise escaping his throat. I scramble away, my fear instincts reacting like crazy.

Mikkalo flashes his fangs and catapults up. "Don't move. Stay where you are, Gwen."

I don't. I stumble from him as fast as I can, my chest heaving. "Leave me alone."

"I don't understand. When? How?" His voice booms with his questions.

Extending my arms, I raise my palms to him. "Leave me alone, Mikkalo. I mean it."

"I can't, Gwen. Please, don't fight me."

I inch my way to the bathroom and try to run in. Mikkalo appears in front of me and grabs my wrists, stopping me from evading him. He spins me around so fast that I don't have a chance to fight, his strength far more powerful than mine. The familiar click of his fangs extending sounds in my ear, and I release a small sob.

"Don't bite me, Mikkalo, please," I beg, trembling so hard that he's the only thing holding me up.

"You should've told us, Gwen," he says.

"Told you what?" I ask.

"That you transitioned." He releases a soft growl in my ear. "Is this why you fought Zaire? Why you killed him?"

My chest clenches at his accusation. "I—I didn't kill him."

"You're lying. Who set this up? Who're you working for? What region?"

Cool metal touches my neck, and I tense at the pressure of a blade against my throat. "Mikkalo, please."

"Bronx will insist I take your head."

"Mikkalo, no, please!" I scream. "Please!"

Through my burning tears, I catch sight of our reflection in the huge bathroom mirror. I stiffen at the sight of silver eyes blinking at me—but they're not Mikkalo's. They're mine.

"Just tell me the truth, Gwen. Who sent you?" he asks.

"No one."

He roars and releases me, the movement sending me sprawling across the bathroom floor. Mikkalo closes the space again, holding up a scary-ass sword. "Gwen, this is your last chance."

Closing my eyes, I summon all my strength. I summon

all my courage.

This is it.

This is the moment I knew would come my whole life.

My life will end by a vampire's hand.

Because with the way Mikkalo roars again, the way his eyes remain completely silver, he's fallen into his nature, and I'm no match.

Something dark burns through me, pushing my fear away. Snapping my eyes open, I stiffen and meet his gaze.

I'm not ready to die.

17

TRAITOR TO HUMANITY

JERKING MY LEG OUT, I attempt to kick Mikkalo in the groin, but he expects it and clutches my ankle, dragging me closer. A figure blurs behind him, and Jameson let's out the scariest fucking growl I've ever heard in existence. I expect the two of them to grab hold of me to rip me apart, but Jameson yanks Mikkalo's arm, snatches the weapon from his grip, and aims it at him.

Thrusting my leg up again, I kick Mikkalo in his junk so hard that he hollers and falls back into his room. I rush forward and slam the bathroom door, shoving a rolling cabinet in front of it to barricade myself in the best I can.

Something crashes on the other side of the door, and I search around the room for anything I can use as a weapon to defend myself. Rushing to the wall near the tub, I yank on the wall fixture and somehow manage to rip the screws free to use the towel rack as a rod.

Mikkalo growls again. "She's a fucking vampire, Jameson! Do not get in my way. It's my duty."

"Are you crazy? I spent the last twenty-four hours with Gwen. She's not. You're delusional," Jameson says, his voice growing soft. "And I need you to back the fuck up. You're ruining everything. I will not stand here and let you hurt my girl."

"She's not *your* girl," he snaps.

"Well, she'll never be yours after this shit you pulled. You'll be lucky if Bronx doesn't throw you to the shadows, you asshole."

"*Me?*"

I wince at another crash.

"Mik, calm the hell down. Even if Gwen is a vampire, you can't just go trying to kill her." Jameson's voice turns into a whisper that I shouldn't be able to hear. "But I know you're wrong. You're stressed out and probably nervous."

"Her eyes flashed silver, Jameson," Mikkalo says.

"Are you sure? If you scared the hell out of her, she could've been crying and catching the reflection of yours."

Mikkalo groans. "She pushed me into a wall."

"Maybe she caught you off guard."

"But look. There is no fucking way she would be able to shove me hard enough to crack the plaster."

Jameson doesn't respond.

"You know she was bitten by that asshole in the city. What if this was all some sort of plot to take over our region?" Mikkalo asks. "It would be perfect. She already killed Zaire."

"But she didn't. I watched the videos. So did you. There was nothing vampiric about Gigi. You saw how distressed she was. Everett didn't see anything in her tests, either. People drank her blood."

"Maybe it took time."

"She doesn't have fangs, brother. Whatever you saw with Gwen couldn't have been what you thought."

"But—"

"Stop it, Mikkalo. You're wrong. If she were a vampire, she'd need blood. Human blood. She wouldn't be able to stop herself. I drank blood in front of her, and the look she gave me...there was no way she wanted any. And now you possibly traumatized Gwen so much that there's no fucking way she's ever going to let any of us get close to her again. If that happens, you're dead."

Silence falls between them, and I clutch the rod, still ready to fight.

A soft tap sounds on the door. "Hey, Gwen. It's just me. Can you open the door?"

I press my lips together, suppressing the small whimper threatening to escape my mouth.

"Please, Gwen. I swear you're not in any danger with me. Mikkalo isn't here."

Still, I don't move. I don't know if I can. My whole body hurts. My mind. I can't believe this is happening. Had Laredo not bit me, I know I'd have been okay. Now? I'm certain that I'll be caged. Mikkalo wants me dead. I shouldn't be so upset, but I am. It hurts because of how much I like him.

"Gigi, please. I need to make sure you're okay," Jameson begs, his voice growing more desperate.

The door shudders as he bangs on it but not hard enough to break it down.

I try not to react and to stay quiet. If I can get him to leave, I might be able to steal one of the weapons Mikkalo has hanging on the wall. That will give me a fighting chance to get out of here.

"Jameson, it's no use. Just wait until Bronx and Everett return," Mikkalo whispers. "I'm sorry that I fucked up. It's just my job to—"

Jameson releases a deep growl. "I said stay out of here."

Something—no someone—slams on the door. It shudders on its hinges. Mikkalo and Jameson break into a fight I can't see, igniting my fear instincts like crazy.

And then I smell blood.

Agony explodes through me, and I scream out, my

stomach seizing. The door to the bathroom flies open, the rolling cupboard crashing to the tile floor to spill towels and toiletries all over the place.

I blindly reach out, looking for the rod I broke off from the wall, but it rests out of my reach and next to the steps that lead to the tub.

"Gwen, fuck. Gwen," Jameson says.

Mikkalo appears behind him. "Careful, brother."

Jameson snarls at him and closes the space to me, turning my closed eyelids from red to dark. He scoops me into his arms, hugging me against him. My stomach releases the most incredibly loud noise, drawing silence through the room. I inhale a sharp breath and immediately regret it. Jameson's scent intoxicates me, his blood stronger smelling than ever before. I don't even have to look at him to know that Mikkalo split his lip.

"Gwen." My name comes out a plea on Jameson's lips. "Please, look at me."

"I can't," I say. "I'm in so much pain."

"Gigi—"

I crash my mouth to his, unable to control the need burning through me that drags me toward the blood I can smell so strongly that I can taste it. Jameson reacts to my ferocity with a soft moan as I suck hard on his bottom lip, drawing as much of his blood as I can into my mouth.

His fingers tighten around me, and he shifts my body in his arms, allowing me to wrap my legs around him. I don't think he realizes I'm seconds away from pulling back to bite him because his massive boner presses into me. He slides his fingers down my back to pull me to him by my ass, feeling the smooth skin of my butt cheeks peeking out from my panties.

"You have to get away from me. It's not safe for you to be this close," I whisper, kissing him deeper, sliding my tongue into his mouth.

He pants a breath, tilting his head as I break from his mouth to kiss along his jaw. "I can't unless you let go of me."

"I'm not going to. Shove me away. Hard," I say, gliding my tongue down his neck.

"Huh?"

"You have to or I'm going to bite you," I murmur, locking my fingers to his shoulders. "I can't control myself, and I don't want to hurt you."

"You won't hurt me, Gigi." Moaning again, he spins and rests my back on the cool shower door. "I don't care if you bite. I like it."

"Jamie..."

"Do it. I want you to do it."

I can't resist his words and sink my teeth into the softness of his neck hard enough to break his skin. He releases another moan, digging one hand into my ass cheek while trailing his other hand between my legs to touch me in a way that has me sucking harder.

My whole body explodes with tingles, the fire burning in my stomach subsiding the longer I drink. Pulling back, I bite him again and moan so fucking loud that Jameson's fangs click in my ear.

The soft sound of footsteps taps in front of me, though I doubt Mikkalo could ever get through Jameson to me as he cages me in.

"What the hell, Jameson?" Mikkalo asks, his voice booming through the air. "Is she...?"

Jameson shifts my weight, lifting his arm up to his brother. "Don't. Something's wrong with her. This is...unlike anything I've ever experienced."

"I'm so sorry," I murmur, burying my face in the crook of Jameson's neck. "I'm just so hungry. You taste amazing."

Mikkalo groans, his feet squeaking as he spins on the tiles. I summon my courage and open my eyes, glimpsing his broad back as he faces the other way, staring into his dark bedroom. "Gwen, you need to be honest with us. I mean it. Did someone transform you?"

I can barely get my mouth to ease from Jameson again. "I don't know what's wrong with me."

Jameson eases away to search my face, tensing under my sudden stare. I don't have to look at a mirror to know that my eyes still flicker silver. I see the reflection blinking in the green depths of his gaze.

I expect him to slam me into the wall. I prepare for him to shout for Mikkalo to help him rip my heart out. But he does neither. He continues to stare into my watery gaze.

His jaw tenses. "Gwen, your eyes. Was Mikkalo right ab—"

"No, I'm not a vampire. I know I'm not," I say, my chest heaving. "I swear."

He licks his lips, turning his attention to my mouth like he wants me to smile to be certain I don't have fangs. "You were possibly bitten with venom."

I bob my head. "I know. Laredo thought I would be caged otherwise. He was trying to stop that from happening because...I'm different. But it didn't work."

I open and close my mouth, trying to push out the words, but fear squeezes me so tightly that all I can do is rest my forehead on Jameson's shoulder. He surprises me by enveloping me in his arms only to stroll from the bathroom and past Mikkalo.

Jameson sets me on the edge of the couch bed and doesn't take his arms off me. He just holds me close, running his fingers over and over through my hair. I breathe into his shoulder, my lips begging me to latch on again, but I know I've already drunk a lot. Like humans, vampires have limitations. Too much blood loss will weaken them, and it'll take longer for them to regenerate. I've seen it once in an unwilling blood source rebels baited by pretending to have been lost outside one of the cities.

My stomach growls again, and Jameson adjusts me and pulls his collar down on the other side of his neck. I tense, fighting against my uncontrollable need awakened by the length of time without blood, feeling threatened by Mikkalo, and just freaked the fuck out. I'm my most powerful when I feel the weakest.

"Can I take her, Jameson?" Mikkalo asks softly from a few feet away. "I think you've given her too much."

Jameson tightens his hold on me. "No."

Mikkalo groans and risks coming closer. He gulps, swallowing whatever nerves he has, and sits beside us. "Gwen, I fucked up. I'm so sorry. I just thought—you scared the shit out of me, if I'm being honest."

I slowly ease back from Jameson to tilt my head to meet Mikkalo's eyes.

"I don't know what's going on with you, but I know you're not a threat now. I regret my actions and understand if you don't want me around. But please, let me give you some of my blood. Just this once. I'm pretty sure Jameson will happily die under that kissable mouth of yours, and I kind of want him alive."

The sincerity of his words cuts through me so deeply that I believe him. And I agree with him. I don't want to risk Jameson's health. I know we've only known each other for a short amount of time, but this weird-ass circumstance brought us closer. I can tell Jameson's grown possessive of me, but I kind of feel a bit possessive too.

And the thought of tasting Mikkalo? It excites me way more than it should. I just know with the way Jameson's currently completely invested in me that he will protect me. He stood against his brother to do so. That's basically treason within a coven.

I ease away from Jameson to meet his eyes. Cupping his face, I kiss him for a minute. "Thank you, Jamie. You have no idea how grateful I am for what you did. But Mikkalo's right. I can't drink anymore from you, but I still need more blood to get my crazy ass under control."

His face softens, and he relaxes his hold on me. "Your crazy ass is so fucking hot. I kind of like how wild you get."

My cheeks burn so hard that Jameson grins and kisses each of them, his cool lips helping to suppress the heat in my face.

Shifting on the bed, he turns slightly to glance at Mikkalo. "You try anything stupid, and I will kill you."

"I won't. You can stay right here if you're that concerned," Mikkalo says.

Jameson's eyes flash silver. "If Gwen wants me to, I will. I don't care how awkward as hell it'll be. You already got my show."

Mikkalo chuckles. "Talk about a bonding experience."

The light teasing of their voices suppresses the jitters engulfing me, and my fear instincts finally subside completely. Mikkalo no longer feels like a threat, and Jameson doesn't look ready to slay his brother on my behalf, so I think I might survive a bit longer. Neither of them asks me anything, nor do they freak out even more about what the hell is wrong with me. Instead, Jameson slides me off his lap so that I sit between him and Mikkalo.

"All right, Gigi. Go on and ravage the hell out of Mikkalo," he says, nudging my knee with his knuckles. "Don't be gentle either. He doesn't deserve it."

Mikkalo scrunches his nose, twisting his lips to the side. "He's right." Inhaling a deep breath, he tilts his neck to the side in silent permission, tense and too brave to admit he's nervous.

"Why don't you go get some blood?" I ask Jameson, keeping my voice even. "I'll be fine for a few minutes with Mikkalo. You look like you could use something to eat as much as me."

Jameson droops his shoulder with a heavy breath. "I appreciate it, Gigi. It's taking everything in me not to pull you back to me."

I lean in and kiss him. "Don't you start getting all possessive on me."

"You make it incredibly hard."

I lick my teeth. "I know."

With a shake of his head and a fake glare, Jameson disappears from my side, though a cool spot blossoms across my cheek, the whisper of his quick kiss lingering on my skin. The door clicks closed, leaving Mikkalo and me alone in his room, and I do my best not to make a big deal.

"Gwen, thank you for still managing even to be in the same room alone with me," he murmurs, peeking at me from his dark shadow of thick lashes. "I was just...surprised. I'm an ass."

I bob my head, suppressing the fear he elicited inside me. "I can't fault you. Your job is to protect your coven and region. You probably feel so betrayed that I didn't tell you about...my needs."

Twisting his lips up, he offers me a small smile. "I can't blame you for that, Gwen. You drink vampire blood. It's unusual."

"Weird, right? Now you know why my family tolerated Laredo and kept him around. I've been like this all my life, but not so bad until you caught me in the city," I say.

Dozens of thoughts cross Mikkalo's face, but he doesn't ask me any questions. Instead, he leans into me and bends his neck again. "Why don't you save all of this information for when my brothers return, and we can all sit together. You still look on edge. Go ahead and...bite me."

I reach for his hand and lace my fingers through his. "You know, I don't bite like that all the time. Just when I'm in certain moods." I lick my lips with my admission. "It's easier if you bite your arm for me. You look kind of tense and that makes it tough. Painful for you. Despite what Jameson thinks you deserve, I don't want to hurt you, Mikkalo."

A soft smile crosses his face, his hard features reacting to my words. "I feel like such a dick, you know."

I shrug. "It's not the first time someone tried to kill me.

I mean, I'm pretty certain my own brothers want to kill me. They *will* kill me if they find out that I told you as much as I already have."

"I'd never let them," he says quietly.

"Hopefully not by assuring they go to auction to be killed before they can try," I say, tilting my lips down. "Because they're my family. I love them."

He doesn't respond to me. I know it's because he won't make me any promises about my brothers. He doesn't even know what's going to happen. If it's anyone I need to plead with, it's Bronx. But now? I don't even know how he'll handle this news. But I know I have to tell him and Everett. Mikkalo made it pretty clear. I doubt they keep any secrets from each other, and especially not one like this about me.

It's just—

Mikkalo bites his arm, drawing my attention away from the silence growing between us. I inhale a soft breath at the delectable scent of his blood that wafts around me, warm and almost spicy like cinnamon—not sweet like Jameson but still alluring.

I clasp his proffered arm in my hands and ease it to my lips, feeling his anticipation so strongly that it's nearly palpable. His gaze locks to me, though I don't meet his stare. Laredo had always watched me too. I know it partly has to do with the fact that vampires don't just give their blood freely to humans—mostly only during acts of intimacy— and another part is because I can still sense Mikkalo's attraction toward me. He can certainly feel mine toward him as I release a hum against his skin, latching my mouth to the puncture wounds.

And fuck does he taste amazing. Warmth floods my mouth, buzzing down my throat to settle in my stomach. I relax under the sudden good feelings igniting inside me, sinking into Mikkalo until he pulls me completely onto his lap to stroke his hand along my back.

"Gwen," Mikkalo whispers. "I know I fucked up. I know I don't deserve another chance. But I want you to know that whatever this is—it's incredible. Jameson was right. You're amazing. I hope you can forgive me."

I ease my mouth away from his arm and finally peer at him. "Of course I can. I already do. I don't know what's going to happen when you tell Bronx and Everett, but if you guys still want to spend time with me, I'd love it. For the first time in my life, I don't feel like the world is out to get me." I rest my head on Mikkalo's chest. "I know this might be weird, and I don't know if you believe in fate, but that's what this feels like. Destiny. You and your brothers have already changed my life."

He runs his fingers along my cheek. "You've definitely changed ours."

"But now what?" I ask.

He shrugs. "I don't know, but whatever happens, I'm not going to fuck up again. If you give me another chance, I'll prove myself good enough to be your Blood Match."

I close my eyes. How could I forget about that? "If you even want it after I tell you about me."

"What do you mean?"

"Mikkalo, you freaked out about thinking I was a vampire. What I'm about to tell you is worse. Much, much worse."

18

CLAIMED

"WHAT THE FUCK?" BRONX'S SOFT voice trickles through the air.

"Shhh," Jameson whispers. "Do you know how long it took her to fall asleep? She has been awake almost the whole time since you dropped her off with me."

"And there was a small incident with me," Mikkalo murmurs from in front of me. "So like Jameson said, shut the fuck up."

Mikkalo's weight shifts closer, and I can't stop myself from sinking more into him, though I clutch Jameson's hand as he cuddles me from behind. The last place I ever dreamed I'd find myself was between two very hot vampires, but Jameson was pacing so loudly in the hallway that I got the nerve to ask Mikkalo if it was okay for him to come back in.

And then I fell asleep between them, and it looks like they never left, squeezing with me on the nearly too small pull-out bed that forces us all to lie on our sides.

"You said an incident?" Everett's voice trickles through the air. "Is Gwen okay? You didn't accidentally hurt her, did you?"

Jameson releases a quiet laugh. "No, but this asshole had a wicked bruised cock for hours."

I scrunch my face at his words. I knew I kicked Mikkalo hard, but I must've missed him telling Jameson just how hard.

"Fuck, why did she do that?" Bronx's voice rises through the air, his inability to keep his voice in control making both Jameson and Mikkalo growl softly in warning.

I can't stand just eavesdropping a moment longer, so I release a small breath and groan, stretching my arms up over my head, taking Jameson's hand with mine. Fluttering my eyes open, I meet Mikkalo's intense stare, though they don't lock onto me nor do they make me turn away. I lean forward and brush my lips to his, making him smile. I wasn't sure he'd be able to again after everything.

"Damn it, Bronxy. We told you," Jameson snaps.

GINNA MORAN

I roll over and offer Jameson a kiss next, stopping him from releasing his wrath on Bronx. The last thing I need is to have Jameson piss Bronx off, especially if I'm going to have to tell him the truth about me.

A gentle hand touches my foot. "Hey, Gwen. Are you okay like my brothers say?"

I turn to lie on my back and meet Everett's gaze as he sits on the end of the bed. I'm rather surprised he risks it, considering how snuggled up his brothers are to me. I offer him a smile and sit up more to reach out and touch his hand.

Bronx's gaze bores into me from over Everett's shoulder, though he keeps his expression in check so I can't read him.

I bob my head, turning my attention back to Everett. "Yeah, I'm a lot better than I was."

Everett frowns, automatically assuming that whatever is going on might have to do with my reaction toward what happened with my brothers. "That's good. I know all this must be hard for you. I promise your brothers are okay, though."

"But we had to mind manipulate them," Bronx says, speaking up. "And I'm sorry. I made sure they were safe and unharmed. It was fast and only to make them forget what they saw."

I tense, trying not to react even though it bothers the hell out of me. I know why Bronx did it. Not only to protect them, because they'd have fought like hell and ended up doing something to get themselves killed, but also to protect his coven.

I take a breath and scoot to the edge of the bed. Standing up, I motion for Bronx to come closer to me. He remains rigid as all get-out, his gaze darting to Mikkalo's. He doesn't know yet that I want a say in the rules, and both Mikkalo and Jameson have already agreed that I'm not going to be included with whatever the hell boundaries they set in place. Until I manage to spill my secrets, I'm doing whatever the hell I want. Right now, I really want to hug Bronx and show him that I'm fine.

I also want to hug him in case this might be the last time he ever lets me.

My heart aches at the thought.

Touching his cheek, I guide his face away from his brothers to look at me. I offer him a smile, getting him to relax, and then I stand up on my tiptoes and kiss him. "First, thank you for letting me see my brothers. I'm sorry if it put you in a tough position, and even though it kills me that they're there, I appreciate you trying to do what you can."

He bobs his head. "I want to do more for you, dandelion."

I smirk at the nickname he uses on me. "And second, I missed you." Pulling back, I smile at Everett. "And you too. Things have been rather tense. I'm just glad you're back."

Everett reaches for my hand. "Me too. I look forward to our upcoming time together, Gwen. I have a few things planned out."

I can't stop my mouth from grimacing, and it catches Everett off guard. His smile fades, his blue eyes flicking from Bronx and then to Mikkalo and Jameson, before returning back to me. Before he can even think for a second that I don't want to spend time with him, I squeeze my eyes shut and gather my nerves.

I force myself to smile. "And I hope I get a chance to enjoy it."

"What's that supposed to mean, Gwen?" Bronx asks, speaking up to ask the silent question that crosses Everett's face.

Jameson groans, sits up, and scoots across the bed to me. He grabs my hand and pulls me back to him, motioning for Mikkalo to take me. The sudden action leaves both Bronx and Everett in confusion.

"Okay, I know there isn't ever going to be a good time for what we need to discuss, so I'm just going to say it," Jameson says.

Mikkalo tightens his hold on me. "And you two better keep your shit together. If you so much as raise your damn voices at Gwen, we're going to have a huge fucking problem."

"Shit," I whisper.

Bronx growls. "What the fuck is going on?"

Jameson flashes his fangs. "Cool it, Bronxy. We mean it. Gwen has been through too much already that she doesn't need any more bullshit. None of this is her fault, and I don't know about you, but I like the hell out of her, and I don't think it's that big of deal."

"Can you spit it out? You're making me nervous," Everett says.

Jameson sighs and twists to look over his shoulder at me. "Go on, Gigi. You can tell them. We won't let anything happen to you."

I clear my throat, antsy at the sudden scrutiny. "Um, so..." I can't do it. I can't fucking do it.

Jameson groans and whips his attention back to his brothers. Straightening his shoulders, he yanks down the collar of his shirt to expose the still healing bite marks I left on him. I really did drink too much from him. What should be bruises are barely scabs. And ouch.

Bronx's mouth falls agape. "Whoa, fuck."

Everett stretches his neck closer, inspecting my bite. "Damn. That's one helluva mark, Jameson."

Jameson chuckles, his chest puffing with pride, making my cheeks burn because both Everett and Bronx look at me. "So, Gwen happens to be a little...aggressive."

"I wouldn't say she's aggressive," Mikkalo says.

"Okay, more like fiercely wild. Hot. Insatiable," Jameson says.

Mikkalo nods. "Definitely all those."

"You guys. I'm not."

Jameson scoffs. "You totally are, Gigi."

I groan. "No, I was just...starving."

"You didn't feed her?" Everett asks.

Mikkalo and Jameson both look at each other and laugh, and I mean full-on barking a laugh with so much amusement that I consider smacking the both of them upside the head.

"Oh, we fed her. And you are going to have to be next," Jameson says. "I mean, if you're up for the challenge."

Bronx fists his hands, scowling as Jameson glosses around what's up without just saying the words. Then he looks at me. "Gwen? What is he talking about?"

I squeeze my eyes shut.

"Gwen drinks vampire blood," Jameson says, answering for me.

Silence greets his comment, and I refuse to look.

"I mean, not the hot way she sucks on my neck for funsies. She drinks vampire blood because she has to."

"She survives on it," Mikkalo adds.

"Survives on it?" Everett asks.

Sighing, I finally open my eyes and meet Everett's gaze, trying my best not to react to the heat of Bronx's stare locking onto me. "That's right. I get sick without it. Out of control. You can say I'm different."

"Are you sure?" Bronx asks. He's not asking me but his

brothers.

"I thought Gwen was a vampire," Mikkalo says softly.

"But I'm not," I'm quick to say. "I'm only half. An anomaly. A symptomatic carrier of a mutation. One of my ancestors caught the Blood Hunger Plague while pregnant. It had an effect on my great-great grandpa in utero during the uprising."

"There is no plague, Gwen," Everett reminds me.

"She means her ancestor was bitten with venom." Bronx frowns at the idea. "I don't believe it."

I press my lips together. "It's true."

He closes the space to me. "No, no. That's not what I meant. I believe you, but I can't believe you just told me that you're a dhampir. I didn't think there were any around."

"You know about dhampirs?" I ask in surprise.

"I told you I was familiar with Blood Rebels, Gwen. But dhampirs have also been more of a story to me. I never truly believed it was possible."

"Oh, it's fucking possible all right," Jameson says. "But something's wrong with her."

"What do you mean?" Everett asks.

I reach out and touch his hand. "I don't know. But I was hoping you could help me find out."

"So tell me everything that has changed about you since Laredo bit you," Everett asks, sitting on one of his reading chairs with his tablet on his lap.

I stretch my legs on the floor in front of me and bend forward to touch my toes. Mikkalo follows my movement, continuing to hug me from behind. Bronx sits on the other chair by Everett, watching me without a word, and Jameson perches on the coffee table, still holding a bowl of yogurt Everett said I shouldn't eat. He wants to draw my blood for more extensive blood work as soon as the vampire blood I consumed runs through my system. I'd have hung out with Mikkalo for the rest of his time until it did, but I think all the guys are a bit antsy and in need of each other, so I suggested we hang out together.

I finally meet Everett's gaze. "Before I could go for two or three weeks without blood consumption. It was uncomfortable, like I was starving, but I never felt like I was going to attack a vampire."

Everett glances at his tablet. "Were your dietary needs like this all your life?"

I shake my head. "I don't think so. I don't remember much about it from my childhood. I think I could go months or longer."

Jameson grimaces. "How fucking weird. There is no way I'd let a kid—"

Arching forward, I flick his leg. "I drank blood from a glass until I was seventeen. My dad insisted it be that way. I actually snuck behind his back with my previous blood source, which..." I let my voice trail off. I don't even want to think of him and what happened.

"Did something bad happen with him?" Bronx asks softly. "I've noticed you never say his name while you will mention Laredo."

I stare at my toes. "Because I can't. I no longer know it."

Silence draws around me, and I try not to let it sink into my bones. The four of them stare at me as I continue to gaze at my feet, wishing Bronx never asked me the question.

"He's the one who killed your father, isn't he?" Jameson asks.

I nearly forgot that I told him about my dad's death. We skimmed over the subject of my parents fairly quickly. I couldn't give him anything about my mom, since she died when I was a baby, and he saw how hard it was to talk about my dad, so we just switched the conversation to his life.

"And I killed him for it," I finally say. "It was the first time I realized I was physically stronger than all my brothers."

"So you've always been strong enough to send me through a wall?" Mikkalo asks, redirecting the conversation.

I release a breathless laugh. "Actually, no. That was new. I don't think I could do it again either. At least not right now."

"What about those wild eyes?" Jameson asks.

"That's new too," I say.

"Given that dhampirs carry some of the same traits as vampires, I can only guess that you react like we do when we experience blood hunger."

Jameson gently kicks my foot. "And blood lust."

My cheeks burn, and I glare at him.

"Nothing wrong with that, Gigi," he says, lowering his voice. "I like your wild side."

Bronx leans across the table and whacks his back. "Knock it off." He flicks his gaze to me but keeps his mouth tight. Then he whispers, "You're going to embarrass her. Not to mention we discussed this, Jameson. You know the rules."

"The rules bug Gwen," he retorts just as quietly.

Bronx growls lowly. "Doesn't matter. We need them. It's important. Not only for her sake but for ours. I already see how possessive you're getting, Jameson. You won't even give her two feet of space."

"You did threaten to murder me, brother," Mikkalo says to Jameson from over my shoulder.

Bronx flares his nostrils. "You did what?"

Everett meets my gaze, and I rub my lips together. He must notice that I flick my gaze to whoever's talking, because he leans forward and touches his index finger to his ear, silently asking about my hearing.

I smirk and bare my teeth at him, crinkling my nose.

"And you also tried to claim her," Mikkalo adds.

I grimace at his words.

"Which Gwen obviously doesn't like," Everett says, raising his voice to a normal human pitch.

"Yeah, Jamie. I'm going to tell you the same thing I told Bronx," I say, turning my attention to Jameson. "You try to claim me and you'll be on the floor, clutching your cock."

He raises his eyebrows.

"And not in the good way. I'm not a possession."

Everett tips his head back and laughs so loudly that the sound fills me up with something unexpectedly good that I can't stop myself from smiling at him. He leans across the table, stretching out his knuckles to me, and I graze mine to his. His brothers sit in utter silence, watching the two of us laugh.

"You fucking asshole," Jameson says, finally pulling himself from his frozen shock at the realization that I could hear his whisper. "You could've said something before—"

"Before Gwen realized that you might not be the best choice to Blood Match with?" Everett asks.

Ah, hell.

Pushing to my feet, I grab onto the back of Jameson's shirt before he lunges at his brother. Jameson freezes, his muscles tensing as I lean into him and slide my arm across his chest to pin him to me.

I breathe softly against his neck, sending his heart racing. Everyone watches the two of us, but I don't glance to look at them. "Jamie, don't even think about it. I just got my human instincts under control, and I don't like when they're set off. Especially by you. It confuses the hell out of me."

He brings his hands up and hooks them to my arms, hugging them into his chest. "Sorry, Gigi."

"You better be," I tease. "And this is me calling your ass out about talking about me like I'm not here."

Groaning, he stretches his neck in an attempt to meet my gaze. "So when you told me you knew we were talking in front of you because of your experience with Laredo...?"

I bite my lip and smile. "That part was true, but it also seems that his bite gave me super hearing and your whispering about me seriously tested my restraint, especially when I first got here."

"Damn it," he mutters.

I brush my lips to his cheek. "I forgive you. I mean, how could I not?"

"You're only saying that because I feed you," he murmurs.

I laugh. "You've got that right. Now, you might want to pull away. I'm starting to feel extremely bitey, and you're awfully close."

He releases a throaty purr, shivering under my words. It's enough to make me graze my teeth over his shoulder through his shirt.

Everett suddenly stands up, drawing my attention to him. "Jameson, give her space."

Jameson growls.

"I mean it," Everett warns. "If she bites you, we're going to have to wait a few more hours before I can run any tests. I don't want to have to turn my time with Gwen into that. Please."

His words are enough to get me to release Jameson and scoot back to put space between us. Jameson makes it way too easy to play around with him. It's now that I realize how important boundaries might be. Not because vampires have a deep-seated nature to possess things they want or because it could lead to a fight, which I don't want. But because I can see how hurt Everett would be if he doesn't get the chance to hang out with me. He obviously looks forward to it—and I do too. The last thing I want is to make any of them feel badly.

Inhaling a small breath, I turn my gaze to Everett. "I'm sorry. I didn't mean to get carried away."

Jameson twists and smirks at me. "Her blood lust is a real thing, and I have to admit. I think I'm addicted to her. So, what she said. Sorry, Ev."

"And you too Bronx and Mikkalo." I stroll a few feet away from them and sit cross-legged on the coffee table so that I can face all of them. "I don't want to upset any of you."

"Which is why I wanted to set some rules," Bronx says, scrubbing his hands over his face.

Jameson reaches over and playfully punches Bronx's

leg. "Come on, she's a rebel, remember? She's going to do what she wants."

Bronx groans.

"Our girl hates rules," Jameson adds.

I blink a few times at him referring to me as their girl. It ignites a bunch of confusing emotions through me. He technically didn't claim me as his, but...shit. My stupid body tingles, and I'm pretty sure my nipples harden enough to give them a show, even with my bra.

"Whoa," Mikkalo whispers. "She liked that."

I squirm under his stare as Mikkalo drinks me in. His brothers turn and stare at me just as intensely, trying to figure out what he's talking about.

"The idea of breaking the rules?" Bronx questions just as quietly.

Jameson chuckles. "Of course she likes that, but I don't think that's what he meant."

"She liked being referred to as our girl, right Gwen?" Everett asks, directing his attention to me instead of forgetting that I can hear them.

I lick my lips, taking a few soft breaths.

"See?" Mikkalo says, his smile widening.

"You guys," I say, inching back far enough to feel the edge of the coffee table. If I'm not careful, I'll fall.

"No shame, Gigi," Jameson says.

"Our girl," Mikkalo says. "I like it."

Fuck. Me.

"Would it bother you if we said it?" Everett asks, keeping his face expressionless. "Our girl."

My heartbeat picks up pace, and I reach out and grab the nearest thing I can find—an actual book—to chuck at him. Everett laughs and sets it on the coffee table. He totally said it on purpose to see if I'd react. And I did.

"It would help with our possessive tendencies," Bronx says softly. "If Gwen's okay with it, I'm okay with it."

They all look at me, waiting for my response. I wait until my body chills the hell out before I even meet any of their gazes.

"If you're all going to claim me, then I get to claim you then," I say, pressing my lips into a line. "You're mine."

"Hell yeah, we're yours," Jameson says, flashing his fangs at me.

I can't stop myself from smiling. If only I knew exactly what the hell I'm getting myself into.

"At least until you make your decision," Bronx says.

My smile falters, and I close my eyes and take a breath. Now that's a thought I hate. I mean, how the hell will I ever choose?

19

SURPRISE

"SO, WHAT DO YOU SEE?" I ask, standing behind Everett as he looks over a document there is no possible way I'd be capable of reading on his tablet.

"It's strange. Nothing is too out of the ordinary. There are traces of a chemical found in vampire blood, which only looks like you've consumed it. It hasn't changed since I tested your blood at the Blood Match Center either."

I frown. "You tested my blood?" I know it was mentioned before, but I hadn't really thought about it.

"Part of your health exam," he says. "Since, you

know..."

"I wouldn't let you play health keeper with me?" I say.

I don't think I've ever seen a vampire blush so brightly before. And I get a kick out of it. Spinning him around in his rolling chair to face me completely, I peer down at him and run my fingers over his cheeks, warm despite the coolness of his chin.

"Gwen..."

Leaning closer, I brush my lips to his. "I'm teasing you, Everett. I know you don't play doctor. By the looks of whatever the hell all this stuff is, you obviously take your job seriously."

He stretches, wanting more of my affection, which I give to him with another kiss. "Don't be mistaken. Yes, I take my job as head of the donor division seriously, but you're not a job, Gwen. I care for you not because I have to but because I want to."

I smile at his words. "Even though I could be the cause of your demise?"

He chuckles. "I highly doubt that."

Slightly bending his head, I draw my lips to his neck. "I'm technically a trained predator. I survive on your blood."

"And I survive on yours." His voice grows soft, and he doesn't move under my touch, under the graze of my teeth as I run them along his skin until I bite his collar and stretch it to explore just a little farther.

"You wish," I say.

"You're right. You'd have to choose first. You couldn't sustain the four of us."

"But the four of you could sustain me..."

Everett inhales a small breath at my words, his hands trailing around my back until I find myself straddling him in his chair. Desire crashes over the two of us as he meets me for a passionate kiss far better than the tease of one he gave me before. I hook my fingers behind his neck, kissing him deeper, sliding my tongue into his mouth to feel how soft his tongue is against mine.

His fangs extend, accidentally poking my tongue, and he stiffens. I don't. A good shiver rolls through me at his reaction, at his desire toward even a drop of my blood, and I rock my body to his, letting him suck my tongue just hard enough to taste a bit more.

"Gwen," he whispers into my mouth. "You taste...unlike anyone."

I hum, my heart banging against his in an attempt to be together. "Is that so?"

"I've thought about this so much. I want more of you."

"I want you too."

Tightening his hold on me, he digs his fingers into my legs, pulling me more firmly into him. His body arouses with my closeness, and I can't stop my fingers from running down his chest until I reach between us and stroke his erection through his pants to discover exactly what I do to him.

He releases a soft moan, sliding his hands to my ass to pick me up with him. Spinning me once, he tosses me toward his bed where I land on my back with a screech. And holy shit. Everett yanks his shirt off, looking so ready to tear my clothes off too. He misinterpreted my comment, his lust darkening his blue eyes. Part of me wants to tear my own damn clothes off and throw myself at him. That part nearly wins. I twist my fingers around the hem of my shirt, my body unable to stay still under the heat of his intensity, drinking in every inch of me.

Kicking off his pants, he stands at the end of the bed in his boxers, his toned body rippling with hard muscles as he bends forward, resting his palms on the bed without moving for a minute. Everett licks his full lips, his bravado surprising me even though I know it shouldn't.

I cross my ankles. The anticipation of what might happen next sends heat and electricity humming from between my legs and up my torso to my breasts. The world flies around me, Everett moving too fast for me to keep up, and I shriek with a laugh as he pulls me closer to him by my ankles.

Everett bends down and kisses me, leaning over me while spreading my legs to rest between them. I gasp into his mouth, my mind whirling. Jameson has mentioned blood lust, and I'm nearly certain I have a case of it. Like bad. Everett too.

"You can tell me to stop at any time," he says. "And I

won't bite you."

I swallow, my head automatically nodding.

"Is there anything specific you like?"

Oh, fuck.

"Of course, I'd love to figure that out for myself."

Double oh, fucks.

I blink a few times, my chest heaving, my body tingling.

His face softens at my lack of response. Releasing a breathless groan, he eases his way from between my legs and sits on the bed next to me, automatically twining my fingers through his. "Gwen, I should've asked. Are you a virgin?"

I shake my head. "No, I'm not, to Grayson's dismay. He threatened basically every guy we ever came across that he'd murder them if they even glanced at me. But his best efforts to try to assure I didn't accidentally expand the donor population...or pass on my dhampir mutation, fell short."

"Laredo?" he asks.

"One of my brothers' best friends."

"I bet that killed them," he says. "Humans tend to be protective, and rightfully so."

"It didn't kill them. It killed him. Actually, Laredo killed him."

"Shit. He must've had some plan in his mind for you. I mean to risk—"

I groan and flop back. "He thought he was hurting

me."

He raises an eyebrow like he doesn't believe it. I barely even believe it. The more I hang out with the guys, the more I realize I knew practically nothing with Laredo. He probably was just like the blood source before him but smarter. Strategic. What if Bronx was right?

"I made too much noise." I don't know why I say it, maybe to try to convince myself that the whole thing with—I can't even remember his name—was an accident.

Everett raises his other eyebrow now.

I cover my face with my hands. "And now I made this awkward as fuck. I'm sorry."

Gently grasping my wrist, he eases my hand from my eyes to hold it between his. Everett offers me a smile to show that he's fine.

"I don't think getting to know you is awkward at all," he says. "And I should be the one apologizing. It's just...your blood."

"You want another taste?" I ask, my voice softening at the suggestion.

He shakes his head. "As much as I want to, Gwen. I shouldn't. I want you too badly. It's strange. I've never had such desire—like a need almost."

"I feel it too," I say. "It confuses the hell out of me. I never got this way with Laredo. Sure, I liked sucking on his neck on occasion, but I never desired him. Not like I do you."

His eyes flash silver. "You know, since we're already...in this position. Can I feed you? I don't need to draw any more blood for testing. You're probably hungry."

I bite my lip. "Starved. It's actually what I meant when I said that I wanted you."

Humming deep in his throat, he pulls me a bit closer, his eyes capturing mine like he loves my admission just as much this time even if it's not what he had originally thought. "So I assume you don't want a glass?"

I shake my head. "Unless you don't think you can handle me...or you're into role playing."

He gets a kick out of my teasing, his eyes lighting up. "What am I going to do with you?"

"What do you want to do with me?" Damn. My. Mouth.

"It's best if we try not to test our restraint," he murmurs.

Climbing into his lap, I wrap my legs around his waist. "You sure?"

"No, but if we do test it, I'll have time to take you where I wanted to. If we give in, I'm nearly certain we're never leaving this room."

I inhale a shuddering breath. "I don't want to go anywhere."

He groans and kisses me. "Gwen, you have to tell me to stop."

"I don't want you to stop."

Everett's com device chimes from his desk, but he ignores it and flips me onto my back. This time, I don't just play with the hem of my shirt. I twist it in my fingers and take it off, giving Everett a complete view of my black bra. He kneels between my legs, just devouring the sight of me with his eyes.

He trails his fingers up my hips, across my stomach and higher until he reaches my bra. Linking his fingers between the cups, he tugs hard enough to rip the fabric in two, revealing my breasts to him. My body hums with desire, my chest rising and falling as Everett bends down, pressing harder between my legs only to glide his tongue over the curve of my breast and to my nipple, gently sucking it into his mouth.

"You're so beautiful," Everett whispers, gliding his lips to my other breast. "I just want to taste every inch of your skin."

And damn it do I want him to.

I moan as my only response, clutching his head by his hair. I tilt my head back wriggling as he kisses ever so slowly down my stomach until he reaches the waist of my pants and stops. I gasp at the release of the button, arching up so that Everett can tug my pants off me.

He peers down, his handsome, rugged face drinking in every inch of me. Instead of undressing me completely, Everett brings his arm to his mouth and bites down to send blood pooling on his skin. I can't stop myself from sitting up and practically throwing myself at him as the scent of his blood wafts through the air.

He catches me, spinning me so that my back rests to his chest. Lying down with me, he holds me from behind and slides his arm under my neck so that I can drink from him while he hugs me close. He moans, deep and throaty, his voice humming over my skin only to make me suck harder. His erection pokes between my legs, and he rocks against me, just feeling me through my clothes.

His free hand maps my side, grazing across my smooth skin until he slides his fingers into my underwear to touch me in a way that makes me gasp and release his arm. His lips brush my shoulder as he sneaks his now free hand between me and the bed, lifting me up to drag my panties down enough to tease me with his erection without going any further.

"Gwen, you feel so good," he whispers. "Let me face you."

I hum my agreement and roll over. He reaches for the blankets, pulling them around us, and I kiss him deeper, grabbing his stiff as all get-out erection in my hand to rub against my clit, the slickness of my building excitement making it slip back and forth to set me off.

"Gwen," he murmurs. "Let me take care of you. I need to take care of you."

A tap on the door draws Everett's attention, and he closes his eyes for a moment without proceeding.

He kisses me softly with a breath and stretches his neck to glance at the door behind him without moving. "That you, Mik?"

"Yeah, man. Corona just arrived. I caught some of his staff members sneaking to the basketball courts. They said they were supposed to meet you."

"Tell them I'll be there in a bit? Keep track of Corona. He can't know," Everett says.

"I brought them here."

Everett slumps against me and meets my eyes.

"I don't feel like babysitting," Mikkalo adds.

Everett sighs and kisses me softly, pulling himself away. "I'll be right back."

I sit up, wrapping the blankets around me. I watch Everett stroll across the room butt-ass naked, not even attempting to cover up. And damn. He must sense me watching him, because he turns his head and smiles at me, holding his hand up.

I smile back at him, biting my lip between my teeth. "Hurry," I whisper.

Swinging open the door, Everett stiffens, steps back into the room, and slams the door. He spins around and faces me, his eyes widening.

"Gwen, get dressed," he says.

"Huh?"

"Hey, asshole. We don't have all night. This is the first fucking time I've had my freewill for this long, and I'm not wasting it hanging around, waiting for some stupid fuck of a vampire." The familiar voice trickles through the door.

My thudding heart threatens to give out on me. "Kyler?" My voice comes out loud, strong, desperate almost, and I scramble from the bed and rush to the door.

Everett intercepts me, hooking his hand around my waist to lift me off my feet. I thrash and scream, trying to get him to let me go.

"Was that Gwen?" Kyler asks. "What the fuck, Frankie? Why didn't you tell me this was about my sister? You said that—"

"Sister?" Mikkalo asks.

"Kyler!" I yell again.

The sudden confusion and then annoyance in a soft growl from Mikkalo sets me off.

Everett cups my face, getting me to look at him. "Gwen, please. You have to calm down. You can't just go running out there. You're naked," he says, holding me tighter, my body tangled around his.

His words act as an instant pause button, and I freeze in his arms and jerk my head up to meet his blue eyes.

"Ev, what the hell were you thinking?" Mikkalo calls. "Get your ass out here."

Mikkalo cracks the door and catches sight of me in Everett's arms. He immediately slams the door shut. Something crashes, and Mikkalo releases a scary-ass growl. I tense, pushing away from Everett until he sets me on my feet.

"Dude, Kyler. Stop. He's going to kill you if you don't chill out," an unfamiliar voice says. "This is Mr. Royale, part of the coven that controls this region."

"And who's with my sister?" Kyler asks.

"She Blood Matched with Zaire, the coven leader," the guy responds.

"You said we were meeting some guy named Everett."

Mikkalo growls again. "Both of you shut up. Someone is coming."

The world spins as the door to Everett's room opens, and I land on my feet inside the bathroom. I hunch forward, clutching my knees, gasping a breath. Everett relocates me so suddenly that I struggle to orient myself.

And then my stomach heaves, dizziness washing over me.

I throw up, sending dark blood over the floor of the bathroom. Everett swears from the other side of the door.

"Mikkalo, go to Gwen," Everett says. "Take her some clothes."

"What? Why would she need clothes?" my brother asks, his voice rising.

Everett doesn't respond to him but addresses the other guy. "Frankie, what were you thinking? You were supposed to tell me where Kyler was. Not bring him here. I was going to take Gwen to him when I could guarantee it was safe."

"Well, I took the damn opportunity I was given. Now, give me what I asked for."

"You will get what you asked for after Kyler makes it back to Corona unharmed. You jeopardized not only him but my coven," Everett says.

"You fucker."

I heave again at the sound of another crash. A cool hand touches my shoulder, and Mikkalo scoops me up from the floor and strolls with me to the shower, turning it on. He steps inside, keeping his eyes trained on mine even though I'm naked.

I don't move.

I don't speak.

All I can find the will to do is just rest my head on his damp shoulder and wait for my insides to stop tormenting me. Mikkalo draws a washcloth over my face to wipe away whatever blood lingers on me, taking care to clean my skin without making me feel exposed to him. Just tending to me because he cares.

"Gwen, I'm sorry. I didn't recognize Kyler," Mikkalo says, turning off the water. "He looks..."

"Awful?"

He shakes his head. "Well taken care of."

I scowl. "Impossible."

"I've seen some personal donors look on the verge of death. Frail and anemic. Uncleanly. Lifeless. Kyler looks healthy. Fresh clothes, a neat haircut. He's even free from mind manipulation."

"I need to see him myself," I say, trying to remain calm

as Mikkalo wraps me in a giant towel and sits me on the counter.

"In a minute. You have to calm down first."

"I don't want to calm down."

Mikkalo strips from his wet clothes, standing completely naked before me. It's enough to shut me up. Turning his gaze to me, he watches me watch him, but he remains utterly expressionless as he dries off. "If you go charging out there, your brother will think the worst. You have to show him that you're better than okay."

I inhale a long breath. "You're right."

"You also need to remember to watch what you say. You're Zaire's Blood Match," he reminds me.

"Then why am I in this room?" I ask.

He grimaces at me. "Uh..."

"Because I'm sick," I say more to myself. "Everett is my personal health keeper."

A smile lights Mikkalo's face. "Maybe you should be the one in charge of strategy around here."

"Careful what you suggest, Mikkalo."

"What did I tell you before?"

"I could get used to telling you what to do," I tease, hopping off the counter.

"Is that so?"

The bathroom door cracks open, and Everett sneaks inside and shuts it behind him. Silence comes from within the room, and I automatically look to the door and close my eyes, listening for my brother.

"He's waiting, Gwen," Everett says. "But we have to hurry. I got an alert from Bronx calling us to see Corona off in ten minutes, which gives us five now."

Everett helps me slide into a dress, skipping over the undergarments in a state of hurry. I quickly rub a towel through my wet tresses, and glance in the mirror to make sure I don't look as crazy as I feel. Because I'm freaking the hell out. This is the first time I've seen Kyler in person since we've been separated. It's the longest amount of time we've been apart.

Taking another deep breath, I step from the bathroom and search around the room to catch sight of Kyler facing the wall, looking at a small shelf of books. He was always the big reader in our family. The brains to the rest of my brothers' brawns, but books were nearly impossible to come by. If he thought he could get away with it, he'd shove one in his jacket now.

I clear my throat. "Kyler?"

Kyler spins around and faces me. I stare at him as he rushes to cross the room. Mikkalo was right. He does look different. Clean shaven instead of his wild beard, his hair cropped and styled short with product he's probably never used in his life, and his skin looks rosy, glowy almost—not pasty like someone who gives way too much blood.

"Oh, God. Gweny." Kyler envelops me in a bear hug, lifting me off my feet to spin me around.

Two soft growls trickle to me from the bathroom, and I tip my head to look at Mikkalo and Everett hovering in the doorway, looking like they want nothing more than to pull my brother from me to force a few feet of space between us. Their reaction goes unnoticed by Kyler, and he grabs my face in his hands and plants a kiss on the top of my head.

"I can't believe it. You're here," I say. "I was so scared for you. Are you okay?"

Kyler pulls back and tightens his jaw. "It's awful, Gweny. I feel paralyzed in my body. Unable to move or speak half the time. I only get reprieve when guests visit or when Asshole Anderson sleeps and Frankie breaks me from the mind manipulation."

Tears well in my eyes, and I blink hard, trying not to let them fall. He'd whack me upside the head for crying on his behalf because I'm not even the one experiencing such torture. Empathy leaves me weak when I need to be strong.

"Gwen, I fucking swear," he mutters. "Those oncoming tears—"

I press my hand to his mouth and shut him up, slightly afraid that if he did raise his hand to me, Mikkalo or Everett might snap it off without knowing that it's just something we do. I've slapped all of my brothers dozens of times in my life, but from how intently Everett and Mikkalo gaze, they wouldn't understand, and I'm not willing to let Kyler risk it.

"I'm sorry," I whisper. "It's just—I was hoping it wouldn't be so bad."

"What about you?" he asks. "Is your match...like Laredo?"

I lick my lips. "He's better. I haven't even been bitten, Ky." And technically, I'm not lying. Zaire's as good as Laredo. They're both dead.

"But you're with the health keeper," he says, flicking his gaze behind me where I know Everett listens.

"I was feeling sick." I stand up on my tiptoes. "You know why."

"Shit," he whispers.

I hate that I'm lying to him, but I don't know how else to explain it. I never got sick before—except when it came to the blood hunger.

I clutch his shoulders. "But don't worry about it. I can handle myself. You guys trained me well."

Everett clears his throat from behind us, his soft footsteps drawing closer, making Kyler tighten his grip on me. Mikkalo's footsteps sound next, slower, more cautiously, and I realize he's circling the room, probably heading toward the door.

Everett stops close behind me. "Gwen, I know this is difficult, but Mikkalo has to take Kyler back."

My heart clenches in my chest, and I try to pull myself away from my brother. Kyler doesn't let me, spinning me away to cage me against the wall like he knows Everett will drag me from him if given the chance.

"I can't, Gwen. I can't go back," Kyler says.

I suck in a shudder of a breath. "It's going to be okay, Ky. I'm figuring it out. I will get you back."

"Gwen, please. You know our pact. You know what you're supposed to do. You have to do it. I can't go back." Kyler digs his fingers into my shoulders, tilting his head a bit to expose his neck. "I can't do it myself. Every time I try...he's in my head, even when he's not here."

"Fuck," I whisper. "Kyler, please."

"You have to, Gwen. I can't live like this."

His words stab me so sharply that I can't stop my eyes from watering. I release a ragged breath. My brothers and I made a pact when we were teens, when we realized the truth to the state of the world outside the bunker, and we promised each other that if something horrible were to happen, if vampires got into our heads, that we'd...

Ugh. I can't. I can't think the thought.

"Gwen, please tell your brother to release you. We have to go," Mikkalo says. "If we don't return him, it'll cause tension, and we need to be careful with the alliances in our region."

"Gwen, just do it," Kyler begs. "Bite me. Do it as hard as you can where Laredo showed you."

"Ky..."

Mikkalo grabs the back of Kyler's shirt while Everett slides between me and my brother, blocking him from lashing out and trying to snatch me back. Kyler hollers, thrashing in Mikkalo's arms, his whole face twisted in a snarl.

"Gwen! Gwen! Do something!" Kyler shouts.

I take a step forward, pressing my chest into Everett. "Please, you guys. We can't just send him back."

Mikkalo flashes his fangs, set off by Kyler's fighting. "We have to, Gwen. We're not going to risk our region. We're not going to risk you either."

"Please, Mikkalo," I say, my whole body roiling with my oncoming despair.

Everett spins me around and touches my cheeks, quickly swiping away my tears. "I promise you that we'll figure this out. He won't be with the Anderson Coven forever. But we have to send him back. It'll be worse if we don't. Corona will come looking. He'll think he tried to run."

"Gwen, do what I asked. Please!" Kyler yells.

But I can't.

I can't just end his life. He's my brother. My family. And I believe with everything in me that we'll be okay.

Sucking in a breath, I pull away from Everett and close the space to Mikkalo. He holds Kyler tighter to him, and Kyler stops thrashing with my approach. I cup my brother's head in my hands and stand on my tiptoes to plant a kiss to his cheek.

"I need you to be brave, Kyler. I have a plan. You have to trust me."

Kyler stiffens under my words. "Gwen, please. I'm not you. I'm not strong enough."

I pull away, searching his face. "I'm strong because I

have to be. Now so do you."

Everett strolls to the door, meeting the unfamiliar guy in his late twenties, around the same age as Grayson. "I want you to continue to look after him, Frankie. A transfer will be given for not only you, but your family once we come to an agreement in the negotiations."

Frankie nods. "And my reward now?"

Everett walks to his lab table and pulls out two small vials from a drawer. Biting his arm, he drizzles blood into each of them, shocking the hell out of me. Mikkalo too. Mikkalo's wide eyes say everything. Everett must be breaking some sort of rule by handing Frankie one of the vials. Stopping in front of my brother, he tucks the other vial in his pocket.

"Use it wisely," Everett tells him. "And don't get yourself killed."

Mikkalo gets Frankie to jump onto his back while he still clutches Kyler, and the three of them disappear from the room.

Everett closes and locks his door, resting his back on it before sliding to the floor. I stand, shifting on my feet, staring at the drops of blood running down his arm. I don't even know what to say. How to feel. Everything inside me is a jumbled mess.

Getting my legs to kick into action, I close the space to Everett and sit on the ground beside him.

I stare at the side of his face. "I hope you know that

what you did—"

Everett turns to look at me, puffing out his bottom lip in a pout. "I'm sorry, Gwen."

I lace my fingers through his. "You should be." Pulling his arm to my mouth, I glide my tongue over the blood trail, humming softly as it tingles across my tongue. "I mean, do you know how incredibly jealous I am right now? I thought we agreed that you're all mine...including your blood."

His pout pulls up into a smile, and he releases a chuckle. "It won't happen again. Promise."

I slide my arms around him. "And as crazy as this night was...thank you. What you did, what you're trying to do. It means a lot to me."

"Make sure you tell my brothers that," he murmurs. "I can already hear them all charging this way. They're going to kick my ass."

I get to my feet and pull him up to hug him. Trailing my hands lower, I squeeze his ass. "No, they won't."

"Is that so?"

I hum my agreement. "Yup. Because that ass is mine as well."

He laughs and leans in for a kiss. "God, I want this always, Gwen. I know it's been so little time for you, but I just know how great our lives can be together. If I would've been able to apply to Blood Match with you, I know I would have beat everyone."

"You think so?"

He kisses me again. "I know so. You're the perfect match for me."

20

DANGEROUS LINE

I NEVER THOUGHT THERE WAS something scarier than a shouting vampire, but as it turns out, an angry, whispering one is worse. Much worse.

Sitting on the leather couch in Bronx's room, I twirl some spaghetti on my fork, listening to the hushed argument outside the door. Everett was right in his assumption that his brothers would try to kick his ass.

The second they came bursting into Everett's room without even knocking, I also discovered something else I didn't realize. While enraged, whispering vampires are scary—those same fuming, whispering vampires are scared of protective, possessive, feisty blond dhampirs—Jameson's words, not mine.

Let's just say I got my guys to cool off. Apparently, staking a claim on them and telling them if they even dared raise their voices at each other, they'd be in trouble by me worked in my favor. They were too shocked to do anything other than listen to me, so now here I am, eating the delicious spaghetti Jameson made me while they all whisper in the hall.

I clear my throat and set my fork down. "You have two more minutes. I'm almost done eating."

"Damn," Mikkalo whispers. "I wish it was my time."

"I might be willing to trade," Bronx says, releasing a low groan. "Whatever gives me more time to—"

"Don't you even think about it, Bronx," I say. "You can't just swap days because you're afraid to face me."

Bronx groans again. "Damn it, dandelion. I'm not afraid to face you. I just—"

"Then come in here and prove it," I say.

The door to Bronx's room swings open, and he steps inside, crossing his arms over his broad chest. His attempt to intimidate me with his overly broody, moody face works, and my dumb mouth chooses now to quiver.

Now that's one way to soften one hard expression.

Bronx closes the space to me, leaving his brothers in the hallway, just gazing at the two of us. They won't come in unless invited, a rule I thought was fair enough, but I don't speak up to tell them it's okay for them to come in. Now might not be the best time to test exactly what I have control over.

Plopping down beside me, Bronx leans his elbows on his knees and finally looks at his brothers. "I need ten minutes with Gwen. Go pack your bags. I'll call you when we're ready."

Jameson closes the door, and I listen to the three of them scatter as they head to their suites. Bronx shifts his legs, touching his knees to mine with what looks like a dozen thoughts flickering across his face.

"Are you leaving again?" I ask, taking his hand.

He squeezes my fingers, leaning in even closer, silently begging for my attention without asking. I react to his quiet need and swing my legs over his, hugging my arm around his muscular back while still holding his fingers. Closing his eyes, he just breathes a few deep breaths like sitting with me, feeling my arms around him, is all he needs to relax.

He finally opens his eyes to meet my gaze. "We're all leaving. Just for a night or two."

"Oh."

"You're coming with us," he says, answering my silent question.

"I am?"

Bronx scoots me completely onto his lap. It's like whatever awkward, infuriating shit that happened between us when he dropped me off with Jameson is long forgotten. And I'm grateful. I know certain vampires can't let things go—my previous blood source before Laredo was definitely one of them. "Yes. I don't feel comfortable leaving you here with the four of us having to go to the city."

"You think I'll try to escape?" I rest my head on his shoulder without meeting his gaze. I can't blame him if that's the reason.

Reaching his arm around me, he touches my cheek, getting me to look up. "Should I be worried? That thought didn't cross my mind after everything..." His voice trails off. He rubs his lips together. "I know we're still trying to figure things out and all, and it's been an adjustment, but I thought you liked it here."

"I do," I'm quick to say. "More than I ever imagined. I just thought you might think I would try to leave because of who I am. What I am."

He releases a soft chuckle. "If anything, I'd think that would be your one reason to stay with us being your food source and all."

I grimace. "It's not like that, Bronx. Yeah, I need vampire blood to survive, but I don't know. I'm not sticking around because some of you will let me devour you."

"Definitely Jameson," he says, his serious face breaking into a smile. "Don't tell him I told you this, but he begged the rest of us to let him continue to feed you even if you don't pick him to fulfill your Blood Match contract."

My whole body explodes in heat at the thought, and I totally squirm a little too much, turning Bronx on in the process. How he manages to keep a straight face with me sitting on top of his boner? I nearly ask him.

"I guess it's good to have a backup, huh?" he teases, his dark eyes lighting with a smile even though his lips remain firm.

"Considering the odds of the rest of you forgetting to feed me? I'd say yeah." I grin as I say the words, teasing him right back.

"Hey, I never really had forgotten..."

I snap my teeth at him. "You're just scared to do so with me."

"Not scared. Cautious."

Leaning in, I can't stop myself from meeting my mouth to his. I suck in his bottom lip between my teeth and bite only hard enough to get a reaction out of him. His heartbeat thrashes wildly, his hands tightening around me, but he doesn't attempt to pull back.

I release his bottom lip and then flick my tongue over it. "Admit it. You're scared of this wild beast."

"Careful, dandelion. We only have a couple of minutes, and it's not enough time to prove that I'm not." His comment digs under my skin in a good way, and I bow my head against his, trying to catch my sudden panting breath. My attempt to tease him totally backfired. I know it. He knows it. But neither of us will acknowledge it.

Shifting my weight, he hooks his arm around my ass and stands up with me in his arms. I've never been carried so much in my life compared to the last couple of days. I don't know if it's because I move too slowly or what, but I'm not going to complain. Who knew Bronx's hard-ass muscles could still feel comfortable as they wrap around me?

Sitting me on the edge of his bed, he reaches for a thermos on the nightstand, one that looks like the one he had the other night when he drank blood in front of me, and I can't stop myself from frowning.

"What? You just mentioned that I have trouble re-membering to feed you. I'm showing you that I'm plenty capable. I'm completely prepared." He grins at me, handing me the thermos. "You drink and relax. I'll pack our bags."

I twist open the thermos and bring it to my nose, sniff-ing its contents. Bronx watches me from just inside the wardrobe where he unzips a duffle bag.

"This isn't your blood," I say, dipping my index finger into the warm liquid to bring to my mouth for a small taste. "It's none of your brothers' either. Whose is it?"

Bronx grabs a few shirts off their hangers and folds them neatly into his bag. That seems like an excessive amount for only a day or two in the city, but I don't say that. Maybe he expects to get dirty. I don't even know why we're going. "The Royale blood supply, mixed just for you. Does it taste okay?"

I take an actual sip and close my eyes, letting the mixture of all four of their blood coat my tongue before I swallow. "It's good. Not as good as if I drink yours alone, but I understand why you don't want me to."

His eyes flash silver at my words. "I can promise we'd never leave this room if you did, and we have things to do."

I grin at him. "Yeah, sure. Whatever you say."

"You're teasing a dangerous line, dandelion," he says, his voice low.

Drinking a long sip of blood, I gaze at him while doing so, taking up his dare to participate in his staring contest. His arms flex as he curls and uncurls his fingers, his broad shoulders straight, his chest slowly rising and falling with his breaths.

I gulp until the thermos is empty and then run my finger along the rim to clean the side and pop it in my mouth, slowly pulling it out. Bronx's fangs peek from beneath his lips, and I set the thermos on the night table without breaking eye contact. Leaning back on my elbows, I smile and shift, uncrossing and then crossing my legs again.

Bronx disappears from the wardrobe only to materialize next to me. He stands at the end of the bed, sweeping his gaze across my body, desire burning silver in his dark eyes. I can't stop myself from smirking at him. Locking his fingers to my ankles, he tugs me so quickly to him that I can't stop myself from screeching and then laughing as I find myself sitting on the edge of the bed with him kneeling between my legs.

He runs his finger along my jaw, combing my hair from my face. "You love torturing me, don't you?"

"And teasing this so-called dangerous line."

Bronx releases a soft, husky noise from his throat, leaning closer. I can tell how much he wants to kiss me, but I don't let him. Instead, I press my hands to his chest and smile.

"Careful, Bronx. I'm still hungry," I say. "And I don't know if I've told you this, but you're fucking delicious."

He disappears from between my legs, leaving me in a state of buzzing desire. I don't know what has gotten into me, but Bronx might be right. I do love teasing danger. I like it a lot. He's far more reserved than his brothers, though he'd never admit it.

Sliding off the bed, I pad my way toward the wardrobe, listening to Bronx continue to pack his bag. I stick my head in and stare at him holding up two pieces of my lingerie before he sets them back in the top drawer. He doesn't meet my gaze, deciding just to grab handfuls of my clothing to pile in another bag.

I close the space and touch his shoulder. "I'm sorry. I didn't mean to get carried away."

He stops what he's doing. "I know."

"If I'm too much to deal with, you can always swap days. I was only teasing you earlier," I add. "Though I don't want you to. I wasn't kidding about missing you and your infuriating intensity."

"Gwen." He groans, lacing his fingers behind his head.

I grimace at the way he says my name and wonder if I might have read too much into this. He claimed he liked me, but maybe I just like him more.

He's quiet for a long moment, just staring past me at the hanging clothes. "What are we doing?" he whispers, still not looking at me. I don't have to ask him to know that the comment was meant for himself. He's still not used to the fact that I can hear him.

Closing the space, I hug my arms around him and nudge him with me until he sits down on the bench at the end of the closet.

"Bronx, what is it?" I ask, speaking first because I'm not so sure he will say anything. "What's the matter? Did I do something wrong? You tease me and then push me away. One moment you devour my attention, and in the next, you want nothing to do with me. One of your brothers said you were going to back out and not give me the option to pick you, you know. If that's what you want...you need to tell me now."

He releases a breathless laugh. "Fucking Jameson. He has such a big mouth."

"So is that it? Because I like you. I have this crazy, unexplainable attraction to you, Bronx." I inhale a small breath, trying to suppress the strange ache squeezing my heart. "I thought you felt the same."

Jerking his head up, he finally meets my gaze. "I do,

dandelion. You've managed to get under my skin and in my mind in the worst and best way possible. I want nothing more than to just—I can't. I can't even say it. I know better."

"Is this because I'm a donor?" I ask. "I know you've never been—"

His eyes flash silver. "No. And you're not a donor, Gwen. Not to me. It's just, what we're doing is crazy. Maybe with other covens it would be different, but something about you...I'm afraid of what will happen when you do decide. I don't want to lose what I have with my brothers—our coven."

Sadness washes over me as he admits his feelings.

"That's the reason I considered backing out. But the stubborn, out-of-control part of me that you love to tease just can't do it. Because I don't want to give up what I feel for you."

"Oh," I say softly. A dozen emotions explode through me at his words.

He rests his hand on mine. "Come on. We're running late already. You make it too easy to forget the world outside."

I want to grip his hands and to ask him to stay. I want so badly to tell him that this whole situation sucks. That I don't want anyone getting hurt nor do I want Bronx to feel like he'll lose something he has with his brothers...or me for that matter.

Bronx doesn't give me the chance to stop him from getting up. Strolling to my part of the closet, he pulls out a few articles of clothing—all in black—and holds the pieces out for me.

"I need you to wear this," he murmurs, keeping his gaze trained on the floor. "Your hair needs to be pinned up as well."

I tilt my head as I look at the ensemble. "That's a bit much. I don't even know where to start."

"Here, I can help you if you'd like."

I give him a once-over and bob my head, hooking my fingers to the hem of my dress to pull it off. He inhales a soft breath at the sight of me in only a bra and thong—sheer lace and soft cotton from the collection Everett had for me in his room.

Reaching forward, he gently turns me around and combs my cascading hair from my back to push it to my shoulders. I shiver as he unhooks my bra, taking just a second to run his fingers over my skin.

"This won't protect you from the strength of a vampire, but it'll lessen any damage if you're attacked," Bronx says, holding some sort of body armor made from thick yet breathable material a Blood Rebel would probably kill to get their hands on. "You can't wear anything underneath or it won't properly compress if you get hurt."

"Okay." My voice comes out as a whisper as he helps me pull it over my head and fastens the clips that stretch the fabric tightly against my chest, smooshing my boobs.

"Here are the bottoms."

"So, I have to lose the thong?" I ask, shifting to look over my shoulder.

"I can step out."

"I'm fine. Not exactly the reason I want to undress for you..." I let my words trail off at his silence and step out of my panties.

"You love torturing me," he murmurs.

I step into the pants made from the same material and turn to face him with a smile. "I'm nearly certain you like it."

His eyes flash silver, proving my point. "I can think of a few other things I might like more."

After helping me slip into a long-sleeved, high neck black shirt that connects to the slim-legged black pants with a complicated belt with built-in sheaths for various weapons, Bronx waits for me to tie my hair into a bun at the nape of my neck before tugging a weird-ass cap onto my head. He hooks the long flaps that cover my ears into the shirt neck to assure that none of my skin apart from my face shows.

As a Blood Rebel, I've always worn quite a few clothes and never showed off more skin than I had to, but this seems excessive. Even the boots lace up to my knees with a steel toe that can most definitely send any asshole vampire to the ground with the force of my kick.

Bronx slides a few weapons into the belt and nods his approval. "Perfect."

"Perfect for what? Battle?" I ask.

He chuckles. "Dandelion, as much as I want to take you into the city and show your cute little ass off, I kind of need to make sure no one realizes who you are. You're coming with us as part of our daylight staff."

I raise my eyebrows. "Because I'm supposed to be here with Zaire?"

"Exactly. As first in line, I must handle a couple of grievances in the city brought to my attention by one of the local coven leaders."

"My brother's Blood Match?" I ask.

He tightens his jaw and nods. "Hopefully not for long."

I turn my gaze to him. "What do you mean?"

A knock on the bedroom door draws our attention away from each other, and Mikkalo says, "Hey, we're ready when you are. Going to have to rush if you take any longer. You want to just meet us there in the evening?"

"No, we're coming," Bronx says, not giving me a chance to plead with him to say yes.

I want more time to ask him all my questions. He must sense my spinning thoughts because he adjusts me in his arms, allowing me to wrap my legs around his waist. He tosses our bags to Mikkalo, and I spot Everett and Jameson waiting a few feet down the hallway.

Bringing his lips to mine, he kisses me softly in front of

his brothers. "We'll talk more in the car," Bronx says.

"Promise?"

"Promise."

I wiggle my fingers at his brothers as they follow us down the hallway to the stairs that'll take us to the ground level. "You guys look hot," I say, noticing they're all wearing suits.

"And you look..." Jameson crinkles his nose at me, letting his voice trail off.

"Overdressed?" I ask.

"Never thought so many clothes could look so sexy," Everett says.

I laugh.

Jameson flashes his fangs at me. "He's only saying that because we're all imagining how much fun the uniform would be to rip off."

I wag my finger at him. "It's unfortunate it's not your night. Don't you dare ask Bronx about it either."

"Damn it," Mikkalo says. "You sure no trading time?"

"You heard our girl earlier," Bronx says, his hard features lighting with something more playful than I've seen on him. "I'm stuck."

"He says it's torture," I tease.

Mikkalo howls a laugh. "Double damn. Bronx likes that kind of shit."

I beam him a teasing smile. "I'm nearly certain you might too, Mikkalo."

He shrugs. "Only one way to find out."

"You still have forty-eight hours," Jameson says.

"But I technically have thirty minutes left." Everett playfully punches Bronx's arm. "So hand our girl over, Bronx."

Bronx eases back and grins at me. "He's right, dandelion. Ev, catch."

I screech as he tosses me to Everett, who plants his mouth to mine in a long kiss that steals the noise from my lips and leaves me breathless. I pat his chest and lean back to fake-glare at Bronx. "You're in so much trouble for doing that."

"What's his punishment, Gigi?" Jameson asks.

"We're always down to help," Mikkalo adds.

I smile at the four of them. "I think I have something in mind."

Bronx raises his eyebrows. "No biting."

"It's worse," I say, snapping my teeth.

"Uh-oh. I have a feeling we're not going to like this," Jameson says, flashing his fangs at me.

I shrug and smile wider. "Maybe not. Your punishment is letting me be the one to drive."

21

REBEL VAMPIRES

"DAMN, DANDELION. ARE YOU ON a mission to hit everything in our way?" Bronx braces himself against the dashboard.

"You drive like Jameson," Mikkalo says, leaning his head between the seats.

"I'll let you suck my neck if you actually hit the next fucker," Jameson says.

Everett hooks his hands to my shoulders even though he assured my seat restraints were firmly in place when Bronx flicked off the autopilot. "Don't instigate her. If she crashes, she could get hurt."

"I'm not gonna let that happen," Bronx says, fully prepared to take over.

"To your right, Gigi!" Jameson calls.

I jerk the wheel, and everyone braces as to not slide around the car since I'm the only one buckled in. Stomping the throttle, I send the car barreling forward toward a vampire just minding his own business.

He spins at the flash of the headlights and darts out of the way, leaving about twenty feet of space between us and a wall. Bronx swears and hits a few buttons on the dash. The brakes and steering wheel lock up as the car screeches to a halt only to turn and drive itself back to the street.

"Damn it," Jameson and I say in unison. We both laugh.

"All right, Gwen. I think we've been punished enough." Bronx quickly unfastens my restraints. "We're coming up to Night Shadow Drive. You can't be seen behind the wheel."

I pout, not moving from the driver's seat. The whole no donors allowed to operate vehicles law is the lamest ever. I mean, shadow vampires are fast as hell. I don't think I could actually hit one.

Bronx reaches out and pokes my bottom lip. "I promise you can drive most of the way back."

"Fuck," Mikkalo says.

I swivel in my seat and look at him sitting between

Jameson and Everett. "I'm not that bad."

He smirks at me. "It's not that."

"Mik's jealous, Gwen," Everett says. "Bronx never lets anyone drive him."

Grinning, I turn back to Bronx. "Is that true?"

He shrugs, keeping his face straight for a minute before smirking at me. "I guess I'm a glutton for your kind of punishment."

"Well, I'm happy for it," Everett says, reaching forward to hit a button on the side of my seat, sending it falling back. Hooking his fingers to my sides, he tugs me from behind the wheel and onto his lap. He brushes his lips to my ear. "I love seeing you smile like crazy."

"That laugh too." Mikkalo grabs my legs adjusting me so that I sprawl across him and Jameson.

"The best. Those fucking snorts. Hilarious. That's how you really know she thinks something is funny." Jameson clutches my feet to stop me from attempting to give him a little kick.

He laughs and scrunches his nose before Mikkalo swings his hand out and clocks him in the chest for me. Jameson heaves a breath and sticks his tongue out at me.

I fake-glare at him. "You just wait."

"I don't know if I can," Jameson responds, releasing a playful growl.

"Well, you're going to have to," Bronx says, his once light voice turning deep and serious. He swivels in the seat, now behind the wheel, as the car drives closer and closer to the tower I wish with everything in me that we didn't have to return to. When Bronx said we were going to their headquarters, I didn't realize it was at the Blood Match Center, but I guess the top couple floors belong to their coven, and it's where they stay when they come to Crimson Vista. "Remember, hands off Gwen. Treat her as you would any other staff."

"Hardest order of my life," Everett whispers into my ear. "One more kiss?"

I shift and graze my lips to his, sinking into him as he tightens his arms around me. I know our time together really ignited whatever attraction we had between us full force. If Mikkalo hadn't had shown up with my brother, I know I would have had sex with him. Just the way he made my body sing...

He hums into my mouth, trying to pull away from me as I take our sweet kiss to passionate, drawing silence from his brothers. It makes me blush like hell, and I detach myself and rest my head on Everett's shoulder.

"You guys, I'm sorry," I murmur. "I don't know what's up with me. It's like I can't control myself."

Bronx clears his throat. "You don't need to apologize. We discussed this, remember?"

I nod. Because it was my biggest thing—not wanting to feel like I did something wrong by giving my attention or affection freely to whomever or whenever I wanted without having to worry about making anyone jealous. "I know. It's just—I'd like to kiss all of you. If that's okay."

Everett kisses me softly once more. "Fine by me."

"I wouldn't deny you," Mikkalo says.

I lean forward and meet Mikkalo's smiling mouth, brushing my lips to his. He rubs his fingers over my leg, sending tingles through me. I hum and ease back but then meet him once more with a tease of a kiss.

"Jamie? Can I kiss you too?" I ask, licking my lips.

"You don't have to ask me. I'm down for whatever," Jameson says, wiggling his fingers to me so that I slide off Everett and onto Mikkalo until I can play lapsies with Jameson. He obviously loves it a little too much with his hard on flexing under my ass as he tries to get a reaction out of me. I nip his lip, making him do it again, and then I break away and giggle, patting his chest.

"You're so bad," I say.

"And you're way too fun to tease."

I swivel on his legs to face Bronx, who trains his eyes on the road ahead. "Bronx?"

Turning in his seat, he finally meets my gaze. "You'll be able to kiss me all you want when we get to our suite."

I swallow my disappointment. "Oh."

He sighs. "I'm sorry, Gwen. I didn't mean that I don't want you to kiss me now, but I don't want you to feel like you have to because you want to be fair. It's going to end up not being fair, and some of us need to get used to it."

My chest tightens at his words, and I turn to look out the window as the car comes to a halt. My stomach clenches, my emotions suddenly turning wild. What's wrong with me? My brothers would kick my ass if they knew it pains me, makes it hard even to breathe, thinking about hurting any of them—and not only that but hurting myself. This is so fucking crazy. It goes against everything I was raised to be.

But the Royale brothers aren't like the vampires I grew up fighting. Grew up fearing.

They make me feel like I'm not a donor.

They make me feel exactly as I should—powerful. Equal. On their level.

Before I realize what's happening, my body kicks into action. I shove Jameson against the seat and fly from the car, nearly eating shit on the pavement. I make a mad dash for the building, needing to get as much space as I can between us. If I don't...I don't know.

"Fuck, Mikkalo. Stop her," Bronx says.

Something whacks me right in the chest, knocking the wind from me. Four deep-ass growls sound through the air, but I can't see my guys. I can barely see the world above me, my vision shadowing as I open and close my mouth, unable to breathe.

A strange vampire hoists me to my feet, dangling me in front of him. "Where is your night pass?"

Swinging out, I slap the vampire across the face.

"Mr. Sur, release her," Bronx says from somewhere close behind me. "She doesn't need a night pass. She is here with me."

"She was running alone. It is my right to punish unescorted donors how I see fit," Mr. Sur says, flashing his fangs. "If you cannot keep your household staff in line, it is in the law to let me do so. You may have her back when I'm through."

I squeeze my eyes shut, my whole body tensing. "Please, no!"

"Fight and I'll make it hurt."

Hands lock onto me, ripping me free from Mr. Sur, and three figures blur, flying at the vampire. A big hand cradles my head, gently pressing my face against a hard chest, and I inhale a soft breath of Bronx's familiar scent. Wind whips around me, making my eyes water, and the temperature turns from cool to warm as Bronx rushes me into the quiet building.

"What were you thinking?" Bronx asks, his deep voice laced with anger. "I told you, Gwen. Stay close. Keep your gaze to the ground. Don't fight back."

"I—I'm sorry," I say, my voice hitching.

Bronx suddenly sets me down in the middle of a grand room with a view of the sprawling city behind tinted glass. "You could've been hurt."

Bending forward, I clutch my knees, trying to orient myself to the fast as hell relocation. I didn't even know we went up the stairs.

He releases a deep growl. "You could've been killed."

"I'm sorry," I whisper again.

"Have you been playing with us this whole time, Gwen?" he asks, lacing his fingers behind his head.

Fury rushes over me at his words. Striding closer, I grab his shoulder and spin him around to face me. I jab my finger into his chest, glowering. I can't believe he even suggested such a thing. I can't believe the thought crossed his mind.

"How could you ask me something like that?" My voice quivers no matter how hard I try to keep it strong.

His dark eyes flash silver. "Because you tried to kiss all of us, making us believe we had a chance with you, but then the second you got your chance to escape, you ran. You were willing to risk your life to get away. So, yes, I'm asking you now if all of this was some kind of game to you."

"Bronx," Jameson snaps from the doorway.

"Go to your rooms, brothers. I'm handling Gwen," Bronx says, his face hard and cold, his eyes practically penetrating me to pierce my heart.

Jameson growls. "No. She's our girl."

Mikkalo locks his hand to Jameson's shoulder, stopping him from rushing Bronx, but he, Everett, and Jameson still enter the room, letting the door close behind them.

"Can't you see? She's not *our* girl," Bronx says. "I knew this whole thing was crazy."

"Of course it's crazy!" I shout.

"What did I say?" Bronx asks his brothers.

Flying at Bronx, I surprise the hell out of him by knocking him off his feet and landing on top of him. I snatch his wrists and pin him down, my chest heaving, my heart aching. Tears escape my eyes and splash across his cheeks, making him freeze. The anger flashing silver in his eyes disappears until all I can see is the reflection of my own silver eyes, blinking back at me.

"I wasn't suggesting this situation was crazy because of some game you think I'm playing." I bow my head, squeezing my eyes shut to get my tears under control without letting him go. "It's crazy because you guys think I'm going to be capable of choosing between you. I don't want to be unfair to any of you. I can't explain it, but I just—you're my guys. Mine."

"Gwen," Bronx says softly. "Your contract—"

"I don't fucking care! Don't make me do this. I can't do this. I won't. I will not be responsible for hurting any of you. I'm not doing it. I want you all too much. Equally. Even when you say idiotic shit and accuse me of betraying you—of playing games with you."

I release Bronx and roll off of him to curl in on myself. A soft hand touches my back as Jameson sits on the floor next to me.

Mikkalo joins him, grazing his fingers over my legs in soothing strokes. Everett takes the spot at my head and gently unfastens the ugly hat from my head and loosens my bun, combing his fingers through my hair.

Big fingers slide into mine, and Bronx pulls my hands away from my chest to hug against his. "Gwen, I'm sorry. I'm an asshole and a dumbass. I just—when you fled the car, it scared the shit out of me. I thought we were going to lose you, and I could only think the worst as to why you'd put us in that position. If something happened to you..." He closes his eyes.

"The whole fucking world would be in trouble," Jameson says. "You should've seen Mikkalo with Ken Sur. Demoted and damned to the shadows."

"He was lucky he wasn't defanged," Mikkalo says.

"Or killed," Everett adds. He gently gets me to roll over. "Are you okay, Gwen? Did he hurt you?"

"I'm probably already getting a bruise on my chest," I say. "Or it could be...this hurting me."

"I'm sorry," Bronx says again, bringing my hands to his mouth to kiss.

I bob my head. "I know. And I'm sorry too. I didn't mean to scare you. I just—I acted without thinking. And now, I'm exhausted. If you guys don't mind, I'd like something to eat and then go to bed." Because I need space to think. To breathe. To get my heart to stop hurting.

"Can I feed you, Gigi?" Jameson asks, rubbing his hand up and down the length of my back.

I shrug and look at Bronx. With the oncoming sun, it's

his time now.

He nods to his brother. "I think that's a good idea. Why don't you take Gwen to the bedroom and help her get settled? If she's hurt, call for Everett."

Jameson scoops me from the ground and cradles me in his arms. "I'm so fucking excited to rip these damn clothes off you."

I shake my head and release a laugh. "Whatever gets me in my PJs the fastest."

"Don't get carried away, Jameson," Bronx says, keeping his voice soft. "As soon as Gwen is comfortable, the four of us need to talk."

A solid body molds perfectly to mine, hugging me from behind. Bronx's soft breath tickles my shoulder before his soft lips brush my skin. Shifting, I slide my fingers through his and pull his muscular arms tighter around me until I can rest my cheek on his fingers. The scent of his skin sends fire through my belly, and I can't stop myself from gently sucking on the skin of his wrist.

"No teeth, dandelion," Bronx whispers, rolling me on top of him so that I lie flat on his chest to stare up at the ceiling. "I have a thermos if you're hungry."

I groan and flip over, straddling his waist between my thighs. Bronx's morning wood flexes against me, feeling just as hard as the rest of his muscles. I suck in a small breath and stare into his dark eyes.

I bend down to kiss him. "That's no fun."

He hums, tightening his hold on me, squeezing my ass to rock me against him. "I want to, Gwen. More than anything. But I don't trust myself not to get carried away, especially with my brothers in the same room. I want things to be better than this. After what you said last night..."

I compose myself and roll off him. "I don't want to talk about it. It's just—I like the way things are now."

"But we should talk about it, Gigi," Jameson says, shifting the bed as he sits on my other side.

I open my eyes and stare up at him, silhouetted in shadows in the dark room with only a streak of light coming in through a crack in the curtains covering the tinted glass windows. Reaching out, I rest my hand on his knee, curling closer to him. The bed shifts again, and Mikkalo touches my leg from above the blanket as he sits at the end. Everett touches my cheek, drawing my attention to him. He climbs next to Jameson and offers me a thermos with what I can already tell is a mixture of all four of their blood. Bronx slides his arms around me and eases me upright and between his legs so that I rest against him.

I bring the thermos to my lips and drink as all of them watch me with anticipation. The sweet mixture floods my mouth and sends tingles across my tongue. It takes everything in me not to chug it, and I force myself to pull the thermos away from my mouth to lick my lips.

"Good?" Bronx asks, resting his chin on my shoulder.

I nod my head. "Would be better if you guys would join me or something."

"You offering?" Jameson teases, shaking my leg. "Because after that claim on us last night, there is no fucking way I'm going to ever drink someone else's blood in front of you. I won't risk you getting jealous."

"Jealous?" I ask. "Yeah, okay. Sure."

He meets my smirk with his own. "I can prove it. You're half vampire, Gigi. Blood exchanges turn personal. Why do you think your brothers always provided blood to Laredo?"

"So I didn't have to."

"Because you'd have grown too close."

Bronx rubs his fingers along my stomach. "Enough, Jameson. We already agreed not to ask Gwen to do this. She couldn't even provide enough blood to sustain all of us. Daring her even to try could put her health at risk, right Ev?"

Everett rubs the scruff on his chin. "I don't know. Gwen's different. A human who drinks vampire blood heals faster, but Gwen's sternum bruising has already healed completely. She regenerates like us, just a little slower."

Mikkalo tightens his jaw, and I can tell just thinking about Mr. Sur pisses him off. "But not as fast as it would have on us."

I raise my hands up. "Okay, you guys. I'm going to

stop you all before you get ahead of yourselves. Even if I heal quickly and could provide blood for all of you...you'd have to bite me, and—"

Everett smirks at me. "We wouldn't."

My body chooses now to react, and I sink my fingers into Bronx's thighs. But not in fear. Why the hell does the idea of letting them taste my blood turn me on? I squirm and shift, drawing my legs to me. Then I distract myself by chugging the whole damn thermos.

Jameson chuckles. "Uh-oh. I know that look."

"Leave her alone," Bronx says. "Gwen, don't let him try to tease you into doing something you're uncomfortable with."

"What are you talking about? Gigi loves the idea," Jameson says.

I shiver and wiggle more, causing Bronx to lock me in place to stop me from continuing to rub the small of my back against his raging boner. "This is crazy," I whisper.

"See?" Bronx says.

Mikkalo chuckles. "She's saying it's crazy because Jameson is right. Look at her face. Fuck, I need to get out of here."

Jerking my hand out, I grab onto Mikkalo's leg, stopping him from getting up. "Wait...I want to do this. I mean, if Everett thinks it's safe and does the whole blood draw thing."

"Let us give you more of our blood first. Just in case. I

mean, if you really want to try." Everett leans closer. "You know I haven't been able to get the taste of you off my mind."

Goosebumps prickle over my skin at the memory of him accidentally poking my tongue with is fang during the most passionate, hot kiss.

"Shit, what did you whisper to her?" Jameson asks. "I need her to react to me like that."

Everett kisses my cheek without looking at his brother. He ignores his comment completely and says, "Fill up her thermos."

Bronx releases a small groan. "Wait, Ev. I know the four of us talked last night, but we need to talk to Gwen first."

His words pull me from my sudden desire aroused by the idea of this little blood exchange. Silence draws between the five of us, and I sit up straighter and scoot out from Bronx's legs to sit between him and Mikkalo.

"What do you want to talk about?" I ask, managing to find my voice even under all their hot intensity burning over me. I'm surprised my clothes haven't vaporized yet, considering Bronx only grabbed me tiny nighties in his rush to pack.

Bronx clears his throat when his brothers look to him. "Last night."

I lick my lips. "Oh, I said I was sor—"

"Not that, dandelion." Bronx takes my hand in his.

"What you said after."

Mikkalo slides his fingers through my other hand. "About how you didn't want to be in the position to choose."

"Yeah, because...it's not fair. I like and enjoy being with all of you. The thought of hurting you kills me, and you all want me to pick you to take my contract. One I shouldn't even have in the first place."

"You're right," Bronx says. "And I'm sorry for that."

"We're all sorry, Gigi," Jameson says. "The last thing I wanted to do was hurt you or make you unhappy. You've been fucking amazing to me. I've never talked so much to anyone in my life."

I touch him with my foot. "I seriously look forward to all the blanket mansions with you."

"Admit it. You just want the chance to suck my neck," he teases.

I blush. "That too."

Jameson reaches out to me and touches my chin, getting me to meet his green eyes. "And that's why I'm fine with your decision not to pick between us."

My brows furrow.

"He's right, Gwen," Everett says. "I can't suppress this innate desire to care for you...in every way you want and need. I don't want you to pick either. You give me so much attention that I don't even feel jealous. All I feel is anticipation—I've never looked forward to anything in my life like I do now waiting for my next day with you. It doesn't bother me that you like my brothers."

"Except when someone thought you were some badass spy trying to ruin our region," Jameson says, knocking his knuckles to Mikkalo.

Mikkalo scrunches his face. "I've never been so nervous of someone in my life. Our girl is such a fucking badass. I can't wait to see what else she's got."

"You want to train with me?" I ask, smiling. "You sure that's a good idea?"

He slides his hand around my back. "Hell yeah. I've never met someone as fearless, strategic, smart, and all around as fierce as you. I feel like you can teach me a thing or two. Help assure our region is safe and secure."

"As long as I don't have to watch any of those crazy-ass security feeds," I tease.

"Ah, come on, dandelion. You know you like those kinds of videos," Bronx says.

I tip my head to the ceiling and laugh. "Maybe if there was some kind of plot like..." I blush, thinking of our first real morning together after I stole his bed though he refused to give it up.

"Shit," Mikkalo says. "She's going to get all sorts of ideas..."

I stick my tongue out at him. "You know you look forward to it. There might be some baths involved after."

Bronx chuckles and brings my hand to his mouth to

kiss. "I know I do...if you're okay with this."

"With what exactly?" They keep saying they're okay if I don't pick, but I need to know what it means.

My heart flutters at the sudden silence that draws between the five of us. I turn my attention to each of them, drinking in their various expressions. Mikkalo remains tight-jawed, nervous almost. Everett smiles softly while he strokes my leg. Jameson's anticipation matches mine, his heart beating wildly. And Bronx? He looks a bit afraid. Not of me, but of what he's about to say.

"Are you guys deciding for me?" I ask, wondering if that's why we sit here together with each of them telling me that they don't want me to choose but also want to be with me.

"No," Bronx says. "That would still be unfair."

Jameson squeezes my foot. "So we agreed to fight to the death."

My eyes widen.

He jerks his head back and laughs until Everett rams his hand into his chest and sends him backward off the bed. Jameson heaves, but then laughs again, darting behind me to climb onto the bed next to me.

He kisses my cheek. "Sorry, Gigi. I couldn't resist. That reaction of yours...pretty sure I'll never have even a small argument with my brothers again. Can't upset our girl now."

"If you agree," Bronx says. "Because we all don't want

to give you up or make you choose between us."

I blink a few times. "I—I don't understand. The contract—"

"Like you said. Fuck the contract," Bronx says with a smile.

"What about everything with Zaire?" I ask. "Don't you have to report his death?"

"Not as long as we can keep everything in our region in order," Bronx says.

"So, this means I can be with all of you?" I need to hear them say it again. I need to make sure I'm not just imagining things.

"In any way you choose," Everett says. "No obligations. No stressing. Just you and us together. Our girl."

"Are you sure?" I stare at the blankets between us, my heart crashing out of control. "This is so crazy."

"We all know it," Jameson says.

I swing my gaze to each of them. "You'll be my guys."

"Damn straight, dandelion," Bronx says.

I lick my lips and nod. "Okay then. No choosing. No contracts."

Mikkalo smiles at me. "Claimed by all of us."

Claimed. Hell, what am I getting myself into? Apparently something I really, really love the thought of because I nod my head. "Okay. Claimed by all of you."

"And us claimed by you," Jameson says, flashing his fangs. "Kind of funny. I never knew I'd be a rebel vampire."

"We might have to be," Bronx says.

"I don't care regardless." Everett stretches forward to take my hand. "I'm pretty dead-set on doing anything for Gwen."

Mikkalo nods. "Yeah, we'll do whatever it takes to make this work."

22.

VISITATION

"OUR GIRL JUST TURNED ME into a blood snob," Jameson says, kissing the spot on my arm Everett extracted blood from. "I mean it, Gigi. I'd rather starve than swallow another ounce of gen. pop. blood again in my life."

Everett grabs me by my ankles and drags me to him only to lie back and set me on his chest with my knees digging into his shoulders. "I can't wait to taste the rest of her."

My whole body reacts to Everett's words, and I intake a small breath. Hooking his fingers to my hips, he tugs me forward to see how far I'll let him pull until I'm only an inch from practically sitting on his face.

I bend down and press my index finger to his mouth. "Don't you guys have somewhere to be?"

"Yeah," Bronx says from his place strapping weapons to his body. "So save that for your night."

Everett chuckles and slides me off of him. "A couple of minutes is long enough for just a taste."

"And to leave her sexually frustrated," Mikkalo says, whacking Everett on the leg.

I cover my face with my hands, inwardly groaning but trying not to react to their teasing. They make this all sound so normal. And I guess it will be.

Everett brings his lips to my ears. "That's what he thinks."

"Shit," I whisper under my breath.

"You two knock it off. I need your heads clear for the extraction. If we fuck this up, Corona won't even consider allowing us to buy out Kyler's Blood Match contract," Bronx whispers. Jerking his attention to me, he meets me with wide eyes, realizing that I just heard everything.

Jameson hugs me from behind. "If we didn't know about your super hearing, we would've now with that face you're making. You're going to need to work on controlling your reactions, and I think I know a few things to help out."

I scramble away from him and stride toward Bronx. Jameson cuts me off and opens his arms for me, catching me in my tracks. Flipping me onto his shoulder, he hangs me upside down. I smack his ass, making him chuckle.

"Your distractions aren't going to work, Jamie," I say, resorting to pinching him next. He jumps at my efforts to get him to let me down and ends up tossing me.

Bronx catches me, his silver eyes enough to leave every noise and argument threatening to escape me locked in my throat. "I didn't want to tell you because I didn't want to get your hopes up, Gwen."

"So, this is legit? We're here because you're attempting to get my brother for me?" I ask.

He slowly nods his head. "It was Everett's idea. We have the power and money, and since your brother was entered as a criminal, the same laws don't apply as the humans who volunteer to sign up to give their families exemption status."

Hope rises inside me despite his words, and I crash my mouth to Bronx's, kissing him so hard with everything in me that he stumbles back and hits the wall. He releases a low moan in his throat, linking his fingers into my hair, drawing his tongue along the seam of my lips until I open my mouth to caress the softness of his tongue to mine.

"Damn it," Mikkalo says. "If she's kissing him like that, Ev—"

Something thuds. "She owes me nothing," Everett says. "I made her a promise."

"And we're assuring your ass gets to keep it," Jameson says. "So try not to make us too jealous and don't get our girl into any trouble. We trust you to keep her safe during her visitation. If anyone even touches her—"

I break away from Bronx. "Wait, what visitation?"

Everett backhands Jameson. "It was supposed to be a surprise."

"Are you crazy? That's something Gigi's going to need to be prepared for." Jameson steps closer to me. "So tell her. Now. I want to make sure she's okay before we have to go."

The four of them suddenly surround me so closely that every time I shift, I touch one of them. Now this is the kind of cage I like—all hot and muscular. The kind of cage that contains only my excitement and anticipation and not me physically.

"We agreed that it would be okay for you to visit with your brothers," Everett says. "Under my supervision. I need to perform a couple health checks while I'm here. These guys usually do the field work while I process things, so I have to prep for the extraction of Corona's runaway staff members that are suspected to have taken shelter in another coven's household."

My eyes widen. "Oh."

"We're in charge of handling any coven disputes in our region," Bronx adds. "Zaire usually took care of everything overall, and we worked under him to assure we remain strong."

"Will you guys be safe?" I ask.

Bronx meets me for a soft kiss. "You bet. Now, we have

to go. The faster we get this taken care of—"

"The faster we can have our time together," I say, smiling at him.

I hold out my hands to Jameson and Mikkalo. "So you two take care of his ass, okay?"

"Why, because Bronx might be into spanking?" Mikkalo quips.

Bronx punches his brother, shaking his head. "Enough. You don't need to give our girl any ideas. She drives me crazy enough as it is, and I don't know how much longer I can handle her testing my restraint."

I wiggle my fingers to Bronx and kiss him again. "Take care of them too, okay?"

"Always."

Jameson sneaks between us and lifts me off my feet, kissing me before I can even make a sound. "Be good for Everett. I don't think he can tell you no. I want you to be nice and hungry when I get back...and expect me to be starved."

I laugh and kiss him again. "We'll see."

He spins me around, and Mikkalo meets me next, engulfing me in a hug I can sink into. Brushing my hair behind my ears, he meets me for a hot kiss that leaves my body buzzing. "I want you to take this," he says, handing me a dagger. "You know, in case Everett needs to be rescued or something."

"I'll protect him with my life."

Mikkalo releases a small growl. "You better not have to."

Everett scoops me up, spinning away from his brothers so that they can have the space they need to leave. I'm not so sure they'd manage to go otherwise. "We got it handled here. You guys go already."

The three of them disappear, leaving me with Everett in Bronx's suite. He sets me on my feet and smiles, giving me a once-over.

"I hope you know how much it pains me to put clothes on you instead of take them off," he murmurs, zipping up my jacket to conceal the weapon Mikkalo gave me.

I pat his cheek and smile. "Good. I hate these clothes."

"I know, but we use them on the humans of our staff to help deter any incidents. We get a lot of guests both here in Crimson Vista and at the Night Palms Castle. Those dressed like this have no-bite contracts. Everyone else has contracts that include donating blood to our coven, though only Zaire had that sort of relationship, which was another reason we were pissed off that he applied to Blood Match with you."

"You know, I know he was your brother, but he was a total dick," I say.

Everett remains expressionless. "He wasn't always. But with the power shift in our coven's favor and his invite to join the Donor Life Corp board...it was all really complicated."

"Sounds like it."

He takes a step back from me and pulls my hair forward over my shoulders. "Bronx's going to kill me for this, but I'm not putting that damn hat on you."

I laugh. "Fine by me. It was the worst."

"Terrible."

Holding his hand out, Everett says, "Come on. I need to get to work to distract myself from thinking about everything I want to do with you."

"Another couple days seems like an incredibly long time," I tease.

"You're telling me." Everett kisses me softly and lifts me up, carrying me to the door of the suite. I expect him to hold me all the way to where my brothers remain locked up, but he sets me on my feet. "We're going to walk at a human's pace. Remember what Bronx said. Don't look at anyone, okay? You might be wearing employee clothing, but there are always people who like to test humans."

I gulp and bob my head. "Got it."

Everett exits the suite before me and leads the way in tense silence. Not being able to talk or look at him makes me really fucking angry with the laws of the city. I know why he asked me to do it, because it's safer not to show any interest or show other vampires that I could be persuaded into something, but still. This sucks.

"Good evening, Mr. Royale," a sultry, feminine voice says. "You look quite handsome tonight."

I stiffen as I stare at the high stilettos of a woman—a female vampire—saunter from behind a desk. Her black skirt sways around her smooth calves, and I can't stop from tilting my chin up just a little to gaze at her perfect manicure and sparkling jeweled bracelet.

"Hello, Francisca," Everett says. "My apologies for being short tonight, but I must prepare for a few arrivals."

"Perhaps you'll come find me when you're through? It's been weeks since we've had a moment alone together," she whispers too softly that I shouldn't be able to hear. "Don't you miss me?"

Everett clears his throat, aware that I'm listening. "Francisca, have you forgotten why?"

"Oh, come on, Everett. It was nothing, and we had fun, didn't we?"

"Bronx didn't find it amusing at all. Neither did Zaire," he says.

I hang onto every single one of their whispers. Jameson was right about me needing practice in controlling my reactions because I inch closer to Everett. He senses me and reaches behind him to brush his hand to mine.

Francisca huffs. "They need to lighten up."

Everett steps back as she steps toward him, keeping the same amount of space between them. "I'm sure they will. Things have just been hectic lately."

"Even more so with Zaire taking a Blood Match, huh? Such nerve of that uptight brother of yours to insist on so much time off to celebrate such a trivial thing. It's not like he proposed a Blood Vow." Francisca touches Everett's arm. "Which is why I think he'd understand if you wanted a break for yourself."

"I'm sorry, Francisca. I must be going."

Everett steps forward to walk past her, but the woman blocks his way. He's quick to take a step out of her reach again and crashes right into me. I stumble back and nearly eat shit before Everett catches me and lifts me to my feet.

"You okay?" he asks me, patting my hair without meeting my eyes.

Francisca hums in her throat. "Oh, I see the reason now. You've always had a thing for donors, haven't you, Mr. Royale?"

Everett guides me past Francisca without a word. From being around Laredo, I know a few vampire customs, and when they're done talking, they're done. If a vampire is of higher rank, they don't even have to respond.

Francisca laughs. "You know, had she been mine, I'd have let her fall to show her that she needs to watch herself. I'm surprised you even let her come along or that Zaire granted you permission to take one of his playthings. His Blood Match must be something else."

I fail to resist looking back at her, and the beautiful blonde parts her lips in a smile. She twitches her fingers at me, her eyes flashing silver.

"You really like your mister, don't you? Poor little doll.

He's going to break you, and you won't even know it because he's an expert at putting things back together again just the way he likes."

Everett releases a small growl.

"Enjoy her while you can, Everett. Little dolls don't last forever," she calls, purposely loud enough for me to hear. "Don't come running to me when she can't do everything you desire, but you know that. A donor can never keep up."

What the fuck? Everett spins me through a door and slams it shut. Turning away from me, he rests his arms on the wall and bows forward, taking in a few deep breaths. I close the space and touch his shoulder, his tight muscles rippling under my fingers.

"Is she always that...pleasant?" I ask, trying my best to keep my voice low, even though I have this strange, deep-seated annoyance sneaking up on me from replaying her conversation back through my mind. I can't be jealous of her, can I? I mean, it was obvious something happened between them but whatever it was ended badly enough that he looks like he wants to punch a wall or something.

"I'm sorry, Gwen. I shouldn't have let her talk to you like that," he says.

"Of course you should have. Bronx said—"

"Bronx wouldn't have. I just—"

I sigh. "Hey, look. I'm not going to lie. I'll probably think through a dozen scenarios about your past with her or whatever, but all that other stuff about you breaking me? I know that's not going to happen."

He meets my gaze, his tight mouth so needing a kiss. Stepping closer to him, I brush my lips to his until he takes a breath and relaxes. "Thank you for saying that, Gwen. If our positions have been switched, there would've been no way I could have handled that as well as you."

"Had we been somewhere else, I might not have. Because the thought that you were..." I shake my head. "Nope. Not going there."

"She's the one who might be jealous."

"Of me? Yeah right."

He chuckles. "Of me. Because you're ours."

I laugh and suck his lip hard enough to pull a soft moan from him before I ease myself away. Everett looks ready to relocate me into one of these medical offices to show me that there is nothing I have to be jealous of.

I straighten my jacket and comb my hair over my shoulders, preparing to bow my head to take on my employee persona again. Everett surprises me by lacing his fingers through mine and tugging me with him down the quiet, sterile hallway until we reach another set of double doors.

"You can relax, Gwen. Only authorized personnel in this hallway, and they're all doing rounds on another floor. I've marked this section off-limits while I perform my exams."

I smile. "So is it safe to kiss you again?"

He leans in. "Completely dangerous. For me. Not you.

Bringing you along guarantees I'll get nothing done."

"I'm sure Mikkalo would love for me to be his backup. Bronx might assure it if you don't...though if you don't, I wouldn't have to imagine you with—"

He kisses me again, pulling me up into his arms until our bodies touch together.

I release a small breath against his mouth. "What was I saying?"

He hums and sets me back down, keeping his arm around me. "You were just imagining how good I'll be to you on our night alone."

Blush crawls up my neck at the thought. Everett is careful yet bold like he's in constant control over himself except in regards to me. And I love it.

He gazes at me with his dark blue eyes, his smile widening as he notices my reaction. Instead of teasing me some more, he pulls me along, keeping at a brisk pace that I can manage to match. I can feel his attention on me, but I can't stop myself from looking into the door windows of each room. Most of them are empty apart from one or two, but the figures sleep on cots with their backs facing the door.

We enter another hallway, one Everett must open the door to with his palm print, and he finally lets go of my fingers to pull his com device from his pocket to tap it a couple of times to bring up something I can't read.

"We couldn't fit all your brothers in one holding room, so we put Grayson and Porter in one room and Declan,

Ashton, and Silas in another. Who do you want to see first?"

"I need to see Grayson," I say automatically. He's my eldest brother and has been assigned as my guardian and protector. I always go to him first. He's the one who found Laredo for me. He's probably also the one the most worried.

Everett nods and heads to a wall cabinet across from the doors to gather a few things. He picks up a box of what looks like some sort of food bars and hands them to me to hold. "Just in case they haven't eaten. Humans and vampires are alike in the way that we're both easily agitated when hungry."

"Only agitated?" I ask.

He chuckles. "You're right. You get full-on wild."

I play-smack his arm. "You like my ferocious ass."

"I like your ass regardless."

Tipping my head back, I release a laugh loud enough that Everett covers my mouth to stifle the noise. With his playfulness, it's hard to remember that we're not alone, and even if vampires might not be in this section, if I'm loud enough, they could tune in and hear me. But hopefully, the music trickling in from hidden speakers helps somewhat with the noise. I've grown so used to hearing music at Night Palms Castle that I've been tuning it out. I hadn't realized it was to help give those with super hearing a bit of privacy.

"Go ahead and take those to room four. It should open for you. I'd like you to warn your brothers that I'll be there in a minute so that they don't try to attack me," he says.

I grimace. "I can't promise you they won't try anyway."

He flares his nostrils with a breath. "Okay, I'll give you a couple of minutes alone first so that you can visit. I don't want to ruin your time if I have to sedate any of them, but I'll be right outside."

"I'll be fine," I say. "They're my brothers."

"I know, Gwen," he says. "But humans do drastic things sometimes. I just want you to be careful."

"I will."

Turning away from Everett, I stroll a dozen feet from him and to room number four. I nearly startle at Grayson standing a few feet from the door, just staring at me through the glass. Porter sits on the edge of one of the cots behind him, also staring at me.

I rush to slap my hand on the palm pad to open the door, and it lights up under the glow of my hand. Grayson waits for me in his spot, and I realize he's chained to the wall and unable to close the space to me.

"Grayson!" I say, dashing to him, dropping the box of food bars on the floor.

My brother envelops me in a hug, lifting me off my feet to rock me back and forth. He sets me down only to have Porter spin me around so that he can hug me too. I can't stop the tears from escaping my eyes, and Porter swipes my cheek.

"Knock it off with that shit, Gweny. Crying does nothing to help any of us," Porter says, blinking his own glassy eyes.

I pat his chest. "I'm so happy to see you both. How are you holding up?"

"Doesn't matter. All that matters is that you're here." Grayson touches my shoulder. "I knew you'd come for us. What are we dealing with? How much time do you think we have?"

"A couple of minutes," I say, trying to hug him again.

He stops me and grabs onto the chain around his ankle, easily pulling it from the wall like he managed to unscrew it. I gape at it, and he offers me a smile like I should know him well enough that he could be in this room, in this building, guarded by vampires, but nothing is ever going to stop him from fighting back. We've been doing it all our lives.

"One of the guards unhooked us in exchange for a bite," he says, pulling down the collar of his shirt to show me the two scabs of a circular wound. "Fucking vampires. So easy."

Porter wraps his chain around his fist. "Do you have a weapon, Gweny?"

I automatically nod, my mind whirling and unable to process what's going on.

"Well, give it to Grayson. Come on. You said we have minutes. We gotta move," Porter says, giving me a shove.

A soft growl sounds from the hallway. "Gwen, you need to get out of there. Just run. I'll get the door," Everett whispers softly, too lowly for my brothers to hear.

I open and close my mouth, trying to get the words out.

"Damn it, Gwen. Get it together. I know it's been tough and you had to do things you didn't want to, but you're a fighter. Now, give me your weapon. Let us handle getting out. We know the way." Grayson reaches for the front of my jacket and unzips it when I don't move.

I don't get a chance to stop him before he slides the dagger out and inspects it.

"No blood," Porter says. "How the—"

"Gwen, run," Everett says, raising his voice.

"What the fuck, Gwen? Who is that?" Grayson asks.

I clear my throat, the words hard to get out. "I'm sorry, Grayson. Porter. You guys are confused. I'm only here to visit."

Grayson stiffens. His hazel eyes shift to glance behind me at the door. Without having to look, I can sense Everett looming behind me. He releases another deep growl as Grayson inches closer.

"Gwen," Porter says. "I don't understand."

"Please, you two. You have to calm down. It's okay. Everett won't hurt you," I say. "He's the one who brought me here to visit. He and his coven are working on buying Kyler's Blood Match contract as we speak. Then we're going to figure out you next."

"Is that what he said?" Grayson asks, clutching the dagger. "What do you think will happen after?"

I shift on my feet. "I—"

"Gwen, you need to leave the room now," Everett says, drawing my attention to him.

"Fuck you!" Grayson yells.

Grayson rushes past me in an attempt to get to Everett, and I snatch the back of my brother's shirt, yanking him so hard that his feet fall out from under him. He lands on his back, gasping a breath, and then his wild eyes meet mine.

A dozen emotions flicker through his pinched expression—shock, anger, grief. This is the first time that I stood up—against him—and for a vampire no less. One of the vampires behind Grayson being here in the first place.

"I'm sorry," I whisper to my brothers. "I can't let you hurt Everett."

"Gwen." My name sounds sharp on Grayson's lips. "Don't do this."

I take a step back. "I have to. You'll get yourself killed otherwise."

"Gwen!" he shouts again.

Porter tries to rush me, but Everett knocks him back, sending him sprawling into the cot. The world spins, and I find myself in Everett's arms. He kisses the trembles from my lips, holding me close like he's afraid if he doesn't I might fall apart.

Soft footsteps sound from behind us, and Everett sets me down to spin around. He snarls and pushes Grayson back into the room only to have Porter come after him with the dagger Grayson took from me.

Something moves in my peripheral vision, and I startle at the sight of Frankie standing next to the asshole vampire from last night.

"Everett!" I shout, but he's not fast enough.

Mr. Sur rushes past me and collides into Everett. The two of them skid along the hall. A firm hand grabs onto my shoulder, and Frankie jerks me back a few feet and shoves me toward another door.

"Unlock your brothers' cell," he says. "Hurry. We're running out of time."

Frankie doesn't give me a chance to react and takes my hand, slamming it hard enough against the palm pad to make me wince. Everett roars from behind me, rushing toward us.

The door to the cell flies open, and Silas jumps between me and Everett, knocking Everett with him into the wall.

"Frankie!" Grayson yells. "Get her out of here. We'll follow as soon as we take care of this guy."

"Gwen, fight," Everett calls. "Don't let him take you."

I realize a little too late that Everett isn't talking about Frankie. He's talking about Mr. Sur. The asshole vampire flies at me and Frankie, scooping the two of us off our feet. The last thing I see is Everett flashing his fangs at Grayson.

Grayson yells.

23

BLOOD REBELS

COOL AIR ENGULFS ME AS Mr. Sur races us from the building and into a nearby alleyway. A car idles in wait, and Mr. Sur throws me into the backseat and slams the door.

Frankie slides into the passenger's seat and twists to look at me. "You have to trust me that you're going to be okay."

Mr. Sur materializes behind the wheel and hits the throttle, sending the car barreling forward. "Don't give her hope. I want to hear her cry when she finds out where we're going."

I lean forward and attempt to punch Mr. Sur upside the head, but he grabs onto my wrist and squeezes so hard that I can't stop the scream from screeching from me. He lets me go and shoves me back.

"Do that again, and I'll crush your bone," he snaps.

I cradle my arm, glaring at him as he flashes his fangs at me. I want to yell at him that he's making a big fucking mistake, but I can't waste my breath on threats. I need to get out of this car. Vampires not only move fast, they also act fast. I might only have minutes.

"You can't do that. She has to be uninjured. That was the deal," Frankie says.

"I know what I'm fucking doing. This isn't my first sale," Mr. Sur says.

"Sale?" I can't stop the word from escaping my mouth.

"You cost me my life, you bitch. My coven shunned me for losing my position." Mr. Sur pushes back his scraggly hair from his forehead to reveal a deep blue line—a tattoo. It's like the faded ones I saw on both Mikkalo and Jameson, but this one is different.

Again, I keep my mouth closed. I want nothing more than to tell him his asshole ways were the reason he got himself into whatever the hell position he's in, but it'll only piss him off, and I wouldn't put it past him to break my arm. What I don't understand is what the hell Frankie is doing with this guy and how it involves my brothers.

But I'm not willing to find out.

Unlacing one of my boots, I ease it off my foot, trying my best not to draw attention to me. I release a few fake whimpers, summoning all of my fear to coil into a ball of anger to make me stronger.

"Up ahead. Two more blocks," Frankie says. "Once the transaction is complete, you'll get your cut and a bonus for the five you released at the Blood Match Center."

"This better be fast," Mr. Sur says. "The Royales have security all over the city. They won't be far behind us."

"Only need a minute," Frankie says.

And I only need twenty seconds.

Slipping my boot onto my hand, I pull it up my arm to protect me better. The armor I'm wearing under the uniform will help against weapons but not a vampire's strength. The steel in the boot should help my hand and stop Mr. Sur from sinking his fangs into me.

The second Mr. Sur turns the wheel, I swing my arm and shove my boot against his face as hard as I can. I grab onto the wheel and jerk it, sending the car skidding and grinding against the brick wall of a building. Metal screeches out, and Mr. Sur growls. Frankie doesn't even try to stop me. All he does is reach for the dash and cuts off the engine.

"Gwen, keep him still," Frankie says. "I'm taking his heart."

Mr. Sur thrashes and screams, trying to fight me, but he can't move as I shove all my weight at him, crushing the boot into his face. The wheel prods at my back, and I ignore the pain the best I can. It's the only thing stopping Mr. Sur from getting a grip on me as I now sit in his lap.

"Yank him forward," Frankie says. "Hard as you can, dhampir. Show me what the Gallagher name taught you."

Reaching my free hand out, I lace it behind Mr. Sur's neck and tug him to me until I hear the gross sound of something wet and squishy slap against the leather seat. Mr. Sur stops struggling, the scent of his rancid blood engulfing me in a cloud of nastiness I thrash to escape. The smell of his blood reminds me that not all vampires are delicious and this asshole's blood is as vile as he is.

I hit the pavement with a thud and somersault backward to land on my knees to push myself up. I jerk my attention around the street, fear tugging at my heart. I can hear several people around me, but I can't tell where they are or if they're vampire or human.

A hand touches my shoulder, and I spin around and hit Frankie so hard that he skids across the ground with a groan. The distinct sound of someone turning off the safety on a gun clicks through the air, my super hearing struggling to decipher the city noise as my heart pounds in my ears.

"Take it easy, Gwen," Frankie says from his place on the ground. "Xavier, move slowly. She's nervous and doesn't know we're here to help her."

Scrambling back to the car, I drag Mr. Sur's body out and feel for a hidden sheath with a blade tucked inside his jacket pocket. Vampires remain armed at all times, just like

Blood Rebels. You can always count on finding a weapon on a dead body if you need something.

I grip the dagger in my hand and straighten my back. "You're not fucking selling me."

"Of course we wouldn't sell you, Gwen. Your life is a precious gift," a man says, inching his way from the corner of a building. "We only told the blood source that to get him to help us. Those stuck in the shadows can be easily persuaded. You know that."

He's right. My dad always taught us that. It's why my brothers allow themselves to be bitten. They use the one thing a vampire wants most to get things we need. Not all vampires live lavish lives of luxury. Many remain stuck in the shadows.

"You should've helped my brothers," I say. "They were the ones that needed an escape."

"Your brothers only carry the dhampir mutation. You, my sweet Gwen, are a dhampir. You come first. We've been looking for you everywhere."

I grimace in confusion. "What do you mean that you've been looking for me? Grayson has been following the calls like our father showed him."

The man twists his lips to the side. "You're mistaken. He hasn't checked in with us in several years."

"But Laredo—my blood source—had been..." Ah hell.

His eyes soften. "Blood sources are tricky, Gwen. Especially toward someone like you. I bet he set you up. Was planning to take you all along."

I purse my lips, remembering what Bronx had said about getting a tip from a source. What if he was right and it was Laredo? I guess I'll never really know. "Well, he's dead, so it doesn't matter. And I can't leave without my brothers." I'm not leaving at all, but I won't say it. I need to stall. I need to figure this out.

"We will go for your brothers next as soon as we get the chance. But for now, we must leave the city immediately. We have a safe house not far from here," he says. "A blood source is waiting to feed you. You must be hungry. How long has it been?"

I rub my lips together without responding. They don't know that I was bitten with venom by Laredo. They don't know that I've already had plenty to eat. All they know is that I was Blood Matched into the Royale Coven and think I need help.

I shouldn't be so surprised that Frankie is a Blood Rebel. We're spread far and wide—both in and out of the cities.

The man, Xavier, steps closer. "Come along, Gwen. Let's get you home."

"I—I'm not leaving my brothers," I say. "They'll die here."

"Their sacrifice will assure that you live—that you help humanity to flourish," Xavier says.

I shake my head. "I can't leave."

"You don't have a choice."

Xavier rushes toward me, attempting to grab my arm to take my weapon. I automatically drop it, letting it hit the ground. Swinging my other arm, I uppercut hard into his chin to send his head jerking back.

I'm so focused on him that I don't see another guy rush toward me until he's only two feet away. Bending forward, I thrust my leg behind me, kicking him in the gut. More voices sound out, and a gunshot blasts through the air, ringing so loudly that my vision shadows at the noise. I lose my balance and fall to the ground.

"The Royales have been sighted. We gotta move," another man says.

Frankie grabs onto my leg and drags me back. "Come on, Gwen. You can't stay here. Stop fighting. I'll get Kyler. I swear."

But this isn't about Kyler. It isn't about any of my brothers. It's about me and not wanting to leave my guys.

It wasn't until now, hearing this group of rebels refer to me as humanity's gift, that I realize how much of my life I spent fighting. How much of my life I was attempting to help humanity but not getting anywhere. I can't change the world alone. I'm not humanity's gift if these people expect me to fight until I can't any longer. If they think dying does more than just end a life.

I can't go.

"Damn it, hurry. Just pick her up," Xavier says.

Snatching the dagger I dropped, I slice it through the air in an attempt to keep Frankie back. It works for him but not for Xavier. Xavier points his gun at me and shoots. Pain explodes in my leg, the force enough to make me scream and drop the dagger.

"The shot came from over there." Bronx's familiar voice sounds through the air from somewhere nearby.

"Bronx!" I yell. "Over here! Blood Rebels are trying to take me."

"Fuck," Bronx says, his deep voice echoing with a growl. "Take the back, Mik. I'll round them off."

Xavier glowers at me and shoots again—three times right into my chest and torso. I heave a breath at the force of the bullets and struggle to get up. Xavier runs at me and grabs me by my hair, yanking me off my feet again.

"By the power of the elder council, you've been declared a traitor to humanity, Gwen Gallagher," he says. "Your family would be ashamed."

Before I can fight, Xavier drags a blade across my throat and thrusts me to the ground. Gunshots pierce the air as rebels fire weapons from somewhere I can't see. I clutch my throat, feeling my own blood pour over me. I can't scream or breathe or do anything in my state of panic and pain.

"Damn it, Gwen," Frankie says, rushing to kneel beside me. He rips off his jacket and presses the fabric to my neck. "You should've just gone. Your brother traded everything to assure you lived."

I stare up at the sky, wishing I could see the stars above the lights of the city.

"Some went that direction," Mikkalo says. "Jameson they're coming your way."

I open and close my mouth, trying to call out.

But I don't have to. Frankie surprises me by yelling, "Help! Over here! She's over here." He continues to put pressure on my throat, his eyes wild as he looks around. "Just hold on. They're coming. I have to go."

Frankie abandons me on the ground and dashes toward the car. I blink through my hazy vision, trying with everything in me to hold onto my consciousness. I'm bleeding everywhere out in the open where any shadow dweller can get to me.

A figure blurs past me, moving too fast to see clearly. I hear the screech of tires, and putrid smoke fills the air. Bright light illuminates above me, stinging my eyes and blinding me. I try to move, but I don't get far. Two cool hands lock me in place. Panic rushes through me, clenching my heart. I'm too weak to fight.

Something sweet trickles over my mouth, pulling at my deep-seated nature as a dhampir. The sudden explosion of delicious warmth summons my last bit of strength, and I manage to lock my hands onto a muscular arm.

"I got you, dandelion," Bronx says, shifting me onto his lap. "Everett's coming. Just hold tight."

"Bronx, rebels have been spotted around the block,"

Mikkalo says.

Bronx releases a deep growl. "No captures this time."

His words ignite fear inside me, and I flail in his arms, digging my fingers into his legs. No captures? He just sentenced a bunch of people who thought they were helping me to death. My people.

"N-n." I can't say the word but manage to push the sound through my lips. The wound on my throat already heals without me having to look at it. But damn it do I hurt.

Bronx bows over me, his dark eyes capturing mine. "They tried to kill you."

"Trai...tor." It's what Blood Rebels do. Vampires are no different in that way. Treason is punishable by death—no matter if it's a human or vampire.

"You are not," he says, combing his fingers through my hair, pushing the sticky strands away.

I nod. "Y-yes." To them, I am. I've betrayed my people.

Bronx hugs me tighter, breathing in a few deep breaths of my hair. Straightening his back, he looks at the world around us. "Mikkalo, call everyone back."

"What?" Mikkalo asks, his voice booming through the night.

"Just do it. And come here. Gwen needs you."

Mikkalo materializes next to us, crouching down. Before my mind realizes what my body's doing, I yank Bronx's arm back to me and bite him myself. He releases the sexiest moan, suddenly tightening his arm around me.

"Fuck, I can't let her go. You're going to have to help me," Bronx whispers to Mikkalo.

Mikkalo gently grabs my hand, and Bronx growls. He wasn't kidding about not being able to let me go. My mouth doesn't plan to let up either.

"Shit. Get yourself together, brother," Mikkalo whispers. He touches my legs, ignoring Bronx's threatening reaction. "Sorry, Gwen. I can't let you devour Bronx."

Glass shatters, the noise enough to startle me. The second I release my mouth from Bronx's arm, Mikkalo pulls me away and gathers me to him, jumping up to put distance between me and Bronx.

A scream rips through the air, sending a wave of panic over me. Mikkalo doesn't give me a chance to make any noise, biting his arm to bring it to my mouth to drink his blood next. The sudden flood of tingles suppresses my out of control body struggling between fear and the blood lust Bronx ignited in me.

"Gwen, help me!" Frankie yells. "I saved you!"

"You're the reason the Royales lost their donor in the first place," Corona says. "You nearly cost me an alliance."

"Gwen!"

I don't get the chance to move or try to scream. Corona restrains Frankie in front of him and bends his neck, biting him hard enough to send blood pouring from the artery he punctures with his fangs. It's a kill bite. I've seen them enough to know. I wince and release a cry at the horrifying crack that soon follows as the vampire breaks the Blood Rebel's neck.

Mikkalo shifts me, trying his best to cover my ears even though it's too late. Bronx closes the space to us, his eyes flashing crazy silver. Jameson materializes in front of me with a familiar figure on his shoulder, but Everett appears to block my view. His wide eyes search my face, and he peels away Frankie's bloody shirt from my neck.

"Give her to me," he says to Mikkalo.

Mikkalo's not quick to react.

Jameson touches his shoulder. "We have to get her out of here, brother. He can't see her. And Bronx needs you to stay. You're our head of defense."

Blinking his eyes a few times, Mikkalo finally loosens his hold on me and hands me over to Everett. Everett plants his lips to mine, kissing me softly like he needs to be close to me, to feel our bodies touch. And I need it too.

Because fuck. How could my life end up like this? I've been deemed a traitor. I can never go back to the life I had before...not that I want to.

But my brothers?

I suck in a sharp breath at the thought. "Grayson?" It's the only word I can manage to spit out.

"Gwen, your brothers are fine. A little roughed up. I'm sorry. I had no choice," Everett whispers. "I had to act fast. You should've never gotten as far away as you did from me."

"Damn fucking straight," Jameson says. "He'll be lucky to get another moment alone with you because of that shit."

"Jamie!" I snap, anger rushing over me, pushing my voice to rise louder. The bleeding in my neck stopped. All that remains is the burning.

Jameson heaves a breath. "I'm sorry, Gigi. I didn't mean...fuck. Just sorry."

The world comes to a halt, and Everett takes me into one of the exam rooms used during the Blood Matching process. The place is empty this time of night, most humans assigned an application time during the day with their matches retrieving them in the evening if they do get assigned a vampire.

"Jameson, take Kyler into another room. If I need you, I'll call you," Everett says.

"But—"

Everett cuts off Jameson's complaint with a growl. "This is a medical exam. Gwen deserves privacy."

I almost open my mouth to tell Everett that Jameson can stay, but one look at Kyler knocked out in his arms freezes my insides. So many unbidden emotions crash through me, and to my despair, my eyes cry without my permission as everything that happened tonight tumbles back to me.

"He's fine, Gigi. Sedation not manipulation. Promise," Jameson says. "He's safe with me. I swear."

I bob my head. I'm too afraid my voice will crack if I

try to speak. It kills me that I can't get my body under control. My brothers would call me out—they'd...

Fuck.

They're going to kill me.

They won't have a choice if they find out that an elder sentenced me to death. I've seen it happen before when I was a kid. A man felt bad for a vampire caged as a blood source. He made the mistake of trying to free him. It was the first time I saw a man die. My dad rarely traveled with me after that.

Cool fingers touch my cheeks, pulling my attention from my thoughts. Everett stands next to me as I lie on an exam bed. I hadn't realized he put me down nor did I notice Jameson leave the room with my brother.

"I want you to take a few deep breaths with me," Everett says, keeping his voice even. "Nice and slow."

I inhale a breath, my chest aching. "It hurts."

He frowns.

"I was shot," I add.

Closing his eyes for a second, he composes himself as to not react to my words. Instead, he gently eases me up and wraps his arms around me again, just hugging me for a moment. I breathe in the scent of his skin, savoring the weight of his body with mine.

"I'm so sorry, Gwen. I've failed you," he whispers.

I rub my hand along his back. "You haven't. I'm okay."

"Can I check for myself to make sure?" he asks, easing

away from me. "The body armor should've protected you, but you'll be bruised. I'd like to clean your neck to take a better look as well, but I'm pretty confident the damaged tissue is regenerating since you're conscious and talking. Only slightly pale from blood loss."

"It hurts a bit too," I say. I attempt to bring my hand to my throat to touch it, but Everett stops me.

"It's best not to mess with it. I'll give you something for the pain."

I bob my head. "Can I have some of your blood too? I feel so out of control. Those Blood Rebels..."

"Were lucky. They should be grateful that Bronx let them go," he murmurs. "He did so for you. But be prepared, Gwen. He's going to want to know why especially after they did this to you."

I close my eyes. "I don't know. They're my peo—" I snap my mouth shut. Because they're not my people. Not anymore. "I didn't want to prove them right. They attacked me because I betrayed them."

His brows crinkle. "What are you talking about?"

"They were here to rescue me...and I chose you. I fought to stay. I'm a traitor now," I whisper, the words burning through me worse than the damage to my body. "If they catch me again, I'm dead."

"We won't let that happen," Everett says.

I tighten my jaw. "I will not allow anyone else to die because of me, Everett. I will not prove them right about being a traitor to humanity. I won't. If that's how this is going to end up, then..." I let my words trail off. I can't say them out loud. My mind refuses even to think them.

"Gwen, I promise you that we'll get this all figured out," he says.

"The five of us together," I say, squeezing his hand.

"The five of us together," he repeats.

I never knew how much I'd love the sound of that.

Together.

24

TOGETHER

"YOU DON'T HAVE TO BE careful with me, you know," I whisper, watching as Everett meticulously cleans every inch of me in the grand shower of his suite. The second he assured I was healing properly and free of pain with the help of a numbing cream, he relocated us back to the top floor.

"Not careful. Professional," he says, not even glancing at my bare breasts as my chest heaves and my heart races, his hand gently rubbing the sponge past the killer bruise on my shin from one of the bullets.

"You don't have to be that either. I'm done letting you

play health keeper. I'm fine." I graze my hand along his muscular shoulder, glistening with shower steam.

He slowly raises his gaze to mine. "Gwen, I'm not playing. You've been through a lot."

I rub my lips together. "Don't remind me."

"Gwen." My name sounds just above a whisper on his lips, sending goosebumps prickling over my skin.

Touching his cheek, I lean in for a kiss that sets him off like it has taken everything in him not to react to me until I made the first move. Lifting me against him, he slides his hands to my ass, holding me in place, his arousal growing at the deepness of my kiss as I cling onto him, squeezing him between my thighs.

Flicking the water off, Everett grabs a towel and wraps it around us, strolling with me in his arms out of the shower and into his room only lit with a small lamp on his bedside table. Our damp skin slips together with the movements, and I can't stop myself from releasing a moan as the length of his shaft rubs between my legs, awakening my desire for him even more.

Setting me on the edge of the bed, Everett breaks from my mouth to search my face, drinking me in inch-by-inch as I clutch the towel to my shoulders but leave the rest of me exposed.

"I haven't been able to get you off my mind," Everett murmurs. "And then after everything—"

I hook my fingers to his hips and pull him closer. "No

reminding me, remember? I'd like to forget."

He leans into me as I scoot further onto the bed, inviting him to join me. Bending down, he brushes his lips to my jaw, breathing a small moan into my ear as he trails his fingers to my breast to graze my hard nipples.

Everett kisses his way down my throat, gliding his tongue along the sensitive skin of my healing neck until he finds what he's yearning for, and he sucks my breast into his mouth, twirling his tongue around my nipple while massaging my other breast with his hand.

I dig my fingers into his taut shoulders, squirming under his touch. His hand trails down my stomach at a torturously slow pace. His mouth finds mine again, and he draws my bottom lip between his teeth just hard enough to make me gasp. I slip my tongue into his mouth, reaching down between us until I lace my fingers around the stiffness of his erection, flexing in my hand as I stroke it with my fingers, using his body to tease mine.

Everett pulls back, kneeling in front of me, resting his hands on my knees. His eyes flash silver with the desire that matches how hard I make every inch of his body. I slowly open my legs for him in silent permission, holding his heated stare.

I know it hasn't been long since we've met but after everything—I chose to stay. I chose to see where all of this will take me. To find out how strong I am. How different the Royale Coven is. I decided to take my life into my own hands to do with it as I please.

I'm all in.

As I lay in front of Everett, exposed and vulnerable, a dozen emotions flitting through me, I realize that my people were wrong. Humanity doesn't need to destroy vampires to thrive. They don't need me as a weapon or a predator to fight until I can't any longer. What humanity needs is to realize that we can't fight alone. That not all vampires want to ruin the world or me.

I need vampires—I need my guys.

And they need me.

We can survive on each other.

Thrive.

Stretching forward, I grab onto Everett and pull him closer to me. He smiles through another kiss, taking a moment to trail his finger between my legs to feel exactly what he does to me. I hum against his mouth, rolling my hips, letting him rub my clit while teasing me with his tip without fully entering.

"Everett," I whisper under the incredible weight of his touch, my whole body growing with tingles.

"You like this?" he asks, his voice low, breathless.

"Don't stop."

I moan and clutch the blankets, my body buzzing with electricity that makes my fingers and toes curl. My back arches, begging, pleading for my body to find the release it needs before I explode. Everett licks his lips, watching me watch him and continues exactly what he's doing. The quick, desperate rhythm of his finger works me over in a way that has me panting and squirming, reaching for him. He links his free hand through mine and sinks into me the moment my muscles tighten and release, pleasure crashing over me in a wave so intense that I scream out in ecstasy that makes Everett hum and kiss me.

"So sexy," he murmurs, flexing his erection inside me as he feels my body pulse.

I release a breathless laugh. "Next time smother my damn mouth with a pillow."

He smiles and combs my hair from my face. "No way."

Meeting him for another kiss, I slide my hands up and around Everett's shoulders, exploring the smooth muscles of his back.

He rolls his body into mine, slow at first like he wants to take his time enjoying me, and I lean up and graze my teeth to his neck without biting.

Pulling back just a bit, he adjusts my body, sliding a pillow under me to raise me just a bit. He straightens up to kneel, using my knees to thrust deeper into me as I lose myself to the pleasure of our bodies aligning so perfectly to be as one.

I've never felt anything like this, the sensation of his body in mine, the rhythm of his movements showing his obvious experience as he drags out another moan from me.

Everett whispers my name, moaning with his own passion compared to the silence I've experienced before. I was always taught to be quiet no matter what, but something inside me awakens, and I lose myself with Everett, enjoying every single sound, every sensation, every plea of my name so hot and deep like I'm all he wants and needs. All he'll ever think about.

His fingers massage my knees, his body rocking perfectly with mine until he bends into me and kisses me again, grazing his teeth across my lip. I gently prod my tongue to his fang to send a drop of blood splashing into his mouth. He releases the sexiest noise that vibrates across my mouth to trail through the rest of me. He kisses me deeper, just tasting my lips, exploring my tongue, sliding his arms around my back to hug me to him with his final thrusts that leave the both of us gasping.

Everett continues to caress my lips through his hard breathing, his fingers playing with my hair, his body now completely on mine but not squishing me as he guarantees no space dare get between us.

"You are the most incredible being I have ever met, Gwen," he whispers, propping up on his elbow to glide his finger across my cheek. "I'm so lucky that you give me even a second of your time."

I smile. "How could I resist?"

He brushes his lips to mine again. "I want to do right by you. What you've given me—I can't even explain. I feel so connected to you. How I'm going to even step a foot away from you..."

"Everett," I say softly. "You'll be able to. You know why?"

Lifting his gaze, he stares into my eyes without responding.

"Because I'm not going anywhere."

"Promise?" he asks me.

"Promise."

"I need that mouth of yours all over me," Jameson says, whispering into my ear.

The second the words come out, I shift on his lap to face him. He meets me with a teasing, almost daring smile. I snap my teeth, making him laugh and then turn back around and sweep my hair from my shoulder just to mess with him.

"All right. My mouth all over you it is then," he murmurs, kissing the sensitive skin of my throat, turning me on with the click of his fangs.

"Damn," Mikkalo says, kicking my foot with his. "I can't wait for our time."

I grin, reaching out to squeeze his knee. "You better plan something fun."

"Then you better not let Jameson try to keep you up all day," he teases with a smile.

"*Me* keep *her* up? I'm nearly certain it's the other way

around. I mean, you try to sleep with her insatiable need to suck your neck," Jameson says, sliding his fingers over my hips. He rubs my body against him. "Or the fact that my dick can't chill the fuck out with her so close. Never-ending boner. I bet if I applied to Blood Match with her, I'd have matched a hundred percent with her body."

"Me too," Everett says, drawing my attention to him standing over Kyler, who remains unconscious on a cot Everett set up in his room until we know what to do with him.

My face warms under his scrutiny. I still can't believe we had sex—mind-blowing sex. I don't know if the others know, but if they do, they haven't mentioned it. I know we have this arrangement, and they agreed that they'd rather I be with all of them than risk a whole bunch of hurt feelings, but I'm still a bit nervous. This far exceeds a Blood Match contract. All I know right now is that I'm staying and seeing where this leads...and having fun while I'm at it.

I squirm a bit as Everett tests my resolve not to react. "You guys need to knock it off," I say.

"No, Gigi. Look what you do to me," Jameson says, flexing his raging hard on under my ass. "It's only fair if you're in a constant state of sexual frustration too."

I tip my head back and laugh. "Jamie."

He purrs in his throat. "Bronx needs to hurry his ass up and come home."

"I know," I say, sliding my hand between my legs to squeeze his thigh. "I just want to recreate a blanket mansion and see what I can do...to help that."

Mikkalo groans, and I slide off Jameson's lap and in between Mikkalo's legs to kiss him sweetly on the lips.

"None of that," I say, patting his cheek.

He smiles at me. "Then just one more."

I kiss Mikkalo again and laugh into his mouth as Jameson squeezes my ass since it's in his face. I squeal and spin away from him before he can grab and pull me onto his lap for another round of lapsies that he's right about leaving the both of us on the verge of something we definitely need to control in front of his brothers.

Jameson just makes it so easy to feel like the world isn't going to collapse on us at any second. His constant state of playfulness really helps keep my heart light, though I know it wants to constantly slide into my stomach the second I think of something other than my guys sudden mission to keep me smiling.

Mikkalo and Jameson both stand up, each going in the opposite direction to try to close the space to me, which will surely turn into a game with me in the middle. I spin and crash right into a muscular chest that sends me sprawling back. Bronx catches me by the waist and stops me from eating shit on the floor.

Our eyes meet, and I intake a small breath, my body doing all sorts of crazy things as I remember how good his blood tasted even if it was only a moment of need and not the desire I most definitely want to explore. Just his closeness, his delicious smell, reminds me how alive I felt even with all the blood loss. How I didn't want to stop. How drinking from him went beyond something explainable for the both of us.

Silence draws through the room, and instead of pulling myself away, I hop up into Bronx's arms and kiss him, hugging him so close that I hear him grunt under my sudden need to smother him with all my affection.

"I missed you," I say against his lips, kissing him a few times more, determined to have him yell for mercy against the desperation of my mouth.

He doesn't. He devours every single kiss I offer, smiling and laughing, the smoothness of his voice such a relief to me as it softens the nerves clinging to my tense body. It's me who pulls back for a breath, and Bronx rests his head on my shoulder, just continuing to embrace me because I refuse to let him go.

"I missed you too, dandelion," he murmurs softly, stroking the length of my back over and over again, gently digging his fingers into my muscles, trying to get me to relax. "I had no idea how much until this second. Are you okay? Have my brothers been taking good care of you? I'm sorry I took so long." Bronx didn't come back with us to Night Palms Castle, having to act on behalf of Zaire under his supposed absence.

I turn my head to smile at Everett, Mikkalo, and Jameson. "They've been amazing."

"And you?" Bronx didn't miss that I haven't answered the first part of his question.

"I—" My voice quivers, and I stop talking.

"It's okay. You don't have to say anything. Can I just hold you for a bit?"

I smile and nod my head.

Bronx carries me to the empty reading chair beside Jameson and sits with me on his lap, wrapping his arms around me while I face him. I run my fingers through his hair, resting my forehead to his, letting our breaths mingle. Mikkalo plays with my long tresses, teasing my waist as he draws his fingers along the small of my back. Jameson moves his chair closer and caresses my knee while Everett joins us, sitting on the arm of the chair until they all engulf me in the best hug of my existence.

Everett, Jameson, and Mikkalo pull away from me, and I brush my lips to Bronx's once more, twisting on his lap so that I sling my legs over the arm of the chair and rest my head to his chest to listen to his heartbeat.

Jameson holds my feet on his leg, stroking the tops without getting carried away to try to rub the rest of my bare leg since I'm only wearing one of his T-shirts. After wearing all of the body armor, I barely even wanted to wear what I have on.

"So the rebel nest left Crimson Vista to head north. We managed to tag three out of the four gas guzzlers, but they abandoned them outside of the Aku Region," Bronx says, keeping his voice even, knowing that I'm gobbling up whatever information he has to offer.

"They'll come back for them," Mikkalo says. "They always do."

"What then?" I can't stop myself from asking the question.

Bronx rests his chin on my head so that I can't meet his gaze. "As long as they stay away from our region, we won't act, Gwen. Crimson Vista is under quarantine for the foreseeable future. No transfers of donors in or out until some things get figured out. There was a decline in the population, and we must show growth or else our coven risks a region split for another board member to take over. But if they do come here—we can't just ignore it."

His words sink into me, and I can't stop the grimace from crossing my face. "Oh."

"Your declaration as a traitor was very much real," Everett says softly. "I called my source in the city, and he said that if you're caught, they will try to kill you. We can't stand by and wait for an attack if we know it's coming."

I close my eyes. "My brothers. If they know..."

Mikkalo releases a soft growl. "You don't think?"

Turning my head, I meet his dark gaze. "It is our way of life. They will believe that I'm not here by my own freewill. I'm too dangerous if I'm not with them. I know too much. Sacrifice is something we're all quite familiar with."

Mikkalo reaches out and touches my knee. "Then we

relocate them and keep them locked up. We can't risk them going to auction and escaping. You're not the only one who knows too much, Gwen."

I groan, scrubbing my cheeks with my hands. "We can't just lock them up forever."

"Then we'll change their minds," Bronx says.

My muscles tense at his suggestion. "We can't just mess with their heads."

"She's right," Everett says. "It's not a foolproof plan."

Jameson squeezes my feet. "Then what do you suggest we do, Gwen?"

"I want to bring them here," I say.

"Are you kidding—"

Reaching out, I press my finger to Mikkalo's lips, stopping his argument. "Just hear me out, Mikkalo. You said you wanted to relocate them, and I think this might be the best place. It's secure. You have plenty of space. Maybe just letting them see us will change their minds."

"I don't know, Gwen," Bronx says, hugging me tighter. "That puts us all at risk. Having Kyler here is bad enough. He's unpredictable. All your brothers together pose a huge risk not only to you but to everyone here. We have staff—human and vampire. Our protection is in their contracts. Now with having to take over the region...I don't know."

"I say we give it a try," Jameson says. "It's only her brothers. It's not like she asked us to house an entire rebel nest."

I tilt my head to look at him. "And if it's too hard, then I won't complain if you relocate them until we have a solid plan."

"I'm going to need time to prepare," Mikkalo says.

"As will I," Everett adds.

Bronx presses his back into the chair, pulling his hands from me to cover his face. He releases a deep growl, and I know he's trying to think of a reason not to agree.

After another moment, he finally looks at his brothers and then to me. "I should say no."

I poke his tight mouth with my finger. "If you are really against it..."

"I honestly don't know whether I am or not, but it's important to you. They're your family," he says quietly. "It would be unfair to you if I didn't try to make this work. You've had so much taken away already. I—we can't do that. Not after what we've asked of you."

My pouty mouth turns into a smile, and I grab his face in my hands and wiggle my nose to his. "Thank you. This means so much to me. I know what kind of risk you're taking and that you don't have to do it."

"Of course we do, Gigi," Jameson says. "You're our girl."

"You had the chance to leave us," Mikkalo says, lowering his voice. "But you didn't."

"You chose us," Everett says.

Reaching out, I grab Everett's hand and lace my fingers

through his to hug it to my chest. "Can I be honest?"

Bronx stiffens while Mikkalo remains expressionless. Jameson fake glares at me, and says, "Depends. Are you going to say you don't like my blanket mansions?"

I release a loud laugh and playfully kick him in the stomach. "Definitely not. What I want to be honest about is...this, you guys." Swiveling, I glance at each of them.

"You can be honest about that, Gwen," Bronx says, kissing my shoulder. "Always."

I lick my lips, summoning my nerve to spit the words out. But I have to say them. I need for them to know. "Everything about our situation is...crazy? Wild? Maybe just different. I don't know. But every time I think about you—each of you separate and together—something feels so utterly right. Like fate, you know? Something unexplainable draws me to you."

"Your insatiable desire to devour us," Jameson says, grinning.

Mikkalo backhands him. "I can't speak for my brothers, but I feel it too. Like somehow the world is better if we're together."

I bob my head. "And that's what really got to me when the Blood Rebels came to take me away from you. I just couldn't stop thinking that even though it hasn't been a lot of time, it doesn't matter."

"Time doesn't mean anything to us, Gwen. We have so much of it..." Bronx lets his words trail off.

"I know. And even so, I don't want to waste it," I say. "I want to see everything we can do together."

"I bet amazing things," Everett says. "Especially with everything in our control."

"As long as it remains," Bronx says.

Mikkalo flashes his fangs. "No one can stop us, brother. We got a badass dhampir on our side."

Jameson musses my hair. "Yeah, she'll just devour them...and make me jealous as hell."

I laugh. "I'd love to see them even try."

25

THE CHOICE

I STAND OVER KYLER AS he breathes evenly under Everett's sedation. As much as my guys didn't want me even within a foot of him, they didn't argue that I wanted some time at his side. It's the first time I've been alone since the incident with Mr. Bevaldi breaking into my mind, but now it's impossible for anyone to attempt such a thing. Jameson would never allow it.

Running my fingers through Kyler's dark blond hair, I push the strands off his forehead. "Kyler," I whisper. "I'm sorry. I'm so, so sorry. What you went through...I can't even imagine. I failed to protect you like I promised. But things are going to change. I swear. You just have to go with it and trust me, all right?"

Kyler continues to lie there, and I can't handle seeing him like this a moment longer, so I kiss his forehead and shuffle my way to the door. Mikkalo leans against the wall in the hallway outside, waiting for me. I smirk. I had a feeling he'd still be nearby since it's his time.

"Will I ever get more than twenty feet out of your reach?" I ask, stepping into his arms to push him into the wall, caging him in with my body.

"Can you blame me for not wanting to risk it?" He tilts his head, meeting me for a kiss. "I'd put a tracking device on you if I knew you wouldn't complain."

I laugh and hold up my arm to show off the sparkly ruby and onyx bracelet Jameson gave me. "You mean like this?"

He purses his lips, turning my wrist back and forth as he inspects the first bracelet I've ever worn. I hadn't expected to like it, but I guess Jameson was right. I appreciate pretty things as much as he does, but I'd never admit it.

"How did he get you to agree? I know it's not just because you like the jewelry," Mikkalo says, raising his eyebrow.

Sliding my hand into my pocket, I tug out the com device Jameson also gave me. I smile and tap the button on the screen, pulling up the map. Holding it out to him, I point at the small blue star that draws quick circles around the screen. It looks like Jameson's pacing laps around his room. "He's wearing one too. You can have access to mine, if and only if I can stalk your every move as well. It's only fair."

He chuckles and kisses me. "Jameson thinks he'd be your body match, but I'm certain he'd have matched with your mind. You two are ridiculous."

"So is that a yes?" I ask. "You going to let me creep on you?"

"Would you like me to set up a camera in my room too?"

My smile widens. "If you insist. I wouldn't mind."

Tipping his head back, he thunks it into the wall with his loud laugh that lifts up my heart with the lightness of his voice. Mikkalo nudges me back, but I stand firm, getting him to pick me up so that I can wrap my legs around him to see how good he is at navigating the house with my lips attached to his.

We bump into one doorway, a decorative table, and knock a glass vase of flowers over, but Mikkalo makes it to the stairs to climb to the ground floor, liking the challenge instead of using the elevator.

"You hungry?" he asks against my mouth.

"Starved."

He moans as I nibble on his lip. "Want to get out of here?"

I pause and pull away, my eyes widening. I was nearly certain I would never see outside of their floor of the house ever again considering how protective they've grown even after so little time.

"Where?"

"Just for a drive around the property. We have guests."

I fake-glare at him. "So that's why. You're trying to hide me."

"If that were the case, we'd never leave our room." Our room. It's still so strange to hear. Any time I ever thought of something as *ours*, it's always been something I shared with my brothers. Jameson offered to move to the upper level so that I could take his room for when I need my own space, but I felt kind of bad that he'd have to upend everything for me. We decided just to see how this goes. I'm so used to always having people around that it doesn't bother me. I like the company.

"We can't have that now, can we?" I ask, biting my lip with a smile. I spent the day in Mikkalo's room, but we didn't do more than kiss and cuddle. It was like he knew that was exactly what I needed. I slept so much better than the last time. No couch beds this time. Or kicks in the groin.

He licks his lips. "Careful, Gwen. There's still time to turn around. I know Jameson might want to live with you forever in his room, but I like getting out. You haven't even had a chance to see the whole estate yet."

I snuggle against him. "Okay. I'd love that. Let's go."

The world suddenly blurs around us, and I screech as Mikkalo purposely tosses me into the air only to catch me to set me on my feet. A sleek silver car idles on a black-paved path only wide enough for the vehicle. Mikkalo opens the passenger's side door to let me in.

Reaching into the backseat, he pulls out a small basket and sets it on my lap with a smile. I lift the napkin and meet his excitement with a grin and a kiss, knowing that he put a lot of effort into making this sandwich.

"This looks great," I say, bringing it up to my mouth to take a bite. "Tastes amazing too. So much cheese."

He chuckles. "I know you like it."

"Because I rarely got it before."

I take another bite and purposely hum my content-ment, loving how proud he is in himself. Mikkalo can prob-ably murder another vampire before I can even blink, and he looks intimidating as all get-out, especially with his col-lection of weapons, but I'm nearly certain none of that will ever bother me. Even my brothers have never made me a sandwich.

Mikkalo sets the car in gear, choosing not to use the au-topilot. I gape out the windshield at how magnificent the property is, even in the dark. Bright spotlights line the out-er-perimeter, creating huge bar-like shadows from the palm trees surrounding the place. Mikkalo points out the basket-ball courts, a game I've never played, and then he motions to a huge block wall that supposedly contains a swimming pool.

"Too bad I can't swim," I say, reminding him of our first day together. "Our bath was the deepest water I'd ever been in."

He swings his arm over my chest, stopping me from flying forward as he slams the brakes. I screech and clutch the grab handle, not even getting a chance to orient myself. Mikkalo tugs me from the car and tosses me onto his shoulder. I smack his ass, my hair flying around like crazy.

"I wasn't planning on this tonight, but since you mentioned it..." Mikkalo sets me on my feet and spins me around to face an enormous, blue-lit swimming pool with a cascading waterfall, steaming hot tub, and a secluded changing area.

I place my hands on my hips. "Not gonna happen."

He slides his fingers through mine and swings our arms. "Come on. It'll be fun."

"You know you don't need an excuse to get me to cling onto you," I tease, sauntering closer to the pool but stopping a few feet away to peer into it.

"Is that so?" His voice lowers, turning deep and husky with desire.

Wrapping his arms around me, he hugs me from behind. "How about we just dip our feet? If you can do that for me, I'll take you to my favorite spot on the property next."

"I've been to the gym," I say, smiling.

Mikkalo rests his chin on my shoulder. "Definitely not there, though I wouldn't mind teaching you a few moves."

"Or I could teach you something."

He chuckles. "I'd like that. So, test the pool, discover my favorite place, and then a little gym time?"

I tug my fingers away from his and saunter forward, hooking my fingers to my shirt to pull it over my head. "No pool."

"Then what are you doing?"

"Get undressed and find out," I say, slipping out of my pants to toss at him.

He catches them with a grin, striding ahead of me to drink me in as I make my way around the pool. I swirl my finger at him, getting him to take off his shirt, and his pants soon follow, making me flush in excitement seeing his muscular body shadowed in the soft light of the pool.

"Lose it all," I say, tightening my mouth. I can't help myself from commanding him. I know he likes when I'm bossy and don't put up with anything.

Licking his lips, he does as I say, undressing completely. I stop a few feet short and give him as much attention as he gives me, just taking my time to memorize his body all over again, throwing my nerves to the ground with the release of my bra.

"Can I come closer?" he asks breathlessly, shifting on his feet.

I wag my finger. "Not yet. We won't make it into the hot tub if you do."

Mikkalo's eyes flash silver at my comment, and he inches closer like the few feet of space between us kills him. I hold up my hand, attempting and failing to gracefully undress completely, but the desire lit on Mikkalo's face never changes.

"Gwen..."

I smile at the way he says my name. "Just another second."

Strolling to him, I run my finger along his arm as I pass by, making him hum deep in his throat. He keeps his hands to himself but turns to follow my movements, watching me with an intensity that sets my body ablaze. I step into the steamy water of the hot tub and dip lower, letting the hot water drench my hair.

I straighten my back and smile. "Are you going to just stare at me all night?"

Mikkalo moves so quickly that the water waves against my stomach a second before his naked body presses into mine. He slides his hand to my lower back, holding me in place with the rocking of the water.

His gaze trails from my face, glistening with steam, and down my clavicle. Grazing his fingers along my sopping hair, he pushes the tresses away to get a better look at my excited body, prickling with goosebumps under his touch.

"You're beautiful," he whispers. "I never knew someone

could make me this happy. I'm so grateful that you chose to share a part of your life with me, especially after everything."

"I chose to share a part of my life with you *because* of everything. As much as your distrust toward me—" I shiver, pushing the thought away. "I love your protectiveness over your brothers, the region. I understand it. I can't blame you for reacting the way you did to my secret. I'm just so grateful you've welcomed me into your life despite it. My life doesn't make yours easy."

He caresses my cheek, enveloping me in his arms so that not even the water can get between us. "It makes it interesting."

I kiss him. "Yeah?"

"Entertaining."

"It's definitely that."

"Complete."

I grin and kiss him again, lacing my hands around his neck. His body teases mine, and I stretch on my tiptoes high enough that his erection presses between my legs. He inhales a deep breath at the movement, at the closeness of our bodies, without proceeding further.

"Also kind of torturous," I whisper, grazing my fingers down his back.

"Doesn't have to be."

I moan softly under the sensation of his hard on sliding more between my legs, just grazing my skin until our hips meet. Pushing his shoulders, I nudge him toward the ledge of the hot tub, so slowly that we never fully part but I can enjoy the friction of him rubbing against me.

"Mikkalo, you here?"

Mikkalo's body tenses at the soft sound of Jameson's voice. I ease myself away from him and dig my fingers into his broad shoulders, trying to stop him from reacting.

"We're here, Jamie, but don't come in," I say.

Mikkalo rests his head on my shoulder. "This is our time. You shouldn't have used the bracelet you gave Gwen to find us."

"You weren't answering my call." Jameson's voice rises in annoyance.

"Jameson, give us a couple more minutes, okay?" I say, pressing my finger to Mikkalo's mouth to stop him from responding in what I'm sure might be a yell.

"I'm sorry, Gigi. You can take some of my time with Gwen if you want, brother. It's just the Anderson Coven—"

Mikkalo releases a soft growl. "Okay. We're coming."

Picking me up, Mikkalo plants his lips to mine as he heads toward the changing room and grabs two towels for us to dry off with. I let him assist me, biting my lip to keep quiet. He groans, touching the warmth between my legs, looking ready just to set me on the counter.

"And you say I'm torturing you," I say, my body unable to chill the hell out.

"It'll be worth the wait," he murmurs.

I smile and kiss him. "Still torture."

Mikkalo helps me dress, and we meet Jameson outside the gate. I thought he'd look cockier that he interrupted something between us, but he surprises me and pats Mikkalo on the shoulder.

"I'll hold Corona down while you punch him," Jameson says, getting a chuckle out of Mikkalo.

"What about for me?" I ask.

The two of them look at each other, their eyes flashing silver. Mikkalo hooks his arm around me, holding me tightly against him.

"You're not getting even a foot within his reach, Gigi," Jameson says.

"But you said Mikkalo had—"

"Bronx has something else for you to do." Jameson bumps his shoulder to mine. "Should be easy enough."

I crinkle my nose. "You say that now."

Instead of taking the car back the short distance to the estate, Mikkalo carries me on his back with Jameson running so close behind us that I can feel him playing with my damp hair. Avoiding the main entrance, we head through the door near the gym building and make our way to Mikkalo's room.

Everett stands outside the door, searching over me, something strange flashing through his eyes—fear? Maybe. It's the same face he gave me after the attack at the Blood Match Center.

"I need you to take a breath, Gwen. Do you remember

Francisca, the vampire from the Blood Match Center?" Everett asks.

"How could I forget?" I say, keeping my voice even.

"Well, the Anderson Coven isn't happy about their inability to reach Zaire. We need you to lie and tell them that he left you in our care to hunt down the Blood Rebels Corona's employee was working with."

I'm thankful Everett doesn't say Frankie's name out loud, because for some reason, he stayed with me after I refused to go. He helped me. Because of that, Corona killed him.

I swallow, shifting on my feet. "I think I can manage that."

"You have to act as if you're under mind manipulation."

"Ah fuck." I can't stop the words from coming from my mouth. I've practiced faking it through mind manipulation a hundred times, but just the thought of it freaks me out. My fingers tremble as I silently count back the hours to when I last drank blood. It might be cutting it close.

Everett touches both my shoulders. "Deep breaths. In and out."

I do as he says, closing my eyes as I inhale and exhale. "And if I fail?"

"You won't," Mikkalo says, pressing his chest into my back.

I shift and look at him. "I need to know."

"We'll just have to file the proper paperwork to announce Zaire's death to the board." He doesn't have to tell me to know there's more. From what Bronx mentioned, I know it's a lot more complicated than that. It risks the Royale Region and will open it for other covens to apply to take over.

"Shit," I whisper again.

"You got this, Gigi," Jameson says.

I bob my head. "I got this...but you'll back me up if I don't?"

They all surround me in a hug tight enough to get my fear under control. I only wish that Bronx was here to join us. I could use one of his smothering-in-the-best-way-possible embraces.

"We're all here for you. Only one Anderson Coven member will witness. Bronx and the others are across the estate in Zaire's study. He'll call in."

I drag my hands down my face. "All right. Let's get this over with. I want to get back to my date."

Mikkalo slaps his hand onto the palm pad, unlocking his door. "So do fucking I."

He takes my hand and tugs me inside when I'm not quick to move with his brothers following behind us. My eyes automatically dart across the room and land on a familiar face from the Blood Match Center.

I can't stop the scowl crossing my lips. "She's the witness?"

"Hey, dolly," Francisca says, standing from her spot on the couch. She gulps the rest of the blood from a clear glass and sets it on the table in front of her. "You're not broken yet. Or did Everett fix you?"

I spin around and turn my back on her to look at my guys. I open my mouth to tell them that this isn't going to work, but the three of them release deep ass growls. A shiver runs down my back as Francisca's sudden closeness sets off my fear instincts.

"I should've known that Zaire would never give away a plaything. Does he know you're fucking his brother?"

My eyes widen, and I swing my arm out to punch her, but Mikkalo catches me by the wrist and restrains me against him.

"How dare you," I say, clenching my fingers into fists. "Zaire had Everett escort me to Crimson Vista only to see my brothers." The lie comes so easy that I almost believe it myself.

"That explains your presence then." A smoky, snarly voice cuts through the room, igniting my rage and anger even worse. "I suppose you wouldn't mind if Francisca verifies for me?"

I gawk at the projection I didn't notice now lighting the wall. Corona Anderson leers at me from his spot next to Bronx, sitting behind a gleaming desk. I can't see anyone else, but I can hear the whispers of the other vampires on their side of the line.

"Ms. Royale, please allow Francisca to get a good look at you." Bronx's voice remains even, though his eyes flash silver with annoyance.

I clear my throat, accepting the plea from his gaze, and decide not to argue. It helps that I kind of like hearing him use his coven name on me. "Yes, Mr. Royale."

"Damn, I liked that," Mikkalo whispers oh-so-softly from behind me—too softly for Francisca to hear.

Francisca strides closer with a smile. Sparkling earrings dangle from her ears to match a strange pendant on her throat. She reaches up her hand to touch my face, but Everett cuts between us so fast that she touches his chest instead.

A weird noise comes from me, and Jameson releases a soft chuckle but doesn't comment on the fact that I totally growled. I couldn't even control the damn noise. My body just doesn't want her anywhere near Everett, and it takes Jameson pinching my ass to get me to back the hell up, so I'm not pushing against Everett.

"You do not need to touch her to ask your questions, Francisca," Everett says lowly. "Nor are you allowed to ask anything invasive in regards to Zaire or our coven. She is not a tool to use at your disposal and don't think I won't consider your attempts to be a breach in our alliance. Understand?"

"Thank you, brother," Bronx says. "Keep your confirmation questions to the point. If she does not, as acting coven leader, I grant my brothers permission to punish your heir appropriately, Mr. Anderson."

"That is fine." The vampire turns his attention to Francisca. "Mind your manners, darling."

Everett squeezes my hand and steps out from between us, and Francisca inches close enough that she's in my same breathing space. I try my best to stay still, meeting her brown eyes rimmed in perfect makeup that makes her look more doll-like compared to me.

"Ms. Royale," Francisca says, attempting to capture me in her gaze.

I relax the best I can, hoping that one of my guys remembers that she technically would hold me up since my mind would be under her manipulation if she could actually do it. Mikkalo eases his arms around me, supporting my deadweight, and I keep my eyes locked on the beautiful vampire's.

Her eyes flash silver. "Please tell me the reason the Royale Coven brought you into Crimson Vista."

"To visit my brothers."

"How did you convince Zaire to let you do such a thing?"

A dozen responses flit through my mind. "He wanted answers about Blood Rebels."

"And your brothers would know the answers to that?" she asks.

"Yes."

"Ask her why he chose not to go himself," Corona says,

his voice booming through the room.

"Why didn't he go himself?"

"He was busy," I say.

"With what?"

"He was—"

"Francisca, that's none of your business," Everett says, covering my eyes with his arm to break my eye contact. And I'm so thankful for that. I had no idea what to say. I wanted to tell her he was probably busy being an asshole.

She sighs. "Fine but one last question."

Everett removes his arm from across my eyes.

Francisca leans into me, her mouth smirking in a smug as hell smile. "Ms. Royale. Did you know that your last visit to your brothers would be the last time you see them?"

"What?" I can't stop the word from coming out of my mouth. I turn to look at Everett. "What the hell is she talking about?"

Francisca tips her head back and laughs. "You were right, Father. She's consuming their blood."

"Mr. Royales," Corona snaps. "I demand to talk to Zaire right now."

Francisca disappears from the room, leaving the door to the hallway open behind her. Jameson chases after her, and Mikkalo picks me up and relocates me into his office. He stares at his monitors for a moment and swears under his breath.

Without saying what he sees, he points at the screen to

show Everett.

"Gwen, Mikkalo's going to take you to my room, okay?" Everett says.

"What's going on?" I ask.

"I need to go to Bronx. It seems the Anderson Coven didn't just come here to question us about Zaire. They've started a blood feud. Something must've tipped them off," he says, keeping his voice even.

I grab his hand. "Shouldn't we come with you?"

"You will as soon as Mikkalo grabs your brother. I have a feeling Corona had never planned to let us keep him."

Fear clenches my chest. I grab Mikkalo's hand and pull him with me. He doesn't let me walk on my own for long, scooping me into his arms. Jameson materializes in the hallway, swinging his gaze from me to his brothers.

"I lost her," Jameson says. "But we have a bigger problem. Found a warning to us outside."

"We saw it," Mikkalo says. "Go with Everett to Bronx. Gwen and I will meet you there. I'll set off the alarms as soon as you're close enough."

Jameson leans in and kisses me. "No panicking, Gigi. We're good. Corona's coven is weak. Diluted by a few recent additions. There is a reason he's not in control of the region."

I tighten my jaw. "Do you think he lied about my brothers?"

None of them respond. The answer is written all over

their faces. They don't have to confirm for me to know that they're gone. Corona used our sudden disappearance from the city and Zaire's absence to his advantage. It was probably Francisca who took them.

"We'll discuss this later," Mikkalo says, hugging me tighter.

I nod. "Okay. Let's get Kyler."

Everett kisses my cheek and disappears with Jameson. The world blurs as Mikkalo rushes us to Everett's room. I half expect to find Francisca or someone else by my brother's bedside, but he remains exactly as he was.

Mikkalo's quick to remove the medical equipment without having to think about what to do, and he lifts my brother into his arms. He squats down, letting me climb on his back, not wasting a moment standing around. Wind whips through my hair, sending it cascading behind me, and I bury my chin into his shoulder.

Jameson materializes outside the door that will lead to the gym building. "The Anderson Coven backed off. Bronx says to take them back to your room and double check all the feeds. I'll do a manual sweep with Bronxy and Ev."

I release a breath. "I don't understand."

"Corona backed off after Bronx..." Jameson doesn't finish his sentence. "Just know it's all good."

"My brothers?" I ask.

"They're going to be fine, okay? Just let Mik take you back in."

I bob my head, turning my gaze to peer down at Kyler in Mikkalo's arms. Snapping his eyes open, he looks at me and smiles a moment before swinging his fist up to punch Mikkalo right in the nose. Mikkalo jerks his head to the side, and Kyler sinks his teeth in his neck, biting him just like the times he's seen me do it.

The surprise move throws Mikkalo off balance, and Jameson lunges forward to grab hold of my brother. Jameson flashes his fangs, releasing a growl. I heave a breath, hitting my back to the wall as Mikkalo crushes me against it.

A figure materializes behind Jameson. No one has time to react, Jameson's attention drawn to Kyler now on his hands and knees. Francisca locks her arm around Jameson's throat, causing him to yell. I smell the scent of his sweet blood before I spot five blossoms of blood stain and grow over the front of his shirt.

"Give the Gallaghers to me or I'll finish pushing his heart through," Francisca says.

Mikkalo growls.

Jameson snarls. "Don't do it, brother."

"Five seconds," Francisca says.

Mikkalo heaves, his breath pushing his back more into me. "Be brave, Jameson."

Francisca's eyes turn silver. "Four."

"Take care of our girl." Jameson releases another yell, sending my own heart crashing against my ribcage to attempt to fly at him.

His words send a wave of panic through me, and I try to push against Mikkalo, but he refuses to budge. He's not giving me up.

"How honorable. Sacrificing your life for hers. I'm sure your brothers will quite enjoy her," Francisca says, her sultry voice turning my fear into full-blown rage. "Maybe he'll change his mind in three..."

"Mikkalo!" I scream, shoving against him. "No. No! You can't choose me over him."

Kyler gets to his feet and stumbles forward. "So it's true," he says, looking at me. "You're a traitor."

Francisca heaves a sigh, and Jameson yells again, the front of his shirt now covered in his blood. "Two."

"Mikkalo!" I scream. "You can't do this!"

"Gigi, he's not. I am. I choose you not him," Jameson says, his eyes flickering silver so fast they look nearly solid.

Francisca smiles at me. "One."

Something snaps inside me, and I summon all my strength and shove Mikkalo so hard that he stumbles and hits the ground under my strength. Francisca's eyes widen as she drops Jameson to his knees to snarl at me.

Kyler rams into my side, knocking me off course. Mikkalo yells. An alarm blares.

I open and close my mouth in an attempt to scream, but someone locks their hands under my arms.

"Got you, little sis," Kyler says.

I blink through the haze, my ears ringing from the intense sound of the alarms. As I look into my brother's eyes, hard and cold and lacking everything familiar I love about him, a part of me dies.

Epilogue

UNBREAKABLE

"COME ON, GWENY. YOU HAVE to eat something," Kyler says, holding out a cup of dark red liquid to me. He sticks his hand through the bars of the small cage that doesn't give me room even to stand.

I smack his hand away, sending the blood cascading across the dirty floor. The second the scent hits me, my stomach screams in pain, and I curl in on myself. I don't know how long I've been here, but it feels like forever.

"See what you did? You're making this hard on yourself." Kyler glides his fingers through the blood and tries to scoop the dirty liquid back in the cup. "This is all you're getting for the month. Corona knows that you don't need blood like a vampire."

Except I do. I need it even more. Everett said that I drink twice as much. But Kyler wouldn't know that. He doesn't know Laredo bit me with venom.

I groan and turn my back on him. "Why did you do this? You were supposed to protect me. I did everything to get you away from him."

I don't know why I ask. Corona was in his head. If he was powerful enough, he could've broken through the mind manipulation Laredo performed to protect me.

"Because you're a traitor, Gwen. A disgrace. Dad would kill me for even sparing you this much. You should already be dead," he says, his voice laced in something impossible. Concern? Regret? He's delusional if he thinks he's doing me a favor.

"Then why didn't you just do it? Why work with the very monsters who will put you in a cage beside me?"

"Because you chose those same monsters, Gwen. You ruined everything. Frankie was—" Kyler thrusts the glass at the wall, shattering it. "Never-fucking-mind. You don't care. You let those damn blood sources keep our family."

I glare at him. "I don't fucking care? Are you crazy? I was getting you out."

"Liar."

Sitting up, I jerk my arm through the bars and manage

to snatch the front of his shirt. I drag Kyler toward me, my strength preventing him from doing anything except hitting the bars hard. His wild eyes meet mine and widen, and I know he sees the silver in my eyes—my deep-seated blood hunger as a dhampir.

My body disregards my mind's pleas to pull my shit together, and I lock my hand around Kyler's wrist and bring his dirty, bloody hand to my mouth. I barely touch my tongue to the blood before Corona rips him away from me, flashing his fangs.

I thrust against the bars so hard that the cage knocks forward, and I hit my knees on the metal slats.

"I told you to give her the blood and leave," Corona says.

"I'm sorry, Mr. Anderson. She wouldn't drink it," Kyler says.

"Then she starves."

"But you said—"

Corona thrusts my brother into the wall, and I can't stop myself from screaming out. Kyler lands with a thud on the floor and curls his knees to his chest. I yell again, drawing Corona's attention away from my brother, and he materializes in front of me. I squeeze my eyes shut and scramble as far away from him as possible.

"Beautiful dhampir," he whispers without touching me. "There is no need to be afraid of me. As long as you learn your place, perhaps I'll consider allowing you a room."

"My place?" I wish I could've ignored him. "I belong to the Royales."

He clicks his tongue. "Do you really think the Royale Coven was willing to jeopardize their standing with Donor Life Corp all for a donor? We have come to an agreement, and you now belong to me. Lucky for you, I know how to properly care for you, thanks to your brothers. You will make quite the asset, lovely."

I inhale a few sharp breaths. "They wouldn't do that."

"I'll prove it. Shall we see if Mr. Royale answers?" Corona asks.

I don't respond to him but hear a familiar, nearly unnoticeable intake of breath. My chest tightens. I can't bring myself to turn over. I can't bring myself to look. If I look, I'll lose my shit. Or they will. I can feel it deep down inside me. They have a plan.

"Ms. Gallagher has something she would like to say to you," Corona says, risking touching my shoulder.

A com device thumps in the cage next to me, and I can't resist reaching to grab it. Clutching it in my fingers, I finally bring it up to look at the screen, but I can only see Bronx's face. He remains utterly expressionless as our eyes meet.

He doesn't say anything. Doesn't even blink.

"Go on, lovely. We don't have all night," Corona says.

I clear my throat. "I hope you fucking know that my nickname isn't dandelion for nothing."

Bronx's eyes flash silver as he gets my message loud and clear. His features soften for a second, just a glimpse of the truth telling me that something happened. Because I know there is no way in hell my guys would have ever let someone take me without a reason. All I can think—

My brother yells, drawing my attention from the com device and to him and Corona. Kyler grabs him by the throat, holding onto him from behind.

"Give me the phone," Jameson says, his voice trickling to me.

Tears burn my eyes as I meet his green gaze. "Jamie."

"I know you, Gigi. I know you want to be brave, but I need you to be afraid. Don't fight."

"Strategize," Mikkalo adds.

My brother screams again. I jerk my head in his direction and stare in horror as Corona extends his fangs longer than I've ever seen them.

"And hang tight. We're coming for you," Everett adds.

I don't look at my guys, unable to take my eyes away from my brother.

"Do you hear us, Gwen?" Bronx asks.

Something feral snaps inside me, and I shove myself into the side of the cage, dropping the com device in the process. The cage rolls again, the bottom now above me. Corona draws his attention to me and snarls. Shoving my shoulders upright and into the solid metal panel, I smash the bottom of the cage off. A few growls echo from somewhere nearby, coming through the line of the com device.

Corona throws Kyler to the ground. "For that, I'll proceed with my plan for your brothers, Mr. Gallagher."

"You fucking asshole!" Kyler shouts. "You lied to me."

Closing the space to me, Corona restrains me against his chest. The soft click of his fangs extending sends panic through me, and I buck and kick until I slam my head hard into his face, and he drops me.

Corona doesn't react further, just cupping his bloody nose while looking at Kyler. "You didn't actually think I'd work with a Blood Rebel, Mr. Gallagher."

Kyler's eyes flick to mine. "I'm sorry, Gweny. I thought—"

Corona lifts him up again and covers his mouth. "I don't think so. You will die a traitor to your sister. She will always remember you as the one who gave her up...and for what? Your brothers don't even care about you. No one does."

"Fuck." Bronx's whisper trickles to my ears, too soft for Corona to hear as my brother screams.

"Don't look, Gwen," Everett says. "Please, close your eyes."

But I can't

I gawk as Corona bends my brother's neck, exposing his throat to him.

He flashes his fangs in a smile at me. "This will teach you your place. Break the cage again, and you'll be next."

Corona bites down so hard that Kyler's blood squirts from his body, his screams piercing my ears until his neck breaks and cuts off his voice. I heave and clench my stomach, my ears ringing, my heart smashing into a thousand pieces.

I rush toward Kyler but don't get within a foot of him as Corona lifts me up and drops me back into the cage, hooking the bottom in place. He kicks the cage over, and my world spins until I land on my back. I don't move. I don't speak.

All I can do is stare into Kyler's empty eyes.

"That's better," Corona says.

I press my cheek into the bottom of the cage, spotting the glow of the com device on the floor. Sticking my arm through the slats, I link my fingers around it and gaze at my guys one last time. The line drops as a shadow falls over me. Corona clicks his tongue and steps on my fingers, forcing me to jerk away as he smashes the com device.

Corona stands over the cage, startling me by biting his arm. "Shall we try again with your dinner?"

I don't get a chance to respond as blood drips over me, and my mouth opens, tasting the bitter liquid that drags out everything horrible inside me.

"This might be easier than I thought," he says, humming under his breath.

He's right. Because now I've had a taste of his blood.

It's all I can think about.

"Good, yes?" he asks, smirking at me.

"It'll do," I respond, turning over on my side.

"I look forward to our life together, beautiful dhampir," he says. "We'll control things in no time."

Power. It's all assholes like him ever want. He thinks he's in control of me, but he'll soon realize that's impossible.

No one controls me.

I'm a dhampir. Wild. Ferocious. Unbreakable. Hungry for his blood.

Corona might claim I'm a beautiful dhampir, but I'll be his ugliest nightmare. A predator who will live to hear him scream.

His blood might taste bitter now, but his death will be sweet.

To be continued...

Thank you so much for reading *Rebel Vampires!* Don't forget to check out *Rebel Match*, the second book in *The Royale Vampire Heirs* series.

Want more of the *Vampire Heirs World* and haven't read *The Divine Vampire Heirs?* Check out *Blood Match*.

To stay up-to-day on new and future releases, follow Ginna on Amazon or Bookbub. By signing up for Ginna Moran's newsletter or joining her Facebook Group, you will also gain exclusive access to special content on her website, including the serialized retelling of *Blood Match* from your favorite blood brothers' points of view!

OTHER REVERSE HAREM NOVELS BY GINNA MORAN

THE VAMPIRE HEIRS WORLD

The Divine Vampire Heirs
Blood Match
Blood Rebel
Blood Debt
Blood Feud
Blood Loss
Blood Vows

The Royale Vampire Heirs Series:
Rebel Vampires
Rebel Dhampir
Rebel Match
Rebel Heir
Rebel Fight

Academy of Vampire Heirs Series:
Dhampirs 101
Blood Sources 102
Coven Bonds 103
Personal Donors 104
Blood Wars 105

THE MATES OF MAGAELORUM WORLD

About Ginna Moran

GINNA MORAN IS the author of over fifty novels, including the popular The Pack Mates of Lunar Crest, The Divine Vampire Heirs, and The Royale Vampire Heirs Why Choose novels.

She always carried a fascination for all things paranormal and wrote her first unpublished manuscript at age eighteen. Her love of the supernatural grew stronger through her adult life, and she now spends her days with different creatures of the night. Whether it's vampires, werewolves, dragons, fae, angels, demons, or mermaids, Ginna loves creating and living in worlds from her dreams.

Aside from Ginna's professional life, she enjoys binge watching TV, crafting and design, playing pretend with her daughter, and cuddling with her dogs. Some of her favorite things include chocolate, mermaids, anything that glitters, learning new things, cheesy jokes, and organizing her book-shelf.

Ginna is currently hard at work on her next novel and the one after, and the one after that.

Made in the USA
Columbia, SC
23 June 2021

40842796R00255